Company of Spies

Code Name: JANA

A Novel By

Dr. Margaret S. Emanuelson

authorHOUSE

1663 LIBERTY DRIVE, SUITE 200
BLOOMINGTON, INDIANA 47403
(800) 839-8640
www.authorhouse.com

This is a work of fiction. Names, characters, organizations, places, events, and incidents are either the product of the author's imagination or are used fictitiously. Any resemblance to actual persons, living or dead, events, or locales is entirely coincidental.

© 2004 Dr. Margaret S. Emanuelson.
All Rights Reserved.

No part of this book may be reproduced, stored in a retrieval system, or transmitted by any means without the written permission of the author.

First published by AuthorHouse 08/16/04

ISBN: 1-4184-1651-7 (e)
ISBN: 1-4184-1649-5 (sc)
ISBN: 1-4184-1650-9 (dj)

Printed in the United States of America
Bloomington, Indiana

This book is printed on acid-free paper.

Acknowledgments

How can I say "thank you." Let me count the ways: there could be none to express sufficient gratitude to those who suffered long months of listening to my incessant questions: read and re-read my unedited—and I do mean unedited manuscript; yet nevertheless spurred me on to touchdown.

To Elizabeth McIntosh, author of "Sisterhood of Spies," long an icon of the women of OSS, who inspired and encouraged me to begin a story long in my head but still unwritten.

To my priest Ed Pippin and my prayer group, who know that Christian faith walks into any situation — even war, and who pray that somehow this book would show it; to Cyndra Van Clief, my friend and attorney and to Jan Karon (Mitford Series) and Merry and Frank Thomasson for their advice and support.

To Pat Brooks my friend and author, "Aftermath," who insisted I write my first book — "Lost Yesterdays" and continues to give support.

To Fred Hitz, former inspector general of CIA, and Mary Bufford Hitz, his author wife, "Not without Permission," and Charlie Pinck, President of OSS: and to those of my friends in CIA who know who they are.

To Howard Jackson, a WWII hero in his own right, a buddy of my husband's in Hargrave Military Academy, who guided me in several technical matters.

To Bill, my favorite pilot and husband of a life time, who advised me on Naval flight and ship technicalities and who still continues to think there is no limit to what I can do; and to my daughter Laura, who "couldn't put it down" and has been a major source of assistance.

And to Jane Rafal, my editor, who no doubt thinks I should rewrite it even now, but who became my friend in the process and has been an invaluable asset in teaching, guiding, trimming, shaping an otherwise unruly document.

This journey has been another learning experience — just one more adventure in a life filled with unexpected turns and twists and I am happily compelled to continue — as I launch into Book II of Company of Spies.

Dedicated To

The men and women of O.S.S., that elite idiosyncratic group, who dared to conceive inconceivable feats; contrived unbelievable means to accomplish the unaccomplishable; and conjured up the insurmountable courage to achieve them …….

And to Elizabeth McIntosh, "Sisterhood of Spies," whom we'd all like to clone.

COMPANY OF SPIES

Dr. Margaret S. Emanuelson

CODE NAME: JANA

.... For such a time as this...
Esther 4:14..

Foreword

No American living at that time will ever forget that Sunday morning of December 7th, 1941. That "date that will live in infamy," when the Japanese attacked and devastated Pearl Harbor. Immediately, the United States declared war on Japan and rapidly a frenzied attempt was openly underway to formulate a war machine capable of overcoming the enemy forces on both sides of the country's oceans.

America became fully awake that spring. Troops were being prepared and sent both to the European Theater, (ETO), and the Pacific Theater, (PTO), a mammoth undertaking for the entire country, and all Americans were intent on doing their part in winning the "war to end all wars."

The military had been, not so quietly, expanding both defense and readiness for some time, under the guise of lend-lease, assisting its European allies in their efforts to defeat Hitler; but now it was all-out open preparation for war, no holds barred, against an enemy on both sides of the continent.

Heretofore, intelligence gathering had been left up to the separate efforts of the burgeoning FBI, State Department's Foreign Diplomatic arm, the Naval (ONI), and the War Department's Military Intelligence unit (G-2). Never had there been a central organization to receive and coordinate all of the information obtained by these sources.

As a result of the reluctance and inability of these separate entities to share, information was fragmented and lost its usefulness. With the threat of war imminent, in light of the mandate to protect and defend the nation, it was instantly obvious that all out war required a complete reorganization.

To that end in June 1941, the Coordinator Office of Information (COI) was formed. President Roosevelt appointed Colonel William Donovan, a decorated WWI army colonel, currently a civilian multi-trust New York lawyer, as its head.

In July 1942, because of the numerous ensuing power struggles and America's declaration of war, COI was replaced by the Office of Strategic Services (OSS) and Donovan was given the full power and authority under the President to accomplish its task.

Thus, OSS became America's first Central Intelligence Agency. Its mission included not only espionage and counter-espionage, but research and analysis, propaganda, morale, special operations, disinformation, command operations, and all other forms of physical and psychological warfare. And like lightening, under Donovan it quickly covered the globe.

Fired by the fuel of patriotism, propaganda, and oratory, every man, woman, and child became either in fact or vicariously part of that war machine. Production of weaponry, ships, and planes reached a new unbelievable high. And more and more young men and women volunteered or were conscripted to service. Doctors, nurses, lawyers, high school and college kids, farmers, office workers, homemakers—Uncle Sam's long arm reached into every area of life to rally his people to action.

America was fully abuzz by the spring of 1942. The country was abruptly awakened by six months of the atrocious devastation of our own men and women, our own ships and planes and our very own outposts. The war was no longer "over there." It was in our very own back yard; and the realization came with a jolt that this was "our war" now and unless these two insane enemies were stopped they might very well conquer the whole world.

But on that fateful Sunday morning of December 7, 1941, America was happily unaware of the utter catastrophe and cataclysm that was to come.

Chapter 1

He awoke with a start. Whether it was the motion of the boat or the constant drone of the engine, he couldn't tell. But then, he was always super alert when a new leg of his mission began. Sleep had never been a primary requirement for him. On the contrary, he often found that a few minutes at a time could renew him for hours.

He looked at his watch; it was almost 3 AM. Soon the sub would surface and he would be on his way. He would be glad to leave these cramped quarters. Being buried under the sea was definitely not for him; besides the uneasiness, it was somewhat tedious. He had taken his meals and had conversed to some extent with the captain, an interesting fellow, the epitome of a highly efficient and disciplined German officer, who would carry out explicit instructions to the letter. But he had had little to no contact with the crew. No need for any excess exposure.

He checked off his requirements in his mind. Yes, it was all there. He had carefully eyeballed his equipment the day before, and checked the items off one by one. Now all that remained were those things he had requested be waiting for him.

At times he thought that his mind was like a vast file cabinet, filled with well-organized folders of information. He had always had a knack of keeping past and present details of operations, people, and events in his mind. Habit had made it easy to open those folders, one at a time, if reviewing an area of concern or a specific operation at an instant's notice. His memory had never failed him. It was one of those endowments that had given him the edge to achieve his ends.

From the onset of his operations from Czechoslovakia through Poland, Austria, and on to France, England and all their conquests, he still had his fingers on all the trigger points. And now, on the eve of an all out expansion of the American caper, he felt he was well equipped. His memory prevented the need for written records. They could be captured, intercepted. No need. His own capture was the only chink in a meticulously well-built armor. But that would never happen. He had taken care of that. No one knew his identity. His pyramid contained few but trustworthy intelligence officers, placed in key areas, who had the authority to carry out his orders, each protected from the other by total ignorance of who they were or what they were doing.

The engine noise suddenly increased, and the boat lurched forward. He felt that strange phenomenon—the pull of gravity against his body as the sub rose—up—up. Soon he would be resurrected into the dim light of the mild March night and a new leg of his mission would begin.

He felt a cool excitement as he gathered his gear and stepped into the narrow corridor. He heard the captain's voice over the intercom, "Alles ist klar."

Quickly, he followed the crewman up the ladder to the surface. The small boat had been inflated and four crewmen were waiting to row him ashore. The brisk sea air filled his grateful lungs as he stepped into the boat. "Ah, fresh air, at last." He shivered as the cold sea-spray touched his skin. But for the lapping of the waves as the sailors dipped their oars, all was silent.

The night was dark with the cloud cover, but he could make out the silhouette of the shore close by. Seven minutes later they reached land. He swung his gear over his shoulder and stepped onto the sand. The head crewman saluted, pushed off, and without a sound they rowed back to the submarine waiting in the distance.

He watched them reach the boat. Soon, quietly, it submerged and disappeared from sight, and he was alone. How easy it had been. Miles of unoccupied virgin beach, in constant patrol by our fleet of U-Boats. Yet, almost five months into the Americans' entrance into the war, the beaches were still wide open for entry.

During the past ten years, he had planted several groups of agents in a number of areas, Florida and New York, for instance. And they had all come by submarine. Espionage was a tricky business—even boring at times. Sometimes it took years of planning and waiting—for just the right moment. Some of his operatives had been functioning within the U.S. government all this time—even in the State Department, *right under their noses.* He laughed. But then, the Americans were so naive about security, unlike the Europeans, who periodically found the devastation of war at their doorsteps. It never seemed to occur to the Americans that the enemy could walk right in or out of their borders, completely unnoticed, and create havoc.

He smiled. *Well, they were about to find out.*

He climbed up the dune to the top. Ah, there it was, only 15 feet away, on the side of the road. How clever we are, he thought. Our calculations are immaculately accurate. He brushed the sand off his jacket, and got in the driver's seat. The keys were in the ignition. He checked his disguise in the rearview mirror, and started the car. Yes, everything had gone off like clockwork. Now all he had to remember was to speak English with perhaps a little of that North Carolina drawl he had been practicing.

At present, he was a professor-tourist, fascinated with the Wright brothers and the development of flight. He would check into the Carolinian later that morning and begin his venture.

He had the perfect cover, for now.

Chapter 2

They had risen early that Sunday morning. Shipmates on weekend leave, Andrew and Brett had grabbed a bite of breakfast at the officers' club and headed straight to the golf course.

"God, it's a beautiful day." Brett waited patiently for Andrew to tee off.

"Yeah! But oh boy, do I have a head this morning. Wish I felt as beautiful." Andrew swung his club at the ball, stepped aside, and handed his club to his caddie.

"Didn't the coffee and aspirin help?"

Andrew groaned. "Not much."

Brett gave his friend an empathetic glance. "What you need is a couple of whiffs of oxygen. That's what the fly boys do." He teed off and handed his club to his caddie. They walked along the course to the next play. "I didn't notice you were drinking that much last night."

"I didn't either until this morning," Andrew groaned again.

"Sorry 'bout that, old boy. I wish you felt better." Brett looked at his friend thoughtfully. There had been times in the past when he had wished his friend would be more prudent. "Maybe you should cut down a bit."

Andrew frowned. "Oh, hell! You sound like my father."

Brett decided to let it pass. "But it really *was* great party, Andrew. Your sister's grown up into quite a beauty. And she's a wonderful dancer. Nice gal."

"She's a sweetie all right." He squinted in the bright sunshine.

"I'm glad you asked me to escort her. She looked like an angel in that dress—sent down from Heaven."

"Yeah, Valentino, I think. Mom got it in Paris." Andrew yawned. "It *was* a good party, wasn't it? My parents really know how to throw one."

"Do they ever!" Brett recalled visions of the night before—the men in full dress and the women in their stunning gowns; it reminded him of a Royal Ball.

They walked on. The next hole was still yards away.

"My Mom's really the one," Andrew said. "She's known for her fabulous parties. I've heard to be invited is known as the stamp of approval in Navy and Diplomatic circles."

"I believe it." Brett nodded assent.

Andrew walked slightly behind Brett toward the next play.

Brett looked at his watch; it was 7: 50. What a glorious December day. But then, the weather was always perfect in Hawaii, no matter what the season.

"The golf course is really busy this morning. I thought I saw the Admiral and his party on the forward tee," Andrew said.

"I'm not surprised," said Brett. "You know very well Sunday morning golf is a tradition around here. I've seen a number of the top brass raring to go, including several ship's captains."

"Well, there are plenty of them here. We must have—maybe 100 ships in the harbor right now."

"We'll just about have time to play 18 and get back to your parents' place in time to change for the luncheon." Brett chuckled. "You can get a little hair of the dog there."

"Yeah, that's right! There'll be plenty of champagne. Thank God for wedding anniversaries!" Andrew stopped near his ball. "My parents really do deserve a lot of credit. They've earned a lot of accolades over the years in the Service. I think my dad's one of the fair-haired boys by now."

Brett admired Andrew's father. An Annapolis graduate, he was the epitome of 'an officer and a gentleman' in every sense of the word. He nodded. "I'd say he's definitely destined for one of the most distinguished careers in the Navy."

"Yeah, I think so too. You know, my dad has to be the luckiest man alive to pull duty here. Pearl Harbor is the playground of the Pacific—the pipe dream of all of us. Wish I —" Andrew stopped in his tracks, his face contorted with a strange, apprehensive look. "What was that?"

Brett stopped and looked curiously at Andrew. "I don't know, probably just bombing practice." He frowned. "But on Sunday morning? You think?—Oh my God—that's a Japanese plane!"

They looked at each other in utter shock and disbelief. "There's another one!" Andrew shook his head incredulously. "This simply can't be happening! It's crazy!"

They heard the escalating sounds of other planes, flying overhead. And sounds of explosions in the distance.

"I don't believe this!" Brett exclaimed loudly. "Battle stations! Run! We've got to get back!" They began to run to the Jeep. Their first thought: to get to the ship as quickly as possible.

Brett threw a few dollars on the grass in the direction of the caddies. "Take care of our clubs," he yelled as he ran.

Another plane suddenly appeared and headed straight for them, strafing as it flew overhead.

"Hit the dirt," yelled Brett. "You too," in the direction of the caddies. Totally bewildered, they dropped the clubs and ran for the woods.

"Screw the clubs," Andrew said as he hit the ground. When the plane had cleared they resumed their run to the Jeep.

The sounds of the bombing became more frequent and more intense. Planes were flying over, strafing as they fled. Brett reached the Jeep first and jumped in the driver's seat. He turned on the ignition and was pulling away as Andrew jumped in.

"We have to get to the ship!" Brett said. "What the hell is happening? I can't believe that those Japs would have the insane stupidity to attack the U.S." He stepped on the gas. "But those planes are Zeros—and they're not fooling."

"My God! They're strafing all over the place." The expression on Andrew's face reflected the sheer horror that he felt.

"This is crazy. Why didn't we know?" Brett drove as fast as he could. "This will go down in history as the biggest foul up of the 20th century."

The road was beginning to fill up with people running and vehicles of all kinds coming from all sides.

"How could they! How could they leave so many of our prize ships and men gathered together in one harbor? We're just sitting targets!" Brett's anger was rising to a boiling point. "Somebody had to know!"

The jeep bumped along as Brett turned and wound around to avoid the burgeoning traffic.

"Somebody had to know." The realization of the far-reaching implications of this attack on an unknowing United States base was beginning to dawn on a sickened Andrew. Yes, somebody had to know. Someone in the know. But it couldn't have been anyone who is in command on this island. That would be like committing professional suicide.

"Son-of-a-bitch! Somebody is going to get the blame and two to one, it won't be the real culprit." Brett said.

Andrew knew how the Service sometimes worked. He had seen a number of brilliant careers ruined by the acts of someone else, and sometimes it had been an enduring deliberate cover-up. He thought of his father. He felt sick. Though his father was not in a critical strategic command post, would this be a 'guilt by association'? A smear on a magnificent man, who had given his life to defend and protect his country?

All of a sudden, he was overtaken with fear. Not only for his own life but for his father, his mother, his sister, his friends.

This is *War* and people are going to be killed.

All along the road people were running, their screams joining the escalating noise of combined battle sounds. Cars, bicycles, and trucks sped in both directions. There were numerous accidents, as frightened people attempted to run and speed away from the strafing of planes and unexpected bombs. Smoke and fire answered the bombs in different places.

People were falling on the roadway, on the grass, as the bullets from the strafing planes made their way to their unknown targets. Speeding vehicles were everywhere. Brett narrowly avoided a couple of near misses of vehicles and bodies, as he drove through the confusion to reach the harbor—and their cherished ship.

Soon they came in sight of the harbor. Brett stopped the Jeep in horror at the sight of the carnage. The harbor was bathed in a blanket of smoke and fire. Burning vessels, burning men were trapped in a bloodbath of inconceivable proportions. Ship upon ship was burning, exploding. Some were returning fire, if they were able. Men were either trying to defend and save their ship, shoot down the oncoming planes, or defeated in their efforts, jump into the flaming water. It was a scene of utter horror, devastation. Smells of death filled the air.

"Oh my God, Andrew! Oh my God!"

At that very moment their ship, the majestic Arizona, exploded. The smoke began to rise and engulf her. Unexpectedly, a fireball shot up into the air like a rocket until it reached 800 feet. The flames were mind-boggling. It was as though Hell itself had erupted. Like some evil volcano was pouring out its wrath in envy against the beauty and tranquility of the landscape. They stood there, frozen for a moment in unbelief. Then gradually their beloved ship, the pride of the Navy, leaned over on her side—and sank into the water.

The fire quickly spread across the oil slick. They could see the men, their shipmates, jumping into the blazing water.

"No! No! My God, the men, the guys!" They glanced momentarily at each other. Andrew jumped from the Jeep and began to run. There was no way to drive the Jeep much farther. The congestion of traffic almost prevented escape. Brett brushed silent tears away as he drove as far down the slope as he could, pulled up, cut the ignition, jumped out, and followed Andrew. They ran toward their shipmates as fast as they could. Perhaps in some way they could help save some of them.

Chaos was everywhere. Bombs kept bursting. The noise of battle was deafening, overwhelming. The Oklahoma and a plethora of other ships were also hit and burning. Smoke and debris were flying through the air as other explosions mingled with the screams of the burning and wounded men struggling to survive in this hellish holocaust.

Andrew had almost reached the water when a plane came out of the smoke, strafing every moving target in sight. Brett, several yards behind, saw him crumple and fall.

"Oh, God! He's been hit." He kept on running toward him. "Oh God! Not Andrew."

Then abruptly, Brett felt as though a mountain had come down upon him. He found himself falling, falling. Blackness began to enfold him as he struggled to catch a full breath. He felt a warm wet liquid creeping over him as though he were in the water, and then the blackness had its way with him and he passed into another dimension.

That was the last thing he ever consciously remembered of that horrifying day…..

Andrew had fallen just in time to prevent worse damage. He felt hot explosive stabs hit him in the leg. The shock stunned him, but he soon got his bearings. Instinctively, he looked back for Brett to help him, but Brett was down, not moving.

He panicked. He had to get to him. He tried to rise from the ground, but his right leg was dangling and there was bleeding from somewhere else, he didn't know where. Still, he managed to half crawl, half walk on one leg and two hands the 20 yards to where Brett was lying. He was out cold. Apparently, he had had a hard blow to the head, but he was breathing. Blood was seeping slowly from some unidentified wound, and kept spreading, soaking his clothing.

From deep in his belly, a terrifying reality came over Andrew: Brett was dying and he was unable to help him. He looked around but no one was near.

In his panic, he called out, "Oh God.... please… don't let him die."

People were running up and down the slope trying to get away or rescue the men in the flaming water, but they were yards away. All of a sudden, out of nowhere, Andrew spied two large men dressed in white coats running toward his direction. Andrew reached out and called to them as they ran:

"Stop! Stop! We need help here. My friend is hemorrhaging. He could bleed to death. Help us!"

The stranger stopped and took in the situation. True, they needed help all right. In their golf shorts they could have been from anywhere, but one of them seemed critical. He spoke to the other rescuer. "We need to do something quickly for these two."

"Our jeep is right up there," Andrew said with a shaky voice. "If you can get us up to the jeep there and take him to the base hospital—I'm afraid my friend is dying." Andrew began to cry. Silently, tears began to slide down his cheeks. He shivered; suddenly he felt very cold.

"Yes, I see the jeep. O.K. Let's go. No time to waste."

The two men were strong. They picked Brett up carefully and carried him to the Jeep. Andrew tried but could go no farther. He felt excruciating pains go down his right leg every time he moved, but this was no time to care.

Once in the Jeep, one of the men tried to give Brett first aid to stop the bleeding but all he could do was apply pressure points, hoping that he'd found the right spot. A wet crimson was quickly covering Brett's body. He was still bleeding.

As he attempted to pull himself up the slope, Andrew tried to keep his eyes on Brett. He saw the man lay his hands on Brett's body He seemed to be mumbling something, but Andrew couldn't hear him.

The other man ran back for Andrew and carried him to the Jeep. The man lifted his leg carefully to prevent further damage. All Andrew could feel was the hideous pain; but then he felt a tingling sensation and almost immediately, to his surprise and gratitude, it began to ease off.

The man jumped in the driver's seat. Luckily, Brett had left the keys in the ignition. He started the motor and they were on their way.

"You say you're military?"

"Yes, Navy lieutenants. We're from the Arizona. Please hurry! He's still bleeding."

"Right! I think we have to go to the hospital nearest us. I doubt we could even get to the base hospital right now. It's almost impossible to get out of here."

They drove in and out of the crowds and congestion, weaving sometimes on the road and sometimes on the grass. After what seemed to be an eternity, they pulled up in front of the hospital; the scene was utter chaos. The driver jumped out and grabbed an orderly.

"We have two Navy lieutenants here. One is critical and the other is badly wounded. There's no time to waste."

The orderly ran inside and returned with a stretcher and a bottle of plasma. He brought two others with him, one with another stretcher. They lifted Brett onto the first stretcher and soon disappeared through the swinging doors. The other orderly and the driver lifted Andrew onto the second stretcher. Weeping softly, he asked, "Is he dying?"

The rescuer looked at him. His eyes filled with compassion. "He will live and not die," he said.

"What's your name?" asked Andrew, startled.

"Does it matter?" He smiled,

"It does to me," Andrew said.

"Angie Messenger," the man said, and even as Andrew looked at him, he and the other man disappeared into the confusion. Andrew had the strangest feeling—as if that were not his name at all…

He began to feel the stretcher under him rolling swiftly toward the hospital entrance.

Suddenly, an overwhelming sensation came over him—and he was at peace.

Chapter 3

The train rocked on down the interminable tracks. The rhythm of its motion was repetitive, the sounds—hypnotic. Brett Whitney stared unseeingly out of the window as the landscape sped by. He was tired; his legs were cramped from the long journey and there were still miles to go. Lulled by the cadence of the train, he let his mind wander back to that day six months ago. Yes, he could remember it now. It was no longer a vague nightmare. He could remember it all—as though it were yesterday.

The dream had been recurrent at first—vivid, frightening, unrelenting. But that was during that first two weeks while he was half-conscious. Then, as those months in the hospital continued, he had dealt not only with his wounds but the nightmare as well.

The doctors had said, "Talk about it and it will become less fragmented. Those memories will come together for you in another form—and subside." They had been right. Eventually, he had been able to deal with it, bring it into the realm of reality.

Luckily, Andrew had insisted that the nurses place their beds side by side in the same ward, so they had been able to discuss what really happened at length—work through it together—bring it into full recall without the emotional pain. What had happened after he had blacked out, Andrew had filled in for him during those months in the hospital, where he, too, had been recovering. His compound fracture had taken long weeks to heal and required a series of intricate operations, the outcomes of which were the pride of the surgeons there. But he was well now, thank God. Better than ever, and raring to go.

God bless Andrew! If it hadn't been for him! Brett knew that they had been saved by an unseen hand. All of the doctors had looked at him in disbelief. He could see them now, shaking their heads and making all kinds of comments:

"This is a medical and biological impossibility. There is absolutely no way a man could sustain that much blood loss and survive. Son, you're a walking miracle!"

He knew it was true. He had had a strange feeling throughout the entire ordeal. He knew that he had been spared for some purpose; and now he was headed to fulfill it, whatever it was.

It had been therapeutic to have Andrew so near. After all, they had been close friends ever since Annapolis and they had been in that hell together. It was no longer a fragmented terror now. It was true. He remembered it in its entirety, the surroundings, the weather, even the conversation. But it was over now, and he was well and strong again. He was thankful to be alive and he was ready for the future—whatever it might bring.

Andrew had left two months before for some new duty in Washington. Brett missed him, but it was time to get on with it. He wondered where his next assignment would take him. There seemed to be some secrecy around it, but he was accustomed to not knowing. He'd been trained as an intelligence officer so they would probably assign him to some other field—that was the typical Navy for you, particularly now, with the nation six months into the war, and officers being reassigned hurriedly, and sometimes inadvisably due to a surplus of necessary posts.

Dr. Margaret S. Emanuelson

Well, he would soon know. He stretched his legs out as far as he could and settled back down in his seat. The train was beginning to slow as it pulled into the station.

The conductor came down the aisle again. announcing the next stop.

"Raleigh, Raleigh …. next stop …Raleigh."

Abby tapped her foot impatiently as she waited on the train platform She looked admiringly at her new watch, a graduation present from her mother, and checked the time. Ten minutes of 10. And the train was already forty minutes late. Well, what did she expect? Everything was late these days in the transportation department. She sighed and sat down again on the bench next to her one large piece of luggage remaining from those she had shipped from her dormitory a few days before.

Thank God, that's over, she thought. Remembering the turmoil of the past few days, an emotionally drained, almost battered feeling came over her.

One would have thought that she would feel triumphant at receiving her degree, an achievement by few women of her day. After all, it *was* from a top-notch university—and two years earlier than normal. But as usual, she felt robbed of any feeling of joy.

It had been a truly impressive and moving ceremony and series of events. But by the time she had tried to meet the demands of her mother, who had come with her two sisters, on the one hand, and those of her father, accompanied by his present wife, on the other, she had given up any hope of saying good-bye to her friends or pleasure in her accomplishment. However, this was nothing new. Constantly torn between the two, there was no hope of salvaging any feeling of value for herself. They were 'joy-killers,' her parents—though they didn't mean to be; nor had they any idea of how their behavior affected their only daughter.

She shrugged her shoulders and sighed. It was the same old thing, they would never change.

She stamped her foot. Well, they called it 'commencement,' and that meant a new beginning. She was *not* going to be defeated by this albatross for the rest of her life. It was time to get on with it.

The whistle of the train pierced her perception as it rumbled in the distance. Suddenly energized, her spirits lifted. Yes, this was a new beginning. And she was ready for it. What better way to begin than to serve her country, particularly now, in such a time as this.

The Silver Comet was full of soldiers, some even sitting on luggage in the aisles. Abby boarded the train amidst a chorus of whistles and approving looks by the young men. She was accustomed to being admired, but in this situation she felt a lot less comfortable. The only female within sight, she felt lost, surrounded. There was no place to sit except the aisle and that was crowded.

Frowning, she looked around. This was an entirely unanticipated situation. She muttered under her breath, "Oh, lord! What am I going to do?"

Unexpectedly she heard a familiar sound, a deep melodious Southern drawl. "Miss, here, please take my seat," the voice said. "I'm getting off at Norfolk, the next stop. It's not too far from here."

Abby turned in surprise and found the voice. She hesitated. "Oh, dear! That's very kind of you. But really, I couldn't. You've probably been traveling a long way. I really couldn't think of taking your seat."

The voice was pleasant, and persistent. It had the familiar flavor and comforting chivalry of the "Old South"—and it belonged to a very attractive, even handsome young naval officer.

"Yes, Ma'am, It *has* been a long journey and I'm just about ready to stretch my legs. Please—allow me to trade places with you."

"I would hate to inconvenience—"

The voice smiled, "But I insist!"

"Well, if you're really sure—I do appreciate it."

"Good! I'll help you get settled with your luggage and all. The next stop is not too very far. That's where they're waiting to pick me up."

"Really? Even so, it's wonderful of you to offer. Thank you so much. I feel as if I've just been rescued." She looked up at him gratefully. "Incidentally, I'm Abby."

"And I'm Brett Whitney," said the young man as he stood untangling his long legs. He put out his hand and took hers in that typical way that a gentleman greets a young lady. His smile broke out of a handsome tanned face. It was contagious.

Abby found herself laughing, looking up into the bluest eyes she had ever seen. As he stood to full height she could see his tall athletic frame as he moved to the aisle and assisted her into the seat where he had been before.

"Thank God for Southern gentlemen," she said.

"How do you know I'm from the South?" asked Brett, laughing.

"I should think it would be obvious." Abby gave him a mischievous look.

"Guilty as charged," Brett smiled as he moved Abby's luggage close to the arm of the seat. Suddenly he felt rejuvenated, restored, his weariness melting away.

She wedged her small body into the seat next to a sleeping soldier. He was a huge young man in a marine uniform. Probably a football player, she thought. To make matters worse the seat facing her had two more of the same sort; but they were awake and they were so accommodating it made her feel a little more comfortable. They must have sisters at home, she thought.

Brett stretched his legs and back for a while and finally sat down on her large suitcase in the aisle. They chatted back and forth. The bars on his shoulder indicated that he held the rank of Navy lieutenant.

He was from Memphis, Tennessee, on the way to a new assignment. He talked of his home, which had been in his family since the early 1800s. Among other things, his family raised thoroughbred horses and maintained quite a large farm. Fulfilling a tradition set by his grandfather, he had finished his college degree at Annapolis and had apparently been stationed somewhere. But now he had been called to a different branch of service. He didn't specify what that was. In fact, he seemed reluctant to talk about the war.

He wanted to know all about Abby. She told him about her home, also a very old antebellum one, in Atlanta, and a bit about her family.

"My father was a career officer," she said. "He retired after thirty years and a four-year tour of duty in the Orient. Afterward, he joined a large corporation as an executive. He loves horses too. Until my early teens he used to take me riding. I can remember as a little girl feeding the horses sugar cubes. My daddy would say,

'Now keep your hand very flat, little Abby, so the horse won't bite you.' It was so exciting to feed those enormous animals. But he would never let me feed the polo ponies. They were too dangerous, too frisky."

"He was right about that! All thoroughbreds can be hypersensitive, but particularly polo ponies. It's not a good idea to spook them, and believe me, they can be easily spooked. I've been thrown a few times myself."

"So you play polo?"

"Yes, but not in a while," he said wistfully.

"And that *is* dangerous!" She remembered the mishaps she'd seen on the field at the old fort.

"I suppose so, but luckily I never broke a bone."

"You were fortunate," Abby said. "So many of my friends have had pretty serious accidents just learning to ride, particularly to jump."

"Oh, it *can* be a particularly dangerous sport. It takes a person with exquisite timing and a very close fellowship with his horse."

"Well, more power to you." She sighed. "I have other things on my mind at this time of my life. I'll worry about horses and riding again tomorrow."

"Just like Scarlet O'Hara," Brett said, with his captivating smile. Brett looked at her long dark hair. He found himself enchanted by the way she tossed her head to one side and flashed those impish green eyes at him. "Oh yes, just like Scarlet O'Hara."

Abby chuckled, "I've been called that before, you know."

"I can see why, you look like her."

"That may be, but I can assure you, that's where the resemblance ends."

"Yes, probably so, but actually, I've always thought her to be an exceptional young woman. Quite a courageous girl for her time."

"That's true, she was all of that" she said. "I suppose a war can bring out the best and the worst in those it touches."

"I'd have to agree with that," said Brett, remembering the heroic deeds he'd witnessed, not so long ago.

"Nevertheless, I loved *Gone with the Wind*. It premiered in Atlanta, you know, three or four years ago. I was even fortunate enough to attend the great ball. It was quite an affair. People are still talking about it, and probably will be years from now. It will always be a great classic epic of a terrible time for our country."

He looked at her intently. "And I suppose years from now there will be other great classics depicting *this* war too, when we're both old and gray."

Abby laughed, "No doubt, only *we're* the *real* characters in this one."

The train sped on as they talked for hours about many things. Their absorption in one another was like magic, so powerful that time seemed to vanish. Suddenly, the train began to lurch and slow down. The conductor came through announcing the next stop, weaving his way through the aisles down the overcrowded train.

"Norfolk, Portsmouth… Next stop… Norfolk, Portsmouth," he called out in that typical singsong voice.

The train slowed and finally came to a full stop.

The soldiers had begun to rouse and move into the aisle, collecting their packs and other belongings. The noise became louder, and grew to an almost deafening pitch.

"I'm afraid this is where I get off," said Brett, raising his voice. "I'm sorry to have to leave you." He looked at her, wistfully, gathering his gear.

"Oh, no, I can't believe it! Where did the time go?" Abby said.

"Looks like it vanished, unfortunately. Do you have a phone number? I'd like to call you."

" I can give you my mother's number. I'll be staying with her a while. She hurriedly wrote her mother's number down on the end of an envelope. When she looked up, he was some distance away from her, surrounded by the crowd of young soldiers scurrying to depart to their destinations. He was hardly in sight. She passed the envelope to him through the soldiers lined up in the aisle.

"What's your last name?" Brett, yelled, as he made his way towards the door.

"St. Giles," she said loudly.

"St. James?" Brett said over the increasing noise. "Great, I'll call you." With that he disappeared in the crowd.

Her heart sank. *Oh dear no! He didn't get my name.* She looked out the window of the train to see if she could spot him, but he was nowhere in sight. What an exciting fellow! She hoped he *would* call. But would he?

There was something about this young man. She couldn't tell quite what it was, but she had felt very drawn to him. To be realistic, she'd probably never see him again, but then, one never knew with a war going on. Of course, according to the rules, she was never to consider going out with someone to whom she had not been formally introduced. But this was wartime—and he *was* a young officer, and indeed a gentleman, at least he seemed to be.

Brett grabbed the envelope with Abby's telephone number from the hand of the last soldier in line, and stepped down off the train. Immediately he was surrounded with the other debarking service men. He looked back to see if he could get one last glance at her. It was hopeless, but he knew he would always remember the image of her beautiful face.

From deep within came an overwhelming thought, more like a decisive resolve. *That's the girl I'm going to marry.*

Abby settled into the almost empty car. She felt dirty, sooty. By now the train was a mess with all the empty cartons and wrappers of food and drink. She was an orderly person, so this kind of disarray was disturbing. But there was very little she could do about it, so she settled down and tried to relax. Staring out the window the countryside sped by, her thoughts wandered—where was Brett going? What would the future bring for him? Would she see him again?

The train pulled out of the station, lurched off and on and finally settled into a continuing melody of rhythm and sound. Exhausted, soon she fell asleep, nodding off into her own dream world.

Suddenly the sky lit up with red and yellow lights as a loud roar exploded in the foggy night. She struggled to come awake but the effort was fruitless. There was an overwhelming feeling of terror, fear, confusion in her half-consciousness. Suddenly out of the darkness she felt strong arms pick her up. She caught a glimpse of startling blue eyes looking down at her, as the light broke through the clouds. Then the darkness overtook her again.

She awoke with a start. In her half-waking state the dream was still vivid. What did it mean? It was significant, otherwise she would have paid it no attention. It was not just one of those everyday dreams one had that were gone by the time one was fully awake. This one was different, not soon forgotten.

Abby was well acquainted with dreams and prophecy. Though some people called such things coincidence, extra-sensory perception, or intuition, she knew that these occurrences were gifts, although sometimes they could be disturbing, particularly for the one who received them.

Her mother had those gifts. She seemed always to know of things and events she couldn't possibly have known. Once when Abby was in college, she had had a sudden attack of appendicitis and was rushed to the hospital in another town. The doctors had decided to operate immediately the next morning.

She had asked her housemother to notify her father. Since she was underage, her father had to give his permission for the operation. But she had requested that her mother not be notified until after the operation was over. She had her reasons. Twice when she was small she had been in the hospital near death. The hysterical scenes had been indelibly impressed upon her memory. She wanted no recurrences.

The operation took place early in the morning. Back in Washington, Miranda, her mother, had dreamt that Abby was in the hospital calling for her. The sound of the doorbell ringing awakened her. At the door, a Western Union boy handed her a telegram saying that Abby's appendectomy had gone well.

To Abby, even as young as she was, it was better to be operated on alone, miles away from school, family, or friends than to subject herself to what she had experienced in the past.

Yes, her mother was gifted in more ways than one: She was beautiful, intelligent, and a talented artist. She was also educated—

a connoisseur of the arts, literature, music. She carried herself with the natural poise and confidence of one of the manor born. She had a keen sense of humor, which endeared her to her many friends.

But where her daughter was concerned there was another side to her of which Abby was very much aware. A side which she wanted to keep private. Her mother was a good and moral woman. She had no desire to besmirch her mother's reputation in any way or cause others to think ill of her. Nor did she want the conflict between her and her mother to be exposed. Things like that were family matters. Not for prying eyes.

As she had grown older she had begun to understand how her mother had become the way she was. It all had to do with the conflict between her father and mother and the relationship among the three of them. But no matter how she tried, she could not change anything. By now, the situation seemed as though it was written in concrete, and she had accepted it, resolving to keep herself as far away from it as she could.

The conductor began to come down the aisle again. "Washington, Washington. Next stop Washington."

Abby began to realize that she had been dozing for some time, but she couldn't stop thinking about the dream. What did it mean?

The train was creeping through the long rail yards into the station. The landscape rolled by, an ugly, endless chain of boxcars and occasional huge black engines, waiting to move down the endless rails to a new destination.

She made a quick run to the restroom to freshen up. She looked in the mirror. Oh, dear, this would never do. Her mother would think she'd been in an accident.

Quickly, she ran a brush through her long, dark hair, washed her hands, and refreshed her lipstick. She returned to her seat and gathered her things. The train was beginning to slow.

The large, heavy suitcase was still in the aisle. Perhaps she could get one of the young men to help her carry it. Porters were hard to come by since the war had started, so that and her small cosmetic case were the only things she had brought with her. Her steamer trunk had been shipped ahead as well as several boxes and pieces of luggage she had had at her dormitory at school.

Abby loved the old trunk. In a way it symbolized her father. It still had stickers on it from all around the world, most of which were her father's from places he had lived and many of his travels. Only some of them were hers. Her other things were still in her grandmother's old colonial home outside Atlanta, where she had lived with her and her mother after her parents' divorce, which was as long as she could remember.

At last the train pulled into the station. Through the window, she could see quite a crowd gathered on the platform. Parents, wives and children, friends and lovers, all were there to meet their loved ones, soldiers on leave, friends, or business associates.

She rose from her seat, gathered her things, and stepped into the aisle. Two young men dressed in naval uniforms stepped aside for her so that she could get in line. She had chatted with them briefly during the trip. Abby leaned over again to look out the window. She couldn't see her mother but she was sure that she was there. Little by little the line of passengers moved up as the crowded train emptied. Then she was at the steps. She looked around. There was her mother a few yards away, waiting.

One of the young naval officers brought her heavy suitcase down to the platform for her. She thanked him profusely.

"Maybe we'll run into one another sometime," he said.

"Great! I'd like that. Good luck to you." Abby turned her attention to finding her mother, who by now had spotted her and had taken in the whole scene.

"Darling, it's so good to see you." They hugged one another and began to look for help with the heavy luggage.

"Who was that?" her mother asked. "Where did you meet him?"

"Oh, he's just a young man who helped me with my luggage. I met him on the train."

"On the train? I see." Her mother gave her a disapproving look.

"Yes. His name was George something or other—yes, that's it—it was George—George Bush, or something, I think."

"Now Abigail, you know very well you should never talk to strangers on the train or anywhere else."

"Yes, Mother, I know, but I don't know how I would have managed that heavy suitcase this far without him. Besides he's a very nice young man."

"And handsome too, but he could be a serial killer, you know."

"That's right, and one day he also might also become President of the United States." They both laughed. Finally they found a porter to handle the luggage and took a cab to the apartment.

Abby was glad to see her mother. She loved her dearly, always had. It had only been in the past few years that they hadn't gotten along so well. She was growing up, asserting her independence. As long as she was away from her mother's domination they did very well. But when she was near, her mother seemed to think it was her lifetime job to direct her every waking moment. She had been away a long time with only short vacations in between, which had gone very well. Whenever she had left to return to school, her mother seemed to release her control a bit, knowing that the one or two universities who were now allowing women had strict rules and too, since her father was also a primary figure in sending her, her responsibility had lessened. However, even so, there were times when her mother had checked up on her without her knowledge. All to her chagrin.

Over the next two or three days, Abby unpacked and settled in. The apartment was considerably smaller than to what she was accustomed, but elegantly appointed. Her mother's artistic touch was clearly obvious and she recognized a few favorite antiques and paintings brought from the old house in Atlanta. If, temporarily, this was to be "home away from home," it was certainly not bad at all.

She made a few phone calls to her father, her grandmother, and a few of her remaining friends who were still in Washington. For the next few days, she and her mother enjoyed each other's company. They went out to dinner, visited with friends, and developed a lighthearted banter between them. Abby realized, however, that this was the honeymoon period and that once things settled down the old dragon of conflict might well rear its ugly head again. Nevertheless, she proceeded as though she expected nothing untoward.

Tomorrow she would begin a new venture, into a new and unknown territory. A mixture of excitement and uneasiness crept over her. Her anxiety might have been greater had she known where it would lead her.

Chapter 4

The French Embassy was abuzz with the usual high-spirited gaiety associated with its many parties. He had come under his present cover as "Jacques D'Arcy," a French diplomat, to instruct Louis Cabot, his key contact there. He hadn't intended to join the affair, so they had met on the dark terrace. No chance of being bugged or overheard. Too, it was cooler in the warm spring's night.

He was pleased with the developments of his organizational efforts so far. He knew how to delegate operations to trustworthy agents. With only one or two key contacts he could oversee the entire operation and instigate the total scope of activities, without disclosing his identity.

He had finished his instructions. Louis, his key man, he knew, would carry them out to the letter. But tonight, Louis seemed to be annoyed about something. He listened to him as he complained.

"There's a problem with this arrogant contact. He's getting very fidgety. Seems to be afraid someone in Congress is going to find out about his connection with us. He's demanding more protection. What shall we do?"

"Tell him to calm down. We've covered any possibility of detection. All he has to do is keep his mouth shut. There is absolutely nothing to worry about—that is, unless he's spouted off to someone."

"That may be why he's worried. He's quite a blowhard, a real braggart." Louis frowned.

"Who is this idiot, anyway? I don't recall any dealings with him."

"You've never met him, but you know about him. 'Razor' is the code name he chose." Louis chuckled with a smirk. "Apparently considers himself pretty sharp."

"Sounds like it. Delusions of grandeur."

"He's the one who got surreptitiously involved with us before the war some years ago through his congressional dealings with us. He was involved with the Congressional Trade Committee or something. He made us some confidential, secret promises and deals that have worked out to our advantage for several years."

"Yes, now I do recall the details about him." Jacques nodded. "He's also made some investments in our economy and our future to his advantage, and he's been given some valuable art treasures as 'presents.' I think he sees himself as a big-wig in our regime after we win the war."

"Yes, I'm sure he does. He's been ecstatic till now, but suddenly he's getting extremely paranoid." Louis took a long drag on his cigarette. "I see him now and again at different functions, but he has no idea that I'm his contact—I use a drop zone for him. But I can tell his behavior is increasingly nervous."

"Jacques" gestured impatiently. "You tell that 'Razor' that we have everything under control. But if he has anything specific that we need to do to protect the secrecy of our operations here, he'd better tell us now, or he may be in more trouble with us than with his own government."

Louis grinned. He didn't like "Razor." "I'll be sure he gets the message, but don't be surprised if we hear from him again."

"You'll handle it with finesse, I know. But if you can't pat him down gently, let me know. We'll take care of it."

They stood and chatted about trivia for a few minutes, like two Frenchmen catching up on past events.

Unexpectedly, out of the corner of his eye, Jacques was attracted by something that aroused his curiosity. He turned so that he could take in the whole scene. Through the open French doors, he saw a wisp of pale golden hair curling from under the back of her uniform hat. Though she couldn't have been over five feet seven, she looked tall, perhaps because of her willowy figure, slim, but well proportioned.

He stood there transfixed. It was impossible, but there she was, talking to a group across the room.

Before she turned, he knew what she would be like beneath that unsightly uniform. He watched her, captivated. At last she turned and his heart jumped. He caught his breath. There was that beautiful face, the finely chiseled classic features, that air of calm measured grace that set her apart. That unique genteel quality which separated her from all the other women in the whole world. Everything in a woman he had been waiting for all of his life.

Suddenly, their eyes met—and he was not disappointed. He approached her.

Chapter 5

By June of '42, Washington was no longer just that beautiful classic jewel of a city. It was the capitol of the nation. It was where the action was; where the orders and planning for conquest and defense were formulated. Washington was the center, the hub, the headquarters, the core of activity, and everything else flowed from there.

Into this swarming, bustling headquarters of the nation came the young, the mature, the educated, skilled and the unskilled, and hundreds of people of all kinds, eager to contribute their multiple and diverse talents to the defense of their beloved country and its allies, to conquer and defeat the enemy.

And on her way into this melting pot of diversity came Abby St. Giles. She was ready for the adventure of starting a new life on her own. She was excited. What better way to begin than to serve one's country, particularly in the midst of a world at war.

On Monday Abby reported to her new position on Constitution Avenue. For lack of a more specific placement, Civil Service had placed her initially in the Bureau of Ships.

Once she was inside the building, a counter barred access to the inner offices. Armed guards were on duty around the clock to check identification. Personal or other unofficial packages were inspected and kept at the security station until one left the building. Security was tightly observed, imperative. Employees were made very much aware of how vitally critical safety measures could be.

Immediately, she was sent for a security badge, to be worn at all times while in or around government establishments. Further, she was instructed never to reveal even the most seemingly trivial part of her work to anyone outside her work environment, or within it, only on a basis of the "need to know." It was emphasized how those with ulterior motives could piece little bits of information together to discover troop and ship movements and all sorts of other important clues valuable to the enemy.

Large posters around the walls with illustrations and slogans gave warning: "Mum's the Word," "She's not so Dumb," "Loose Lips Sink Ships."

The interiors, painted battleship gray and white throughout, gave a sparse, clean-cut, no nonsense, almost antiseptic feel about the place. In fact, it was rather dismal. Entering the inner offices, the only bright spot that caught her attention was a solitary vase sporting a single red rose on one of the desks.

At least intelligent human beings work here, she thought, and for an extremely urgent purpose. Otherwise, the atmosphere itself would be too depressing to tolerate the surroundings. It has to be the ultimate goal and the people involved, which serve as the motivation to continue here.

Abby waited impatiently for several days while the "powers that be" decided what to do with her. To keep her occupied, she was given organizational charts of the government of the United States, the Navy, and the Secretary of Navy, and the extensive organization of different branches over which he had purview.

It was impressive; things she would never have suspected. She doubted seriously that many of her college colleagues were aware of the intricacies or expanse of the way the government worked, and certainly even fewer average citizens.

But the waiting was agonizing. When would they finally decide what to do with her? To make matters worse, she was informed that Civil Service workers were required to be on duty six days a week and sometimes seven. Quite a change from her stimulating but casual college lifestyle. If it were absorbing, interesting, it was acceptable, but she couldn't bear to think of her future employment as this dull, colorless, existence.

At one point her temporary supervisor brought in a large stack of invoices to sort out. She felt like a complete idiot. Had she said "bills," then Abby would have known what she meant, but she had never been trained in office procedures and certainly to this point she had never paid an "invoice" in her life.

After an interminable week of waiting, a middle-aged, pleasant looking naval officer strode in to the office where she was sitting behind a desk. He pulled up a chair and sat down.

"I'm Commander Logan," he said. "I'm with the Bureau of Naval Personnel. We're right under the Secretary of the Navy. I thought perhaps you might be more suited to be employed by my office, and I'm sure by now you're getting somewhat eager to get going."

"That is the understatement of all time," Abby said, laughing. "Thank heavens! I hope you're here for the rescue."

The Commander's blue eyes lit up with a warm empathetic glow. "Truth is, there is so much to be done around here, our people sometimes get lost in the shuffle. But after looking at your credentials and qualifications, I think you're just what I'm looking for. Besides, I think you'll enjoy this kind of work. So if you'll come along with me, we'll get on with it."

She wasted no time. Delighted, she gathered her things and gratefully accompanied the Commander to the main building.

The Commander was a pleasant but no-nonsense guy. Abby liked him immediately. He seemed to know exactly what he wanted and made it clear that he wasn't used to compromising. He turned out to be extremely courteous, considerate, encouraging, and businesslike. He let one know what he expected precisely. Usually, there was no second-guessing. She liked that; it made things a great deal easier, especially while she was becoming oriented not only to a new job but working itself.

He escorted her to his office and introduced her around to some of the staff. As with many other government offices, the staff included officer, enlisted, and civilian personnel. The Commander, of course, was the C.O. His assistant C.O. was a chic well-groomed blonde woman, Lieutenant Commander Marie Swenson. She had joined the WAVES several months before and had risen quickly in rank, partially because of her expertise as director of personnel for a large international retail store that had branches all over the world. Marie was a very charming and personable young woman and Abby liked her immediately. She seemed compassionate and friendly while at the same time a seasoned professional.

Marie introduced Abby to some of the other girls in the office. There was Barbara, a newcomer, and Bunny, who was engaged to a bombardier, and could talk of nothing else.

Lt. Suzanne Davenport was Commander Logan's confidential executive secretary. Tall and willowy, Suzanne was an unusually attractive woman. Her gray-blue eyes and long dark lashes alone set her apart. But her sometimes-unruly pale gold hair, which framed an oval face, completed the picture. Despite Navy regulations about short hair and uniforms, nothing could deny her Dresden-like femininity.

Suzanne was sophisticated, well traveled, educated, and somewhat worldly. By twenty-seven, she had gotten around a bit as executive secretary for an airlines magnate for a while and then settled for a job as an executive secretary for a senator. Leaving the senator's employ, she had been assigned to Commander Logan as his confidential executive secretary. At the onset of the war she had joined the WAVES, and received an immediate commission as an officer while continuing in that position.

She and Abby clicked immediately, finding they had much in common. They had even attended the same school in Switzerland, though not at the same time due to the differences in their ages.

Among the enlisted personnel was Joe, who was usually assigned to courier service and other odds and ends, yet all essential to a smooth operation. There were other employees, some older experienced Civil Service workers who had been with the Service for quite some time before the war. In addition to the other employees, there were temporary enlisted personnel assigned from time to time. They would come and go as needed.

At the time Abby was assigned to this office there was something of an upheaval going on because of so many transfers of the officers and enlisted personnel to sea duty and overseas assignments. The war, now in full force, was fairly new and re-organization was constantly necessary to provide for the increasing demands for personnel on land and on sea.

She found herself at home with most of the people in the office. Barbara was an upbeat girl, and since they lived near one another, sometimes saw each other outside the office for lunch or dining. Abby admired Marie Swenson. Although they maintained a certain level of professional distance, there was a mutual level of respect and unspoken comradeship which they both recognized. She affectionately nicknamed her "Mither Sweeney," though it was never used openly.

But her closest confidante was Suzanne. She particularly enjoyed the easy rapport between them, since they shared a number of interests in common—classical literature, architecture, music, and paintings of the old masters included, and some of their experiences abroad.

From time to time they would attend functions together, as singles or with their respective young men. They, laughingly, concocted a signal between them, a sort of code. If either one became bored or compromised in a situation and felt the need to be rescued, it meant: "Help! Get me out of this." A forefinger on the side of the nose had unobtrusively saved a number of awkward situations.

One afternoon Suzanne asked if she would like to go up to Capitol Hill for a party being held in a senator's office suite. Abby readily agreed. It would be interesting to get a closer look at some of the people who now made the laws and the policies, as well as get to know some of them here in Washington. Her family had been actively involved with politics and with most of the primary senators and politicians in their state. In fact, her grandmother, in her girlhood, had been best friends with the mother of a later Governor of Georgia, and was on a first name basis with most of them.

"When is it?" Abby said.

"It will be Friday evening around six. We can go from the office if you like."

"Great! What do we wear?"

"Well, of course I'll be in uniform," said Suzanne. "But you can wear something a little dressier to the office if you want. You'll find all sorts of outfits there."

"Wonderful, that'll be great! It would really take too long to go home to dress. I'll find something appropriate."

Abby knew she would have to explain to her mother why she wasn't coming straight home from work on Friday. When she usually went out on dates it was from home, where her mother could meet the young man, in case she hadn't met him before. To her delight, most of the young men she knew came through Washington on their way home on leave or on new assignments. There were also invitations from some of the older friends of the family, who had long been there, so she had had no reason to feel left out of the social scene. It had been fun, getting reacquainted with the many of the young men she had known in college. Besides, her mother knew most of them, so she was less demanding. Some she had dated off and on, and had even continued a correspondence after they had left for the service, or graduated. But this was different—a chance to size up what was really going on in this fascinating city of intrigue.

Friday arrived at last. After work she and Suzanne took a cab to the Capitol. Along the way Suzanne said, "I feel like I'm leading a lamb to the slaughter."

What in the world did she mean by that? Abby thought. But they chatted on the way and Abby thought no more about it. She asked who was giving the party.

"Senator Dudley Downs," Suzanne said. "I used to work in his office some years ago. I know him pretty well. He's having a party for his staff and some of the other senators and congressmen. He does this every now and then for those who continue to support him and his bills that he introduces to Congress. It's something of a PR activity that he can charge off on his expense account—

all, of course, intended to endear him to those who support him. He's quite a character."

"Sounds like it," Abby said. "I'm beginning to realize that politicians do an awful lot of things the public doesn't think about, little more have any knowledge of."

"The Capitol," said the cab driver as he stopped at the nearest approach. Abby felt an inner tug of patriotic pride as she viewed the shining dome and the symmetrical beauty of the architecture. She thought of the Founding Fathers as they laid out their designs for the premises and laws for the new nation.

She thought of twilights with her father as they stood on the parade ground of the old Fort and watched the soldiers as they carefully lowered and folded their treasured flag.

"See, little Abby, how cautiously they handle it, never to let it touch the ground?" Her heart filled with love for her father, her homeland, her heritage, and those who had instilled it within her.

The vast expanse of the Capitol steps reached out before them, as they proceeded up to the offices of Senator Downs. There was a small mixed gathering in his office, maybe 35 or 40, mostly men, although four or five young women were there, dressed to the nines in cocktail dresses, and what looked to be a couple of secretaries scurrying around.

Abby was beginning to feel uncomfortable. Not only did she know none of these people, there was an underlying element here that was disturbing. What had she gotten herself into? Surely, Suzanne would not lead her into a lion's den.

The senator was very gracious, excessively so. He was an attractive man, tall and boyish looking. Indeed, he was obviously quite young compared to his colleagues. He began to introduce her around to several of the men.

"This is Congressman Wallace, and this is Senator Brooks," he said, as he moved her around to several others, acquainting her with a number of the partygoers. The bartender was busy filling glasses. The drinks were flowing freely and after a while one could sense spirits rising. There was a great deal of laughter, and the jokes were getting a little smuttier.

Abby chatted with several of the guests. There were one or two attractive women and men who obviously were well versed in small talk and interesting banter. They talked about where they were from and what they stood for politically, and some of the comments they made had to do with bolstering up the war effort and of course the latest Hill gossip. She made an effort to be congenial, chatting with some of those she felt were interesting.

Suzanne suddenly caught her by the arm "I'll be back in a little bit," she said as she looked at her watch and then at the door. With that she disappeared with a young man whose image was scarcely visible through the outer door. Abby caught a brief glance at him before the door shut.

Strange, she thought. He was not a part of this gathering. He didn't even make an entrance. Why the secrecy?

Now her guard was up. It wasn't just Suzanne's peculiar behavior, it was also the realization that, although she had walked in some high and important circles before, and with ease, this was a different situation and these people, for the most part, were different. They each seemed to have an ulterior motive for being there. It seemed to Abby, that, like hawks, all were on alert, seeking what information could be ascertained from little bits of conversation and innuendo.

Out of the corner of her eye, she occasionally caught a furtive look from some of the men. They seemed to be waiting for something. Finally one approached her and began to make extravagant complimentary remarks, but there was something in the way he made them and the tone of his voice that she found offensive. She didn't like such outlandish flattery or the innuendos in his suggestive tone.

One of the guests continued to ask so many questions about her job that she began to feel she was getting the third degree. She instinctively dug her heels in, evading and throwing questions back. She was becoming more and more irritated, and it was becoming more and more of an effort to conceal it.

After two or three like encounters with some of the others, somehow she extricated herself and sought refuge with one distinguished gentleman she had gotten to know slightly. He seemed almost protective, as though he had summed the situation up pretty accurately. Abby decided he was a family man and a good one at that. She continued to look around for Suzanne but she was not there.

Eventually, the crowd began to thin out. Suzanne had still not returned. By now there were only two or three couples huddled in different corners totally absorbed with each other. Rather too absorbed, in her estimation.

Senator Downs approached her. "Well, my dear, are you enjoying yourself?"

Abby tried to be genial. "Your friends are very interesting. I've had an informative chat with several of them. You're fortunate to have such solid support, but then I'm told you deserve it."

"It's very good of you to say that," said Senator Downs, beaming. "Are you interested in Civil War history? I understand you're from the Deep South."

"I suppose I would have to answer yes to both questions," Abby said. "Atlanta has quite an extensive history, particularly during the Civil War."

Dr. Margaret S. Emanuelson

"Ah! Indeed," said the senator. "Step into my office a moment, I want to show you something. You're from Atlanta—it should be of great interest to you."

The way he looked at her prompted something in Abby to recoil. *Me thinks he has a lean and hungry look.* Abby looked over at the open door of his inner office. *Like a spider to the fly.* She supposed stepping in for a moment was safe enough but she still didn't feel very comfortable.

"Really? Anything about Atlanta is always of interest to me," she said. They went into Senator Downs's inner office. The door stayed open; but the people had virtually disappeared from view.

Senator Downs pointed to some innocuous document on his wall that had something to do with the Civil War but of very little importance to Abby. She knew it was a ruse to get her alone. All she wanted to do was leave.

"You really have to admire those Johnny Rebs," he said. "They were committed to a cause and they stood up for it. Too bad most people today can't think for themselves and choose what's best, even if no one else agrees with it."

"True," she said. She wondered where he was headed with this, but she really didn't care. There was something obnoxious about this man. She wanted it to end. By now, she was getting annoyed and more than ready to leave. Where in the world was Suzanne?

Senator Downs changed his tactics. "You know, Abby, you are a truly beautiful girl," he said. "You really ought to be in the movies." He stood, leaning against his desk, his eyes taking her in. "You know, some of the girls who win beauty contests have no trouble at all getting movie contracts. I know some of the movie tycoons. I could speak to them about you."

Oh, no! Abby was stunned. She couldn't believe what he was actually saying.

The senator prattled on. "They're always talent-scouting, you know. As a matter of fact, I know of a contest that I could sponsor you for. I'd be most happy to do so." The look in his eye and his syrupy tone turned Abby's stomach. It was clear he was waiting to see if she were going to play his game before he went further.

What kind of an idiot did this man think she was? How could she get out of this without insulting this fool—but Senator Downs interrupted her thought.

"Now, dear, just stand right there and let me see your legs. Just raise your skirt a little and let me see if the rest of you is as beautiful as I think."

That did it! Abby pulled herself up to her full height. Trying to adopt a soft and amiable tone, she forced a smile. "Senator Downs, I really have absolutely no interest in becoming a movie star or competing in any beauty contests. I appreciate your interest, but I can also assure you that my family would *never* permit such a thing." Trying to control her inner outrage, she looked directly into his eyes. "I appreciate your asking me to attend your party, but it *is* getting very late and I really must go. Thank you for your hospitality but I really must say goodbye."

The look on the senator's face told the story. He had gotten the message. Apparently, he was not used to being rebuffed, even in a relatively gracious way. He frowned and snorted but Abby turned on her heel and walked out of his office. She spied her coat and quickly put it on. She couldn't get out of there fast enough!

Suddenly she saw Suzanne coming in the outer door. Abby gave the signal. Suzanne headed for her immediately.

"Thank heavens you're back. Shall we go? I think this party is *over!*"

Suzanne looked a little sheepish but she ignored Abby's annoyed tone of voice. "Sure! Let's go, I'm ready."

Together they walked out and headed down the long hall.

"What happened to you?" Abby said. "I thought you were *attending* this party; instead you left me with a pack of—I don't know what—to fend for myself."

"Well, I guess I did, I'm sorry. But it looks like you handled it all right. Downs must have offended you. He used to be a rather sweet man, but I think his power has gone to his head."

"Or somewhere else," Abby said. "You could at least have warned me."

"I thought I did. Please forgive me. The last thing I want to do is to offend you. I know I owe you an explanation. I should have told you before we came."

On the way home Suzanne tried to explain why she had disappeared. She was very much in love with the young man she had met there.

"His name is Jacques D'Arcy. He's attached to the French diplomatic corps," she said. "Apparently he's assigned to some of the governmental operations in the Capitol in some type of arrangement. His work is very confidential, so he ordinarily doesn't appear in many public gatherings. We've had very little time to spend with each other, and this seemed to be a convenient time. He travels a lot, and when he's in town he stays in different places, so with his unpredictable schedule it's hard for us to see each other alone very often."

That afternoon she had met him on Capitol Hill so that while the party was in progress she could meet him and slip out to one of the empty offices for a while to be alone with him.

"How long have you known him?" asked Abby.

"About three, four months. He's the most fascinating man I've ever met."

"But what do you really know about him?"

"He's French, attached to the French Embassy. That's where I met him—at a party. He's told me all about himself, as much as he could. His work is pretty confidential, you know." Suzanne paused, as though she were struggling with a decision. "Can I tell you a secret?"

Abby nodded. "You can count on me."

"We have plans for the future but that's strictly confidential." Suzanne's eyes lit up like a child at Christmas. It was easy to see she was totally smitten.

Abby was beginning to understand what kind of relationship Suzanne had with her Jacques D'Arcy. She assured her that she understood and that everything was all right, even though she didn't approve. Suzanne was a big girl. There was little she could do except be there for her as a friend.

Nevertheless, she didn't feel that Suzanne had been honest with her about the party in the beginning and that she actually had perhaps "led a lamb to the slaughter." Still piqued, she shuddered to think what could have happened had she been left alone with that pack of wolves.

As for Suzanne's relationship with her "Jacques"—Abby smelled a rat. But she said nothing. Time to talk to Suzanne about it later. Or so she thought.

Something in Abby was disillusioned. In her innocence she had looked at senators and congressman as being the cream of the crop. Brought up in a tradition of honor, country, duty, she had been taught reverence for God, the flag, and everything they represented. As far as she was concerned, to serve ones country was to serve God as a sacred trust and privilege. It was abhorrent

Dr. Margaret S. Emanuelson

to think that her beloved country could be lead by any except those with the highest integrity, morality, and ideals.

But she was also a realist. She knew it was time to grow up. She had already had a few rude awakenings, which had alerted her to the fact that some people were not to be trusted, and her tendency to think the best of all those she met would have to come under closer scrutiny.

Washington might be one of the most beautiful cities in America, with its classic architecture, and its cultural and historical treasures, but there was intrigue, conspiracy, and immorality underneath the masks that many of the leaders and others wore. She decided that she would be very careful in the future, She was almost grateful for this last experience. It had taught her a valuable lesson.

She returned home that night to the third degree. Whom had she met? Where was the party? What went on? Why was she so late? It was only 10:15. What had they served to drink? How much had she had?

She politely answered all of her mother's questions—but the more she asked the more upset her mother became.

"And who is this man who keeps calling and asking for Miss St. James? Have you changed your name? It looks very suspicious."

Abby's heart sank. "What did you tell him?"

"I told him there was no one here by that name, and after the third call—not to call again."

Abby knew there was no point at this juncture to explain. "Mother, it was just a wrong number." But she knew it was Brett. He was in Washington and had tried to call.

"It's not only all this mystery," her mother went on, "You go out all the time and leave me here alone to worry about you. How can you treat me like this."

Exasperated, Abby threw up her hands in defeat, "I'm sorry, I'm sorry you feel that way. Please forgive me."

But for what? She had done nothing. This is what it was really about. She wants to be included in everything I do and think.

It was fine for her to leave when her mother had an engagement. There had been a number of times when she had left Abby alone for an evening. But for Abby to have a date or go to an old girlfriend's for the weekend—that meant she was ungrateful, inconsiderate, or up to some immoral, degenerate activity which only her mother's vivid imagination could conjure up.

Abby was becoming sick of her mother's behavior. She was totally unpredictable. But her accusations were what hurt the most. Had she been having some furtive affair it might have been different, but that was not the case. She had always been honest with her mother. But after finding her opening her mail and calling her family, even her father, and friends and checking up on her and telling all sorts of stories, she was finally getting angry. She began to tell her mother very little, which did nothing but make her more curious and suspicious.

I'm not going to live the rest of my life this way, she thought. My only hope for any peace of mind is to leave.

But she would have to find a way that was acceptable if she was to do it.

Brett hung up the pay phone. He was sure this was the right number, but the voice on the other end was not Abby's. By the third attempt, it even had a hostile and snobbish ring. He felt as though he had tread on a sacred flowerbed in one of the palace gardens that were indeed forbidden to all but the "inner circle."

But he wasn't about to give up. I'll find her, he said to himself as he stepped out of the phone booth. He didn't know how, but he knew he'd find her.

He walked through the lobby of the Union Station to the curb outside and hailed a cab. He had been given orders to report to a strange address in Washington for his next assignment. But he had no idea what that was to be. He was about to find out, and no one could have been more surprised.

Chapter 6

The next month or two Abby's work went fairly smoothly, considering that these were abnormal times. There were some inconveniences, even some small hardships, but nothing compared to what others overseas were experiencing. Because of the war, all government offices were open seven days a week. Civil Service workers were scheduled for six days a week. It was very difficult to find any time at all to shop during her brief lunchtime for even a pair of stockings, to say nothing of groceries.

Many foods and other fairly common essentials were rationed: sugar, meats, shoes. Many were impossible to find. Housing was almost non-existent. The only hope was to find a place that had been occupied by someone who was being reassigned. Even those who could afford luxury quarters had to settle for less.

Shoes, gas, cigarettes, tires, and other items were being shipped overseas by the ton for use of the servicemen. Gas was a real problem. Those people who had brought their cars to Washington frequently had to leave them in the garage while they took public transportation or called a cab. Car-pooling became common, particularly to get to work.

Abby had to laugh when her boyfriends, already overseas, sent her cartons of cigarettes. What an ironic reversal, she thought. Many was the afternoon she and dozens of others stood in line in the main building on Constitution Avenue to obtain what few packages were left by then. Once or twice there was nothing available except Turkish cigarettes. They were so terrible Abby decided that if this continued she would have to stop smoking.

But everybody smoked. One could blow off a lot of steam that way and it seemed to give one an air of sophistication. It was fashionable, completely acceptable, in contrast with some of the other things people were doing. Heavy drinking and partying was common and extra-marital affairs were rampant. With so many married men and women away from home, while the cat was away, the mice did play. There was a Zeitgeist of "eat, drink, and be merry, for tomorrow we die." And the latter was true for too, too many.

As the weeks turned into months, Abby began to realize how protected she had been. Even in college where she had had a great deal of freedom there were still rules and limits to what was acceptable behavior. The honor system was quite clear. One didn't violate the rules unless one were willing to take the consequences, and they could be severe. There were many things she was beginning to see.

The trip to Capitol Hill had opened her eyes to part of what was really going on in Washington. The stars in her eyes when she had thought about her government were quickly fading. No matter what their title or rank, these were simply people sent from a diverse cross-section of the country. And some of them were morally decadent. She was learning a hard lesson—one must be careful about trusting anyone, particularly in this setting.

It was wartime and security had become of primary concern.

Within three months, Abby was given a commendation for a chart she had devised to show important essential personnel vacancies to the Secretary of the Navy. Commander Logan was very pleased, and so was the Sec Nav. Shortly thereafter, she was given a two-grade raise and was made a supervisor.

Ninety days of officer training had been instigated because of the immediate need for eligible officers. Those who went through that training were jokingly referred to as "90-day wonders." She laughingly considered herself a "90-day wonder" also.

Barbara became her secretary, which was a godsend, since Abby typed only by the hunt-and peck system. Barbara was a lovely girl and had become a good friend. She was lonely in Washington, and since everyone worked six days a week there was little time to cultivate new friendships except in the office, and that was very limited. Her boyfriend was overseas and she heard from him infrequently by V-mail, which was often censored to the point it was almost unreadable. Barbara had no idea where he was except that he was somewhere in the Pacific.

She and Abby would sometimes take a brisk walk at lunchtime across the Park to Garfinkels for a quick shopping spree, or simply have lunch together in the cafeteria where most people ate because of the time limits.

One day they arrived back in the office to find Bunny in tears. She had just received a phone call from her mother in Maryland. Her fiancé, a bombardier, had been killed in action. Bunny was inconsolable. Abby went to her and took her in her arms.

"Oh, Bunny," she said. They stood there for a long time slightly rocking back and forth while Bunny erupted in paroxysm after paroxysm of tears. Finally the torrent subsided and Abby let her go.

"How could God let this happen," Bunny sobbed. There was no answer.

"It's the war," Abby said. "It's this horrible, evil war. Brought about by horrible, evil men."

But Bunny's war, and her world, were over. As far as she was concerned God had betrayed her. It was impossible for her to see the bigger picture. Jimmy was her whole life, her future, her everything. All her dreams had centered on her future with him. Now it was over, as though some evil hand had wiped it all away.

The office took up a collection to send flowers to the memorial service. There was no body, no remains, so, of course that was all the family could do. The military stepped in to assist and provide the patriotic touch.

Bunny took a week's leave and went home. She would be surrounded by family and friends. Some of the girls helped her pack and saw her off on the train. It wasn't far to her home in Eastern Maryland so all felt it was safe to let her travel alone. By the time she left she had a grip on herself. But Abby was concerned. Sweet, sweet Bunny now had a hardened, cold demeanor. She seemed different, mechanical, almost like a robot. Going home to the closure of a funeral and all the attention might help a little, but Abby knew Bunny's world had vanished. She was a nice but very plain girl. She had put all of her eggs for the future in Jimmy's basket. With him gone, there was no wedding, no marriage, no children, no chances, no future.

But Bunny was not alone. By now, all throughout America, parents, wives, and sweethearts were being greeted with that deadly telegram, "I regret to inform you"—usually followed by personal letters from commanding officers and sometimes comrades extolling the virtues of the dead. Lives were changed forever, halted in their tracks. Hearts were broken—beliefs questioned—futures obscured by a dark cloud of uncertainty.

The world is changing, Abby thought. *My world is changing. What is this evil, diabolical war going to do to the world we've known? To our cherished beliefs in God, in country, in honor, integrity, fidelity, morality? And what is it going to do to us?*

Abby shuddered to think of what was coming. The signs were all there. Hegel was right. The pendulum was swinging. From the old Judeo-Christian thesis—old codes of ethics and morality—to its antithesis: "the end justifies the means" and "if it feels good—do it." And somewhere in between the thesis and the antithesis, the synthesis would come. But for how long? And how far would the pendulum continue to swing before corruption, deception, and immorality were accepted as normal.

Yes, the signs were there. That beautiful, gracious, genteel world that she had known would never be again!

By August '42, the war had escalated to a fever pitch. Every day reports of battles, loss of men, ships, and equipment were paramount in the news.

France had been under the occupation of the Germans since the Blitz of 1940. After the German invasion, France had surrendered in six weeks and had signed an Armistice. Southern France had been designated as "neutral" under the command of General Petain, the "leader "of the Vichy government. But it was well known that the Germans were really in control, though they made a feeble outward attempt to disguise it.

The "New Germany," allied with Italy, extended all across Europe to Russia, including Czechoslovakia, Poland, Austria, and beyond, as Hitler continued to gobble up as much of the known world as he could.

Many Jews and dissidents continued to attempt to flee to Spain, Switzerland, America, or elsewhere. Some succeeded, however others were caught in a trap if their "papers" were not in order or they were discovered or deemed to be involved in subversive activities. And in some closed circles, incredible information about terrible atrocities, torture, and concentration camps was coming forth, mainly heretofore unknown to the general public.

Abby found the office had also become more active. It was amazing to her how many new assignments and transfers were being made and the incredible number of men and women appearing to fill those new and empty billets. To her surprise, many of the young men she had known in college were increasingly streaming through Washington on their way home on leave or on their way to a new assignment.

Though it was pleasurable to reminisce over college days and renew some of her old friendships, one could not deny the underlying anxiety which lurked like a dark shadow behind the light banter and joking laughter. No matter what the façade, the truth couldn't be avoided. These were transient times. Nothing seemed permanent. It was impossible to make long-term plans in a world gone mad. The hopes and dreams of the young were on hold. For some, those dreams had already been shattered along with their limbs and even their lives. And for those who were left at home, their dreams as well.

Chapter 7

Abby returned home one evening exhausted after a very busy day. Joe had been away on another assignment that day, leaving his courier post unattended. There were many more officers and enlisted personnel coming through for their assignments. She and Barbara had volunteered to fill in as escorts for the men, taking them down the interminably long halls and corridors to other offices to finalize their orders. The miles of corridors had taken their toll and Abby found herself done in.

No sooner had she tossed her things on the table and plopped down in an easy chair than the phone rang. It was Uncle Robert's wife, Cameron, calling to invite her for a weekend at their country house in Virginia. Abby was delighted.

"Could you come this weekend? We would so love to have you, dear." Cameron's melodious voice and precise British accent were unmistakable. Abby would have recognized either anywhere.

"Actually, Cammy, this is a perfect time. Mother has gone to Atlanta to visit Grandmother. I would dearly love to come if I can get leave."

"Do you think you can, m'dear?"

"I think so. I have a few days coming to me and as far as I know there are no pressing reasons why not. I'll check it out tomorrow and let you know. Wonderful! I can hardly wait to see you."

"Mutual here. We'll be waiting for your call. Robert will be ecstatic."

Abby had always felt close to Cameron and her husband whom Abby had known as "Uncle Rob" ever since she could remember. Sir Robert St. Giles was her uncle, her father's younger brother. He was a charming, educated, and distinguished man who had spent many years in the diplomatic service before his retirement, though she had always wondered if he were really retired. He and Cameron were always taking trips abroad to their English estate, the original "Allistair," and somehow Abby knew they were not just touring otherwise.

They had two children her age, now out of college, and she remembered many great childhood days visiting the family. The wonderful parties, holidays, historic garden tours, and the fox hunt breakfasts—all were treasured memories.

Their American home was only a short distance from Washington—an old antebellum treasure set in acres of rolling hills and magnificent mountain views. They raised horses, cattle, and probably the most beautifully landscaped gardens in the area.

Cameron Allistair St. Giles was a handsome, well loved, and admired Englishwoman and had always been a favorite of Abby's. An aristocrat, her father had been a prominent member of the British diplomatic service. He had married a French noblewoman, and together they had made quite an impression on many an elite circle. Cameron's mother, since her husband's death, still resided at her original family's chateau, situated in a magnificent part of southern France.

Their daughter, Cameron, was as elegant and graceful as a ballet dancer. Even when, in some situations, protocol required a certain correctness and distance of manner, she was able to project a warmth and charm rarely seen in one with her background. But in more relaxed moments with her family or friends her quick wit and funny quips betrayed a childish abandon meant only for those close to her.

Abby remembered private conversations with her over the years. Cameron knew all about the terrible conflict between Abby's parents, and she was one of the very few people with whom she ever confided. Cameron didn't like Abby's mother, although she was always courteous, even empathetic with her. And she understood much of the trauma that Abby had experienced as she grew up.

Although she had been there many times, she wondered if anything unusual had brought on this particular invitation. She guessed that her mother had been calling Cameron to complain about her, and heaven only knew whom else.

The next morning she asked permission of the Commander to take two days of leave.

Commander Logan agreed. "You've accumulated several days leave and even worked on Sundays at times to help catch up," he said, "and I think we owe you a little time off. Suzanne will be taking leave next week but you'll be back by then. Go ahead."

She and Suzanne lunched together that day. They were both excited about their leaves. Abby explained the connection between her father, Uncle Robert, and Cameron, relating some of the treasured times she had had as a child growing up at their homes in Virginia and abroad.

But Suzanne's mind was elsewhere. Her eyes sparkled as though she were lit up from some fire within. "I can hardly wait. A whole week. I can't tell you how long I have waited for this."

"Yes, I know," Abby said." It seems like an eternity since I got a weekend off, but actually I took a weekend last month and flew down to Virginia Beach to visit friends." She sipped her coffee. "Still, working six days a week—it does seem like an eternity, doesn't it? I can hardly wait."

Suddenly curious as to what Suzanne might be up to, she asked, "Where are you going and what wonderful things are you planning to do?"

"Oh, a little of this and a little of that," Suzanne said. "I like to ski, you know, and I'm really thinking of a trip—maybe north for a few days." Suzanne seemed unusually evasive.

Abby decided to pursue it. "Sounds wonderful! Going with company?"

Suzanne looked at her watch. "Oh dear, it's later than I thought. We'd better get going. I'll get the check, you leave a tip."

They rushed back to the office. As they reached the outer door, Suzanne looked at her very intently, straight into her eyes. Then, suddenly, she grabbed her and gave her an affectionate hug.

"Bon voyage, Abby, au revoir," she said.

"Vous aussi," Abby said, in startled surprise. "You too."

Chapter 8

Thursday mid afternoon, Abby drove the fifty miles to Allistair House. It was a beautiful fall day. The countryside was emblazoned in vibrant, multi-colored leaves. The rolling hills and the tall trees signaled the changing of the seasons.

All along the road came the aroma of burning leaves and the smell of freshly mowed fields. It was reaping time and the farm hands were out gathering the harvest of grass for feeding the cattle. Abby remembered being part of the celebrated hunts. She had mind-pictures of the beautiful horses as they galloped up and over the hills with the dogs chasing the fox chosen as the prize. And after that, the wonderful smell of Smithfield ham, eggs by the dozens, hot biscuits, curried fruit, grits, and other delicacies served on traditional hunt tables by the uniformed servants.

As she drove along she thought of Brett. Where was he right now? Would she ever see him again? Abby let her imagination roam freely as she drove.

Where was she headed? What was the future hiding from her? She knew there was something—something exciting—she could feel it hovering over her. But what? And when?

Suddenly, she recognized a familiar curve in the road and the white four-board fence that extended acre after acre, guiding guests to the entranceway. She could see the cattle grazing in patches over the hills and she knew that she was close to her destination. Around the bend in the road she spied the two brick posts supporting the two large Lions which signaled the entrance to Allistair. As she came nearer, the tall iron gates came into view.

Abby stopped at the intercom box and buzzed the house. She heard the click of the opening gates and she began the long drive to the top of the hill. The tall oaks formed a canopy over the car, providing a colorful protection from the outside world.

If there were ever a romantic setting, this was it. Ahead, the tall columns of the house accentuated the symmetry of the architecture and whispered of plantations of yore when maidens danced in silk draped hoop skirts with gentlemen adorned in fine full dress uniforms.

She pulled up to the portico over the slate portion of the drive. There stood Uncle Robert with his arms wide open.

"Darling little Abby." Uncle Robert enfolded her in his arms. Instantly she felt like a little girl again with her head against his shoulder and his strong arms embracing her. Only this time she wasn't small enough to be bounced on a knee or held on a lap while being read a Mark Twain or a Dickens story. Uncle Robert had always had a penchant for reading classic literature to young minds. She fondly remembered many warm and delightful occasions when Robert gathered her and the other children round his knee to read a story or a poem or two.

"Abby, darling! How wonderful you look. You're just in time for tea." There was Cameron, tall, regal, and gracious, with that way she had of making one feel more than welcome.

Jameson took her bags up to her usual guest room. They sat down to chat and partake of the lovely tea which had been prepared and placed outside on the patio off the library. After the usual pleasantries and inquiries about family and friends, Abby asked Cameron about her mother. "Is she well?"

"Yes, indeed. You know Ma Mere! She's fit as a fiddle, and just as stubborn. We cannot get her to leave France. She absolutely refuses. And you must know that it becomes more dangerous every day. Vichy France is teeming with Nazis and who knows what else. But she says she is happy there and no one, not even the Nazis, are going to run her out of her own home."

"Good for her," exclaimed Abby. "How wonderful to know that grand lady has not lost her spunk. She will probably outdo us all before it's over."

"She is resolute," Robert said, "but we're becoming concerned for her safety."

"I can see why—who knows what mischief she may be into."

Abby had always admired Ma Mere. She was definitely of the old school with her regal, formidable manner. Abby thought of the old days when she and her family had come for the hunts. Ma Mere had been there, joining in with her characteristic humor and grace, so reminiscent of Cameron, her daughter. Her chateau, situated strategically in southern France, was quite capable of providing escape routes for the underground. No wonder they were concerned.

After a thoughtful pause, she looked across the lawn at the beds of multicolored chrysanthemums. "The flowers are lovely this year," she murmured.

"Yes, I love a fall garden," said Cameron. "They're so hardy and so easy to grow. And so colorful as well, it warms the heart." She looked out over the stunning expanse of the grounds she had created. "And how do you like your new position? I should think it would be very interesting. We also hear you're doing extremely well."

"Yes it's interesting and I *am* doing well. Now, how would you know?" Abby smiled.

"Well, now, you know very well Robert has always had his ear to the ground as well as knowing all the informative people in Christendom."

Abby laughed. "True, I should have remembered. I suppose as a child I never even considered what he did, much less how far his influence reached." She glanced at her uncle. "Anyway, I've done well so far. Of course, the pay is minimal and I'm having to learn how to manage my finances since I declared my independence. I'm learning a great many things about life that I was pretty naive about before."

"I suppose that's true for most everyone." Cameron reached for another bonbon.

"True, but sometimes I think there has to be something else out there that I'm supposed to be doing that might be of more help to the war effort, even though I know that my present position is important too. I see so many assignments which seem to me to be a mistake." Abby sipped her tea. "Without qualified personnel in positions that fit their abilities, we would lose the war. There's just no place for misfits and incompetents. But it happens, I suppose. In the rush to accomplish such a tremendous expansion, sometimes one has to place what's available."

"Unfortunately true," Robert said. "But in some branches of the government it's quite a different matter. We always choose our diplomatic personnel very carefully. Not only for their talent and training, but also their character and their ability to keep a secret. Otherwise it would be better to leave a post open until a suitable candidate could be found." Robert filled his pipe.

"Of course, sometimes you would have no choice," Abby said. "But have you ever felt that a mistake in a selection was made?"

Robert took a long drag on his pipe. The smoke curled up over the now cleared tea table and mingled with that of Abby's cigarette. The wonderful aroma of rare blended tobaccos reminded her of her father. He and Robert were brothers, and alike in so many ways.

"It *has* happened, I know—but very rarely." Robert looked out at the distant mountains, deep in reflection.

A comfortable silence prevailed for a few moments.

Finally, Cameron said, "So—you've been thinking of making a change? Would that have anything to do with moving away from Washington?"

"Perhaps. But you know I've already had a number of options which have been interesting and with a great future. One from IBM, another to get in on the ground floor of television, and a few others, but somehow I don't feel any of them are right for me at present. Perhaps later after the war."

"What do you think you would like to do other than what you're doing," said Cameron.

"Oh, I don't know. Getting out of Washington might be good, maybe to do something interesting and important. I feel like there is something else out there that I'm supposed to be doing." Abby shrugged and gave a small chuckle.

"Perhaps that's just the ravings of an impatient college graduate."

"Not necessarily." Robert stretched his long legs further out in front of his chair and turned toward her. "There *is* a new organization underway that I happen to know about. In fact they're recruiting right now. Actually, they're something of an elite group and they're looking for top-notch talented people from excellent schools and prominent backgrounds. From what I can gather it is ostensibly by invitation only."

"Sounds fascinating. But what are they doing? Do you know? It sounds pretty vague to me. I wonder what they're up to—and I'll bet you know." Abby gave her uncle a mischievous smile.

"I might know little about it." Robert looked at her closely with his keen blue eyes as though he were accessing her motives. "Do you think you'd be interested?"

"Wouldn't that depend upon where I'd be sent and what it was all about?"

"Suppose I told you it was designed to be a type of communications and information gathering outfit. Do you think that would interest you?"

"Sounds intriguing! It seems to me that that sort of thing would be essential to winning the war. And also brings up a lot of other unanswered questions in my mind. You mean, sort of like the diplomatic service?"

"Something like that. Of course, during war, methodology and operations have to adapt to the situation."

"Yes, of course, I see what you mean." Abby could tell he was holding back. No doubt it was Robert's training in the diplomatic corps that prompted him to frame his words in veiled terms. However, at times she found it somewhat trying. She was one to turn over every stone and look under every boulder. It was part of her investigative nature, which had served her well in the past. "What you really mean is—it's some kind of an intelligence service."

"I suppose you could say that—among other things."

Abby chuckled. "God bless the diplomatic service! You people can never say anything without shrouding it in armament."

"Really, now?" Robert smiled, his blue eyes sparkling.

"Really, now!" Abby gave him a wink. What a marvelous man he was and how dear he was to her. All three joined in a good and hearty laugh.

"So—now—perhaps you have another option," said Cameron. "You should give it some thought."

"Yes, indeed I will."

The next two days were a delightful combination of visits with friends, little gatherings, and riding for the first time in years with Cameron over the beautiful rolling countryside. For Abby, the break was a Godsend. The gourmet food, the laughter, the rides over the fields on Cammy's gentle mare. She felt as though she was back in a different world, the one she had always known before. A sense of nostalgia tugged at her persistently. Would she ever know that life again?

On Saturday evening, Cameron and Robert held a dinner party in her honor at their home. As usual Cameron left her own special mark upon everything she touched. And her hospitality and warmth created an pleasing atmosphere for those who were fortunate enough to be invited.

Abby enjoyed the party immensely, chatting with some of her old acquaintances and meeting a few new people. Some of them were her own age or thereabouts. Some were friends and neighbors, and many were colleagues of Robert's from the diplomatic corps and other governmental posts who had settled in nearby estates.

The conversation covered everything from the war to cultural events, rationing, and the latest benign humor. It was fascinating to be in the company of people like these again, so alert and stimulating in their intellectual pursuits. But she noticed that there was obviously great caution in what was discussed, and a veiled approach to anything that might be considered hush-hush.

Nevertheless, the guests were lively and entertaining and the party did not break up till well after midnight.

Abby fell into bed exhausted with that wonderful fatigue born of pure enjoyment. She fell asleep almost as soon as her head hit the pillow.

She was walking down a long corridor on the second floor. From the architecture and the wall coverings it was obviously an old and elegant French hotel. As she passed from the end of one wing, the corridor extended into an open middle portion. It was barricaded by a beautiful marble balcony, flanked on both sides by graceful curved marble stairs leading down to a large lobby. As she continued to glance down through the open portion she could see a large ballroom on the right of the lobby. There were people dressed in festive attire, dancing to a waltz. As she watched she heard the strains of music. It was the Blue Danube.

She continued past the open balcony to the other wing. As she entered, she passed by one closed-door after another until she came to one door half open. She stopped and looked inside. But it was dark, and all she could see was part of a carved antique chest and part of a bed. Upon it lay a red dress and a long blonde wig.

Out of the dark, a man's voice suddenly said, "Komm nicht herein! Das ist verboten!"

She caught just a fleeting impression of the face of a handsome man as he slammed the door shut. A cold shiver crossed her flesh. Dismay and uncertainty overtook her. She hesitated in the long hall. What should she do?

Suddenly it was Sunday. Abby awoke to the sound of knocking. Jameson called out in his rich baritone:

"Breakfast is served in 15 minutes, Miss Abby."

"Thank you, Jameson," she called out through the door. "I'll be right down." She looked at the clock. It would soon be time for church. She stretched and flexed her muscles. She was still half in the dream. What did it mean?

She rose, showered, dressed quickly, and ran down the long staircase to the main floor dining room.

"Will you join us for church this morning, my dear?" said Cameron, sipping her coffee.

"Absolutely. I love your old Episcopal church here, with all its traditional heritage, and besides your Rector is extraordinary. I wouldn't want to miss it." Abby reached for a ham biscuit from the breakfast buffet and sat down at the table. "And we may meet some of the old troops there. I wouldn't want to miss them either. That is if they can make it."

Cameron laughed, "Oh, I suppose some of them are just a tad short, this morning. But stiff upper lip and all that tommy rot."

Abby grinned. "At least some of us are up and at it. Incidentally, the party last night was lovely. So well done. How do you do it, Cammy? You always have a knack of selecting the most amusing array of people and the most unbelievable cuisine."

"Oh, it goes along with the territory. You know, being the daughter of the Allistairs and the wife of a diplomat. "

"Now it couldn't have anything to do with artistic flair and extraordinary taste, could it?"

"Possibly. C'est la vie de l'artiste, you know!" Cameron playfully waved a graceful arm with an exaggerated flourish.

Abby giggled. "Mais oui, madame, mais oui! C'est la vie!"

After breakfast, they drove the short distance to the church. Abby looked out at the horses grazing with their young colts following them close by, over the green meadows. Here and there several deer and their fawns also grazed some distance from the horses. And once in a while the squirrel and rabbits would run about creating a scene of sheer pastoral delight.

As they approached the church, she began to feel a sense of anticipation. As though there was something around the corner waiting for her.

The sermon that morning was different from any she had ever heard in that church or any other Episcopal one. The Rector was teaching about desire of the Lord to fill those who were willing with the power of the Holy Spirit and equip them with the gifts of the Spirit.

Lord. I'm willing. The thought kept running through her mind.

Suddenly she felt a strange current surging from within. An overpowering sensation. This was something beyond—something mysterious. Abruptly a warm glow came over her. She had an overwhelming feeling of joy; an immediate explosion of energy from deep within her seemed to flood her whole being.

Awestruck, she felt compelled to know more.

She made a mental note of the passages the Rector had quoted from Scripture. Surely, someone could instruct her as to what all of this meant. She had heard of the Holy Spirit all of her life, but she had never heard this kind of teaching before. And certainly she would have no peace until she pursued it.

Abby left the church that day with many more questions than answers. Sometimes her inquisitiveness knew no limits, and this was one of those times, but she was strangely quiet on the way back to the house. Once there, she gathered her things into her luggage and said her goodbyes to Cameron and Robert.

"Be careful on your way home, Abby. Once you hit the Sunday traffic it can be somewhat dangerous, you know," said Robert.

"Yes I know. I keep very much alert. Having had a few close calls in the past I keep my eyes keenly on the road."

"We shall miss you, Abby dear," said Cameron. "It's been wonderful having you here. You know you're welcome any time. Give our love to your mother, and remember, you have another option to consider."

"Yes, I'll give it some thought. You can count on it."

There was a flurry of loading the car with luggage, hugs, and embraces, and the usual goodbyes, and Abby took her leave to return to Washington.

She smiled as she drove the long miles back to "civilization." It was as though she had been visiting her other world and now she was returning to the new real and intriguing, but not so lovely one. She felt a sense of impending excitement, new things to discover, new fields to conquer, an awaiting expectancy of things to come.

Yes, indeed she would give the new group some thought. Who could know what it could bring? Yes, she would definitely give it some thought, some thought indeed.

As she drove back towards Washington, Robert's words came back to her. This kind of position could mean staying in Washington, but it could also mean an assignment somewhere else, even overseas. Would she really be willing to risk her life? She knew that type of assignment could mean exactly that. Yet it would be a great adventure and certainly from what Robert had said it was a vital necessity with the nation at war.

Well, she would just think about it, and she'd worry about it later. Immediately she thought of Brett, and his reference to Scarlett. She wondered where he was now and what he must have thought at her mother's rebuff. Too late now. But in her heart she thought, maybe it's just unfinished business.

Abby let her thoughts wander as she drove along. Almost overnight the leaves had turned to a more brilliant array of color and the countryside had undergone a new burst of glory. She thought of that awesome new burst of glory she had received just that morning.

"How clever you are, God. How could anyone ever deny you?"

She opened the apartment door to the insistent ringing of the phone. Who could that be? Mother wasn't due in for another week. Abby picked up the receiver.

"Abby, have you heard from Suzanne?" It was Commander Logan.

"No, I haven't. Is something wrong? I thought she was going to take leave beginning tomorrow."

"She was. At least that was the plan, but she has been gone two days, AWOL since you left on Thursday. No one has heard from her. Do you have any idea where she was planning to go on leave, or any idea with whom she was going?" The Commander's concern was obvious.

"No, I really don't," Abby said. "But you know there *is* something I've been concerned about. Let me make a phone call and I'll get back to you. Are you in the office?"

"I'm at home. How soon can you get back to me?"

"Almost immediately, I hope, if I can connect with the right person. In any case, I'll return your call within the next hour. Have you checked her home?"

"There's no answer," he said. "Actually, other than Marie Swenson, you're the only one I have called. I kept thinking she would call in. It's totally unlike her not to report. She has always been completely reliable."

"Yes, of course, I know she is. I'm very fond of her you know. Do you suppose she's had an accident? We could check the hospitals. I don't think she has any family in this area."

"Of course, you're aware this is something of a sticky wicket," he said. "Being AWOL doesn't set well on one's record. Maybe I'm being overprotective, but I would hate to see her get into trouble, and besides I'm concerned that something unfortunate has happened to her.

"So am I." Abby began to think back to the night on Capitol Hill. Why was Suzanne so furtive about her relationship with the young man she met there? And who was he? She tried to remember his name—Jacques something?—yes, Jacques—something. Now what was it? She would think about it later. She was almost sure she could remember it, but she decided not to mention it until she had checked it out.

"Commander Logan, let me make a couple of phone calls and I'll get back to you as soon as possible. Give me your number at home. You know I would never use it unless there were an emergency."

"I know that, however I'm beginning to think it's not a bad idea for office staff, particularly when they have top clearance. Thanks, Abby. I appreciate your help. Sorry to break in on your leave."

"No problem. I'm concerned too. We need to find her, the sooner the better. I'll call you back."

Abby suddenly had an overwhelming feeling of fear. The same feeling that had hovered over her whenever she thought of Suzanne and her "French diplomat." What was his last name? Abby sometimes used word association to remember things. Good old Aristotle!

Let's see, when I think of him I think of Paris, and when I think of Paris I think about the Eiffel Tower, the Louvre, and the Arc de Triomphe. Aha! Something to do with the Arc. Yes, Jacques Arc—no—Darc—no—D'Arcy. Yes that's it. "Jacques D'Arcy."

Even his name sounded suspicious. She could hardly contain herself. Her association maneuvers had worked, in perhaps a critical situation. She had meant to ask Robert if he knew of him while she was at Allistair, but there had been so much going on that it had slipped her mind. But now it was a different matter. Abby reached for the phone.

The phone rang again and again. It was dusk by now and she knew that Cameron and Robert were likely to be at a Sunday night buffet usually given by one of their friends. But after what seemed like an eternity Robert answered the phone

"Uncle Robert? It's Abby."

"Abby, are you all right?"

"Yes. I just got home, no problem. But there *is* a matter that is somewhat pressing. I was hoping you can help me with it. Do you think this phone is safe?"

"Mine is, I'm sure, and that should be sufficient."

"OK, then. Frankly, this matter is completely confidential so I will rely on your discretion. There is a girl who's missing from the office. Actually, she's the confidential secretary to the commanding officer. She is a lieutenant in the Navy and has been AWOL since last Thursday after I left the office.

"Ordinarily, she would be at the office all day on Friday and Saturday, but she has neither reported in nor been heard from by anyone we know so far. It's totally unlike her. She has been Commander Logan's secretary for well over a year and has always been completely reliable. She has never done anything thing like this. That's why we're so worried. She was due to go on leave for a week starting tomorrow since I would be returning by then. But the fact that she's missing is very questionable. Commander Logan knows we're good friends and that's why he contacted me. Now, I get to the point in fact."

Robert said, "Yes, Abby, I'm here."

"I feel conflicted about telling you this because about six weeks ago she told me this in confidence. But the situation has changed, and if she's in danger I have no alternative."

"I understand your feelings but this sounds serious. Go ahead, tell me what's bothering you."

"She said she had met a fascinating young man who was attached to the French Embassy. At least that's what he told her, and she believed him because she met him at a party there. But I have been suspicious of this man ever since. I got a brief glimpse of him on Capitol Hill on a night she and I attended a party there." With that Abby related the entire evening's performance on Capitol Hill, including Senator Downs' behavior.

Robert was silent. When she finished, she heard him sigh.

"You know, my dear," he said, "I have known many true statesmen in my life. Some who would give their very lives for their country and their duty. It always pains me deeply when I find a true scoundrel in office. I know this man, and what you say does not surprise me." He paused for a moment. "Now, to get down to specifics. What is the name of the young man who is supposedly attached to the French Embassy? I can make some discreet inquiries for you."

"His name is Jacques D'Arcy. At least that's the name Suzanne gave me. I have only a vague idea of what he looks like. I got only a brief impression of him that night."

"At least we have a name. Let me see what I can do. I'll get right back to you."

"That would be wonderful. That's what I was hoping for. I know that you have connections with all the embassies and particularly the European ones."

"That would be about right," Uncle Robert said. "I'll begin calling now. And I'll get right back to you as soon as I find out anything."

"Wonderful! I can't thank you enough. But bear in mind I haven't told Commander Logan any of this yet. Only that I wanted to check some things out and would get back to him."

"That was smart. I may have to fill him in later, but we'll wait and see." Robert hung up.

Abby called Commander Logan and told to him what she had done, that Robert was a senior diplomat, that he had many resources for information at his fingertips, and would keep it confidential.

"Thank you, Abby. I know that your uncle will be very careful. I prefer to keep this matter completely confidential at present until we know what has happened. But I'm afraid I cannot cover for her any longer once tomorrow comes. I sincerely hope to get to the bottom of this immediately. There is also, from what you tell me, the possibility that this could be more serious than we know. Unless she returns or calls in by tomorrow—" Commander Logan paused. "In any case she's missing and we don't know where she is. My next thought is to call her family, but if I recall, she lost her only relative some time ago, so that could cause another problem." He stopped, contemplating his next move. "I'll simply have to wait until morning to decide the best thing to do. Thank you again, Abby. I'll wait for your call." He rang off.

She was alarmed. The more she thought about the situation the more she feared some sort of foul play. There was really no way to know. Her thoughts went back to the luncheon she and Suzanne had shared the day that she left for Allistair. Suzanne had been evasive about her leave—where she was going, and with whom. But she had seemed excited, unusually so.

She wondered too, about the impulsive hug Suzanne had given her as they parted. Though they were very fond of each other, Suzanne's demeanor was usually very proper. It was unlike her to be openly affectionate.

As she waited for Sir Robert to return her call she unpacked her things and prepared a light salad for dinner.

About two hours later, the phone rang. It was Robert.

"Abby, I've made some calls. I can't check this out thoroughly until tomorrow. But from what I can gather so far, there is no 'Jacques D'Arcy' attached to this French Embassy. I hate to leave you with this dangling, but it will simply take further investigation. I hope you'll be patient until I can get some further data."

"I understand," Abby said.

"I know that you and your commander are worried, but this is going to take some time. You can tell him that I am completely committed to helping in any way I can. Perhaps he would like to discuss this with me on a one-to-one basis at some time in the future. I would be most happy to meet with him if it becomes necessary."

"Yes, I'm sure he would like that."

"Of course his problem is, does he report her AWOL now, or does he wait. There is a problem with waiting. As her commanding officer, he will soon have no alternative. Try not to worry, I'll call you as soon as I find out anything more."

"I'll call Commander Logan and let him know what you said. I suppose there's nothing to be done from this end until we find out more," she said with a sigh. "Thank you so much for your efforts. I know we can count on you to do your utmost. In the meantime, I'll wait for your call." Abby paused in thought. "Incidentally, Mother won't be home for another week, so you can call me here. Since this is confidential, there's no need to get anyone else involved. I'll talk to your later."

Abby placed the receiver back on its cradle. What now! What if this was a case of espionage? Who was this Jacques D'Arcy? Where was Suzanne? Was she safe?

Suddenly, she thought of the dream she had had three nights before. Could it have anything to do with Suzanne's disappearance?

Abby called Commander Logan and told him what Robert had told her. "I suppose there's nothing to do but wait, at least until we can get further information," she said.

"Actually, there *is* something we can do." Commander Logan sounded like a man who had made up his mind. "I've thought about this and I think it's the only one thing we can legitimately do without unnecessarily arousing or involving anyone else at this point. Would you be willing to meet me at the office an hour early tomorrow? I would like you to accompany me to her apartment. Perhaps we can discover something there."

"Of course I'll be willing." Abby hesitated. "But how will we get in? We have no key. You know that she moved to a new place about six months ago. Do you have the address?"

"Yes, I do. Anytime an employee or service person changes their address they are required to report it. I've already looked up her records, which go back before she was employed, including the FBI clearance done at that time. I'm pretty much up-to-date on all the informational data about her. So far, there's nothing suspicious in her background. I think this is the only thing I *can* do legitimately before I report her AWOL, which of course you know I am very reluctant to do."

"Yes I do understand. It's very good of you to go to such lengths to protect her. I know she'll appreciate it. O.K. then, I'll meet you in the morning at the office parking lot at 6:30. No one will know what we're up to."

"No one knows except Marie Swenson, but she is acting C.O. when I'm not in the office. No problem there. So, see you in the morning. We'll play it by ear."

"Roger, see you then."

Chapter 9

The next morning Abby grabbed a cab, arriving at the office in a light rain. Commander Logan was waiting for her.

"We'll take my car," he said.

On the way to the apartment they discussed the pros and cons of what could have happened to Suzanne, why she hadn't notified anyone, and what further steps might be taken. Suzanne's apartment house was a beautiful old building, used by some of the congressmen and assistants when they were in Washington. As a result, there were many months of the year in which their apartments remained vacant. There was little hope that anyone who maintained an apartment there might know her.

They entered the building and Commander Logan went to the manager's door and rang the bell. After a few minutes, the door opened. A well-dressed middle-aged woman greeted them.

"Good morning, I'm Mrs. Lovelace, the manager, what can I do for you?" she said.

"Good morning." said Commander Logan. "I wonder if you could possibly let us have a passkey to apartment No. 317. An employee of mine lives there and has not reported in to work for the past two days. I'm concerned that she is sick and unable to phone in."

"I see," said the manager. She frowned. "But of course I would have to have some sort of identification."

"Yes, I understand. This is her sister and she's very concerned." Commander Logan nodded toward Abby.

Mrs. Lovelace turned to her. She seemed nervous. "Well—perhaps then *you* can give me some identification that would show your relationship."

Abby thought quickly. Other than her security badge, which she didn't want to show, all she had was her driver's license. She pulled it out and waved it by the manager's sight, talking at the same time.

"Yes, I'm extremely concerned about Suzanne. It is totally unlike her not to notify me if she is ill. From time to time she's had dangerous blackouts, which sometimes last several hours. I'm alarmed that perhaps this is another one of those times."

Where did all that come from, she thought.

Mrs. Lovelace looked worried. She frowned as though she were weighing the consequences of not letting them in, and perhaps having a dead resident on her hands.

"Well of course, in that case." She went back into her apartment and immediately came out with a set of keys. "Come with me."

Abby and Commander Logan followed her to the elevator. When it reached the third-floor, they traveled down a long hall to 317. As they reached the door Abby turned to the manager. "Do you mind if I go in first? I would hate to frighten or embarrass her if nothing is wrong,"

"Yes, of course. I'll wait in the hall for the two of you." Mrs. Lovelace unlocked the door to the apartment and stepped aside.

Abby and Commander Logan entered the apartment and closed the door. They went from room to room quickly. The apartment held nothing but the barest of furnishings. There were no personal items anywhere. The desk drawers were empty. There were no *objets d'art* sitting around on tops of the chests. Not even one item!

The bureau drawers yielded nothing. Though the few pieces of furniture were top-of-the-line, there was not a book or any thing else to suggest that someone lived there. The bedroom was the same. The bed had been stripped down to the bare mattress. The closet was totally empty of clothes. The kitchen was spotless, as were the pots and pans. The refrigerator was completely empty…. It was as though some ghost resided there, with no need of physical food, clothing, or accessories in order to exist.

Abby looked at Commander Logan. Her expression reflected the horror and amazement she felt. This was the most bizarre event she could ever have imagined. She said nothing.

Commander Logan raised his eyebrows, shook his head, and shrugged. In silence they walked to the door, opened it, thanked the manager, and walked towards the elevator.

"Did you find her? Is she all right?" said the manager.

"No, but everything is all right," Abby said pleasantly. "She must have gone away for the weekend, tried to call me and couldn't reach me. Actually, I also was away for the weekend. I'm so sorry we bothered you. Turns out it was a false alarm. Many thanks for your help."

As they entered the elevator, Abby looked back at the manager. There she stood at the apartment door, motionless with keys in hand, looking at them. Relief mixed with bewilderment covered her face as though to say, "What was that all about?"

Abby was amazed at how easily she had been able to come up with a story. "Perhaps I should have become an actress instead of what I'm doing," she said as they left.

Company of Spies

"You did an unbelievable job," said Commander Logan, laughing. "You surprised even me. And I'm not so easily surprised," he said as they walked to the car. "But what can we make of what we found? Does she actually live there or is this a front, meant to deceive others? As far as I know, no one has ever been invited to her apartment for any reason, so no one would know that it was bare." Absentmindedly, he took the car keys out of his pocket. "The only other explanation that I can think of is—that someone has gone in there and cleaned that place completely out."

"That's the only thing I can come up with," Abby shook her head. "I don't think I've ever been quite so shocked in all my life as when I walked into the apartment and found it completely devoid of anything."

"Exactly!" He looked troubled. "My next problem is what to do next and I have to make an immediate decision once I reach the office."

"By then, I have a feeling you'll know what to do," she said.

They reached the car and began the drive back to the office. With this discovery, Abby was beginning to feel she should put the Commander in direct contact with Robert. This looked too much like foul play, and suppose this Jacques D'Arcy *was* a spy?

"Why don't you let me out first before you park," she said. "If anyone should see us they might get ideas."

"Good idea. No matter how innocent, we don't need any office gossip. There's enough of that going around as it is."

Abby got out and walked towards the entrance to the building. She said hello to the security staff, said she had nothing to declare, and proceeded to the office.

She was greeted with "missed you" and "how was your weekend?" "It was wonderful," she answered. Her demeanor was important, there could be no hint that something was wrong. This matter was completely confidential and it was very important that it stay that way. However, she did give Marie Swenson a knowing look, since she was the only other one who knew.

In about 10 minutes, Commander Logan came in. He walked straight to his desk, nodding to several on the way, and sat down. Abby saw him reach for the phone.

He's made the decision to report her. Abby cringed in suspense.

Marie interrupted him. "Incidentally, Commander, a messenger delivered this envelope for you. I found it on my desk this morning. You might want to open it before you get on with today's work."

"Right." He hung up the phone and took the envelope from Marie. He opened it and read the note in silence. It was written on a typewriter but it was signed by hand. The Commander was familiar with Suzanne's handwriting. It looked the same. But he supposed it would take an expert to make sure. Anyway, he felt like he had been let off the hook at least for a week.

"Marie," he said, "would you see that Suzanne's leave is extended to Friday and Saturday of this past week and reported to payroll, please. Incidentally, did anyone notice who delivered this message? Was it one of our regular couriers?"

But no one seemed to know. He passed the note on to Marie. "Did you see who left it?"

"No. It was on my desk when I arrived this morning. I never saw a messenger but I assume one delivered it." Marie read the note. A few minutes later she motioned to Abby to come to her desk. She handed the note to her. No one said anything.

Dear Commander Logan,

I hope you get this in time. I have been called out-of-town very suddenly on an urgent problem. Please extend my next week's leave to include Friday and Saturday of this week. I know that I have extra days coming to me, so that will not be a problem. I do appreciate this so much. I would not ask if it were not an emergency.

Many, many thanks,
Suzanne Davenport

Abby heaved a sigh of relief. "Yes, good, she's reported in, no problem," she said, mainly for the benefit of the rest of the office staff, and returned to her desk. But she knew this affair was not over. There were too many questions now. And the results of their visit to her apartment—a complete mystery.

She hoped Suzanne would be back in a week. In the meantime they could still check on Jacques D'Arcy and perhaps eventually know what the cleaned out apartment meant. But somehow, she didn't believe that Suzanne was out of harm's way.

Abby picked up her pen:

In light of what was discovered this morning I'm giving you this private number. I think you should call him immediately, and relate what we found.

887-5454, Sir Robert St. Giles.

Abby walked to the Commander's desk handed him the note, and returned to her desk. He made a record of the number, and put the note in his pocket. Some time later he went to the men's room, tore the note into pieces, and flushed the pieces down the toilet.

Chapter 10

Somewhere in London a light October rain sprinkled down on some of the top brass of British and American intelligence as they and their assistants carefully made their way into the old building through different entrances. This meeting was one of many aimed at the planning, coordination, and merging of wartime intelligence efforts since the Americans had become openly and fully committed to the war not only in Europe but Asia as well.

From the long hall they were ushered into a large room by an armed British soldier in full regalia, obviously proud of his post, and settled down into their respective seats at a long conference table. The faint aroma of ancient tapestries and old leather mingled with finely blended imported pipe tobacco. Were it not for the thick Orientals covering the dark polished floors and the heavy drapery, the height of the ceilings might have made conversation impossible because of the echo.

The discussion involved a number of problems, past, present, and future.

Finally, Lord Smythe turned to the American colonel.

"I say, Colonel, how are your efforts at recruiting proceeding?"

"Actually, they're going full speed ahead. General Donavan has a knack for rapid organization of our new OSS unit. I understand that we are investigating our potential people thoroughly, even without their knowledge, long before they are interviewed. After that they are put through a rather vigorous battery of psychological tests and situational observation as well as a thorough psychiatric session."

"Sounds pretty meticulous. Can't afford any slip-ups recruiting the too risky. Good show, Colonel. You Americans are a Godsend. Combining our resources should begin to pay off toute suite. How soon can we expect another shipment?"

"Two groups of eight are in the finishing stages of training now, being inoculated and cleared by the State Department and put on alert for transport, which is in process of scheduling. They are not told where they're going, when they're going or how they're going."

"I'd say that's pretty cautious." Lord Smythe smiled a lofty smile.

"Yes," said the Colonel, "We'll make a joint decision where they should be placed after they arrive. Some should go to Pemberley for further training, some should go elsewhere, of course, but we'll have more detailed information by the time they arrive."

"Of course," said Smythe. "By then we'll have an even better idea of where they are needed when plans for expansion of our activities unfold." Lord Smythe gave the distinct impression that he alone intended to make that decision.

"Indeed! Of course that would be on an ongoing basis. We have a number of critical spots that need filling now, to say nothing of developments as they unfurl and as the need arises." The Colonel continued with an obvious attempt at diplomacy, and a firm grip on his temper. "However, we may have a bit of a problem. We're beginning to notice that of our people we're sending over here, two out of three of our American candidates are being *rejected* for placement after they finish their stint at Pemberley. You *are* aware, of course, that they were carefully selected, trained, and briefed by our experts in the U.S. before they arrived here."

"Hurrumph!" Lord Smythe made a great to-do of clearing his throat. "Yes, yes, well, you see, unfortunately, we've been somewhat disappointed in some of the candidates you're sending us." He looked away from the Colonel, addressing only the others at the table. "As you know we English are pretty old hands at intelligence. We've decided that only those who meet our high Selection Assessment Board standards are suitable to continue. So sorry if some of yours haven't made it." He turned away as to dismiss him but the Colonel was not about to let the subject go. Though he kept a fairly modulated voice, his face was reddening dangerously.

"Too, too many, I'm afraid." The Colonel fixed a cold glare on His Omnipotence. "Lord Smythe, our candidates are all top of the line exceptional candidates. It's ridiculous that two thirds of them are being rejected. We feel perhaps there has to be a communication problem. Either a lack of understanding by your Brits of the cultural and behavioral differences manifested by our people, or perhaps... something else."

He knew he had to cool down. But he was a no nonsense military man. This game of smoothing over the insufferable arrogance and superior attitudes of some of these "crowned heads" was not only maddening, it was keeping this operation from going full speed ahead. Time was of the essence. *How dare this prejudiced old fool disqualify these men. Who did he think he was!*

"Yes, well, yes. Hurrumph!" Lord Smythe said. "I'm afraid that until your selectees can meet SAB standards, they're out." It was clear he was through discussing it.

The Colonel suddenly rose to his feet. "I see," he said, angrily. "That position is absolutely untenable. In that case, I propose we get some of our expert psychologists with yours to investigate just what the *real* problem is, and in just which areas our operatives are coming up *inferior* to yours!"

Lord Smythe, reacted with feigned shock. "There, there, Colonel. We never intended to imply—"

The Colonel took contemptuous note of the royal "We," as only the Queen used it. A long silence prevailed as the Colonel continued to stare fiercely at Smythe, who averted his eyes.

Suddenly Smythe's voice became sugar coated. "I say, Colonel, you have made an excellent suggestion. We'll see to it. Yes indeed, we'll see to it."

Lord Smythe realized he had gone too far. Like it or not, Britain needed the Americans if they were to win this war. He would have to use more careful diplomacy in the future. But he knew he was prejudiced. As far as he was concerned, the Americans were an arrogant, undignified, and ill-mannered lot. They even had had the affront to send a few *women* as operatives. Indeed, they certainly lacked the traditional protocols and demeanor of the Old Guard. But then, one could probably hardly expect them to, considering where they originated.

"Yes, and *we'll* see to it too!" the Colonel said. "We'll arrange for our experts to consult with yours. I'm sure we can reach an equitable solution." He kept an even tone of voice, even in his anger. He had no intention of letting this stuffed shirt get the upper hand. He had his attention now, so he continued. "I need to point out to you, Lord Smythe, that although we will know where a placement needs to be made, the decision as to who will be placed where needs to be made primarily by the training officers. They will know of the suitability of each trainee for different assignments firsthand, whereas we will have only a paper report at best. It will be risky enough at that, not only for the success of the operation but also for the mortality of the operative."

"Yes, yes, of course. Well, we can get to that later. Shall we proceed to other pressing matters, gentlemen?" Lord Smythe made a gesture as to sweep the matter aside.

The Colonel sat down. He had made his point. Smythe's reluctance to turn over such decisions to what he considered "subordinate" staff was clear. But the Colonel held his tongue. He knew by now that dealing with the British was as much a diplomatic assignment as it was anything else. He would let it go for now but he fully intended to deal with it later.

Lord Smythe continued: "Gentlemen, it seems we have another rather troublesome problem. As you know, we've had a continuing quandary with enemy operatives and from time to time, some success in capturing them, but this one is unique." He looked around to see if he had elicited the intended level of curiosity. "He's been in our sights since '39. He continues to cause a great deal of havoc, but lately his operations, at least the ones with which we can link him, are escalating. Efforts to identify him have been fruitless. One might say he's 'sometimes here and sometimes there,' but, not unlike our Scarlet Pimpernel, 'no one has seen him anywhere.'"

Lord Smythe, glowing with pride, waited expectantly for his attempt at levity to be appreciated. A slight ripple of laughter obediently followed, though somewhat reluctantly.

Lord Smythe continued, "For about six months we didn't pick up on him. We first thought that perhaps he'd been killed, but now we think he's been in another country—probably the United States. But now he's appeared on the scene *again*." He paused, setting the stage for the full wallop. "He's fully operational, obviously with a well-oiled network. We're now thinking that he's some kind of super spy, that he organizes sub-operations and is contacted only at arm's length. He is incognito even from his own. The one or two of his surrogates we've been able to apprehend have no idea who he really is. He's intelligent, clever, cunning, and dangerous. Now he's back, right under our noses, and we're intercepting countless messages with his signature."

Every eye was on Lord Smythe as he finished his dissertation and waited patiently for the expected response. At length one very brave member spoke up with the anticipated question.

"Then who is he?"

"His code name is 'Jana,'" he said.

"Not again!" said another brave soul.

"Yes, gentlemen, yes! I'm afraid he's back again, or rather, he was probably never far away. But this time it's absolutely imperative that we 'get' him."

"Hear, hear!" the group said in unison.

Lord Smythe was beginning to feel exalted, very masculine and suave. He imagined he felt something like that new American movie idol, Humphrey Bogart, who always "got" his man.

"Yes, gentlemen. We'll discuss this fully at our next meeting," Lord Smythe said. "In the meanwhile, if any of you come up with any relevant information about this 'Jana,' I should be absolutely the first to know. And remember, gentlemen, this is TOP SECRET." He gave a dramatic flourish.

Two hours from the time the meeting had begun, the attendees began to leave. One by one they spaced their departures—some through the back entrance, some through the side, and two only through the front doors.

As the Colonel left, he was deep in thought. Still miffed, as he got in the car, he spoke aloud, "Just wait till the Old Man hears about this!"

His aide spoke up. "Is there a problem. sir?"

"None that we can't resolve." He was already thinking of a Yale psychologist he knew. A good friend of his, Dr. Morgan Williams. They could send him to Pemberley. He could solve their rejection problems there.

Chapter 11

Late the next afternoon after work Abby and Barbara had a light supper in one of the many ethnic restaurants along the Washington Mall. They had chosen one known for its superb French cuisine.

"Mmmm, this is so good," said Barbara. "I'm so tired of that stuff in the cafeteria and all that junk we've been eating. This is a real treat."

"You bet. We deserve one after the heavy workload we've had lately. I'm really glad it's let up a little." Abby toyed with her goblet. "We need a little breathing time."

"I'll say. Plus all the worry about Suzanne. I'm certainly glad we heard from her. I was beginning to wonder." Barbara leaned forward, her voice lowered, "But you know there is still a real question in my mind about that message. If it were sent by one of our couriers, why wasn't it here on Friday instead of Monday? Actually we don't really *know* where it came from."

"Your guess is as good as mine." Abby shrugged and thought quickly for a plausible answer, "But you know how things get fouled up around here sometimes, particularly with communications. Somebody probably just put it in the outgoing file and didn't make a note that it was priority."

She hoped she had assuaged Barbara's curiosity. But she had a point. For now the rest of the office staff needed their questions answered also. Their suspicions about Suzanne being AWOL needed immediate squashing.

"Maybe," Barbara said. "I hope she's having a wonderful time. She's a great gal, and we all like her, even though she *is* something of a loner. Abby, you seem to be the only one she's really close to."

"That's probably true, but only because the work we do is more interlocked than with the rest of the staff. You know yourself how little time any of us has to see each other outside the office."

"I suppose you're right. Anyway, I'm glad she's not going to get into trouble." Barbara began to pick up her things. "Guess I'd better get going. It's getting late. I'll get the check this time, you leave a tip."

"OK, see you tomorrow, take care." Abby left a tip on the table and walked to the door.

There were so many unanswered questions. Suzanne had been Senator Downs' confidential secretary before she came to work for Commander Logan. Obviously, in the past, she had known a great amount of secret and confidential information. What was the connection between Senator Downs and the French diplomat? Did he know him? He didn't seem to object to Suzanne's not being at the party for the most of it. Did he know she was meeting with Jacques D'Arcy? And how close was her relationship with Senator Downs? Yes, too many questions.

A light rain had turned into a thunderstorm. The lightning lit up the sky. Abby hailed a cab, got in and soon was homeward bound.

Though it was October, Daylight Savings Time was year round because of the war, and it was still light when the cab let her out at the apartment house. She caught the elevator to the fourth floor and unlocked the apartment door. Immediately the phone began to ring. "Hello," she said, "Can I help you?"

"I hope so. Is this Miss St. Giles?" The pleasing inflection of a British accent came over the wire.

"This is she," Abby said.

"Miss St. Giles, this is Russell Bifford. Sir Robert St. Giles recommended that I call you. He said he had spoken with you, and you were the kind of person OSS is looking for."

"I see! Yes, now I recall, he *did* mention some sort of fairly new organization to me. Is this it? So he *is* really more a part of you than he said?"

Abby heard a light chuckle on the other end of the line. "Oh, I think you could say that," Russell Bifford said. "Even a rather important part. In any case, I would very much like to meet with you for an interview. We're very interested in exploring your interest in joining us."

"And whom would I be joining, pray tell? Do you have a name?"

"Oh, I see, Sir Robert never told you. We're called the Office of Strategic Services. I'll be happy to tell you more about it when we meet. Could you do it possibly tomorrow around 5:30? We could meet for dinner or make some other arrangement, if you like. Would the Peacock Room at the Willard suit you?"

"I suppose so. It *is* a convenient one. How will I know you? I'd just as soon not make a mistake with a complete stranger."

Here came that chuckle again. "Don't worry, I'll know you. Let's see—I'll start with 'Your grandmother sends her love.'"

"Rather cloak and dagger, isn't it?" Abby laughed.

"But that's what makes it interesting, don't you think?"

"Oh indeed it does. It's getting interesting-er and interesting-er. I'll meet you tomorrow then. Put your arm in a sling or something."

"Capital idea! I'll be looking forward.

They rang off laughing.

The next day went quickly. There was no more information about Suzanne, but now Cdr. Logan was in touch with Robert and was receiving guidance and information about protocol. Since this might very well be an espionage matter, the OSS were the ones to conduct the investigation, but it needed at some point to be coordinated with Naval Intelligence.

There was always a real reluctance to get the FBI involved because of J. Edgar Hoover's ongoing insistence on taking complete control of everything he touched. But this was wartime. The FBI's duties were supposed to be confined to the domestic area, while investigations of espionage and national security reached far beyond the shores of the United States and furnished the rationale to keep control in the hands of those better equipped to handle it. Keeping this one quiet was essential to avoid the inevitable squawking when "The Hoover" found out. However the FBI would be called in if necessary.

Too, since Suzanne was Navy personnel, her superiors were very much involved. It was not simply a matter of her safety, but that of confidential and secret information critical to naval operations. After all, she was a Navy lieutenant—and she *was* AWOL.

Abby hailed a cab and arrived at the Willard on time. As usual, the lobby was full of the customary late day crowd. Congressmen, newspapermen, civil service, and military often found the Peacock Room their favorite watering hole. People of all sorts frequented the Willard, and for all sorts of reasons. Clandestine meetings, sometimes extramarital, often took place there. One overheard discussions of governmental matters, elections, critical news events, and all sorts of Washington gossip.

Abby looked around the lobby, but did not see anyone approaching what she felt a Russell Bifford might resemble. Who was this pleasant voice with that charming British accent?

She moved to the Peacock Room entrance and suddenly spied a young man with his arm in a sling. He was an extremely attractive young man between 25 and 30, with sandy hair, astonishing green eyes, wearing a smart but relaxed English tweed coat.

When he saw Abby he began to grin, which turned into a gentle laugh as she approached. Immediately, Abby joined in.

"Your grandmother sends her love," said Russell Bifford, continuing to laugh.

"I was only joking about the sling," she said.

"I know, but it seemed appropriate since you really had no idea who I was."

"Well now, that was very considerate of you. But how did you know me?"

"I was told to look for the most beautiful woman I had ever seen. And so I had no problem at all in recognizing you." His eyes confirmed his sincerity.

"Goodness, Mr. Bifford, I'm overcome with all these compliments. Are you sure you haven't kissed the Blarney Stone recently?"

"Ah, but if it's true it can hardly be Blarney, now can it?" he said, smiling. "Call me Biff. By now no one would know me by my real name."

"And I'm Abby."

"It suits you," he said. "Come, let's find a table so we can get on with our business." Biff, with a mischievous glance at her, took the sling from around his arm and stuffed it in the pocket of his tweed jacket.

The maitre d' led them to a table in the corner. They talked for a long time. Abby was full of questions, and by the time their meeting was over, she had a reasonably complete overview of what the Office of Strategic Services was all about. The fact that she knew no details of any of its operations was routine for this kind of intelligence interview. Actually it was mostly about her. But she came away from the meeting realizing that this operation was absolutely vital for winning the war. There was a deep excitement beginning to rumble in the depth of her being. She knew that much of it had to do with a new adventure at hand.

She also suspected that some of her feelings had to do with the handsome young Mr. Bifford. Nevertheless, she had agreed to come in for evaluation. There was always the possibility that she might be rejected but somehow she didn't think so, and there was something in her heart that said: *this is your path, walk in it.*

Biff had given her an address and the time she was to report for evaluation, and a phone number, which she had memorized, and instructed her to tell them to no one under any circumstances.

As she left the Willard that day, Abby thought of her mother. She would be returning from Atlanta on Friday. That gave her only two days to explain to her mother what she was planning to do. What her response would be was anyone's guess. But Abby was prepared for fireworks if her mother objected.

Chapter 12

On Friday, after work, Abby met her mother, Miranda, for dinner at their favorite little French restaurant in the square. They exchanged hugs and greetings and began to catch up on the events of Miranda's trip.

Atlanta, always the center of the social scene, had been quite prepared for Miranda's visit. Friends had entertained her royally, and it was obvious that she had enjoyed herself immensely.

According to Miranda, Mama, Abby's grandmother, was still full of that exuberance she always manifested. Abby missed her terribly. She had always been a safe harbor in a bad storm, and there had been many during her early childhood. Particularly while her mother and father had been fighting in court for her custody, a fight that had lasted over nine years, leaving all parties concerned not only emotionally wounded but exhausted as well.

Mama had been her anchor in times of turmoil, the one steady rock on which she could depend. She was never critical, always encouraging, always uplifting. Abby adored her. It was in times of stress that she always remembered her grandmother's admonition: "You are in the palm of God's hand, darling, trust Him."

Miranda and she chatted throughout dinner. Miranda was full of herself and all that she had done on her trip. Finally, she asked about Abby's two weeks.

"Work has been pretty heavy over the past week or so," she said. "There really hasn't been much going on here in Washington, but I did manage to get away over last weekend for a couple of days."

"Really? That was nice. Where did you go? To Virginia Beach?" Miranda said, inattentively.

"No, actually I got a call from Cameron and Uncle Robert and I went there for a couple of days. The scenery was beautiful driving over and I really needed to get away. It was lonely here without you, particularly on the weekend."

Suddenly Miranda's eyes narrowed. "You mean you went to see *Cameron and Robert?* Why didn't you tell me when we talked on the phone?"

Here we go again, she thought. "Well actually, I don't think we've talked since before last weekend. I never thought to call and tell you this week because I knew you were coming back today."

"Well, I never! Just let me go out of town for a few days and the conspiracy starts all over again."

"What conspiracy? Mother, what *are* you talking about? You and I both have visited Cameron and Robert many times and they've always been cordial to you. Just because Robert is my daddy's brother is no reason you should feel that way."

"Don't you tell me what I should feel. Your father has done everything he could think of ever since you were born to turn you against me. And everyone else on his side of the family, for that matter. I know how clever he is. I'll bet you anything he put them up to it. So don't try to defend them." She sat back, settling a frozen glare on Abby.

"They really don't need any defense, Mother. The entire time I was there, no one mentioned you or Daddy or anything that has happened in the past. I really wish you would get over these feelings that there is some kind of conspiracy. It simply doesn't exist."

"Oh yes, of course, I'm the one who is paranoid. I'm the one who's crazy. All that bunch has ever done is blame me for everything that has ever happened, particularly to you. If you were sick, it was my fault. Whatever you did or said, it was my fault. I am really sick and tired of it by now." She looked accusingly at Abby. "It does seem that I should have a little loyalty from my own daughter."

Abby was getting that old feeling of anger mixed with helplessness. Her shoulders drooped as she slumped back in her chair. "I have never been disloyal to you, Mother. But to tell you the truth, I'm getting very tired of being torn between the two of you. Neither you nor Daddy has any idea how you make me feel when you put me in a position like this." She sighed a deep sigh. "I sometimes wonder if you *care* about how I must feel. Neither of you seems to consider what your battle has done to *me* for all these years."

"How can you even *think* such a thing," Miranda said, reproachfully. "You've been treated like a little princess since the day you were born. I have done everything in my power to give you everything a child could possibly want. I have sacrificed my very life for you—I never married again because of you. You're all I have left. And yet *I'm* the one who is always wrong. And *I'm* the one who is plotted against behind my back. Don't try to blame this all on me."

Abby had had enough. "I'm sorry you feel that way, Mother, but we've had this conversation many times before, and it never goes anywhere, it's never resolved. There is no conspiracy that I know anything about. And I think at this point we should simply let it drop. There is no point in both of us getting all upset about nothing."

Miranda looked around. They were in a restaurant, a scene in public was unthinkable. She put her finger to her mouth. "Hush up—what will people say?"

Abby looked at her mother for a long moment. It was hopeless. She decided to change the subject. "Why don't we go to a movie or something. There is a good one playing at Loew's. It's with Clark Gable and Lana Turner."

"Well, I suppose so. All right," Miranda said reluctantly, "but I won't soon forget this." Miranda fully intended to give Cameron a piece of her mind. She certainly wasn't going to let *this* go, but time for that later. "I really do like Clark Gable, but I can't imagine him paired with Lana Turner. Some combination!"

Abby heaved a sigh of relief. She determined to be as pleasant as possible during the remainder of the evening, which, unexpectedly, went very well. The dinner was delicious. The movie was entertaining and suddenly her mother's mood seemed to change. But Abby knew she was biding her time. She decided that this was certainly not the time to bring up the subject of OSS. She would have to wait until tomorrow.

She realized she should never have told her mother about her trip to Allistair, but it wasn't her nature to keep secrets from her. Nevertheless, had she thought it through, she would have guessed Miranda would think it was part of the "conspiracy" to get Abby away from her, which was partially the root of the delusion in the first place. However, it was less of a delusion than it was the actual truth.

Abby and Miranda attended their usual Episcopal church that Sunday morning. It was a beautiful uplifting day, the sun was shining, and a crisp autumn wind was blowing the vary-colored leaves helter-skelter. Autumn was well underway, and the landscape was emblazoned with reds and yellows against the fading greenery.

The sermon that morning was about forgiveness and learning to love your enemies.

"Blessed are ye when men shall revile you, and persecute you, and shall say all manner of evil against you falsely, for my sake. Rejoice and be exceedingly glad for great is your reward in Heaven. For if you forgive men their trespasses, your Heavenly Father will forgive you."

Abby listened intently. How strange it is, she thought, that those we love the most sometimes are the most difficult with whom to get along, and even appear to be our worst enemy. How difficult it is to forgive those who inflict such hurt.

After the service, they decided to walk to the little French restaurant on the way back to the apartment. It was such a lovely day and the walk was short. Soon they reached the restaurant and were seated near the window. During lunch, Abby decided she *had* to broach the subject of making a change in her employment, though she did so with some anxiety.

"I guess I forgot to tell you," she said, as she fidgeted with her water goblet. "I've been offered a new job. It will mean a two-grade raise, also in salary, and it's something I'm much more interested in than what I'm doing."

"Really?" Miranda narrowed her eyes and frowned. "Now how in the world did that come about?"

"I'm not really all that sure. All I know is that there are multiple changes in personnel going on right now. It seems that everyone's records are being investigated to see who might serve better in another position. I know I have a good employee evaluation. Commander Logan has been very pleased with my performance. It could easily have been he who recommended me."

"That would be paradoxical." Miranda gave her a piercing look. "If Commander Logan is so pleased with your performance, why would he be willing to let you go?"

"Well you know, it's not always what one wants. It's the powers that be who decide." Abby felt hopeless, her mother was bound to know.

"Now I'm beginning to see what's really going on. It was Cameron and Rob who put you up to this, wasn't it?" She nodded, calculating the odds. "I *knew* they were up to no good. It's just another piece in their diabolical plan to get you out of my life for good."

"Mother, how can you say that? I'm sure Cameron and Robert have much better things to do than to plot against you, much less try to control what directions I take." She placed her napkin on the side of her plate. How could she introduce this prospect appealingly? "Did it ever occur to you that this is something I might really *want* to do? That it really *is* a good opportunity with a position raise as well as a salary increase?"

Miranda drew back from the table and crossed her shapely legs. "All right, let's have the rest of it. What is this new position all about? And what branch of the service is it in?" She fixed a steady glare on Abby. "When you answer *that* question I'll soon know what's been going on and where it's coming from."

Abby gathered up her courage. "It's in intelligence. *You're* in intelligence and *you* love it. Why would you not want me to be in the same field?"

"Of course, why not?" she said. "Now I *know* it was Robert who's behind this. You should know by now that it's hopeless to try to deceive me. Shame on you!"

True, no one could ever keep anything from Miranda. It was as though she had second sight. She could always see through any kind of camouflage.

"The truth is, Mother, I was approached by someone else. He asked me if I was interested in becoming part of the organization. He explained a lot of things to me about the operation itself and it's right up my alley." Abby was becoming more than agitated. She decided that tact was not the answer. "The fact is, I have an appointment in the morning for an evaluation to see if I'm qualified for the job. I *fully* intend to be there, so if you think you're going to stop me, *forget* it! I'm sick of your attitude towards me and your attempts to control every decision I make. Where I go. Whom I see. And everything I think and do." Though she kept her voice low, Abby's eyes flashed her anger.

They sat in silence for several minutes, but Miranda didn't flinch, nor did she remove her frozen stare from Abby. Finally she spoke, "Very well," Miranda said, "You needn't get on your high horse. If you have absolutely made up your mind you're going to defy me, then go right ahead. I won't try to stop you." She frowned and looked away. "Maybe it will do you *good* to get into a field that's so difficult you'll see that I was only trying to protect you and your interests. I suppose *some* people simply have to do it the hard way. Very well, go right ahead. *I* won't stand in your way."

Abby realized that this particularly skirmish was coming to an end.

"Good. I'm glad you decided to be reasonable about this. Remember, I haven't been accepted yet, and there's a chance I won't be. So why don't you wait and see?"

Miranda narrowed her eyes. "I suppose you know that they could send you somewhere else. As a matter of fact, there's a plethora of intelligence going on right here in Washington. It would be very foolish of you to even consider an overseas assignment." She sighed heavily, "but knowing you, that's probably exactly what you'll do."

Abby looked at her mother intently. She knew her mother was only trying to protect her—or was it her obsession with control? "Why don't you simply wait until I'm accepted to start worrying about where I'll be stationed. It might be right here in Washington, for all I know. But even if that were the case, there is quite an extensive training period, so I'm told."

"Yes, I suppose it could be Washington. Well you've made up your mind. So go ahead. I'll wait and see."

By now Miranda had completely changed her approach. Abby heaved a sigh of relief. She changed the subject to more pleasant things as they finished their lunch. But she was leery of her mother's response, and she wondered when the next shoe would drop.

Yes, sometimes it's the ones you love the most who seem more like the enemy.

She awoke abruptly the next morning to find her mother standing over her, shaking her shoulder.

"Abby, I want you to call those people and cancel this appointment. You have absolutely no business in intelligence or being transferred somewhere else."

Immediately she was alert. "Mother, that's impossible. I cannot possibly cancel this appointment at the last minute. And furthermore, I don't intend to."

"Oh, is that so? I demand that you do what I say. I am your mother and I do have a say about what you do and where you go. Now, you get up and call these people. I will not have it any other way."

"All right. I'm getting up now. Go away and let me get dressed." Abby decided there was no way she was going to argue with her mother. Let Miranda believe that she had had her way for a few minutes. She dressed quickly and looked at the clock. She had enough time to arrive promptly if there were no more delays. When she was ready to go she walked into the front room and headed for the door. Here we go again, she thought.

"Where do you think you're going, young lady! You go right over there and pick up that phone. You call them right now and cancel that appointment!"

"Mother, you're being ridiculous! I told you yesterday that I really intended to make this appointment and that's what I'm going to do. Now you can get yourself in a stew if that's what you want to do. But I'm going—and you're not going to stop me."

"Oh, I never heard of a daughter being so ugly to her mother! 'Sharper than a serpent's sting is that of an ungrateful child.'" Miranda began to weep. "After all I have done for you, that you would treat me in such a disrespectful way. Don't think that I won't remember this. I'm only trying to protect you from people who will take advantage of you." Abruptly her voice changed to anger. "Can't you listen to reason?" Miranda had stationed herself in front of the door.

"Move away from the door, Mother. I'm leaving now."

"Oh no, you're not. You're not stepping one foot out of this house until I know where you're going."

"Move away from the door, Mother. This is absurd! Stop trying to block me."

Miranda didn't move. "I demand to know where you're going. If you don't tell me it will not go well with you."

Abby threw up her hands. She knew when she was defeated. She was going to be late. She went to the desk and wrote a number down on the message pad.

"All right," Abby said. "Here is the phone number, but don't you dare call it. If you do you will get me in big trouble and maybe even yourself. I have told you *repeatedly* this is highly confidential information."

"That doesn't apply to me," her mother said. "I'm your mother. Besides, I'm in Intelligence myself."

Abby shook her head, Miranda was impossible. She lowered her voice, "Mother, move aside and let me out. I'll see you late this afternoon when this is over. I have to hurry."

Miranda didn't move. So Abby pushed her aside. As she did, Miranda's voice completely changed. "All right, darling. I'll be here."

She had gotten her way.

Abby fled the apartment. She bypassed the elevator and took the steps to the lobby. She knew that any delay might defeat her once her mother realized that she still did not know *where* she was going. Reaching the lobby in record time, she hurried through the front door, and hailed a cab. She felt completely wiped out. On her way, she tried to regain her composure as she sped through the traffic to her destination.

It was in this state of emotional upheaval that Abby arrived at the confidential address of OSS for evaluation. It was an old spacious mansion, apparently converted to its present use. In a half-daze, she wondered fleetingly, What kind of people must have lived here and how long ago? What must have happened here? Were the people happy?

She pushed open the door gingerly and was met by an armed guard who checked her credentials and ushered her into the hall lobby. *An armed guard! This is no laughing matter*, she thought.

She looked around. No one was there, the waiting room was empty. There was no receptionist no secretary, no one at all. Suddenly the receptionist returned to her desk.

"Just have a seat, Miss St. Giles. Someone will be with you in a moment."

Abby thought she heard soft music playing from another room. What was it? Of course, Mozart. She supposed this was to allay her anxiety. But it didn't. After this morning's fiasco she doubted that anything could.

Selecting a chair along the wall she let herself into it. She felt self-conscious, as though in view of 1000 invisible eyes stationed around the empty room, critically watching her every move. It had been a harrowing morning. She felt guilty, as though she had committed the unpardonable sin. But her determination to get away from her mother had been considerably strengthened.

The inner door opened and a distinguished looking man greeted her. "Miss St.Giles, I'm Dr. Bernard. I'm happy to meet you."

Abby responded immediately to his soft, reassuring manner. "Thank you, it's a pleasure to be here."

"Good. So, shall we get on with it?"

"Yes, indeed. What comes next?"

"Well, first we have some tests to determine in what areas your skills lie so that we can know where best to place you. Some of these are written, some verbal, and some are situational. I think you'll enjoy them."

"All right—you're the doctor." Abby smiled but her thoughts were rattled. If he thought she was in any condition to take any tests today he was sadly mistaken. Oh well. She hoped she didn't shoot herself in the foot.

Dr. Bernard smiled back at her. He was so relaxed it was contagious. "This way," he said and led her down a long corridor where another young man welcomed her.

Abby knew he was a psychologist or a psychiatrist, as was Dr. Bernard. Before the day was over, she knew that they all were one or the other.

He seated her at a table and handed her a some test booklets. "Just follow the instructions. Some of these subtests are timed. I'll administer some of these and keep tabs on where you are and give you go and stop signals. You may begin when you are ready."

Abby took the material, which looked reasonable enough. Even though she still felt anxious, she was fairly comfortable with the verbal part. But then came the timed tests. By then the knots in her stomach had tightened. However, she was in it now so she did the best she could. She knew the young man was observing her, noticing her slightly trembling hand and her mostly hidden confusion. What he couldn't know was the emotional state she was in from this morning's events. As a rule she could handle most any situation with relative calm, but not today.

She didn't like being treated like a guinea pig, but she knew it was part of the game. She also knew that this organization had already done a complete investigation of her to clear her for top security. So they knew by now that she had always tested in the gifted intellectual area. To boot, she had a degree from one of the toughest universities in the nation, a rare feat for a woman in her day.

Dr. Margaret S. Emanuelson

But they had delved deeper than that—into her loyalty to the nation, into her morality, her ability to get along with others, her special talents, her achievements in the past and in her present though short position. So they knew she had received a special commendation from the Secretary of the Navy during her third month of employment, and made a supervisor as a result. She had even been given a personal secretary. Abby had laughed at that. They didn't know what to do with her, so they had made her an executive. A 90-day wonder. Although at only 20, that didn't particularly endear her to *some* of her staff, most of whom were many years older and had been in government for years.

She had no fear of her past. It was pretty much beyond reproach.

Two hours later she finished the tests with a sigh of relief.

"Well, now—all through? Good," said the young man. "Now, just follow me down the hall to the next part." Abby obliged. When they came to a door he said, "It was a pleasure to work with you, Miss St. Giles."

"Thank you, same here," she said, opening the door.

The next test was a situational one. There were several young men in the room and no women. The room was practically empty except for a few wooden chairs, some rope, and a few boards.

Apparently, there was a one-way mirror though which the observers could scrutinize every move, but they were never informed about it. The group was completely quiet. No gab, no introductions, just perfect strangers waiting for instructions. Soon they came:

"The enemy is approaching. With only the materials you find in this room you are to build a bridge over a deep river 35 feet wide. You have 25 minutes to build it and evacuate your people." The instructor walked outside and, before shutting the door, said: "Begin now."

Oh Glory, Abby thought. This was impossible. She didn't swim very well on top of every thing else, but she said nothing. Suppose this were a real situation? The young men were scrambling around placing the chairs and boards in a chain position, but the materials were obviously short of the mark. Many of the people at hand were not consulted, in fact, totally ignored, while one young man took the lead, instructing all the others. Obviously the real goal was to evacuate the people, and they were getting nowhere. Finally she spoke up.

"In view of the time, it would seem to me that the only solution is to form a human chain with the strongest swimmers so the others can get over first. The stronger swimmers can follow. If we start now we can make it."

But her offering fell on deaf ears and was ignored. Of course, she realized later that there *was* no real solution. They were set up to fail while the observers took note of how they approached solving tough problems, and probably more important, who were leaders, who were followers, how resourceful they were, and how they reacted to failure.

The 25 minutes was up, the observers thanked the participants with no other comment, and they began to disburse in different directions. Suddenly here came the young psychologist who had tested her before.

"Miss St Giles, you have a phone call."

"I beg your pardon. I—what?"

"You have a phone call, you can take it in here." He led her to another room where a phone lay on the desk off the hook.

Abby's heart sank. Didn't her mother have grain of sense? Didn't she have any idea what this was going to do to Abby?

"Yes, Mother, what is it?"

"Finally, it's you! How did you know who it was?"

"You're the only one who *has* this number."

"Oh—yes. Well, I was worried. I didn't know where you were so I called to see if you were there. I've called a number of times and I keep getting the run-around."

"Didn't it ever occur to you that you should have trusted me? That you shouldn't have called at all?"

"Now, Abigail, you were acting so strange, not telling me anything. As your mother I have a *right* to know where my daughter is."

"We'll discuss this when I get home. I have to go."

"Wait. I demand to know where you are, *right now*!"

At this point, Abby knew that if she didn't tell her something, she would undoubtedly call again even more irate. She drew on all her resources to come up with a believable lie.

"I'm in an office at 2001 Dupont Circle. Now don't you dare call here again. I will be home very soon."

Immediately her mother's voice changed. "All right, darling, I'll be waiting for you." She hung up. Now that she had gotten her way, she seemed satisfied for the moment. But Abby knew it wasn't over, and that a few days or months or years later it would be thrown in her face again.

The young psychologist approached her at this point. "Miss St. Giles, Dr. Bernard would like to see you."

"Yes, I suppose he *would*," Abby said. Obviously, someone else knew that the conversation had ended. How she wished she could shrivel up and disappear. But she squared her shoulders and followed the young psychologist to Dr. Bernard's office. He rose to greet her and motioned to the chair in front of his desk.

"You almost gave the store away, didn't you?" He smiled.

Abby realized that not only had her mother been harassing the switchboard but that all of the phone calls had been monitored. She threw up her hands and sank hopelessly into the chair. "I feel terrible. I never meant to violate this information. I knew it was confidential but my mother has her methods." She looked away and shook her head. "She works in Intelligence herself, you know, and she does have top clearance. I tried to put her off but I'm so unused to lying about anything."

"It's O.K. In the end you gave her the wrong address. You're a quick study. You saved yourself."

"Yes. Well, it won't happen again. If I'm to work here I suppose I'll have to learn to be a better liar. This morning it was a classic approach-approach avoidance-avoidance conflict."

Dr. Bernard looked at her with a somewhat surprised expression on his face. "We'll help you with how to maneuver these things and train you with other techniques as well. I can see you've had quite a good deal of psychological training already."

"Yes, but I really blew those tests this morning. I was so upset I really couldn't think."

"But you went on with it anyway."

"Yes, I had no alternative. The show must go on, no matter how I feel." She could recall many such occurrences.

"Shows a lot about you—dedication and persistence under pressure. The ability to push your feelings aside in a difficult moment." He smiled, supportively.

"I suppose so. I guess I never thought of it that way." Abby was beginning to feel better.

"Actually, you did very well, indeed. You went on and succeeded in the face of heavy obstacles. It shows a great deal about you." Dr. Bernard gestured with his hand, as if to wipe the entire incident away. They sat in silence for a moment. "Now that that's over, let me ask you a few questions."

"Very well. What do you want to know?"

"Why don't we began by your telling me why you might want to come to work for OSS?"

"All right. Where do I start." Abby paused for a few moments and began: "As you know I have finished my B.A. degree. I came to Washington initially to work in Civil Service. They wound up placing me in personnel directly under the Secretary of the Navy. I've been happy enough there and have had a good deal of success as I'm sure you already know." She stopped, reflecting for a moment.

"I suppose it is normal to want to become totally independent of one's parents, but in my background, a young southern lady does not live alone but remains under her parent's roof until she is married, which, in my case, presents a problem. Under the circumstances, I have decided that the only way I can gracefully leave my mother's home is to be assigned somewhere else, perhaps even overseas. OSS can give me the opportunity of doing so. This is a field I am intensely interested in, and I think I may have the skills and the abilities to contribute something positive.

"However, that aside, I've always been extremely interested in intelligence work, research, and problem solving. Had the war had not come along I would probably have gone into medicine or psychology. In fact, at some point in the future I may do exactly that, but now we are at *war* and I want to contribute whatever I can to ending it. I can assure you that leaving my mother's abode is not my only motivation, nor my primary one."

"I understand. Would you like to tell me exactly what *did* happen this morning?"

"It's somewhat difficult to explain. One would have to go all the way back to the beginning to see how this situation developed."

"Of course, you needn't do that. We know that your mother and father are divorced and have been for many years and that their animosity and struggles seem to continue even now, and

Company of Spies

mostly surrounding you. In a nutshell, just try to give me the scenario of what happened this morning."

"I'll try." Explaining was the absolute last thing she wanted to do, but she had no alternative. She began to explain why and how her mother had behaved the way she had.

This morning's fiasco was typical of her relationship with her mother. In her assumed role as "protector" she insisted in knowing every act and thought of her daughter. Abby had discovered that she was even reading her mail and listening in on her phone conversations.

After four years away at school, where she had had more freedom to make her own choices, she had forgotten how impossible living with her mother could be. She had thought this time it would be different, but if anything it was worse. Had Abby been a bad child it might have been different, but she had always been morally high-minded and upright. It was as though her mother was looking for something, not finding it, yet making her feel guilty anyhow. The theme usually ran "after all I have done for you, that you would treat me like this." Abby was finding it harder and harder to figure out what that was.

So she had decided to get away on her own, and after five months in her civil service position she had been given an opportunity to join the Office of Strategic Services. Her mother knew that she had had the offer, and that she was going through the processing procedure. She also knew how confidential it was. She had seemed to accept it, but that morning they had had a terrible row. Her mother had *demanded* to know where her daughter was going. She pulled every trick she had in her long repertoire. So, against Abby's will and her better judgment, reluctantly she had left her the phone number.

"I honestly never for one moment thought she would actually use it. I'm so, so sorry."

"I understand," said Dr. Bernard.

"So you can see that I arrived here at headquarters this morning in a completely harried state." She leaned back in the chair with a heavy sigh. There were a great many other things she hadn't told him. Always a private person, she was not accustomed to revealing private matters to anyone, not even the rest of her family. Usually, she kept her own council and told no one anything of any real importance, particularly her feelings about things.

"Seems you had a pretty horrible experience with your mother this morning. I can understand how you must feel and how upset you were. But as I said, you saved yourself, so no real problem."

At this point Dr. Bernard asked a few more questions. "Are you willing to be reassigned outside Washington, even for an overseas assignment?"

"Yes, I know how dangerous it could be. But my country is at war. There comes a time in everyone's life when one has to stand up for what one believes."

"Indeed! We all feel that way. That's why we're here, doing what we do," Dr. Bernard said. "Very well, we'll see where we can place you. Of course, first, we would need to put you in a training program. That may take several weeks. Also there are a series of inoculations and a physical. But those details you'll be informed of in the near future."

He asked her a few more questions and finally said, "You know, after taking a look at your records and everything we've come up with about you, I think we've made an excellent decision. We probably know a great deal more about you than you know, and as it turns out we think you're the kind of person we're looking for." Dr. Bernard leaned forward. "So I think we can end this conversation on a positive note. If this is what you want, you're in."

"Wonderful!" Abby smiled, relieved. She felt as though a world of guilt had been erased from her. "It is certainly gratifying to know that you can understand my dilemma of this morning. I'm pleased to be accepted. I can assure you I'll do my best."

"Were happy to have you, Abby. It may take you a little time to get used to the chaos around here but I can assure you, you won't find it boring. And you'll meet some fascinating people."

"I have already," Abby said, looking directly at him.

Dr. Bernard smiled. "Thank you. I assure you it's mutual. Now, let me give you a preliminary schedule. You are to report for a physical and your inoculations as soon as possible, so that you'll be ready to ship out as soon as your training reaches a certain point. Also, if you are sent abroad, you will be put on alert until the opportunity presents itself to schedule you for transport."

"It becomes very involved, doesn't it? All the little things have to add up."

"Yes, indeed it does. And before I forget it, you need to report for your badge. You can do that today, right down the hall—six doors on your left. We'll take care of applying for your passport with the State Department. There are only special passports being issued at this time. Wartime, you know."

Dr. Bernard rose from his chair. "Now, Miss Abigail St. Giles, you're on your way. It has been a pleasure meeting you. If there is anything I can do for you in the future, be sure to let me know. You'll be seeing me—here and there."

Abby left the office that day feeling good about her encounter with Dr. Bernard and actually being accepted, but, on the other hand, dreading to go home to face her mother.

Chapter 13

Suzanne sat up in the big luxurious bed. She reached her arms as high as possible and stretched her sleepy muscles. Her happiness knew no bounds. Jacques was wonderful. She could never have imagined a partner who could make her flesh tingle so completely. He had awakened wonderful new desires within her. She felt completely in his power. He had only to walk in the room and she began to feel those almost uncontrollable sensations.

He was an unbelievable lover. Remembering their encounters one by one, Suzanne smiled a secret smile. These were memories for her alone. Never to be shared with anyone.

Jacques had planned this so carefully, down to the last detail. She had total faith in him. After all, he was completely experienced in diplomatic affairs, actually quite a hero in his own country. Even so, he kept a very low profile. He could handle the particulars. All she had to do was follow his instructions. Jacques said it was important to follow the plan exactly, even though she might not know the reasons why, and she was willing to believe in him.

However, she felt bad about the way she had disappeared. Particularly where Abby was concerned. She was so fond of

Abby. She had come to the point in their friendship where she felt closer to her than anyone else.

The only remaining member of her family, Kippy, her father's sister, had been her surrogate mother through all the teen years after her mother and father were killed in the plane crash. She had offered not only tenderness and affection, but had guided her through her later teens in her educational and vocational choices. But Aunt Kippy had died six months before and left her a complete orphan. Now she was totally alone.

Kippy had been the co-trustee of Suzanne's sizeable estate left her by her father. She had always been fair and understanding when Suzanne wanted extra money, even though to Kippy her wants had sometimes seemed somewhat frivolous, even exorbitant. But now the estate was totally Suzanne's. And although there were still some restrictions on it and she had to deal with the only remaining trustee in Switzerland, she could more or less do with it what she would.

Suzanne returned to her reverie. Jacques would soon be back. She was becoming used to the little errands he seemed obliged to run. Usually it never took very long, maybe two or three hours at the most. Only once recently had he been on an overnight trip. But many times when he was away she simply went shopping for the new wonderful designer clothes she was now able to wear. What a wonderful joy. She was so tired of that uniform. New York City was really the most wonderful place to shop. Outside of Paris, she could think of no better opportunity. During the past ten days, she had certainly indulged herself, but she didn't feel the least bit guilty. After all, she had done her part while in uniform. Now she was still going to contribute to her country, only this time it was going to be in a less conspicuous, even more significant way.

The prospect of a new life was exhilarating. The way Jacques had explained it had excited her to her core. He was so clever. He had taken care of everything, even arranging for the two Naval Intelligence officers to come and explain her new mission to her. Getting her honorably discharged and detached from the Navy and on "special assignment" was one of his incredible feats of the day. But then that was part of his expertise. He was going to take care of her passport as well, through the State Department. She felt totally cared for, pampered, for the first time in years. It was wonderful.

Suzanne looked at the bedside table clock. It was 10 AM. Jacques would soon be back. She jumped out of bed and headed towards the shower. She would put on something especially smart today. They had a number of things to do to be ready to depart and she wanted to please him.

Chapter 14

Abby returned home that Monday evening expecting not only the third degree but forty tongue lashes. Unexpectedly, Miranda was the epitome of gracious charm and good nature.

"How did it go?" she asked.

"Fine. I've been accepted."

"I knew you would be. So what happens now?"

"I'm not really sure of the timeline but apparently there is a period of training. I don't know what my assignment is yet or what I will be doing. I'm sure when they get their heads together they will inform me of the next step. But first, of course, I need to inform Commander Logan of my reassignment."

"So, if you *are* reassigned outside of Washington, it won't be immediate. Good, that will give me time to think about it. Perhaps they won't send you out of town. There's plenty of intelligence to be done right here in Washington."

Abby could see that for the next few days even weeks, there would probably be relative peace. She intended to savor every moment of it.

On Tuesday, the next morning, Abby arrived at the office a few minutes early. Commander Logan was already there. She had told him that she was being interviewed by OSS and tested the day before, so he was aware of the situation. He said he had already been informed through official channels that she had been reassigned. But that he had requested the rest of the week for her to introduce and train her replacement.

They discussed a number of loose ends and then Abby asked the big question. "What about Suzanne? Have you heard anything? I don't know when anything has been so upsetting. Not knowing where she is, or if she's all right." Abby looked directly into his clear blue eyes. "I know you've been in touch with Robert. What does he say?"

"Your Uncle Robert is a blessing. He's digging into all the particulars. Of course, she was due back yesterday. But so far, there is no word. We've had to wait to see if she returned on time. But now, Sir Robert and I are going to coordinate this with naval intelligence and OSS. So I think we're in pretty good hands." Commander Logan swung around his swivel chair to face her directly. "I understand OSS has some significant leads, but they may not be willing to divulge what they find. From here on out we're to treat this as top secret. If I find anything out I'll let you know, if I can."

"Good! I'll be waiting to hear from you."

Commander Logan looked somewhat wistfully at Abby, like a proud father might look affectionately at a cherished child. "I'm going to hate losing you, Abby. Not only have you done a wonderful job here, but everyone is devoted to you." He sighed, resignedly. "We will all miss you terribly. And with Suzanne missing, it adds an even sadder note." He looked away into the distance. "But this is *war* and things can change instantly, I know."

"Yes, indeed they can." Abby paused. She felt a tug of nostalgia. "And I shall miss all of you here. You, in particular, have been so supportive and helpful in making my transition into the workplace so much easier. It has really been a wonderful learning experience for me. I can't thank you enough."

"We should be thanking you." He nodded, smiling. "You're a quick learner, my dear. Besides, you've made a real contribution to cutting the red tape and straightening out the methodology around here." He leaned forward, obviously reluctant to see her go. "But, aside from that, Abby, I want you to know, if you ever need my help, in any capacity, you can count on me."

She knew he was sincere. What a fine man he was, honorable, reliable, steady as a rock. An admirable man, one to be trusted. "Believe me, it's mutual. You can count on me too."

They sat there a moment, thoughtfully. And then Abby broke the silence.

"Now, I guess I should say something to the rest of the troops about my leaving, and get on with training my replacement. I'll talk to you later."

Abby went back to her desk and began guardedly to explain her reassignment to the others in the office. From time to time throughout the day small groups gathered around her desk, all expressing sorrow to see her leave.

In part, she was sorry to go. She had become genuinely fond of many of the staff, particularly Suzanne, Marie, and Barbara and, of course, the Commander. She knew she would miss them all, but it was time to move on.

On Tuesday afternoon, on the shores of Lake Erie, a fisherman reported finding the body of a young blonde woman to the police. When they investigated they saw that the body was naked from the waist down, had been raped, beaten, and then mutilated beyond recognition. The only clues of identification were her remaining clothing—the top of a WAVE uniform, a set of dog tags—and her pale blonde hair.

The authorities immediately reported the incident to the Navy, who instantly put a Top Secret hold on the information.

The discovery was reported very quietly in the small local newspaper on a back page without reference to the uniform or the dog tags.

But this latest discovery was raising eyebrows in certain quarters of English and American Intelligence. It bore too many similarities to the recent disappearances of a number of other young women, in American and European government service.

Chapter 15

The following Monday Abby was instructed to report to OSS. When she awoke that morning the sun was shining and the weather was mild for late October. What a wonderful day to begin a new adventure, she thought. Well, here goes. She dressed, grabbed a cab, and gave the driver her instructions.

The cab driver looked at her curiously when he heard her instructions. "Miss, are you sure this is where you want to go?"

"Yes, I'm sure," Abby said. "Is there a problem?"

"No ma'am, not if you say so. But it just seems a strange place for young lady like you to want to go." He shook his head in disapproval.

"Why do you say that? Is there something wrong with the address?" she asked.

"No, it's just that it's a pretty bad section and it's mostly warehouses."

"I see. Yes, well I have business there. So don't worry." She nervously tapped her foot on the floor. "Is it far from here?"

"It's on the other side of town. Not too far."

"Well that's good. I don't want to be late."

Abby was worried by now. She knew that many of the offices and headquarters were stationed in obscure places. Clandestine operations had to be, to maintain their secrecy. But she didn't exactly relish working in a bad section of town, much less being in the midst of a plethora of warehouses.

About 30 minutes later, the cab driver began to slow down. He appeared to be looking for the address she had given him.

"Are we near the address?" she asked.

"Yes'm, we're about a block away from where it should be. It should be right straight down this street."

"All right," she said. "Why don't you let me out half a block down from here. I'll walk the rest of the way."

"If you sure that's what you want." The cabbie shook his head and mumbled something under his breath.

Abby was simply following her instructions, no doubt formulated to protect the identity of the place where she was going. But maybe she was being overly cautious.

The driver slowed down and stopped. Abby paid him and exited the cab.

"Good luck, Miss! Hope you know what you're doing." The cabbie shook his head.

"Thanks, I appreciate your concern, but I'll be fine."

She didn't *feel* fine. Anxiety and trepidation were creeping upon her. This was unknown and alien territory. But she squared her shoulders, picked up her briefcase, and started down the rest of the block to her destination.

"Be a good little soldier." Her father's oft spoken admonition came back to her from her childhood. It always gave her courage in times of uncertainty. And this was certainly one of those times. Even the cab driver was concerned about her safety.

Abby reached the address on her instructions. It was a large building, three stories high. It looked like some sort of storage warehouse. She went up to the door but it was unmarked except by a number. She entered and immediately was met by an armed guard on duty. He motioned to a desk with a receptionist, who rose to greet her.

"May I help you?" said a pleasant voice.

"Yes, thank you, I'm Abigail St. Giles, reporting for duty."

"Ah yes, Miss St. Giles. We've been expecting you. May I see your badge?"

"Yes, of course." Abby dug in her purse and pulled out her new identification badge. "Here you are."

"Good! Glad to have you on board. Incidentally, I'm Cordelia Simpson. If you have any problems or need any help I'm the one for you to see. Just let me know." Her smile was warm and cordial.

"That's very good to hear," Abby said. "You may be hearing from me sooner than you think."

"That's perfectly all right, I'm used to new people and their problems." Cordelia laughed.

"Well, that's certainly comforting." Abby laughed along with her. She felt as if a load had been lifted off her shoulders. She was not alone. There were people here who would help if needed, and Cordelia's manner was especially comforting.

"Now, let me call an escort to take you to your assignment. Today you're going to see Dr. Warner. He's our director of training and placement. I think you'll like him."

Dr. Warner turned out to be tall, silver-haired, and distinguished looking. He could easily have passed for the president of a University or an honored professor, which, in fact, he previously had been. Poised and serious, he was nevertheless betrayed by a certain unmistakable twinkle in his pale blue eyes that invariably put any of his subjects at immediate ease.

Abby also felt a sense of calm, and anticipation that something very interesting was about to take place. The interview began with the usual greetings and courtesies as Dr. Warner got to know Abby and her background. Then they explored several testing and interest areas. When he came to coding and de-coding, she told him about her sparse past knowledge of the subject.

She looked at the message handed her by Dr. Warner. "You really want me to *de-code* this message?" Abby began to laugh. "Let's see if I remember anything about it. It seems to me coding has to do with substitution of symbols for words. It could be mathematical or it could be word substitution or letter substitution or it might even be some sort of scrambling process that only those who are familiar with it could unscramble."

Abby looked at the message again. She began to laugh. "I have absolutely no idea even how to begin to decode this message. There has to be a key to deciphering it, but I don't have the key or the formula." She shook her head, in defeat. "Although I find this completely fascinating, I can assure you, Dr. Warner, that I could work on this all day and never come up with the correct answer." She gave him a quizzical look, but he just smiled expectantly. "All right then, for the sake of proving my point I'll give it a whirl."

She began a series of operations. Some mathematical, some word or letter substitutions. After about 20 minutes while Dr. Warner observed her working, Abby looked up at him with a mischievous smile and wrote down "the great bird has landed." With that she began to laugh.

Dr. Warner chuckled. "Only the problem is: the great bird was an agent and he sent his message to his enemy." They both laughed together. "You know, Abby, you're really quite methodical in your approach to problem solving. That's really what quite a lot of this testing is all about. To evaluate your ability to approach

Company of Spies

problems and apply good reasoning techniques in finding the solution. You have a good inquisitive mind, and a wonderful sense of humor. And believe me, in this kind of endeavor there may be times when that's the only thing that will save your sanity." He raised his hands in a gesture of acquiescence.

"I really think you're going to enjoy this kind of work as well as become a great asset to it." He leaned forward with one arm on the table. "Are there any questions you have before we stop today?"

"Only about 1000," Abby said. "In fact, there are so many I'm not sure where to begin."

"Well, then." He leaned back, "Why don't we simply take it one step at the time. Your training has already begun. You're going to get a sort of crash course in multiple areas. Then as you progress to your ultimate assignments you'll be able to put the pieces together."

"That sounds reasonable enough." Abby smiled. Dr. Warner was a dear; she could easily become fond of him.

"Fact is—you may ultimately find yourself being assigned to a number of various activities. And this kind of work sometimes requires quick judgment and insight, which really can't be taught. But I'm convinced you'll be able to handle whatever when the time comes." His look was reassuring.

"Thanks for the encouragement. You can probably guess I feel like Alice in Wonderland."

"Exciting, isn't it? Actually no one knows from moment to moment what might come his way in this kind of work. I suppose learning to handle ambiguity in life is the epitome of feeling secure deep within." He paused, looking at her intently. "It's really a matter of trust, isn't it?" He sat quietly for a moment. "In what do you put your trust, Abby? Yourself? Your intellect?"

"Good question." Abby pondered that thought for a moment. "My grandmother always told me I was 'in the palm of the hand of God.' And somehow I know that is true. No human being could be in complete control of all the chains of universal events impinging upon him." She turned the question over in her mind. "Although I do believe God gave us a brain to use and abilities to act and react in reasonable ways. So—I suppose, to a degree, we do have some ability to control our destinies. Beyond that, it's very comforting to know that He is there to keep us out of harm's way."

She looked at him directly. "I suppose I would say that, ultimately, I put my trust in God."

His kind blue eyes smiled at her. "If that is true, Abby, you'll be able to handle whatever comes your way."

Abby left Dr. Warner's office, walked slowly down the long staircase and over to the entrance where Cordelia was busy talking in French with a tall young woman. Abby lingered a moment at the desk. Cordelia almost immediately turned to her.

"There is someone here waiting to see you," she said.

Abby thought she saw a twinkle in Cordelia's eye. "Really? And who would know I'm here? I told no one."

"Over there." Cordelia pointed to a young man leaning on the doorjamb to the conference room, 40 feet away. He was engaged in an apparently jovial exchange with a decorated military man in uniform. But almost at that instant he caught sight of Abby, and laughingly reached in his pocket, took out a makeshift sling and arranged it on his right arm.

Abby burst into laughter. She could hardly contain her delight to find him there—and waiting for her! They approached each other.

"The last time we met you had broken your *left* arm!"

"Yes, well, sometimes my left doesn't know what my right is doing." Biff took the sling off and stuffed it in his pocket.

Abby continued to laugh. He was indeed the most charming person she had met in a long time. "You're impossible! What *are* you doing here?"

"I came to see you, what else?" He smiled.

"I must admit, this is a lovely surprise. But how is it that you always know exactly where I am and exactly what I'm doing?"

"Just think of me as your guardian angel, sent to protect you and keep you out of harm's way." Biff's grin was infectious.

"What a comforting thought." She paused. "But how do you know I won't become a terrible burden to you?"

"I can't think of any 'burden' I'd rather have." Biff looked straight into her eyes.

"Very well. I shall put myself entirely in your hands, but I warn you—you might find me quite a handful."

"I suspect I already know that. If you get too much for me, I'll just scream," he said with a big sigh, eyes twinkling. "Now come with me. We have things to do."

Biff took her by the arm and ushered her out of the building, waving to Cordelia on the way. He kept a firm but gentle grip on Abby's arm as they started walking to the parking lot.

"Do you mind telling me where we're going?" Abby said. "I feel like I've just been caught in a whirlwind."

"Now, little one, don't fret, enjoy it. Everything's under control. First we have a journey to make, and then there are some things I need to discuss with you. However, perhaps that can wait until tomorrow." Suddenly he stopped. "This is my car." He opened the passenger door for her.

"Yes, your majesty. Your wish is my command." Abby stepped into the black Lincoln town car obediently, as Biff continued onto the driver's side and settled himself in the seat.

"Where is it we're going?" she asked.

"We're going to Area F, the Congressional Country Club. It's being used at present for part of our training program. But this evening, a social is being given for some of our newcomers."

"And that includes me, I suppose. But it couldn't possibly include you, now could it? You are hardly in that category."

"Oh but it does. I'm part of the staff and from time to time I have certain duties there. There will be other staff members there. A bus is taking some of the new people over, but I thought perhaps you'd rather drive with me. Was I mistaken?"

"Oh no, kind sir. I shall consider it a privilege."

"I'm happy to hear that." He grinned, infectiously. "Let's enjoy this evening before we get down to more serious things." Biff's tone was slightly different.

"And what might those serious things be? I've already discovered that you *can* be serious." Abby had noticed the change in his voice.

Biff chuckled. "You don't miss much do you, Miss Abby? That's one of your most fascinating qualities. Your manner is so genteel and soft, one might be fooled into thinking that behind it is a helpless dependency, rather than a clever mind."

Abby looked at him with surprise. "That sounds rather ominous, as though I'm sneaky and devious. Is *that* what you think?"

Biff stole a glance at her. "No, no, on the contrary. That isn't what I meant. Let me explain." He smiled. "My dear Abby, your looks are so striking and your manner is so ladylike that, in the beginning at least, one might underestimate how acutely observant and intelligent you really are."

"Really?" She was beginning to understand.

"You must realize that in intelligence work those traits are invaluable assets. Even *more* so if the other one doesn't recognize them."

"I suppose that's actually quite a compliment. I'm sorry I misunderstood you." Abby looked over at Biff's strong and handsome face. He was smiling that concerned but playful smile which so characterized him. "So that's what you really think of me?"

"That and a great deal more. You're really quite a remarkable girl."

"A rare species?"

"The only one in captivity!" Biff glanced over at Abby. They both laughed.

"On the contrary," Abby said. "I'm convinced that it is *you* who is the only one in captivity."

Abby settled down in her seat. She felt comfortable now, protected, appreciated, even admired. She was glad to be there with Biff. He was becoming more and more important to her, although she hadn't yet quite thought of it that way.

They drove through the countryside to their destination. It was a beautiful late autumn afternoon. The shadows were beginning to fall between the rays of sunlight that filtered through the leaves on the tall, tall trees. Both of them remained pensive as the moments passed. But it was a moment that both would remember in the days to come. Those peaceful, exciting, delightful days of their first few encounters.

Finally, they arrived at the Congressional Country Club. They drove up the long driveway toward the impressive entrance of a towering building with a marble facade and enormous marble columns. Biff drove up to the steps and stopped.

"I'll let you out here, Abby. Just go straight up the steps into the lobby and you'll immediately see where the gathering is, off to your right."

"You're not coming with me?" she asked.

"Not at the moment. I have business upstairs, so I'll leave you on your own for a while. By the time for you to leave, I'll come down and take you home. Besides you're here to mingle with the other people. I can't completely monopolize your time, no matter how I might like to."

"Oh all right. If you're going to abandon me to a group of complete strangers! I suppose I will simply have to fend for myself."

Biff grinned his usual. "I have every confidence that you will *fend* very competently." Biff leaned over and opened the door for her.

"Very well! If this is the way it's going to be. I'll see you later." Abby got out of the car and walked up the gentle steps to the main entrance. She was met at the door by a cordial gentleman who directed her to the large room on her right.

There were quite a large number of people gathered there. Among them were officers, enlisted and civilian personnel. She supposed they had some official connection with OSS. Many of the service people were in uniform, including a few young women. By far the majority were men, some younger, some older. Some in uniform, some in civilian clothes.

Abby wondered if she would ever really know any of these people, much less what their assignments might be. She had never been comfortable around complete strangers, but she had been taught to be cordial and to make an effort to get to know a few at the time when she was faced with such a dilemma.

Almost immediately she was approached by three young men, who began a conversation amongst the four of them. The banter was lighthearted and non-controversial, and she found herself joining in with very little effort. From time to time, the little group would shift, one would drop out and another join in. By the end of an hour Abby felt she could identify a few of those whom she had met at least on a superficial level.

But there was a moment at the very beginning of the conversation when she spied four naval officers running down the steps from the second floor. The steps were quite far from where she was standing, but she felt a strange inkling of recognition. Something in her memory, something intangible, something she couldn't get her mind around. What was it? What were her senses trying to tell her?

By the time she had come back to the present the four officers had disappeared out the front door. Abby looked through one of the large Palladian windows that gave a view of the parking area, but all she could see was a large Lincoln town car speeding away.

Biff left the car in the parking area, and walked over to the entrance of the Congressional. As he entered he almost bumped into an old classmate, Captain Jordan Jenkins, who was on his way out.

"Well, now. If it isn't good ole Biff!" He slapped him gently on the shoulder. "They're waiting for your upstairs. What took you so long?"

"Hi, Jinx. I had another assignment that took longer than I thought."

"Well, better get up there. You know how the Old Man is. See you later."

Biff hurried toward the steps, taking two at a time. Midway up the inner steps, four naval officers passed him, swiftly scurrying down to the main entrance. Biff moved aside to let them pass and then continued until he reached the top. He walked down the hall and entered a large conference room.

"Ah. Here he is. Now we can discuss that other matter." The Old Man turned an affectionate gaze toward Biff. Though he was usually fairly rigid about punctuality, Biff was one of the few he was more lenient toward. But it was mainly because he knew that if there was a slight delay in Biff's response, he usually had a very good reason for it.

Biff stood removing his overcoat. "What was that all that about? Those naval officers looked like they were in a big hurry—almost knocked me down flying down the steps."

"Well they *were* in a hurry. Two of them are ready for transport and we had just gotten word that we could get a hitch out from Stuart, our upper New York base. One of our WASPs is ferrying an aircraft over in about four hours. There just happens to be a place for two more. We're in luck!" The Old Man sounded pleased.

"Who are they?" Biff asked.

"One is a guy named Brett Whitney. He was intelligence officer on the *Arizona*. Got badly wounded trying to save some of his shipmates, but now he's fully recovered. So we were lucky enough to nab him before the Navy reassigned him again. We've had him in training for five months. Yale man—at least that's where he was in graduate school. Before that—Annapolis."

"I say! The *Arizona*!" Biff shook his head. "He's really been through it. I can't believe the Navy would let us have an Annapolis man without a fight."

"Well, it came near to that but we have our persuasive techniques, you know." The Old Man leveled his twinkling blue eyes directly on Biff.

"You mean blackmail." Biff gave his superior a sly wink.

Everyone laughed. The Old Man's ability to beg, borrow, and steal the cream of the most desirable personnel was notorious.

"And the other?" Biff pulled up a chair and sat down.

"Oddly enough, a classmate of his, Andrew Worth, also Annapolis. Both assigned to the *Arizona* when it was hit. His injuries were a bit worse than they had thought but he seems to be in pretty good shape now.... Communications officer."

Biff bent over with laughter. "Oddly enough, all right! Highway robbery! We'd better stay away from the Navy brass for a while. I'm sure we're persona non grata!"

"I'm not so sure about that. As I said, we have our ways." The Old Man leaned back in his chair with that playful look he often had when he played his guessing games.

"Oh, yes, we know. What did you promise them? A sortie in Tokyo?"

"Something like that."

"Well, I wouldn't doubt it, knowing you. In a matter of months you've already got us operating all around the globe. It's a real miracle." Biff looked at him with genuine admiration.

"Had a little help from my friends," he said. Everyone laughed.

"Even some of your enemies," Biff said, remembering a few of the battles with Washington insiders.

"Oh, indeed. Well gentlemen, enough of this. Better get back to work. You have your instructions. Good luck, we'll be in touch. Biff, I need to see you about that little matter at hand."

The others saluted and said their goodbyes and began to leave the room. When the last man was out Biff closed the door.

The Old Man got right to the point. "You know about the latest reports on Suzanne Davenport?"

"I understand she's AWOL, but for some strange reason it's not official yet. Some kind of mysterious disappearance." Biff actually knew more but he wanted to hear it from the Old Man.

"Right. Well, we have her body down in the morgue. It just arrived. Some fisherman found it washed up on the bank of Lake Erie. Raped, beaten, and mutilated beyond recognition."

"My God. How ghastly." Biff thought a moment. "But if you can't identify her, how do you know who it is?"

"She was found a few feet from a bundle containing her dog tags and the top of her uniform." The Old Man settled his full gaze on Biff.

"Horrible!" Biff grimaced. "Sounds like—"

"Yes, doesn't it? This is the second girl connected in some way to our government information sources. There are several in Europe too." The Old Man sighed.

"But it doesn't seem to be quite the same M.O. The others weren't mutilated. Weren't there clear identification marks on the other bodies?" Biff asked.

"Yes, but there are other similarities. She had no family, and apparently very few friends. Not too many people seemed to be in contact with her." He looked at Biff with deep concern. "You may not realize it, but the last person she was known to be at all close to is our newcomer, Abby St. Giles. They worked together at Navy Personnel."

A cold wind seemed to hit Biff in the face. "Oh, no. Do you think Abby's in danger? We need to know. And how involved in this investigation does Abby need to be?"

"As far as we know, she's the only one of *us* 'under cover' who can positively identify her." He leaned back in his chair. "It's your case now, Biff. Up to you. Track it down, use your own judgment, then report to me. I knew you'd want to be involved." The Old Man gave Biff a keen piercing look, as though he could read his mind.

Was there nothing that escaped this man? Somehow he knew of the unspoken bond he already had with Abby. He had assigned him to her in the beginning. If he were matchmaking, he'd done a superb job of it. But Biff knew better. The Old Man knew how to put teams together. People who grew into a bond where they were one for all and all for one. And he had put him and Abby together, as though some mysterious hand had guided him.

"Roger, I'm on. Fill me in on any connections and leads and I'll go from there."

Biff spent the next thirty minutes being briefed on the known data. He learned that Commander Logan and Robert St. Giles were also knowledgeable. He would interview them the next day, go down to the morgue and view the body, consult with the coroner, and then talk to Abby. He had no alternative. She was much more involved than he had known.

"What kind of son of a bitch would do such a monstrous thing?" Biff said.

"I'd say a son of a bitch with a monstrous motive. We'd better catch him soon, before he has a chance to do more damage not only to these young women but to our country."

Biff knew in his gut this guy was an operative. Was he also a double agent? No one could identify him. He was slick. A chameleon. No one knew what he looked like or whether he operated alone. The more Biff thought about it, the more determined he became.

He was going to get this guy, if it was the last thing he ever did.

Chapter 16

The next morning Abby and Miranda grabbed doughnuts and coffee at the corner cafe. Miranda had decided to be her usual charming self this morning. "How was the party last night? The Congressional Club hosts some very fine affairs, usually extremely well done."

"This was just an informal get together for the new and old staff. Sort of a getting to know you affair."

"Oh, I didn't realize it was a staff party. Did you meet anyone interesting?"

"A few attractive young men. I came away with several invitations: one for the horse races, two for dinner, and one for the theater. I really can't remember any others."

"And who might these young lotharios be? Do any of them have names?"

"At the moment I can only remember a Buck, a Winston, and—an Averil. At least, I think those were their names. Don't ask me to come up with their surnames. You know I never catch them on the first go around."

"Yes, I know. Well, we'll see what develops. It's always exciting to meet new people." Miranda looked at her watch. "It's getting late, we'd better run." She grabbed her things and started

Company of Spies

out the door. "Are you coming? Maybe we can grab a cab and you can let me off."

Abby dropped her mother at a favorite spot for employees carpooling others to the Pentagon, and traveled on to the office. She was scheduled this morning for her physical and to begin her inoculations. But first she needed to report.

She had agreed to meet Biff for lunch. He seemed anxious to discuss something with her, but the night before he wouldn't tell her what it was. Probably something concerning work, she suspected. At any rate she would soon find out.

As the cab dodged in and out of traffic, she thought about him. He was so much fun to be with, and so handsome. She was becoming more and more attached to him. But she couldn't really tell whether he was interested in her as a person or as an assignment. He was always so proper. He had never really stepped out of line like some of the other young men she had dated. But she knew he liked her. She wondered if something would really ever come of their relationship. And if it did what would be her response.

The cab pulled in front of the warehouse door. As she entered, she wondered, *could there be any more peculiar place or more peculiar circumstances in which to work?*

Abby waved her badge at Cordelia, and headed upstairs to her new office and the next two hours of instruction in Morse code, cryptography, deciphering and writing in code.

Cordelia had said the best time to go for her physical was right before lunch. "Somewhere around 11 or 11: 30." It didn't take Abby long, once she reached her destination, to realize why Cordelia had suggested that particular time.

Once there, she entered a very large room. Along the side of the room at one end were several long tables, behind which, seven or eight men sat wearing long white coats, with stethoscopes hanging around their necks. Abby assumed that these were doctors. Several nurses in uniform scurried about assisting the doctors and engaged in various other duties. They were at the moment, each examining several young men in various states of undress. There was a short line behind each one.

Suddenly she was struck by a number of large posters placed high on the walls, some almost reaching the ceiling. One in particular stood out more than the others. It was a picture of a voluptuous and beautiful French girl wearing a beret, a short tight fitting, revealing dress and long well shaped legs. She stood in a provocative position. The caption said "Beware of V. D."

The other posters had something of the same meaning and theme. Abby was somewhat taken aback. She was beginning to realize where she was. This was an induction center where young men and a few women were physically screened to join the armed services. She noticed a large number of young men donning their clothes and their gear and making preparations to leave. The place was obviously beginning to empty out for lunch. She knew now why Cordelia had said to go now. At least she would have more privacy with fewer people around. But there were still a number of young men being examined. Abby averted her eyes to avoid their degrees of nakedness.

"Can I help you, miss?" a burly, crisp, all business Army nurse addressed her.

"Yes, thank you. I'm here for a physical and there was something about some inoculations. I'm here from OSS. Here is my checklist." She gave it to the nurse. "Apparently, everything that's required is on that list, including the list of inoculations."

Abby had been handed the list right before she left the office, but she hadn't really had time to look at it.

"O. K.," she said, glancing at it, I'll get you started. Let's see—I think Dr. Hancock is free at the moment. Come with me."

Abby followed her to a chair across from a young man whom she assumed was Dr. Hancock. The nurse handed him the checklist. He took it without looking up.

"This one is from OSS," she said. She gave Dr. Hancock a look that said *can you believe this?*

"We don't get many of those." He looked up briefly and then did a double take. The expression on his face registered surprise, as though he were saying, Young lady, what in the world are you doing here? This is no place for *you.* But his reaction was momentary and he quickly recovered. "Yes. Well now, let's get down to business. Let's see, this is your checklist. A number of things we have to do here. First, let's get a urine sample and we'll go from there." Dr. Hancock handed her a small glass urinal.

"A urine sample?" Abby looked around. On the opposite wall she saw a number of booths. Though they were separated from one another by partitions, there were no curtains or any kind of door to provide privacy. The participant inside would be in plain view. She was horrified.

Abby looked somewhat helplessly at Dr. Hancock and then at the booths along the side of the wall.

Dr. Hancock began to chuckle. "I see. Modesty is a great virtue but it doesn't work very well in this setting. Well, we didn't promise you a rose garden but I'll see what we can do." He turned and addressed the nurse. She too was trying to restrain a large grin from bursting into outright laughter.

"Lieutenant Lamar, see what you can do for this young lady."

Nurse Lamar took charge immediately. "Come with me." Raising her voice with all the authority of a boot sergeant, Lamar addressed the young men on the floor. "And the rest of you dog-tags, keep your eyes to yourselves." A titter of laughter surfaced around the room.

"And none of that, either!" Lieut. Lamar knew how to bark.

Abby was mortified. *I have never been so embarrassed in all my life*, she thought. *I hope I never see a single one of these people again as long as I live. I would never be able to face them.* Sheepishly she followed Nurse Lamar to one of the booths.

"I'll just stand in front of you. I'm so big they'll never see anything but me."

Abby realized that Nurse Lamar, despite her tough exterior, was actually empathetic with her. As an Army nurse she would obviously have been put in many similar situations. Abby was beginning to wake up to the reality of what she was getting into. She could see the humor and stupidity in the situation. Here were these young men preparing to go to war, and she was worrying about her privacy.

Handing over the sample, she turned to Lieutenant Lamar. "I can't thank you enough. I know I must seem like a blithering idiot but this is all very upsetting to me."

"I understand. I was once in your place, myself. But I can assure you, you'll get over it. When you come face-to-face with life and death situations, particularly on the battlefield, things like this seem like trivia." Lamar smiled tenderly. "You simply haven't experienced that kind of thing yet. I hope, for your sake, you never will. But if you do, I can tell about you, you'll be fine, believe me."

Abby suddenly felt exonerated. There were people who really did understand. If this was the worst thing she ever had to face, she would be more than grateful.

She went back to the table in front of Dr. Hancock. He looked at the checklist. "Well let's see now, I'll do a preliminary examination and then we'll get you to X-ray. After that for your blood tests and inoculations. How does that sound?" Dr. Hancock smiled somewhat gently at Abby. She returned his smile but said nothing.

"O. K. then. Just remove your jacket. You can leave your blouse on." Dr. Hancock went through a few simple steps. He listened to her heart, checked her eyes, nose, throat, ears, chest, and asked her the usual questions about operations, serious illnesses, and so forth. She was given a family history to fill out but was told that she could return it the next day.

Lieutenant Lamar took her height, weight and ushered her down to an adjacent room. "O.K., here we are." She handed a copy of the checklist to the technician.

"Travis, we've checked off everything we're responsible for, so now she needs a chest X-ray, a blood test, and her inoculations. They're all on the list here. When you guys finish with her, send her back to me." She gave him a rather stern, almost warning look.

The technician motioned to Abby to sit down and place her left arm, palm up on the table. He then placed a tourniquet on the top of her arm and twisted it until Abby flinched.

"Sorry 'bout that!" Travis let out a weird squeal. "Guess I'm not use to gorgeous young gals. I keep forgettin' how tender y'all are." He looked at Abby with a malevolent gleam. "What's a beautiful gal like you doin' in a place like this?"

Abby felt shivers going down her spine, but she tried to pass it off. "Looks like I'm doing what everybody else is. Getting ready for the big one."

"Oh, that's right, y'all with OSS, ain't you? They must be *crazy* to send a gal like you overseas. Them hungry soldiers over there will eee*eat* you alive, at least they'll want to." He let out a terrifying cackle.

Abby's stomach knotted. What was this sick feeling she was getting?

"Well, I may not be going overseas at all, and I'm sure those soldiers over there have better things to think of than eating young girls." Abby tried to keep her voice light.

"Really? Now, I don' know 'bout that. Some of those guys is vampires like me." Travis began an eerie laugh. "Ready for the Vampire Man?" With that, Travis took out a long needle and shoved it into the vein puffed up on her left arm.

"Whoa, that hurts!" She flinched and drew back. "I see what you mean about the Vampire Man."

"Oh, sorry 'bout that," he said. "Missed it. Got ta do it agin."

Travis was obviously anything but sorry. His "miss" was deliberate. In fact he managed to miss twice more.

"Do you think I might get out of here *alive*?" Abby said.

"Most people do…. But then you might not." Travis began to cackle again. He looked at her with an wicked grin.

On the next "try" the needle went in. It seemed to Abby that Travis drew out enough blood to sink a battleship.

"Thank heavens that's over. I hope you left a little." Abby was furious, but she smiled her best ingratiating smile. "Where are you from, Travis? Somewhere around Louisiana?"

"Well, I declare, Cher. You done hit me right on de nail. Yes, ma'am, Cajun country. That's me. Now how'd ya know dat?"

"It's your accent. I thought I detected the flavor of New Orleans. I love the food there, the French really know how to cook. I have truly never had better cuisine."

"Yes ma'am, that's because there they… cook little girls." Travis let out a diabolical shriek that sent more shivers down Abby's spine. She realized she'd opened the door for that one.

But she was determined not to allow him to get the upper hand. Abby forced a smile.

"Travis, you are *impossible*! Are we through here?"

"Yes ma'am, unless you—" Travis stopped in his tracks. Dr. Hancock had suddenly appeared in the doorway.

"Travis, what are you doing? I think you'd better come with me."

Travis immediately stood at attention when he saw Dr. Hancock. The sheepish but defiant look on his face revealed that he knew he was already in deep trouble.

"Miss, you're through here. Just go two doors down the hall for X-ray." Dr, Hancock smiled at Abby and turned with a glower at Travis. Dr. Hancock left the room with Travis silently following, his insolence written clearly on his face. He was obviously plotting his next move.

Abby followed directions down to X-ray. The X-ray technician was a small no-nonsense woman who obviously ran a strict assembly line, taking only a few minutes to achieve her results. The last patient was leaving just as Abby arrived. She was grateful that the technician was a woman, since she had to remove her upper garments and don a gown. But no one else was around. It was over in a few minutes. The technician gave her instructions to go down the hall for inoculations.

There were three technicians and three nurses administering shots. Each pair had a different delivery station. Two of the pairs were leaving for lunch. By now, only one young soldier was ahead of Abby and he was rolling down his sleeves preparing to leave. She handed her checklist to the remaining technician. He took a quick look.

"Good grief! Where are they sending you? This should take you around the world." He handed the checklist to the attending

Dr. Margaret S. Emanuelson

nurse. She glanced at the paper, shook her head in disbelief, and began to prepare the first hypodermic.

"Can you roll up your sleeve, please."

Abby obediently rolled up her left sleeve. The technician looked at her arm. It was bleeding and turning black and blue.

"Wow! I'll bet Travis did this—that sadist."

"Yes, you mean the Vampire Man."

"That's a good name for him. He deliberately picks on some people. It's his way of throwing his weight around. Those Cajuns have strange ways, they don't think like we do." He pulled on a new pair of protective gloves. "He's already in some kind of big trouble—I know he's been under investigation. I'll be glad when he's gone from here. He gives me the creeps."

Abby silently agreed. Travis gave her the shivers too.

The nurse handed the technician a hypodermic.

"O. K., miss, this is a tetanus shot and it's going to sting." He popped her with the needle before she could respond.

"Massage it, that will help. Now let's do the smallpox, and then the typhoid. After that I'll switch arms. This poor thing can't take much more." The technician administered two more shots.

"How much more? Surely this can't go on forever," Abby said.

"Let's see, we've done three, we have only six more to go," the nurse said, searching for the right vial for the next shot.

"*Six more?*" Abby threw up her hands.

"We've already done your tetanus, typhoid fever, and smallpox. That leaves…. malaria, cholera, yellow fever, dengue fever, typhus, and a couple of other things."

"Oh, please! That's too much. Is there any way I can do the rest tomorrow? I have a luncheon date and I'm sure I'm already late."

"I suppose so. Looks like you've done everything else on your checklist. Why don't you come in around 11: 30 tomorrow and we'll finish up. I'm sure we'd all like to leave for lunch."

"Great! Maybe I can do you a favor some time." Abby rolled down her sleeve, picked up her things, and made a quick departure. "See you tomorrow."

What an experience. All she wanted to do was get someplace to freshen up, brush her hair, and go to meet Biff. This had been one unbelievable morning.

Abby left the building just in time to see Biff driving up in front. Immediately, her spirits lifted.

"I've never been so glad to see anyone in all my life," Abby said as she slid into the passenger seat. "Forgive me if I'm still flustered. I'll pull myself back together in a moment or two."

"Good grief! What did those big bad people do you in there?" Biff gave her look of concern spiced with humor.

"Don't laugh! It isn't funny." She was in no mood to be patronized.

"I just ran into the most diabolical sadist I've ever met. He gave me the absolute creeps. You should see what he did to my arm."

"That's a shame. But you know, Abby, these Army medics are not all that well trained. Plus the fact that they're used to dealing with male troops in an assembly line fashion. Some of them are pretty brutal when it comes to needles. They made hash out of my arm too."

"But, Biff, you don't understand. If that were all there was to it I wouldn't complain. But this—idiot—was not one of your regular clumsy Army medics. He not only knew what he was doing, but he was so offensive that finally one of the doctors ordered him out. I can only guess that he was already in deep trouble before he was overheard with me."

"What in the world did he do?"

Abby related the incident and the conversation between her and Travis in detail.

"That's appalling! But I'm sure you handled it very well," Biff said. "You have a way of always rising to the occasion."

"Well, that is one occasion to which I hope I never have to rise again. I don't think that I can remember ever having had such a hideous feeling before. I am certainly glad it's over!"

She didn't mention the urine sample. That was too embarrassing. Abby heaved a deep sigh, feeling thankful relief. "Now, let's go. I'm dying for one of those wonderful popovers."

"Absolutely! Let's wipe the slate clean for a few minutes and enjoy our lunch. We can worry about the Travises of this world later."

Biff was thoughtful as he wove through the mid-day traffic. He wondered if this man might decide to harm Abby in some way, since she may have been one of the reasons for a reprimand. He would check him out.

He was well aware that he was in serious danger of becoming overprotective. After all, Abby was now officially a member of OSS. What her future assignments might be there was no way to know at present. He realized he would have to be more objective. He was stuck between his fears for Abby and his concern for carrying out his own assignments effectively.

The Watergate Inn was a popular lunch place in Washington. It drew people from all the surrounding areas. It was a cheerful,

exciting place, where many intrigues had been either perpetrated or plotted. If only one could listen to its walls tell their secrets, but like the Sphinx, they remained silent, revealing nothing.

It was a fine early November afternoon. They arrived a little before two o'clock and were seated at an isolated table that overlooked the river. Their order arrived quickly since it was near closing time for lunch.

Abby arranged her coat on the back of the chair and sipped her coffee, but she was deep in thought. She began to replay the incidents of the night before.

"Before I forget it," she said, "while we were at the Congressional Club last night, I thought I saw four naval officers running down the steps to the front door. They seemed to be in a very big hurry. I thought—I could almost have sworn—that I recognized one of them, but they were far away and it was just an impression. Do you think that's possible?"

"I seriously doubt it. Two of the guys came to us from P. T. O. They've been in training here and were on their way for transport overseas, and they were in a big hurry. We had just been informed that transport was available and they had very little time to reach their target

"I see. Even so, I had the strangest feeling."

Could it have been Brett? Probably not. Still...Why was she still wondering about him six months after their chance meeting? There must be a reason. But why dwell on it? She was here with Biff. Handsome, fascinating Biff. Who could ask for anything more?

Abby glanced through the window at the river. The sun played games with the ripples on the water, reflecting little diamonds of lights sparkling on the surface.

Finally, Abby turned and addressed him directly. "I'm so glad we decided to come here. Not only is the food delightful, but there's something about the ambiance that's really quite charming."

"But you come here frequently for lunch, don't you?" He watched the sun playing tricks on her long dark hair. *How beautiful she is,* he thought. *Beautiful and unassuming.*

Abby began to laugh. "You should know. You always seem to know my itinerary. One would think you're a detective on my trail."

"Aha! You've found me out. Now I can no longer remain incognito. I might as well confess." Biff grinned at Abby in his playful way. "Truth is, we're a pretty close knit group around here, and we keep a close eye on one another. If one of us is in trouble, the others will rush to the rescue."

"An admirable philosophy. One for all and all for one. But sometimes with you, I have the feeling it's more than that." Abby looked directly into his eyes.

Biff knew instantly that his answer to that remark would make the difference between keeping their relationship impersonal or revealing his real feelings for her. He had to restrain himself. The situation was too tenuous at present, it could become too precarious to risk it now.

"You're right. When someone first joins the unit, he or she is assigned a sort of mentor. Someone to help with orientation and making the other feel comfortable with policies and practices." Biff sipped his coffee. "But later on, one is often assigned a teammate, sometimes more than one. That's an even closer relationship. And that puts more responsibility on each one to look out for the other."

"So we've now been assigned to work together? When was someone going to tell me?" Abby said.

"I just did. How do you feel about it?"

"A little confused, but I can't think of anyone with whom I would rather team up. Why didn't you tell me before?"

"You're just full of questions aren't you?" Biff laughed. "It's because I didn't know for sure until yesterday if that was what the top brass wanted. We have to have approval for some of these things, you know."

"And you got that yesterday?"

"A great many things happened yesterday and that was just one of them."

"I knew something was up, Felt it in my bones."

"Well now, Miss Abby, finish your lunch. After the harrowing morning you've had we must see that your bones are strong and ready to tackle our next assignment."

"Oh, Biff. You're always keeping me in suspense." Abby took a big bite of her enormous popover, and finished her shrimp salad. "There now, all through."

"Good girl. Feel better?"

"Unbelievably better! I was beginning to think the Vampire Man had drained me completely. Amazing what a great salad will do." Abby sipped her coffee. "Where do we go from here?"

"Let's go to my office where we can be secure. Something has come up that I need to talk to you about." Biff rose, and helped her with her chair.

"Our first assignment together. Sounds pretty serious."

"Come. We'll discuss it when we get there."

They headed out into the cold crisp air. Biff opened the car door for her and got in his side. He started the motor and turned on the heat. "It's getting chilly, but it's only a short distance to headquarters, it'll be warm there."

"Good. I hate cold weather. I can remember a few terrible ice storms in Atlanta when I was a child. The entire city was paralyzed."

"Most people think of Atlanta as the deep south, all sunny and warm," Biff said.

"I know. What they don't know is that Atlanta is 1000 feet above sea level, in the foothills of the Smokey Mountains."

"That high? It's deceiving." He stole a glance at her.

"The weather can be brutal in the winter and as hot as Hades in the summer. The main problem with snow and ice is that we're not prepared for it with the proper equipment like the North is. Luckily it doesn't happen that frequently."

Abby tried to limit her talk to chitchat. She knew Biff would tell her what was up in his own time. Finally, they arrived at Headquarters. Biff ushered her upstairs to an office on the second floor.

"Here we are," he said. "Make yourself comfortable."

Abby took off her coat and placed it on a chair. Her arm was beginning to throb, and she felt a little shaky but she said nothing.

She looked around the room for some sort of personal artifacts, but there was nothing to suggest that this office belonged to Biff or anyone else. "Is this your office?"

"I use it. At least for the time being. Only some of us have permanent offices. The rest of us never know when we'll be required somewhere else." He pulled up a chair for her.

"And apparently that's so for you? Doesn't the ambiguity of not knowing bother you?"

"If this were peace time it probably would." Biff spoke thoughtfully. "Before the war, I thought my future was pretty well set. But now there are millions of people whose future plans have been ruined forever. Not only their plans but their very lives have been lost or are at stake. At least, if I survive, I have something to come back to—not so with most of them."

Abby looked intently at Biff for a few moments. "I've just realized, I know absolutely nothing about you. Where you live, where you went to school, what you do in civilian life—who you really are."

"Does that bother you?" Biff looked at her intently.

"It hasn't till now, but suddenly I want to know everything about you."

"So, not knowing, you trusted me anyway?"

"Yes. That's strange, isn't it? Not at all typical of me."

"Abby, the fact that you trusted me without knowing is probably the greatest compliment you could pay another human being." He leaned toward her. "I pledge to you, I will never betray that trust. And I can assure you—it's mutual." He never took his eyes from hers. "If you really want to know more about me, I promise to tell you everything you ask very soon. But right now we need to work on this matter. At this point it's somewhat urgent."

"All right, if you say so. I'm listening." Abby settled down.

"You remember Suzanne Davenport? I believe you worked with her at Naval Personnel."

Abby leaned forward in her chair, fully alert. "You've heard from *Suzanne*? Tell me. All of us have been worried to death about her."

"Our efforts to trace her activities after she left were fruitless at first. The speculation was that she left with a young man. And that she had become quite involved with him."

"That's what I believe happened. She was obviously smitten with this man. But I never trusted him or what he had told her." She shook her head. "Even so, I can't believe that Suzanne would deliberately go AWOL. She was always so patriotic, so dependable."

"How much did she tell you about her relationship with this man? Did she tell you who he was, or what he did?"

"She said his name was Jacques D'Arcy. He told her he was with the French Embassy, that she had met him there. She said his work was very confidential and that she really couldn't tell anyone about him. At one point, she told me that they had 'future plans' and asked me to keep it confidential."

Abby took a long pause as she remembered the details. "I felt guilty about breaking her confidence when this first came up, but then I realized something was very wrong and she might be in danger."

"Yes, of course you would feel that way." His voice was gentle. "No one wants to think he's betrayed a friend."

"I always had a bad feeling about him. Obviously, Suzanne knew very little about him. I tried to warn her, but she seemed to be completely under his power. She trusted him implicitly."

"Did you ever see him?" Biff said.

"Not really. But there *was* one night we attended a party at Senator Downs' office. I was annoyed with her for leaving me there while she went off with him. When she came back I got a glimpse of him through the outer door, but it was dark and far away. I didn't really see him. It was only an impression. I doubt I could actually identify him."

She sighed. "Biff, tell me where is this leading? How much do you know about this situation? And why has this become so important now?"

Biff began almost reluctantly. "There have been some recent developments that are going to require our expertise. We believe that this man is a foreign agent."

"Oh, my God! How dreadful!" Abby sat back in shock. "And you know this is the man?"

"We're reasonably sure. We know that he has been operating between Europe and this country since the 1930s. He uses devious means to achieve his goals. As one of them, he selects young women in government or other positions who are knowledgeable about troop movements, weaponry, military intelligence and any other information which can help the enemy. Apparently he is very attractive to women. He courts them, probably offers marriage, all the time gleaning whatever information he can from them." He paused. "And then sooner or later he abandons them."

"Oh how horrible. Poor Suzanne! And you think this is the man she's involved with?"

"That's what we think. His M.O. seems to be very similar to what the investigations in Europe and here have yielded."

"But the young women he abandoned, obviously they can identify him. So you must have a description and obviously some details of what happened while he was with them. And you still have no leads?"

"No. No one has any idea of what this man looks like. All we know is that he's gathering information and using it in an extremely destructive way to either abort or destroy our military efforts." Biff paused, clearly reluctant to continue. "Unfortunately, the young women he's consorted with have either disappeared or …have been murdered."

"Oh, my word! That's why you have no leads. And you think this may have happened to Suzanne." Abby frowned, deep in thought. The pictures running through her mind were hideous. But there was something here that didn't add up.

"I can't believe that," she said. "She may have disappeared, but somehow I think I would know if she were dead."

"Brace yourself, Abby. There's something else I have to tell you. After Suzanne went AWOL, about three weeks passed with no word at all. Then the dead body of a young woman was reported found on the shore of Lake Erie. The body was naked and unrecognizable, but the top of Suzanne's uniform and her dog tags were found in a bundle very close to the body."

Biff reached out and took Abby's hand. She sat silently for a few moments, trying to sort out and analyze the information at hand. Very quietly she began to speak.

"Nothing will convince me Suzanne is dead unless I see her body. We were close friends. I would know if she were dead. No, I will never believe it unless I see her body—" She shook her head. "But then I know that's impossible."

Biff looked intently at Abby. "No, not impossible. The body of the young woman is in the morgue at Walter Reed Hospital. We have been able to keep all of the information regarding Suzanne top-secret. No one knows but us whose body it is."

Abby did not hesitate. "Take me there. I want to see her. I will *never* believe that it's Suzanne unless I know." She squared her shoulders.

"Abby, you have no idea what you're asking. This monster mutilated this young woman. I can tell you, the body is unrecognizable. We have only the circumstantial evidence that it *is* Suzanne."

"All the more reason for me to see her. I have to be absolutely sure in my own mind."

"All right. I've already been there and talked to the coroner. He and the investigators have almost completed their forensics and they've cleaned her up. I hate to subject you to this, but if you insist I'll take you there. Are you sure you're up to it? It's not a pretty sight."

"Absolutely! Suzanne is my friend. It's the least I can do for her."

Biff smiled at her with frank admiration. She had not even flinched at the prospect of viewing the body.

"You're quite a girl, Abby. Quite a girl!"

In a way this had been a test. For all her youth, beauty, and obvious intelligence she had the moral toughness and persistence that it took to be a good operative. There could be no question about it now.

"Very well, if we leave now we can get there before the coroner leaves for the day. Here, let me help you with your coat."

Abby took extra care to protect her left arm as he helped her slip into her coat. Biff stopped her.

"Wait a minute. Let me look at that arm."

Abby slipped out of her coat and silently rolled up her sleeve. Not only was her arm black and blue, but there was an open wound where the needle had torn her flesh.

"That son of a bitch!" Biff said. "He ought to be court-martialed! There is no excuse for what he's done to you. I intend to find out about him."

"I think his superiors have already dealt with him," she murmured, quietly.

"Nevertheless, I need to check him out. When we get to the hospital I'll have someone look at that arm. It could get infected. I'm so sorry, Abby. I didn't realize —" His voice betrayed his concern. "It must be pretty painful."

"Not as painful as what I'm finding out about Suzanne," she said with a sigh.

"Yes, I can well imagine. Here, I'll be careful with your coat."

Chapter 17

They arrived at the hospital just before four. "I wonder if the coroner is still here," Abby said. "I know the nurses usually change shifts at three o'clock."

"You're right. But I don't think he's on a shift schedule—anyway we'll find out. Let's stop and see about that arm first."

"No, no, the arm can wait. Let's get this other thing over with." She was beginning to feel strange, detached.

"All right, whatever you say. We're here. I'll let you out and park the car. Then we'll take care of the rest of this miserable undertaking. Are you sure you're all right?"

"Yes. I'll meet you in the lobby."

Biff joined her in the lobby, then spoke to the coroner on the phone for several minutes. Abby was out of earshot but strangely she didn't care what they were saying. She was beginning to feel very exhausted. Her shots were kicking in and she was finally reacting to the stress of the morning and the horrible news about Suzanne. She didn't feel well at all, but she squared her shoulders and took a deep breath.

"The coroner says he's ready for us. Shall we go?" Abby nodded. Biff took her by her good arm and ushered her down the hall to the elevator. He pushed the *down* button and they were on their way.

"Where are we going?" Abby realized her thoughts were becoming quite fuzzy.

"To the morgue. That's where the coroner is."

"Of course, what am I thinking? It's always in the basement." She was drifting, she knew, but it was almost over. She had to keep going.

"Here we are." Biff opened the door to the coroner's office. He made the introductions and before he could say another word, the coroner reached out and put his hand on Abby's forehead.

"Young lady, I'll wager you have a temperature of over 103. What have you been exposed to?"

Biff answered. "It must be the shots. What did you get this morning, Abby?"

"Tetanus, smallpox, and typhoid," she said.

"It's the typhoid. Not unusual, though some people *do* have a violent reaction," the coroner said. "But you need to be home in bed for a day or two. Here I'll give you some aspirin. That should bring your fever down." He handed her two aspirin and a glass of water. With that he shoved a chair under her. She gratefully plopped down on it and took the medicine.

"It's hit me all of a sudden," Abby said weakly.

"Typhoid'll do that. You must be going somewhere."

"True. I'm going to bed as soon as I can get there."

All three joined in a good laugh. Biff took note of the good humored and clever way Abby had avoided the coroner's question.

"Ready, then, when you are. Are you sure you're up to this?" The coroner stood, waiting.

"Ready or not, here I go," Abby said.

"This way." Biff took her by the arm as the coroner led them into a large room. The smell of formaldehyde was penetrating, almost suffocating. There were several tables in a row with corpses on them, most covered by sheets. Several attendants were working on the bodies.

"You're in luck. She's still on the examining table. We've just finished with her and she's all cleaned up. Now, tell me what you want to see."

Abby approached the table. The body was covered in a crisp white sheet. There was a tag on her right large toe, but she didn't ask what it said.

She suddenly caught her breath as she caught a glimpse of a few strands of pale blonde hair, protruding from under the cover. She moved closer to the table.

"Her hair. I want to see her face and her hair."

The coroner looked at her. "Miss, I won't show you her face. Take my word for it—there's nothing there you could possibly recognize. But I have a sample of her hair I can show you. He turned to a group of test tubes containing various samples from the body.

Abby scrutinized the test tube. "This could be hers, but I'm not sure. What about fingerprints?"

"They've been removed," he said gently.

Abby just shook her head. Her legs felt wobbly. Luckily Biff was still holding on to her.

"Is there anything else at all you can show me? Her arms? Her hands?"

"No, not really. I've uncovered everything I think you might identify. Her hair. You can see her legs there. Who ever did this job on her was unbelievably thorough. There's not a mark left on her."

Abby gave a deep sigh. She felt hopeless, as defeated as a whipped child. She had so wanted to find that it was not Suzanne. But what little she had to go on confirmed that it was she. Her hair was the same lovely color and texture. Her legs could be Suzanne's. Obviously her hands and arms were mutilated beyond hope or she knew he would have shown her.

Fighting back the tears, she turned to the coroner. "Thank you," she said. "I wish I could have been of more help." A big tear rolled down her cheek and splashed onto her blouse.

She turned to Biff. "Shall we go?"

"Yes, of course, let's go." Biff put a supportive arm around her and began to walk her out. He thanked the coroner on the way.

They walked out into the hall where the air was fresher and continued down the long hall. Her fever was still raging and the scene had been indeed heinous.

"Are you all right?" Biff said. "I know this has been terrible for you. I wish I could have avoided getting you involved."

"How could you have avoided it? I was already involved, only you didn't know it. Don't blame yourself. You've done what you had to do." They walked on.

"Thank God, at least we can breathe out here. That was the most suffocating place I've ever—" Abby stopped short in her tracks. Suddenly she felt her thoughts quicken. "Did he say there wasn't a mark left on her?"

"Yes, I think so."

"We have to go back—I just remembered something. Hurry!"

"Roger! About face. Here we go." Biff had to let go of her as she charged back down towards the coroner's office. He trailed after her, laughing at the sight of a renewed and purposeful Abby bursting though the doors of the morgue. The heavy doors flew open, pulling a gusty swish of air with them.

"Where's the coroner?" Abby demanded.

There were three other attendants working on different bodies. All turned and looked at Abby in complete surprise. In unison they pointed in the same direction.

The coroner was in the process, with an attendant, of preparing to remove Suzanne's body from the examining table.

"Stop!" Abby sounded like a drill sergeant in full authority. The coroner dropped the instrument he was holding and looked around. He spied Abby.

"My Lord! Amazing what two aspirin will do," he quipped.

Biff had caught up with her by now. "What a woman," he said. "I'm glad she's on my team."

Abby ignored the quips and laughter. "Sir, did I hear you say 'There is not a mark left on her'?"

"Why yes, I did."

"Then, would you accommodate me for just a moment more, please?"

"Of course."

"Good! You said that her face was unrecognizable, but what about the back of her skull?"

"That's pretty much intact."

"Wonderful! Then would you reexamine the back of her head within the hairline? There should be a small scar, covered by her hair, which might identify her."

"Sure, I'll be glad to." Abby stood toe to toe with the coroner as together they carefully examined every single inch of the back of the skull. The search continued painstakingly through the beautiful pale golden hair until there was no other place to look.

"No, you see, there's nothing there—Wait, you're right, there *is* a tiny half-inch scar on the left side. But it's very small. No wonder we missed it."

Abby sighed. "I cannot thank you enough. That answers my question."

The coroner looked at her with curiosity. "Then you can identify her?"

Biff interrupted, "We'll get back to you. Thank you so much for your help." They said their goodbyes.

Abby turned to Biff. "Shall we go?"

"Yes, of course, let's go." Biff kept a supportive arm around her and began to walk her out into the hall.

Finally they were out of earshot. "That's not Suzanne." Abby sighed deeply, in relief. "Thank God!" Suddenly she began to cry. All the stress and horror of the day had caught up with her. She looked up at Biff. "Not tears of sorrow," she sobbed, "Tears of joy."

With that, Biff took her in his arms. They stood in the hall for several minutes as Biff held her close. Her legs felt weak and wobbly. She leaned against him, held up by his arms. Biff pressed his cheek against the top of her head.

He spoke to her gently, "Let it go, Abby, you're entitled to a good cry." He began to stroke her hair. Suddenly, he put his hand on her forehead. "You're burning up! I'm taking you to emergency."

"Yes, sir," she said.

He swept her up in his arms and carried her to the elevator and down the hall to the emergency center on the ground floor.

"Got a handkerchief?" she said.

"Breast pocket."

Abby took the handkerchief out of Biff's pocket and wiped her tears.

"Blow your nose, like a good little girl."

"Yes, sir." Those fuzzy feelings were closing in. She felt like a sleepy child, totally safe and protected in his arms.

Biff backed into the door of the emergency room. He looked around. A nurse spied him and came hurriedly over to where he was standing with Abby in his arms. Biff asked for Doctor Baxter, whom he knew. The nurse went to fetch him. Luckily he was free at the moment.

"What's the matter, Biff? My! What a lovely package you've brought us. Now, tell me what we can do for her." He gave instructions to the nurse to put her on a gurney and take her in one of the examining rooms.

Biff lifted Abby onto the gurney. "For one thing she's burning up with fever. This morning she had a tetanus, smallpox, and typhoid inoculation."

"Well, it's not the tetanus, she would have had an immediate anaphylactic shock. It has to be the typhoid. It can be violent for some people."

The nurse stepped out of the examining room. "Her temperature is over a hundred and four."

"That's dangerous, we've got to get it down. Start her on an I.V., obviously she's dehydrated—and get some ice, that will help." Baxter turned to Biff. "Anything else?"

"Well, yes. This morning a maniac tore a place on her arm in the process of taking blood. He called himself the Vampire Man."

"That fool? I've run into him before. Why they don't either court-martial him or give him a Section 8, I don't know. He's caused a lot of trouble in one way or another. Anything else?"

"She's also had a terrible shock. We've just come from the morgue, where she had to identify a friend who was literally mutilated."

Company of Spies

Doctor Baxter shook his head and walked into the examining room. "Well, young lady! Looks like you've had quite a day. How are you feeling?"

"Feeling? Loverly! Out of this world!"

"It's the high temperature. We'll get your fever down and you're going to feel much better." Baxter began to give her a preliminary examination. "Heart's O.K.; pressure's up a little. Now, let me see that arm." Abby obediently stretched out her left arm for him to see.

"Damn! Looks like somebody did a hatchet job on your arm. It's black and blue all right. Now, let me see where that tear is." Baxter found the place. There was a small tear on the surface of Abby's arm, but there was a longer tear beneath and into the vein.

"All right, we'll take care of that. Then I'm going to give you some medicine to take by mouth. It will keep your arm from getting infected. It is a new sulfur medication. Be sure to use it according to directions. It's really a wonder drug. Thank God we finally have something effective to give our patients. It's been a blessing to our soldiers on the battlefield."

Abby said, "I feel like a perfect idiot. All this attention to me when I know you must have much more serious patients to look after, particularly the soldiers."

"But you're a soldier too, Miss Abby. I'm fully aware of what you people in OSS do. I know of no greater soldiers than you guys."

"I suppose I never thought of it that way," she said.

"I doubt the rest of you do either. Nevertheless, I know you risk your lives almost every day. Without Intelligence, no one could win this war. Brute force alone won't do it." Baxter finished bandaging her arm. He thought of the men and women of OSS he had seen, some now dead from torture during capture by the Nazis. Some of the things he'd seen were too monstrous to relate.

"Biff tells me you've had quite a shock today. I'm sorry about your friend. It's sad when these awful things happen. But this is an awful, bloody war." He patted her on the shoulder. "You're going to feel a lot better in a couple of days. How many more shots do you have to take?"

"Six more," Abby said.

"Six more? My word! They're getting you ready for most anything and most anywhere." Baxter took a knowing gander at Biff.

He turned back to Abby. "Don't start the other six shots until next week. You need a few days to recover. You're aware, of course, that there are varying times for the rest of the inoculation series. It's going to take you about six weeks to finish up." He gave some instructions to the nurse.

"O.K., I'm going to give you a shot now and—"

"Oh, no!" Abby grabbed her arm and recoiled at the idea.

Baxter laughed. "You won't even feel it." The nurse handed him a hypodermic. He gave it to her while he was talking.

"You should have been a nurse. You're right. I didn't feel it." She laughed. "What time is it? I have to call my mother. If I'm late—"

"Stay here a little while, at least until we get you stabilized and that fever down. Maybe you should stay here tonight."

"Oh no! I'll be fine. I'll call to say I'll be late. I can leave a message with the doorman." Abby wanted no problems with her mother. She had enough on her plate as it was.

"O.K. Your call. We get you back together then, and turn you loose." He turned to the nurse. "They're serving dinner now. Feed her—that will help." Baxter and Biff walked out of the examining room.

"Where did you find such a beautiful girl? She's a knockout! Tough day for her, but she'll be okay. I've given her a hypodermic so she should drift off for little while. Better to let her sleep a little. She'll wake up soon." He paused, in thought. "I don't blame you for being taken with her, Biff. A girl like that—"

"Is it that obvious?"

"'Fraid so, m' boy. At least to me. But then, I've known you since before our undergraduate days. Does she know?"

"No. I've tried to keep it on a business-friendship basis so far. But she knows I trust her, and that I'm very fond of her. I'm sure she feels the same way. It isn't wise to get too involved with the people with whom one works. You know that. Particularly now."

"Do I ever! I see disasters around here all the time. Hospitals are hotbeds for power struggles and strange alliances, both political and sexual. Complicates operations." Baxter shook his head. "Well, pal, glad I was on duty and here to help. I've got to run now, but I'll catch up with you later. I'll sign her out. She's free to go when she wakes up."

"Thanks, Bax, you're a good friend."

"You bet." Dr. Baxter took off down the hall.

Biff returned to the examining room where Abby was now sleeping. The nurse was just leaving. "She ate a little something. Her fever is down considerably. Here are some pills to keep it down. You can give them to her to take in the future." She handed him two prescriptions.

"Thank you," he said.

"She'll wake up in a few minutes. It was a very mild hypo. Just something to take the edge off."

"I'll sit with her till then. Thanks for your help."

"You're welcome. Lovely girl."

Biff pulled a chair up to the gurney where Abby was sleeping, and sat beside her.

He took her hand and looked long at that beautiful face he loved.

Chapter 18

Biff was in his office by 7:00 the next morning. He put a call in to the Old Man's office, and was told to come immediately. He began to relate the occurrences of the day before, in particular, the trip to the morgue.

"So, your Abby ruled out the body as being Suzanne Davenport?" The Old Man leaned toward him.

"Yes, I think that's definitely been ruled out. Suzanne was close to her. It seems they saw a good deal of each other outside the office. Abby told me that after they had been swimming one day, she noticed a dark red birthmark as Suzanne was brushing her hair dry. It was completely hidden within her thick blond hair. Seems she was very sensitive about it. She told Abby she always made sure no one ever saw it. Apparently, they had some discussion about having it removed someday… but she insisted that Abby keep it confidential, even swore her to secrecy."

"Sounds a little strange don't you think? Why should she be so sensitive, particularly if it was covered by her hair."

"It *would* seem so, wouldn't it? But Abby said that Suzanne had an almost morbid fear that others might think there was something abnormal about her. She was also afraid that if she ever had any children they would be marked. She was particularly careful not to reveal it to anyone, particularly any of the men she dated."

The Old Man sighed. "I suppose we all have our demons. So, whoever was trying to erase all identifying marks missed the boat. He didn't know about it."

"Exactly! Abby and the coroner examined the back of this poor deceased girl's head meticulously. The mark was missing. That's how she knows it's not Suzanne."

"I'd say—a real stroke of luck! So—where do you think we should go from here?" The Old Man settled his keen blue eyes on him.

Biff returned his gaze. "I think you would agree with me that this pervert has tried his best to convince us that Suzanne is dead. That can only mean, in light of what we know about her devotion to him, that either he has won her to his way of thinking or he has deceived her and convinced her to follow him to accomplish his own devious ends."

The Old Man tapped the top of his pen on the desk. "That leaves us with a promising option. The only way to go right now is to try to find Suzanne. If we can find her, then sooner or later, we shall find him."

"Indeed. Of course, there are number of other things we need to do. Our investigators will have to follow up on the murder of the dead girl. He may have used someone else to do the dirty work. Someone he knows and is connected to in some way. If we can find who she is and who killed her that gives us another major lead."

"You're right on track. I knew you would handle this well, Biff. Anything else we need to do?"

"Well I'm still thinking about that. If he has a contact at the French Embassy, we might be able to identify him. We need to follow up on that end." Biff looked off into the invisible distance.

"I suspect that he's left the country by now and taken Suzanne with him. As clever as he's been for the past several years, he would know how to disguise himself, cover his tracks, obtain false passports and so forth. I think we're going to have to set up some kind of joint task force between here and Europe."

"I agree completely." The Old Man leaned back in his chair, analyzing the situation as Biff talked.

"I think we should keep the number of people involved to an absolute minimum. This has to remain top-secret and on a 'need to know' only basis. Who knows who his collaborators in this country alone could be. It's hard to conceive that he could operate strictly alone." Biff paused, waiting.

"True. Let me review something with you again that we've known for some time. For some months, even a year or two, our European friends have been intercepting wireless messages, putting two and two together. Considering what they pertain to, and the coincidences adjacent to them, our colleagues believe that this is the same man. They are always signed by one name, 'Jana'."

"So, you also think this 'Jana' is our man?"

"Yes," the Old Man went on. "In the past few months we've been intercepting messages in this country with the same signature. So we know he's operating in America at present. We've broken his code and his messages are consistent. Of course they're then in a verbal type code. He reports sometimes as though he's a shipping magnate. For instance, 'the shipment you ordered on January 1st has been canceled. However, the shipment you ordered on January 11, has been successfully completed and is on its way.'"

"We've also recognized his pattern of sending Morse," Biff interjected.

"Yes, for some time now. Many of these dates line up with either the disappearances of some of these young women or their murders. Many of the other messages line up with obvious devastating interceptions of our military plans of troop movement and plans of attack. They are carefully worded but all seem to fit."

"Destructive little devil isn't he? Amazing to think that one operative working alone can do so much damage." Biff sighed.

"Of course, you know very well that some of *our* operatives have done worse. I'm really proud of our accomplishments so far. This war is going to be considerably shorter because of our efforts. I'm convinced of it." He smiled in satisfaction, his blue eyes sparkling.

In Biff's estimation, the Old Man could afford to be pleased. "So, where do we go from here? What do you suggest?"

"I think we should do exactly what you've outlined. If you can find Suzanne, you can find him. I told you this was your baby, Biff. Just get it done. You know what to do. And I trust you to know how to do it, you've had all the training. Just inform me of your progress."

"I appreciate your support, but there is just one other problem." A look of deep concern spread across his face. "How involved does Abby need to be?"

"You already know the answer to that. She's the only one of *us* who can positively identify Suzanne." The Old man sighed. "Of course, you know this was not our *original* plan for her, but Abby was already involved. And when we take Suzanne in custody, she will be the best one to interrogate her because she's her friend and Suzanne trusts her." He leaned forward, his voice tender, "I know you want to protect her, but I'm afraid the die is cast. You will simply have to use your own judgment." He paused, looking off into the distance for a moment. "I know that you won't allow your feelings for her to interfere with accomplishing your assignment. But you know very well that if he discovers her knowledge of Suzanne's alliance with him, she's in grave danger."

He looked at Biff in silence for a long while. "Ask her how far she's willing to go to get this guy."

"I already know the answer to that. She's a brave girl. I think she'll go to any lengths, particularly to find Suzanne."

"Then you have your answer. *Cherchez la femme.*"

Biff called Abby later that morning. She was at work in spite of her episode of the day before.

"I thought you'd take a day off to recover. After yesterday, maybe you could use it," he said, surprised.

"No, no, the medication is working. My fever is down to 101, and you know as well as I do—the show must go on."

"Yes, I suppose so. No time to waste. I was just concerned about you."

"I know, but you'll find I'm tougher than you think."

Biff laughed, remembering her charge into the coroner's morgue the day before. "I'd say you're practically *indestructible*! Can you arrange to meet this afternoon?"

"Well," Abby giggled, "in addition to coding, they have me submerged in conversational German and French. I may not be able to understand English by noon."

"Then we'll speak French!"

"Mais, non! Heaven forbid! I need a moment to relax into my old comfortable communication shoes."

Biff chuckled. "Very well, I think I can remember a few English words. Purhaps, Miss Abby, we can evan communicate in yoah wundaful Southern tongue."

"Oh, Biff, you stop that! You know what I mean."

They arranged to meet that afternoon. First thing, he related his meeting with the Old Man. "Abby, you know it's important now for you to finish your training here as soon as possible. With your inoculations to complete, I place that time line at about mid-December. At the same time there are preliminary investigations we need to make before we have to leave the States."

"So you think we need to continue our investigation into Europe?" she asked.

"I think it's inevitable. If the imposter and Suzanne have left the country there's no alternative. But I believe we can find out whether they have or not."

"So—then we need to outline our steps of procedure."

"Exactly! First I think we need to check with those who investigated this homicide in the first place. We know she was found by a fisherman, who obviously reported it to the local authorities. They found the bundle of her clothing including her dog tags a few feet from the body. The bundle had been wrapped, secured with a belt, and weighted down. And it had been submerged in water, as though someone had thrown it in expecting it to sink." He stopped as though he had a second thought. "I think that someone intended to give the impression that it had been thrown in but had been washed ashore."

"Yes, that's exactly what I thought," Abby said. "It was found near enough the body that whoever found it would connect it with the body. The more I think about this the more I'm convinced that this was simply an elaborate hoax to convince us that the body *is* Suzanne's."

"I agree completely. That makes perfect sense."

"So when they found the bundle, they informed the Navy?" Abby asked.

"Yes. Obviously, if this were Service personnel then it was up to that branch of the Service to handle the body. The Navy investigators immediately took over both the body and the investigation. That's why they were able to suppress the information about her uniform and her dog tags from the press."

"That was fortunate, wasn't it? No need to alert the enemy."

"Absolutely!" He looked at his notebook. It was written in unintelligible symbols.

Abby glanced at the scribbling and laughed. "It would take Madame La Zonga to figure that out."

"My secret code. You're right, I'm the only one who knows it." He paused, gathering his thoughts. "I've just contacted those who were involved in that part of the investigation. They know this is top-secret and they can be relied upon to keep it that way. They're continuing to make discreet inquiries about this homicide. Making it appear as though it were done by some sex offender."

"Do the locals have any leads?"

"I think the local authorities are probably overjoyed to turn over this case to the Navy. It's a quiet community. They don't want any scandal or sensationalism. So they've pledged to keep the connections with her Navy identity secret and they'll keep the whole incident quiet."

"That's good; that would be important for security measures as well But, Biff, what you're saying is: whether or not he's a local, if the real killer can be found, then under pressure he might lead us to Suzanne and her spy."

"Yes, this imposter may have gotten someone else to commit this crime. Obviously, it was well thought out. First, it had to be a woman the same size, shape, and coloring as Suzanne. So they had to find her somewhere, then they had to stalk her until the right opportunity arose to kill her. Plus the fact that the timing had to coincide with this Jacques' plans to leave Washington with Suzanne. This woman had to have the exact same texture and color of Suzanne's hair. And she had to have all identifying marks removed, including her fingerprints, to prevent the discovery that she was *not* Suzanne." He raised his brows—almost in admiration of Jana's ingenuity. "Actually, it was very cleverly done."

He stopped, gathering his thoughts. "But despite his thoroughness, he missed something. We can believe that it was only because he didn't *know* about it. You know, if you had not discovered the birthmark missing, Abby, that body would have been officially identified as Suzanne Davenport and we would never have known any different."

"Just a stroke of luck, really—and a fortunate memory. Have there been any other young women reported missing in that area?"

"No, it's a quiet community, that's why I think the local authorities are so happy to turn it over."

"Then this young woman with Suzanne's specifications was probably found somewhere else, even killed somewhere else, and placed there." Abby sighed. "So the prospect of tracking down a local killer *could* be impossible."

"True, but we'll keep our investigators on it. Something could turn up. Maybe someone saw her being placed there."

"Perhaps—but what happens to the body of this poor girl now? Shouldn't we let the killers think they've succeeded in convincing us it's Suzanne?"

"Right! Since there is no next of kin, no one needs to be notified. We'll simply identify the body as Suzanne's and bury her in Arlington with a small ceremony. We can list her in the obituaries in Washington and New York. We could even eliminate any cause of death. It will have to look official enough to convince the perpetrators." He thought for a moment. "Would you like to write her obituary?"

"I'd be delighted. Just as long as it isn't true!" She thought for a moment. "But you know, I see a problem with that. Perhaps she should be listed without any fanfare. There are others in this town alone who know her. All of the girls in the office, for instance. Senator Downs, and many of the people she knows there. Also, you know that she worked for an international airlines' executive for a number of years, both here and abroad. Are we to let them all think that Suzanne is deceased?"

Biff shrugged his shoulders. "We may have to, if we are to convince the killer. Not too many people keep up with the obits, or the lists of war casualties, but you can bet the killer will."

"True. I suppose no plan we could come up with will be perfect. I just hate to lead people astray, but I suppose in this case it's necessary. I don't think the girls in my old office would be reading the war obituaries unless someone they know has just died. So many of our servicemen and women have been killed or maimed in this war that there's always a long list. Don't you think that might suffice?"

"We'll consider it. Maybe you're right. Maybe we should simply have this poor unidentified girl buried quietly and hold onto to her information in case we ever find her identity." Biff sat silently for a few moments. "Abby, you mentioned Senator Downs before. Do you think it would be wise to question him? I don't particularly trust him. I don't know many people who know him who do. I wouldn't like to see him throw a monkey wrench into this investigation. Yet we really need to know what his past association with Suzanne was all about. How do we know that he didn't *know* this Jacques D'Arcy? Or was even in some way hooked up with him."

"We don't," she said. "But I think we have to tread very lightly with this one. If he's involved, he could give away the store, or do something worse. Let's think about him for a while before we do anything. Maybe we can sneak up on him without his knowing. I don't trust him either."

"Good point!" Abby was always in tune with his own thinking.

Abby continued, "But it does seem to me that we really do need to investigate Suzanne's past. She speaks several languages fluently. That would make her invaluable to an enemy agent. I know she was educated in Switzerland—we went to the same school, but of course she was older. I know that she also attended the Sorbonne in Paris. Plus she has international connections as an airlines executive secretary. He may use her past associations somehow to get his information."

"Yes, he will probably try. Let's see—Allen Dulles is in Switzerland. He could follow up on that aspect."

Biff leaned back in his chair. "Well, Little One, looks like we have a lot to do." He stared unseeingly out the window, deep in thought. He wondered if Jana knew about Suzanne's friendship with Abby. If so, that could put her in danger. But he put that thought aside for now.

"I think our next step is to try to figure out where they've gone. I doubt seriously that they could have obtained passage very quickly to Europe. Do you have any idea where Suzanne thought she was going on 'leave'?"

Abby thought back to the last conversation she had with Suzanne. "I had a distinct impression that she was going north. She even mentioned skiing." Abby sat pensively. "There are too many loose ends here."

Suddenly she sat forward. "Let's look at this hypothetically. Don't most detectives come up with a theory?"

Biff nodded, "The effective ones seem to."

Abby went on: "Hypothetically, then, suppose he proposed to take her on a lavish vacation. My first thought would be a luxury hotel in New York City for a week or two and then—some kind of trip to—maybe Canada for skiing. That's north, and there's plenty of skiing there. Come to think of it, wouldn't that fit in fairly closely with the fact that the body was found on the shores of Lake Erie? New York borders Lake Erie where she was found, doesn't it?"

Biff rose from his chair and pulled down a map from the shelves lining the office walls. He spread the map out on the conference table.

"You're right. And there's a city not too far from the village where her body was found—Buffalo, N.Y., which, incidentally, is almost on the border of Canada, near Niagara Falls."

Abby was getting excited. Something inside told her they were right on target. "That would make it very convenient, wouldn't it? Convenient to New York *and* Canada.... Maybe he left her for a day or two to make the arrangements for her 'death.' She said he sometimes took fairly short confidential trips. He would come and go."

"That's a good theory, Abby. Let's start with that. Now, the next thing would be how did they get out of Washington unnoticed? Did Suzanne own a car?"

"Yes, but she rarely used it. She complained about gas rationing and scarce parking. She said cabs were so much more convenient."

"Of course, that's it! They're driving. What kind of car is it?"

"I don't know. But I think it's a top of the line convertible. Suzanne was quite wealthy, you know. She had a rather handsome trust fund, set up by her parents before they were killed in a plane crash."

"Well, we can easily find out about the car through her personnel records. Of course he could have a car of his own or he could have changed her tags, but a convertible is easier to trace. People notice them. If they used it to drive through the border guards station in Canada, then that would really be a bonus."

"Yes, it would, wouldn't it?" Abby perked up. "If he didn't use her car, then he had to know we would find it here wherever she stored it, and that could yield information he wouldn't want disclosed. Even the trust fund might be exposable, although the Swiss banks are like the Sphinx."

"That's a thought! Good show, Abby. I think we're on the right track. I'll check out the car, and the hotels in New York. Maybe someone, somewhere will remember them."

Abby felt a warm glow overtake her. Once in a while during her lifetime, she had experienced a sudden infusion of knowledge without any possible way of knowing. This was one of those times. Somehow, deep in her spirit, she knew her theory was true, and that she had been placed in this mission for a reason, and that in some mysterious way He would guide her.

She looked across at Biff leaning against the bookshelves. Their eyes met in an affectionate warm embrace. Her excitement mounted.

Yes, there was a Master plan. And Biff was part of it.

Chapter 19

By the next week, Abby managed to return to the clinic for the beginning of her series of the six remaining shots.

She reported in to Dr. Hancock. "Here I am again for the rest of my inoculations, and whatever else I need to do."

"Yes, we wondered what happened to you," he smiled. "We knew there had been some problems but I think you'll find they have been resolved. Let me take a look at your checklist." He took her chart and scrutinized its instructions. "It seems you still need six inoculations and a tuberculosis patch. And because of an unfortunate mishap, we have to do another blood test."

"Oh, no! Not that again! The last one just about took my arm off."

"Yes I know, but you won't have that problem this time. I'll ask Lamar to do it. She's great with a needle. First, why don't you go on down to inoculations. After you finish up there, Lieutenant Lamar can give you your blood test and your TB patch and you'll be all through."

"Good. I'll be glad to get this finished. But I do want to thank you for being so considerate. I hope I wasn't too big a pain in the neck."

Dr. Hancock smiled. "As a matter of fact, we found you very refreshing. You have no idea how many hard-liners we get around here."

Abby proceeded down the corridor to Inoculations.

The medic checked off the first three shots of the series already administered. "Yes, let's see, you've had tetanus, a smallpox booster, and the first of your typhoid series. So now you need six more: malaria, typhus, yellow fever, cholera, dengue fever, and—there's one other. I can't make this out but I'll check on it. O.K., Miss, roll up your sleeve."

Abby instinctively rolled up her left sleeve without thinking. The technician took a quick look at her arm and grimaced. "Well, I guess it does look a lot better than it did last week. It was a mess back then. Now it's just a beautiful shade of green and purple, but maybe you'd better roll up the other sleeve."

"Yes, I was finally put on a new miracle drug to keep down any infection," Abby said. "I suppose others thought it was pretty bad as well."

"Well, you don't have to worry about the Vampire Man anymore. Travis is gone. I think they threw the book at him. They finally proved he was sabotaging records at his last post, hundreds of them. He was always causing all sorts of trouble. When he found out they were charging him, he went berserk. He tried to sabotage all the records here, but thank God, they caught him before he'd done too much damage. I'm glad he's gone."

"Unbelievable. Is that why I have to take another blood test, because he destroyed my record too?"

"Unfortunately, that's true. He probably blamed you partially for the fact that he got canned. But believe me, he was way over his head before you showed up."

"Yes, I can see why."

Company of Spies

"O. K, you're all through. Now all you need is a new blood test to replace the other one. Lamar will do it. She's an expert. You'll never know what hit you."

Abby laughed. "That's what I'm afraid of." She said her good byes to the medics and went back to find Lieutenant Lamar.

"Ah, there you are. This will only take a moment." Lt. Lamar smiled, looking almost delighted when she saw Abby, despite her ordinarily brusque manner.

"I'm certainly glad it's you," Abby said. "Looks like you people had a little trouble with the Vampire Man. I, for one, am certainly glad he's gone."

"You're not the only one. He was bad news." Lamar administered the needle. "There now, that wasn't so bad was it?"

"You're a wizard, lieutenant, I hardly felt the needle go in. I can't tell you how I was dreading this."

"Well, you don't have to worry about Travis anymore. And neither do we, thank heavens. He won't be bothering anyone else for quite a long time. Now, I see you're all through. So, I wish you well on your new ventures." Lieutenant Lamar looked rather intently at Abby. She smiled a wistful smile. The kind that one would give a daughter if she had had one. "May the good Lord protect you, my dear."

"I can't thank you enough, lieutenant. May the Lord bless you too. Maybe we'll meet again one day, who knows. In this war, people never know where they'll be."

"True, you never know." But Lamar did know. Her orders for the Pacific Theater of War had already been cut. And she had a strange feeling that she would never return.

They said their goodbyes. Abby started down the hall to the entrance. *Goodbye to you too,* she thought on her way out, as she passed the many posters with their warnings of VD.

Dr. Margaret S. Emanuelson

The next few weeks found Abby busy with her training in coding, disinformation, propaganda and other techniques. She was still unsure what her ultimate assignment was to be. Maybe the higher ups didn't know what to do with her either. But she was learning. And there was never a dull moment. She recalled the statement Dr. Warner had made about ambiguity, and she was trying to become comfortable with it as a continuing condition in this type of operation.

It was true. There was no way to dot every *i* and cross every *t*. She began to realize that knowing what to expect in a reasonable routine, even if not a comfortable one, made one feel safe. Gave one a feeling of autonomy, of power over one's life. But yesterday's plans could be today's disaster. Nothing could be written in concrete. Everything was subject to change in an instant.

At least one hour per day was spent in French conversational communication, and another in German. Abby found French easier since she remembered more of it and could translate more readily. The one thing that saved her was the two years she had spent in school in Switzerland, where conversational French and German were faithfully practiced as well as grammar and translation. Her present problem in both languages stemmed from the fact that it was typical of American schools to teach mainly grammar and translation, and she had had very little opportunity to practice in-depth conversational language since her sojourn in Switzerland. She was rusty. Even so, her present tutors were surprised at the accuracy of her French pronunciation. The German was really no problem.

"Now if we can only get you more fluent in conversational language, you could easily pass for a French native."

But Abby had her doubts about that. Many of the French spoke very rapidly and she had a hard time keeping up with them. "I suppose I could feign deafness and ask for repetition," she said with a smile. "Do you think that might work?"

"Quite possibly. But it would also draw a lot of attention to you that you don't particularly want."

One of the primary concerns in espionage was not to draw attention to oneself. The more nondescript one could appear, the better. Any kind of mannerism or gesture or anything that might attract attention could give one away and was dangerous. Recently an OSS agent had betrayed himself by reverting back to the Americanism of switching to his right fork while eating his dinner in a French restaurant. The Nazis had arrested him immediately.

Another compatriot, meticulously trained in the military, had had the same fate when he was met by a Nazi officer who saluted him with, "Heil, Hitler." Instinctively, he had returned the salute with a typical British one, immediately sealing his fate.

Unspeakable horrors were coming forth about the different methods of torture used by the Gestapo from the very few who had later managed to escape. The real truth about concentration camps, heretofore hidden, and the murderous atrocities performed on the Jews, the Christians, and other dissidents, was now coming forth, at least in the small isolated community of OSS in which she found herself.

Massacres of innocents, extermination of thousands of people in gas showers and ovens, bizarre scientific experimentation with living human beings, slavery in all its forms, and torture that even far surpassed that of the Inquisition was a common occurrence.

This spy business was no cup of tea. Cover stories could not simply be memorized. In a momentary lapse, or a daydreamy moment, one could easily be compromised. Cover stories had to be practiced, almost lived, to offer the greatest measure of protection from giving oneself away.

This had to be why some sleeper agents were placed in strategic positions sometimes years before, so that they could eventually become the character intended. That strategy had worked and agents had been accepted and trusted over time by the people in the setting in which they were placed. But unless pre-arranged, in wartime, of course, this was rarely possible.

The enemy was alert to any word or action that aroused suspicion. A heightened paranoia alerted the enemy to arrest first and ask questions later. The narrow escapes of some of her OSS colleagues and others were hair raising.

The war was having its effect on every walk of life. It permeated the mind, body, soul and spirit of all those whom it touched. The moods of the people were reflected in the current music from patriotic themes to love songs of longing for the absent lover, and other loss. Bing Crosby's "White Christmas" became an enduring classic as did Jo Stafford's "I'll See You Again," and Marlene Dietrich's rendition of "Lilly Marlene" became a beloved tune on both sides of the battlefield.

The movie industry was busy portraying heroic battle scenes and underground espionage scenarios to heighten the public's patriotism and support for the war.

There were also counter efforts from the enemy. The rampant ravings of "Lord Haw Haw" were causing great chagrin amongst his British countrymen, as he betrayed them by his treasonous broadcasting for the enemy, aimed at undermining the morale of the British and American troops. An incredible thought, for most British subjects, that one of their own could betray them in such an outlandish manner. However, this subject was not alien to the high command. It brought up an area of vital concern for many in high places, who were privy to the fact that there were strong German sympathizers even among some of the British aristocracy. Some of their peers even courted and plotted to reinstate the former King Edward to power, as an ally to the Nazis' strategy to overcome Britain and make it part of their 1000-year reign.

Abby was learning. It seemed to her that all conflicts had their roots in the psychological attributes, attitudes, and expectations among people. Old prejudices, old hatreds, old conflicts dug deep roots, and the unforgiving and the unforgiven eventually awoke again to a new and worse battle than before. This was no less true between nations. Some of the historical backgrounds of those now in conflict reached back decades, even centuries, before, creating the smaller bonfires that would eventually erupt into consuming worldwide conflagrations.

Historically, the British and the Germans were strongly intertwined. Not only by the constant interaction of ethnic, genetic, philosophical, economic, religious, and psychological factors but by the fact that they both enjoyed common customs, aspirations, and educational goals for their respective children.

These interrelationships were compounded by the continuing arranged intermarriages of the royal families, aimed, of course, at keeping royalty royal, and not allowing common blood to flow in royal veins. A precedent that had existed amongst the royal families of Europe for centuries. This practice sought to ensure that alliances made by marriage between nations remained secure and kept the underling nation under control.

At the time of World War I, the grandchildren of Queen Victoria ruled Europe and Russia. Wilhelm II was Kaiser of Germany. George V was King of England, and Alexandra,

Victoria's exquisite granddaughter, was Czarina of Russia, married to Czar Nicholas II. With so many extended family ties among the three ruling monarchs it was inevitable that many disagreements, political and personal intrigues, and resentments would spring up. One in particular caused an outcry of horror that has never been forgotten.

When, in 1917, the Russian Revolution threatened the very lives of Nicholas and Alexandra and their five children, they appealed to King George in England for asylum. At first he agreed. But, surrounded by his political advisers, he was coerced into denying their appeal. The subsequent murders of the entire family punctuated the outraged outcry of those who regarded the denial as a sentence of death, and accentuated the bitter resentment in some quarters against the British throne. And some of those attitudes and family fingers reached not only into Russia but Germany as well.

An empire whose colonies reached around the globe, "upon whom the sun never sets," was bound to have energetic enemies, particularly among the conquered. That was the case of Germany by the end of World War I. The once proud, intelligent, and industrious Germans were not only defeated and humiliated, but cruelly stripped of even the semblance of dignity and reduced to utter poverty by the Treaty of Versailles. Then a worldwide economic depression hit in the twenties, smashing the feeble efforts of Germany to regain its equilibrium and reenter Europe as a respected and viable nation.

And the stage was set for a megalomaniac to reinstate the idea of order, revitalization, national pride, and supremacy to a nation barely hanging on by its fingernails, whose consuming hatred for the British, French, and Americans spurred their fight for survival and their determination to rise again.

"Deutschland, Deutschland uber Alles"— became not only the German national anthem, but the hope of the German nation as well. It was only later that the truth became evident. That the people had been deceived and had unknowingly traded an old enemy for a more diabolical one from within their own midst.

Introduced to Dr. Karl Haushoffer in 1933, by a young and eager Rudolph Hess, Hitler was intrigued by his theory of world domination. At the time, Hitler was known for the writing of his classic, *Mein Kampf.* Haushoffer's teachings of geopolitik at the University of Munich taught him the keys to the most powerful weapon of all—information—and how to gather it into a meaningful whole.

Information equals knowledge, and knowledge equals power. Information, gathered from bits and pieces of what might seem to be trivia, when pieced together could mean exact battle or attack plans of the enemy, or detailed evidence of the enemy's resources. Information and the control of it gave one power over one's own staff members, one's own people at large, and even more important—one's enemies.

Hitler learned his lessons well. Haushoffer's theories fell in line with his own agenda and he built the most powerful war machine ever conceived. He not only used it on the enemy but upon his own people, as he set out to rule by the tyranny of fear and the totality of armed control.

Abby had always loved a mystery. As a small child she sent off the Ovaltine box top in order to receive the offer of Little Orphan Annie's "secret code watch." Interest in cryptology and solving mysteries was old hat to her. Problem solving was fun. It had always been her favorite pastime. Always a perpetual student by nature, she was motivated to research the subject of encryption and decoding, while at the same time she was being involved in the actual process of both.

Methods of secret writing were what encryption was all about. The key was always the answer to deciphering the message. The discovery of the Rosetta Stone by Napoleon's soldiers had been an exciting key to open up the secrets of the Egyptian hieroglyphics. Of particular interest was her discovery that the English had actually used the novel *Rebecca* as the codebook for some of their operations. The Bible was another.

By 1942, the prized and ingenious coding machine, Enigma, was captured in a series of operations unbeknownst to the Germans who had developed it. An extremely complicated machine, using three keys, it required some of the top cryptologists and mathematicians to conquer it, and it opened the door to invading the Nazis' communications systems.

The solving of the intricate Enigma problem fell to Bletchley Park and Operation ULTRA, who were engaged in receiving and decoding transmitted radio messages. About 200 cryptanalysts were involved from different universities. One of them, Alan Turing, also a mathematician, developed the Turing bomb, an electromechanical machine that tested the fit of the crib to a given message.

The bomb was an enormous contraption that took up a mammoth amount of room, but with the help of the cryptanalysts, it enabled the Allies to intercept a glut of the enemy's messages. Oddly enough, the Germans never knew about the Turing bomb or the activities at Bletchley Park, nor did anyone else. And Bletchley Park remained a secret for 30 years.

Chapter 20

Senator Downs lifted his coffee cup and scanned the newspaper. He lived for the news, the crime stories, the deaths. He needed to know. He needed an answer, *now*. It was already mid-November. Who had been murdered? What bodies had been found? Finally, he turned to the daily obituaries. Again, there was nothing there. He banged his fist hard on the desk.

"Dammit to hell! This is ridiculous! Why haven't they informed me?" He voiced a few more vulgarities and began to look under the service report of Army and Naval personnel who were listed either missing, wounded, or dead.

His thoughts went back some years before, to that glorious trip abroad in 1935. He had recently become one of the youngest senators ever elected to Congress. He was riding a wave of glory, rising quickly to a position of power and his spirits were soaring.

Germany before the war was an exciting place. He could sense the power and the glory of the Zeitgeist of the day, the excitement, the exhilaration. The military parades and celebrations were meant to inspire the young, the soldiers, the entire population. The multitude of soldiers and youth groups marching, standing in attention before their Fuehrer, the music, the anthem, all were orchestrated to instill fierce patriotism, pride, and hope into a nation that had felt rejected and abused by past events. Only a few of the wise seemed to suspect the hidden agenda, to foresee the horror of the deceit of the totalitarian rule that was encroaching upon them. Only a few visionaries projected the disaster that was to come.

Germany is where they had met. The moment he saw her, he was immediately smitten.

Several meetings had been arranged with a number of heads of large corporations including their governmental and diplomatic connections. And there she was—as the executive secretary for an airlines magnate. He had supposed that they were having an affair but he also thought it might be ending. The gentleman was married and probably had no plans to leave his wife and family. But it was easy to see why he had become totally infatuated with this dazzling creature.

Downs had made his first move as a "friend." He had guessed right. Suzanne, feeling that she was wasting her time on a man who would never marry her, began to respond to him. He had offered her a position back in the States in his inner circle. To escape the situation she accepted, packed everything she had brought and returned with him and the group of congressmen with whom he had arrived.

She immediately became his executive secretary. Soon they became intimate. He was totally obsessed with her. He began to trust her with more and more confidential information. She was his confidant, his girl Friday, his everything. For over two years they continued. He even considered obtaining a divorce from his wife and marrying her. He had gone so far as deftly to ask some of his closer colleagues what the chances were for reelection of a divorced senator, but they, all without exception, had said it was taboo.

"The country is not ready for Catholics, Jews, or divorced senators in government. It will never work. Not in 1935."

Finally, rumors began to circulate. His wife, Betsy, suspicious for months, found out that it was Suzanne who was his mistress. By this time, Suzanne was pressuring him to leave his wife and marry her. He adored her, but he couldn't risk divorce. His career was at stake. He could never give up his position, his power. He would be ruined.

Suzanne on the other hand wanted to be a wife, not somebody's mistress. She realized he would never give up his career. She ended it. He pleaded with her that if she could wait a few years things would be entirely different. But it was to no avail.

When he saw that she was determined, he had helped her make some key contacts. And shortly thereafter she accepted a placement that he had suggested to her. Through his glowing recommendations she landed a civil service job as executive secretary to one of the heads of naval personnel. Later, when the war erupted, she joined the WAVES, and received an immediate commission as lieutenant, maintaining the same position.

They had seen each other from time to time, but just as friends. He had always believed that one should keep a potential enemy as close to one as possible. He had always trusted her, she had always been loyal and protective of him, but she knew all of his secrets. Though it had been five years since they were together, she had been his only confidant during those years and there had been much pillow talk. She knew about his past contacts, his friendships with the Nazis. Even his investments and plans there for the future. She knew it all. How could he have been so stupid?

Yes, he had always trusted her. But things were different now. They were at war. What had seemed innocent enough during peacetime now took on a sinister aspect. It could even be viewed as *treason*.

The investigations into the Pearl Harbor incident had helped to trigger his fears. Someone was going to pay dearly for that screw-up. He had had absolutely nothing to do with that scandal, but by now *everything* was under suspicion and surveillance, everything and everybody. If they ever found out about his relationships in Germany—he couldn't even think about it. It was too devastating, too threatening.

He was beginning to panic. She had to be removed. She was the only one who knew.

In September, he had sent a message under his code name "Razor" to his German undercover contact again, at his drop zone. But after that last message from him, that "if you know any reason why our secrecy or position could be in jeopardy, you had better tell us NOW," he was instantly afraid of the Germans as well. He had to extricate himself from their suspicions. He had insisted that this message be relayed to the German High Command. It was best that the order on Suzanne came directly from Germany. That way no one would connect him with her removal. No one would ever know the details, not even he. But over two months had elapsed and they had had more than enough time.

Though there were none officially, he felt the investigations closing in on him. He was agitated, fidgety, nervous. Paranoid. It was affecting his work. He was afraid people would notice.

He looked through the obituaries again, as he had for over two months, ever since the day in September when he had finally requested her removal. There was nothing there relating to Suzanne. Finally, he looked carefully again, down the long list of war casualties and confirmed deaths. Suddenly he saw it— listed under deaths:

Suzanne K. Davenport, Lieutenant, U.S. Navy: WAVES.

There was no mention of how she died, when, or where it happened. But it was there. He read it again and again and clipped it out of the paper. He breathed a deep sigh of relief. She was dead. He was safe.

Chapter 21

Life was busy. Thanksgiving came and went. Miranda had quieted down, probably because a new man had emerged in her life, a distinguished Navy captain who had lost his wife two years before. He seemed very devoted, and was constantly wining and dining her. Abby was happy for her.

Abby had almost finished her shots. She was immersed in what seemed to be a speed course in operational techniques, warnings of pitfalls, and security indoctrination. But as yet no real "assignment."

There were many briefings and she met with Biff frequently. Yet there were many areas of OSS functioning that she couldn't seem to get a handle on. If someone would only provide her with an organizational chart she would feel more secure. But none was forthcoming. As Dr. Warner had said, ambiguity was the name of the game. There seemed to be long periods of waiting—and then a sudden rush of activity when a "special operation" became imminent. Never knowing must be what kept everyone on their toes, but much of the time she felt frustrated, impatient.

It was almost impossible to believe that a year had passed since that fateful day of December 7, 1941. She wondered where she would be at Christmas time this year and she missed the promise of Christmas at home. Yuletide was always a festive and beautiful experience in Atlanta. The extravagant displays of lights, Santa with his reindeer and sleigh on the rooftops of the old elegant houses, and the social whirl of parties and cultural events were always accelerated by that special season.

Although it was very cold at this time of year, there was not always the expectation of snow. The strains of Bing Crosby wishing for a "White Christmas" was heard frequently now and was simply a sentimental reminder of Christmas at home, no matter where that happened to be. Popular songs of the season and Christmas carols were constantly wafting over the radio, engendering a surge of Christmas spirit.

Robert and Cameron had been in contact from their elegant country house in England, the original Allistair, with its tall ceilings and extravagant grounds. They would be there for the holidays, and probably for a great many other endeavors. She knew now that Robert was much more involved in covert activities than she had previously thought, but what he actually did was still a mystery.

She had had several invitations away for the holidays but she had been put on alert and told to stay in Washington until further notice. So Christmas this year was an unknown factor. She was getting impatient. Time to get on with it.

The phone was ringing. It was Biff. "I'll pick you up in 15 minutes at the entrance," he said. "We have a briefing with the Old Man."

She at once became alert. At last. This would be her first briefing with him. She freshened up, donned her coat, grabbed her purse and files, and scurried down the stairs to the front desk.

"Hi, Cordelia. Calm my fears. I'm a nervous wreck! This is my first briefing with the Old Man."

"Believe me, my dear, he doesn't bite. Besides, you'll charm him." Cordelia scanned her from head to foot. "You're looking especially chic to day," she said.

Abby laughed. "You mean 'chicken,' don't you?"

"Hardly! You know what I mean."

"Now, Cordelia, you know that flattery will get you nowhere. I'm completely out of tickets to see Mae West. You'll have to forego the burlesque after all."

Cordelia lifted her hand to her brow in feigned defeat. "How tragic! I'm going to have a nervous breakdown."

"Please don't. You're the only sane one around here."

"Very true." Cordelia exploded in her typical tinkling laughter. "Biff again? Or should I say soul mate?"

"You mean my guardian, don't you? Who else?"

"Now, now, I imagine you have a few other Lotharios hiding in the woodpile."

"Oh, absolutely! All infested with termites!"

Cordelia laughed, "Well now, look who's here, imagine that."

Biff leaned over in a bow, took Cordelia's hand and kissed it, clicking his heels. "Your humble servant, madame."

"Goodness! I'm completely overwhelmed."

"Cordelia, my dear, it would take a tornado to overwhelm you." Biff's eyes twinkled as he took Abby's arm. "We have to go. See you later."

"Bye, bye, you two."

Cordelia watched them as they walked toward the car. They belong together, she thought, a perfect combination.

As they made the short drive to headquarters, Abby sat nervously in her seat. "What's the Old Man like? What's the briefing about? Why am I included this time? What's up? Any new developments about Suzanne?"

"Slow down a bit, Little One. As to what he's like—he's probably one of the most uniquely intelligent men you will ever know. The Old Man is quite remarkable. He's handsome, very charismatic, and can charm the birds right off the trees completely without effort. He's very direct, sees everything, and hears all. He misses nothing. He was a prominent New York attorney before he was asked by President Roosevelt to head up the OSS. In other words—he's quite a man."

"He sounds pretty formidable."

"He is, but I promise you'll think he's wonderful, and he'll think the same of you."

"Oh, Biff, you always know exactly what to say." She looked at him out of the corner of her eye and relaxed in her seat.

Biff leaned over in amusement and wiped an ink smudge off her cheek.

They reached headquarters and headed up the stairs to meet the Old Man. The armed guard checked their credentials and waved them on. The Old Man's door was half-open. He was sitting behind his desk, absorbed in reading a document.

Biff knocked on the doorjamb. He and Abby stood there waiting.

"Enter." The General glanced at the door. Just as quickly he looked again as though he was struck by something. "Ah, Mr. Bifford, I presume. And this is the young lady you've been telling me about." He rose from his chair.

"Sir, this is Abigail St. Giles."

"My pleasure, Miss St. Giles." The General held out his hand and took Abby's.

"And mine also," Abby said.

He motioned to the two chairs in front of his desk. Abby sat down, the two men followed. He looked down at a file on his desk.

"Let's see, Miss—"

"Abby—please call me Abby."

"All right, Abby. I see here you've been put on alert—you know what that means, of course?"

"I suppose that means that you're about ready to send me somewhere."

"Yes, that's the tentative plan as of now. But first, I need to brief the two of you on recent developments, and we need to review where we are now and what we know. Then we can decide what projections for the future may be."

He turned to Abby. "Biff has kept me up-to-date on what the two of you have come up with so far. Now I need to tell you what information we have gathered, and together we can see if any of this makes sense.

"Biff, what further do you have to report? Do you have any leads from your investigation of where Suzanne and her 'Jacques' might have gone?" He turned his swivel chair to the side, and, hands together, prepared to listen.

"I think we do." Biff said. "I found her car by her car registration. Her license number of course was listed in her Navy personnel file. So that was simple enough. The question was, since she used cabs most of the time, where did she keep her car stored? I asked around some of the gasoline stations that she frequented, but no one there knew anything, although they remembered her.

"So then, I decided I would try the Cadillac dealer. It was likely that she would have her car serviced there since it was a Cadillac convertible. The dealer there remembered her quite well. He remarked on how beautiful he thought she was."

The Old Man chuckled. "Yes, a beautiful woman does enhance the memory, eh?"

"In this case it certainly did. She had asked him where she might find a place to store her car when she wasn't using it, and he remembered telling her about a garage he knew about. He gave me the address.

"He was quite curious as to why I was making inquiries. I told them I was her brother and she had asked me to bring the car to her in Maryland, but had neglected to tell me where it was. I told him she was on vacation there and had decided to make some historic side tours. That seemed to satisfy him."

"Good story! What else have you found?"

"I went to the garage. The owner said the car had not been there for several weeks. So it appears that Abby's theory is the correct one—that Suzanne and her 'Jacques' drove the car to their destination. That may be a lucky break. A convertible is easier to spot, and easier to remember."

"Yes, it would be."

"It was a good-looking car," Abby said. "She had nicknamed it the Maroon Monsoon. She usually drove it only on short trips, because then she could save her gas ration tickets for those special occasions. So—they probably had plenty of gas to take them where they were going."

"And where do you think they went?" said the Old Man.

"We talked about that," Biff continued, "and Abby felt that since this Jacques was courting her, he would probably promise her some kind of luxurious vacation trip. By the second week after she was confirmed AWOL, of course, the confidential information had come out about the girl who was murdered and mutilated on the shores of Lake Erie. And we knew that Suzanne's uniform and dog tags were found only a few feet from the body, so it was obvious to us that someone wanted us to believe that it was Suzanne who was murdered."

"Yes, that was clever, wasn't it? It was to stop us from looking for her." Abby gestured with her hands. "Only it didn't work, thank heavens!"

"Right. Since the body was discovered near a little village near Buffalo, Abby theorized that probably Jacques had taken Suzanne to New York City, which is not that far from Buffalo, maybe a day's trip. That perhaps he had left her in the hotel and made a trip overnight to arrange the murder, making sure that all the identification marks on the girl were removed so that the authorities would put two and two together and decide that the murdered girl *was* naval personnel. Which is exactly what they did. If the locals had not informed the Navy because of the uniform and the dog tags, we might never have known about it."

The Old Man turned to Abby. "And I understand that you, Abby, went to the morgue and ruled out any possibility that it could actually *be* Suzanne."

"Yes, that's true. Thank God! I never really believed she was dead. I had to know for my own peace of mind." She paused. "But from what I understand about his past M. O., we need to find her as quickly as possible. Otherwise, I'm afraid that when he tires of her, or has no further use of her, she will meet the same fate as the other women involved with him who've either disappeared or been murdered."

He nodded in agreement. "Of course. We need to find her as soon as possible, for her own safety." He swiveled around to face them. "And in finding her, hopefully we'll find him. So where do you think they are now?"

"We think they must have headed to Canada." Biff leaned forward in his chair. "I checked the hotels in New York City. There was one desk clerk at the Waldorf who remembered an exceptionally beautiful pale blonde woman in civilian clothes. He said she was dressed to the nines in designer couture, but he didn't remember ever seeing a young man with her."

Abby spoke up. "That *had* to be Suzanne. She loves designer clothes, and he would probably take her to one of the best hotels. Hide in plain sight, you know... But they had already checked out, didn't the desk clerk say?"

Biff responded. "Yes, by the time we tracked them down, they had left. After that, I began to check with all the border stations in Ontario. I figured they would probably go from New York through Buffalo, maybe even see Niagara Falls, and go from there over the border."

"Of course, that would fit into his seduction plan. To make it look like a honeymoon trip." Abby said. "Of course, this may simply be part of his strategy to make her a love-slave, obedient and subservient to his every whim."

"Exactly! He knows how to manipulate people psychologically." The Old Man nodded in assent.

Biff continued, "I found one border guard who remembered a French diplomat and his 'wife' going through his gate—perhaps a week or two ago. He couldn't describe them very well. He said it was dark and snowing. I suspected the guard just wanted to stay in his warm hut, and didn't pay much attention. He said diplomats came back and forth all the time, as a rule, and all their papers had been in order. The only reason he had remembered this one was because of the terrible weather, and they were driving a convertible, which he thought was unusual for a diplomat. There hadn't been any others through except this one in a couple of weeks."

"Ah, yes, a convertible. Did he remember a name?"

"I asked him that. He said it might have been Du Bois, Du Veau, or something. Something that started with a prefix."

"Sounds suspicious."

"Yes. He was curious to know why I was investigating. I told him there was someone at our French Embassy who was trying to find him. That he had seen him inadvertently leave a locked briefcase there when he left. Embossed with the initials 'J. D'A.' He wanted to see that he got it, might be important—with the war and all. He perked up a little with that and told me if any one with those initials came through he would certainly contact the Embassy. I told him not to do that, instead to hold onto the information and I'd check back with him." Biff stopped. They sat in silence, analyzing the material at hand.

Abby thought for a moment, and then: "You know, it's curious that a man like this would go to so much trouble not only to deceive but to please a young woman he obviously means to use in some surreptitious way."

"Yes, it is—very curious!" The Old Man sat back in his chair and stared out the window. "Except that the route he's taking seems to fit into his plan to leave the country." There was a long pause.

"Did it occur to either of you that perhaps he's fallen in love with her? That could be the explanation of why he would go to such extraordinary lengths to please her."

Biff leaned forward. "Of course, that *is* a possibility. And if that is true, it becomes much more dangerous for him. Then he would be concerned with trying to protect her."

"Yes, very much so." The Old Man paused. "Protect her not only from harm but from finding out what kind of a man he really is, not only a spy but a murderer. There can be only two scenarios. Either Suzanne is completely unaware of the murder and that she is supposedly dead, and that presents a very large problem for Jacques—to keep that knowledge away from her—or she knows about it. Which presents the other possibility: that he's turned her into his way of thinking. And that now, she has become a counterspy."

Abby sat forward and pounded her fist on the chair arm. "Sir, I will never believe that. Suzanne is one of most patriotic persons I've ever known. That's why she joined the Navy when she certainly didn't need to. She is beautiful, wealthy, well educated, and has some important friends. Yet, despite her wealth and everything else she has going for her, she joined the Navy to contribute to the war effort. No! I will never believe that Suzanne would knowingly become a traitor to a country she loves."

The Old Man looked closely at her. "You care a great deal about this young woman, don't you, Abby?"

"Suzanne is my friend," she said quietly.

"She's very lucky to have a friend like you. Loyalty is an admirable thing. But if you found that she *has* become a spy for the enemy, could you put that loyalty aside in the interest of your country?"

Abby answered immediately. "I would have no alternative and no hesitation."

Abby looked directly into the Old Man's intense blue eyes. He looked at her for a long time, and then he said, "I believe you."

Finally he began to share his thoughts. "This is a terrible time. Brothers are fighting against brothers. Friends against friends. Loyalties are in conflict. The killing fields are red with the blood of those who fight for an ideal— for truth, for freedom, for deliverance of the innocent and the captive. For the belief that we are our brother's keeper, not his killer.

"But at the same time, we are compelled to send men and women out to go against everything they have ever believed in, and everything they have been taught at home, at school, in church. They are sent into battle to deceive, kill, and destroy, when, at the same time, they have been taught to love the enemy and forgive him. Without a strong faith, the psychological inner conflicts alone, generated by this war, will create a unique generation of victims.

"In the midst of this slaughter, it is almost impossible to keep focused on the overall goal, and the ultimate alternative—if we do not stop these madmen, the world will become an impossible place. A place where no man has an identity of his own. Where all of his God-given talents and abilities will be smothered and snuffed out and he will be used to serve the state and the Devil, in total servitude. The world will be ruled by tyrants of the first order, and the dignity and freedom that each man deserves as his God-given heritage, as a human being, will be buried perhaps forever."

The three of them sat for a long time in silence, considering what they had heard.

The world is changing, Abby thought. *That beautiful genteel world that we have known, will never be the same again.*

Finally, the Old Man said, "Why don't we take a break. You two go along for now. We'll resume after lunch."

Chapter 22

When they met again that afternoon in the Old Man's office, the briefing continued. He sat in his swivel chair, check-listing his facts.

"I think we've reviewed most of what we know to date. The murder itself of the unidentified young woman is still under investigation by the Navy and the FBI. No leads as yet. They'll report to us when they have anything.

"And we now have fairly reasonable confirmation that this Jacques and Suzanne have crossed into Canada. I think we can also speculate that they will go on probably to Québec and arrange to gain passage to Europe from there. We need to know when and where they are going. Our agents can then follow them." He paused.

Biff said, "We also know that we have some loose ends. One is Senator Downs and his relationship with Suzanne. Where does he figure in this—or does he? And in addition, the possibility of his relationship with this Jacques D'Arcy. Does he know him? If so, what is a United States senator doing consorting with a German master spy?"

"Yes, what indeed!" The Old man placed his hands together in his characteristic way. "The other is the airlines magnate for whom Suzanne once worked. Who is he? How close were they? And what are his European sympathies and endeavors? Could he have any connection to Jacques D'Arcy?

"And who at the French Embassy here knows this Jacques D'Arcy and what do they know about him? And this could be dangerous. Finding out could tip him off that we're onto him. There are many, many little details that we may need to look into."

Turning in his swivel chair, he addressed them directly. "But right now I think we have a pretty good handle on the situation. At least the pieces of the puzzle are beginning to emerge and I believe we've already put some of them together."

Biff leaned forward. "Yes, I think we've made a pretty good start in a rather short period of time."

"You and Abby are right on track. I salute you on your efforts so far. Now we have to get on to the next chapter."

"And where do we begin?" Abby asked.

"I think we need to get more solid confirmation that they *did* go to Québec and that they did obtain passage to Europe. If they did, then we know we must pursue them to E.T.O. Otherwise, we're going to get two or three steps ahead of ourselves."

"Of course, it would make no sense for us to send *our* agents over there unless we know where they're going or that they have left. I'll get right on it." Biff made a few notes on his scratch pad, and then tore them up.

"Exactly!" The Old Man looked at Abby, she needed a *full* analysis. "Now, let's review: I've recently been in contact with our London headquarters. They've been trying to track down this one particular enemy operative ever since 1939. He's apparently been very active in Europe for a long time. But during the last six or seven months they had more or less lost track of him. So the conclusion was that either he was dead or that he was operating somewhere else—probably the United States."

"Yes, Biff has told me a little about him," Abby said.

He nodded, and continued. "The British have linked him with innumerable events that show he is a master at espionage. Many of the disastrous failures of some of their military plans and operations have been directly attributed to his ingenuity and the intervention of a spy network. We have come to the conclusion that he has in fact been operating in this country for the past six or seven months. But now the British are intercepting messages with his signature again, so they think he's back in Europe, or soon will be." He looked away for a moment organizing his thoughts.

"As you know, he has also been linked with the disappearances and murders of several young women in Europe who were well connected in their governments, rendering them invaluable to the enemy as sources of classified and secret information. And because of the similarity of his M.O. to those young women—and now, to the disappearance of Suzanne Davenport, including the murder of that unknown woman—we have concluded that he is the *same* operative.

"His code name is 'Jana.'"

"And you believe this 'Jana' is *also* Jacques D'Arcy?" Abby asked.

"Yes, that's what we think. Obviously an alias."

"Unbelievable!" Abby said. "A German spy representing himself as an ally, as a French diplomat, working as one of us, and reporting to the enemy." She paused, examining the thought. "Suppose he's told Suzanne he is an operative acting for us—the Americans, British, and French? Suppose he's convinced her that she's been reassigned as one of *our* undercover agents? He could use her anywhere…. And if she believed him to be one of our agents, she would report all she knew to him."

"Yes, we know he's a spy but he may very well be a double agent. And to convince her to join him, he could very well be posing as a French patriot or one of ours."

Abby had just recognized the total picture. "God forbid! He could be someone we trust—someone we see every day—someone we work with?"

Biff picked up the theme. "Yes, a mole! Could that be? But then I suppose anything is possible. As of now, is there anyone else under suspicion? Are there any suspects?"

"So far, we know of none, but there are always undercover agents here and in England, France, and elsewhere." The Old Man frowned. "The worst scenario is those right in our midst, who unknown to us, could be counter spies."

"My God! A German spy right in our midst. Posing as one of us and reporting to the enemy." Abby had never thought of this possibility before.

"Of course we don't know that this Jacques *is* a counter spy. But make no mistake, this guy is not an *ordinary* spy. This Jacques, this Jana, is a super spy—a master spy. There is evidence that he is an organizer. That over the years he has established a network of spies and undercover resistance workers. Not only in England and France, but in other countries. Now, we're very much aware that he's doing the same thing over here in the United States. In fact, this probably has been going on long before the war started. There are many German sympathizers in this nation. And some who would be more than willing to assist him, and the enemy."

"Too true, unfortunately," Biff said, "and they could be placed in strategic positions."

"Yes, they could be, and only too eager from what we're uncovering. He's organized mass sabotage operations, aimed at delaying production and destroying all kinds of targets. Aircraft factories, public buildings, shipbuilding facilities, munitions factories, boat docks, anything that has anything to do with preparation for and execution of war." The Old Man's keen blue eyes never strayed from them. "As a matter of fact, there was recently a devastating submarine attack on a California shipyard…. He's a tycoon in business, industry, and economic knowledge and know-how. And he has his fingers in politics all over the world."

"A regular Meisterspion!" ventured Abby. "This is far worse than I had thought."

"Yes. He's an organizer and a strategist. He chooses his key people very carefully. He trains them, tests them out, delegates them, and if they prove themselves worthy, they move up to his inner circle. They follow his orders unconditionally. As a result, he can operate from a broad base. Obviously, he does little hands-on interaction himself. Most of his operation would be at arm's length. He organizes his contacts, drop points, and establishes all sorts of communication paths and devices. He's a master at disinformation and deceit, encryption, and special operations…. He's also a master at keeping his identity top-secret. I doubt seriously that any but a very limited few, high in the German command, know who he actually is."

"He would have to be some kind of genius," said Abby.

"Yes, but he has a sinister side as well. It's obvious that he has a hit list and that he arranges the extermination of people who get in the way of whatever he intends to accomplish. There is a long list of accidents, suicides, and downright murders of key people. Politicians, diplomats, doctors, professors—and even people we might think are of little importance. But anyone who knows too much or becomes a jeopardy to his goals is probably doomed.

"Amazing," Abby said. "And *this* is the man we're supposed to find and *capture*." She shook her head. "I knew Jacques was a spy but *this*....It's overwhelming!"

She narrowed her eyes, leaned back, and crossed her legs. "Jana.... Isn't that a strange choice for a code name? Did you ever stop to think of what it might mean?" she said pensively. "Remember your mythology? Janus was the guardian of inner and outer gates. He kept watch over beginnings and endings. He had two faces, one in front of his head and one in back..... Jana would be the female form of Janus. How do we know this spy is not a woman? Or that perhaps he sometimes appears as a man and sometimes as a woman?"

The Old Man leaned forward. "That's an extremely astute observation. There could very well be some personal reason he chose that name. And that it does have some peculiar significance."

"And there's something else I keep thinking. That name, that alias he's using—Jacques D'Arcy. Something has been bothering me about that name ever since I first heard it.... But now I remember: Mr. *Darcy* was the name of the hero in *Pride and Prejudice* and his country estate was named *Pemberley*. Doesn't some of the pertinent training of our expert operatives take place at Pemberley?"

"Indeed it does," the Old Man said, his eyes alert. "It's an exclusive English estate and a particularly special part of our English training facilities."

"Then it would seem to me that Jana is playing a very clever diabolical game with us. And that he's just laughing up his sleeve while he's doing it. D'Arcy, indeed! He may even be dangling a flag right in front of our faces—He *must* know about Pemberley. How do we know he's not planting *his* operatives in there so that they will know who *our* agents are? Or even worse, so that we can train them to be *his* counterspies."

The Old Man and Biff looked at each other and then at Abby, aghast.

"Unbelievable!" said the Old Man. "Biff, I can certainly see what you mean about this young woman."

Biff began to laugh. "I told you I was glad she was on our team and not that of the enemy."

But Abby was still deep in thought. "I know what I'm saying is just a wild theory, but just in case it's true, shouldn't we warn them?"

"Absolutely. I'll get on it immediately. Your deductions may not be so wild after all. In fact I think they're downright ingenious. It would seem to fit this man's devious personality to a T. I'm sure he tries to infiltrate our key positions and place his operatives wherever he can…. But Pemberley. That would really give our English colleagues a jolt!"

The Old Man recalled the Colonel's recounting of the put down Lord Smythe had recently levied at our "so-called inferior" American trainees. He made no attempt to stifle a smile: As disastrous as that might be, it would serve the old pompous, arrogant bastard right.

"I wonder why he chose the name Jana," Abby said. "If we knew, it might be a clue to his identity."

The Old Man nodded. "Could be."

Biff turned to her. "Abby, why don't you see what you can conjure up. You've had some psychological training. Maybe some kind of hypothetical description of this man. His background, his personality as you envision it. Something like that may help to pin him down if we knew more about him."

"Roger. Maybe I'll see him in my dreams." Abby laughed.

"Perhaps! But indeed, some of the things you dream up turn out to be incredibly accurate, even prophetic."

"True. They seem to be." She smiled. She knew it was a gift. And she knew whence it came.

They left the briefing that day armed with a list of loose ends. Biff knew what his next steps would be, but Abby wasn't so clear about the role she was to play. There was that old demon ambiguity again. Nevertheless, she would start with attempting to sketch a description of Jana's personality, and continue with her ongoing training.

Biff, on the other hand, could hardly contain his amusement at Abby's perceptions. He had watched as the Old Man's estimation of her had grown in just a few minutes. He felt like a proud parent, basking in the accomplishments of his child.

What a woman, he thought. What a woman. He shook his head and laughed.

The following day found Abby staring unseeingly through the office window. Pen in hand she paused, deep in thought. She looked at the list of loose ends she had written on the paper on the table:

1. Where are they?
2. Senator Downs?
3. Airlines magnate?

She mumbled out loud as she started through the list: "Starting with No. 1, we think they've gone to Canada. Then probably on to Québec."

All of a sudden she remembered the dream she had had weeks ago. She saw it again in her mind's eye—the hotel, the curved marble staircase, the strains of the Blue Danube. She looked up when she heard the door open.

"Hi there, hard at work?" Biff laid his briefcase on the table and pulled a chair up closer to her.

"I was just going over this list. And I remembered something I had forgotten about. Now, all of a sudden, I can't get it out of my mind."

"Then it must be important. Let's have it."

"It's something I never thought to tell you about, a dream I had weeks ago. Oddly enough, it was when Suzanne was first missing—only I didn't even know it then."

"Tell me—you know I've come to believe in your dreams."

"The interesting thing is that I had gone on leave for the weekend. Actually, it was to my Uncle Robert's, at Allistair. Suzanne was to take leave the following Monday, but actually she was missing the Friday, Saturday, and Sunday that I was away. I had absolutely no way of knowing it at the time. It was on that Friday night that I had the dream."

"And what was your dream about?" Biff said.

"As I remember it—I was walking down a long corridor in an old and elegant hotel. I could tell from the architecture and the wall coverings that the entire decor was French and looked authentic. A long corridor led from one end of the building to the other. But in the center was a marble balustrade which made a balcony. It was flanked on both sides by a curved marble staircase leading down into the lobby.

"I was there, looking through the open portion of the balcony. I could see a large ballroom on the right side of the lobby and there were people dressed in festive attire dancing to the orchestra. It was playing a waltz, the Blue Danube."

"Ah! This is getting interesting." Biff leaned forward, listening intently.

"Yes, isn't it? I began to walk past the open balcony to the other wing. I passed one closed door after another. Then, suddenly, I came to the door of a suite. The door was half open so I stepped forward and looked inside. But it was dark. I saw an old antique chest and part of an elegant bed. On the bed lay a red dress and a long blonde wig. Then all of a sudden—out of the dark—a man's voice said, 'Komm nicht herein! Das ist Verboten!' And with that he slammed the door shut.

"But I caught just a fleeting impression of the face of a handsome man. I had an eerie feeling, I remember cold shivers running up and down my spine. I remember hesitating in the hallway in utter confusion. I think, in the dream, I finally said, 'What shall I do?'"

They sat in silence for a few moments looking at each other.

"What do you think the dream means? Do you connect it with anything?" Biff leaned back in his chair, continuing to look at Abby.

"I don't know. Perhaps it has something to do with where they went. Maybe they're still there. And maybe we could find them if we knew what hotel it was. Obviously, the hotel is French—that's what my dream said to me. And they may be in Québec. At least, that's what we think!--- Of course all dreams are symbolic."

"Have you ever been to Québec? Do you know any of the hotels there?"

"No, I've never been to Canada, or to any of the provinces. But I'll bet I know someone who *has* been there. And knows all about the hotels." Abby tilted her head and looked up at Biff with her mischievous green eyes. She was laughing.

"Oh! Is that so?" Biff's eyes twinkled as he took up her challenge. "Very well! Let's see if any of the clues in this dream can lead us anywhere. We know it's a French hotel. We know it's elegant. We know the orchestra was playing the Blue Danube. What else comes to mind?"

"Come to think of it—the whole dream seemed to have a blue cast to it."

"And the Blue Danube?"

"It's a waltz, of course—but the blue is there—and the Danube is a river—maybe water? Could it mean water—blue water? But that doesn't make any sense."

"But it does. Would this hotel, by any chance, have a fountain, a very large fountain in front of it?"

"I didn't see any fountain in my dream. What do you think is the significance of the feeling of blue?"

"Well, it just so happens that I *may* know the very hotel you're talking about. Or should I say dreaming about? I have a feeling you're describing the Fontainebleu, one of the most famous hotels in the world. It's a copy of an old French chateau. It has a magnificent bronze fountain in front of it, which seems to turn blue in the cold atmosphere. That may be why you got the feeling of blue. It was a hint."

"And where is this wonderful hotel, the Fontainebleu?"

"In Québec, of course. Would your dream have led us anywhere else?"

"Incredible! When do we leave?" Abby's eyes sparkled.

"Let me check with my contact there, and if it checks out I'll leave immediately. Abby, you *are* amazing!"

"You mean *we're* amazing, don't you?"

Chapter 23

From the tall, tall windows, Suzanne could see the near distant snow-capped mountains and the shore on the other side. It was an incredibly stunning scene. Snow covered the landscape like a pristine coverlet, attempting to obscure the famous fountain in the center of the entrance circle. But to no avail, its imposing classic presence commanded notice. Although made of bronze, in winter the fountain took on a strange blue cast, which had been the original inspiration for its name.

The first Fontainebleu had been famous for centuries, one of the most cherished chateaus in France, long before the ambitious builder had copied it as a tribute to his skill, to say nothing of his pride.

Suzanne had never been happier. It was like a fascinating, intriguing game, with twists and turns, and maneuvers she had never dreamed of. She realized that up to now, she had had what might be considered an enviably advantaged life. She had traveled around the world, been educated in America but for the most part in England until her parents were killed, and then in Switzerland and France. She spoke several languages fluently, and had moved in some rather high circles most of her life. Aunt Kippy had even insisted that she be presented at the Court of

St. James. She saw now that she was really as much European as American. She even spoke with a watered down English-American accent.

Yes, life had been fun and exciting at times, but none of her relationships had been permanent. She was grateful for her past advantages, but she was just now realizing how lonely she had been. All she had ever really wanted was a man of her own, to love and be loved, to live together with him till 'death do us part'. Her parents had left her that legacy—a happy and devoted marriage. She knew now she could never be satisfied with anything less.

There had been a few short-lived love affairs in her life, even two that endured two or three years. But both men were already married and not about to risk their position or financial status with divorce. Each one was devastated when she ended it, each pleaded with her not to, but she had realized there was no future with either.

Then out of the blue came Jacques. Wonderful, mysterious, fascinating Jacques.

Not only for the first time in her life did she feel completely loved, adored, and protected, but she had never had a lover to equal Jacques. He was tender and so skilled in lovemaking, she tingled when he simply looked at her.

He was generous to a fault financially, fun to be with, and couldn't do enough to please her. Too, there were many things he was teaching her about their undercover assignment, intriguing things she needed to know about handling people and situations. Jacques had convinced her that she could be perfect in espionage for her government. Yet there was still an air of mystery about him—much more she wanted to know.

They had spoken French entirely since they left New York. Québec was, after all, a French-speaking province. She knew she spoke French like a native. Madame du Veau, her headmistress at L'Ecole de St.Claire, had insisted her girls speak a different language six weeks at a time, even outside the classroom. By the time graduation arrived, all were required to be fluent in French, English, and German. And now Jacques and she had switched to German entirely, except in public, just to keep on their toes.

There was only one thing that she missed, but then she knew it was necessary because of their unique situation and the fact that they had to keep such a low profile. Suzanne was by nature a social animal. She loved people, sports, dancing, the theater, parties. Sometimes she wished they could mingle more, but Jacques had said it wouldn't be possible until they reached Europe.

He had taken her ice-skating on the pond near the hotel, and they had done some skiing, But they were so bundled up no one could have recognized them, particularly wearing their ski masks. Here it was so cold that everyone wore scarves and earmuffs. She had taken to hiding her pale blonde hair tucked under her fedora or a woolen cap. They had been careful.

But today, she could hear the strains of the Blue Danube wafting up from the ballroom on the first floor. The hotel had tea dances every afternoon at 4 o'clock, and also dancing after dinner. Suddenly, she had an insatiable desire to dance. Maybe she could persuade Jacques to take her down for dinner and dancing tonight instead of the usual gourmet dinner with champagne served in their rooms.

She would wear the long dark wig he had brought for her to disguise her identity. She had worn it when they had first arrived. Of course, she must darken her eyebrows, otherwise she would give herself away. No one would believe that she was a brunette with blonde eyebrows.

Actually the disguises were quite fun. Jacques was an expert makeup artist and had brought many with him—goatees, wigs, and all sorts of costumes. They had laughingly tried on combinations as though they were actors in some kind of play. Although she wasn't quite sure why they might be necessary, not here, where no one knew them. But Jacques insisted they take no chances.

He would soon be back from arranging their passage. He had already taken almost all of their luggage away to be shipped across. But this was to be their last night in this winter's paradise. Why not? She would persuade him to let it be their last celebration before leaving the States. She smiled with delighted anticipation as she thought of his reaction when he saw her in her gown.

Yes, she would surprise him. She took the one formal dress she had kept a secret, out of the almost empty closet. It was an elegant designer gown that she had bought at Garfinkel's while they were in Washington. It was to be a very extra special surprise for Jacques.

She freshened her makeup and donned the dress. Its smooth white satin glided over the curves of her body. She reached for her long white gloves and had put one on before she realized she had forgotten to darken her eyebrows and don the dark wig. She would do the wig first.

She rose on tiptoe to reach the wig on the top shelf of the closet, when suddenly she heard the outer door to the suite open. He would soon come into the bedroom. She heard him call out, in that tone of voice that meant he could hardly wait to embrace her.

She smiled in elated expectancy and turned slowly around so that he could admire her.

"Liebchen?" He reached the inner door, saw her standing there, and stopped abruptly. The light behind her gave a ghostly specter, glowing on her lovely hair. As in a dream he stood there frozen. She saw the expression on his face change from joy to shock. His face became gray, stricken.

Then strangely he cried out, "Mein Gott! Nein, nein! Das ist verboten."

Suzanne dropped the other glove. *What had she done? What was wrong? What had she done?* She felt strong icy fingers grip her in the pit of her stomach.

A deadly silence permeated the room. They stood there motionless, their eyes fixed on one another.

It was like a movie, of long, long ago, seen in a split second, and then pushed away, forgotten. A memory so horrible, so traumatic, that it had needed to be hidden forever, buried in some deep grave somewhere, safely guarded. But now it was there again—in the fullness of all of its horror—in a split second—as though it were happening again. Just as it had all those years ago.

It was that same panic that gripped him now. Rendering him paralyzed. Lost in another world that no other could enter.

Jacques stared unseeing for a long time, not moving. Lost in that buried episode of long ago. Then finally, almost instantly, the moment was gone, retreating into the long forgotten past.

Could it really be true? He stood, studying this apparition from his past. His vision began to clear. His heart began to slow. He began to gain his composure. The panic was subsiding.

Slowly, emotionally exhausted, he came back to the reality of the present. He knew he would have to sort this out. But it would have to be later. They were in danger. She was in danger. They had to leave—now!

He spoke quietly. "Liebchen, take that off and dress warmly. Quickly, pack what's remaining. We must leave immediately."

In horrified obedience, Suzanne shed her beautiful white satin dress and donned the warm tweed suit and fur-lined coat she had purchased in New York. She moved like a robot, mechanically, unable to think or reason.

Jacques looked at the girl he loved. He suddenly realized that the impact of his panic was devastating not only to him, but to Suzanne as well. He saw the expression on her beautiful face—that look of astonished hurt and horror. *Oh no! What have I done?* He reached out for her.

"There, there, liebchen, don't be frightened. Forgive me." He held her close and stroked her golden hair. "I didn't mean to hurt you. I know you don't understand what just happened—but I will explain it to you later. Right now we have to run. We have to leave here, without delay—the time is short. Our ship is waiting to sail. Grab your things. We leave down the back stairs. Quickly! A car is waiting for us."

They flung the remaining odds and ends into the remaining suitcase. Jacques picked it up with one hand and took her hand with the other. As they reached the outer door, Suzanne took one last glance as she pulled it shut.

She heard the phone ringing as they fled down the hall. She looked at Jacques, her eyes questioning.

"Let it ring," he said.

They reached the back stairs, and quickly went down to the car waiting at the back entrance. It was growing dark. The driver spoke in French, "We go now. We arrive at the dock in about 30 minutes."

Suzanne was silent. Stunned, she stared into space as in another world. He had spoken to her so harshly—he had never done that before. Her dreams of a perfect relationship had been abruptly shattered, and fear gripped her. He had suddenly seemed so very different, so stern. For the first time since she had met Jacques, she began to question. What had she gotten herself into? She had trusted him so implicitly, believed everything he had told her. But now she realized she knew very little about him. Who was this Jacques D'Arcy? What was he really about?

Suzanne was suddenly fully awake. She would continue to play the game, but she would hold her suspicions close to her vest until she was sure. She was in too deep now to try to pull back. She would bide her time.

Jacques hugged her close to him as they drove. Suzanne cuddled into the comforting curve of his arms, After all, she hadn't completely lost faith in him. He had said he could explain. She would wait and see.

The driver soon left the main road and turned right, onto an old road that followed the shoreline. They were on their way.

Chapter 24

The phone continued to ring in the now empty suite.

"Je regrette, monsieur, there is no answer. They must be out for dinner," the desk clerk said.

Biff slipped an official looking badge out of his breast pocket. It signified the credentials of a French diplomat. He flashed it to the clerk.

"Monsieur, I need your careful attention. Is there some way we can check to make sure? Surely you can give me access to their rooms. It's a matter of the utmost urgency."

"Non, non, monsieur, je suis—"

"Then call your manager, s'il vous plait. Toute suite!"

At the tone of Biff's voice, the clerk ran into the inner office. Biff heard a babble of French coming from the inner door. Soon the manager came out speaking in English in a most ingratiating manner.

"Monsieur, is there a problem?" he threw up his hands. "You realize we cannot give you access to a patron's rooms! C'est impossible!".

"Sir, I am from the French Embassy in Washington. This is a matter of life and death. I *must* contact one of our diplomats, whom we believe has been staying here. I demand that you give me and my government access. Time is of the essence."

"But monsieur, I *cannot* give access without the permission of the Canadian authorities, comprenez-vous?"

"Then, I suggest you call them immediately." Biff's voice was courteous, but demanding.

"Oui, monsieur." The manager gave him a frightened look and ran to the inner office.

Biff crossed the lobby and, out of eyeshot, ran up the marble steps to the second floor. He had watched the manager as he rang the suite, and remembered the number. He walked down the long hall, then came to the right door—it was shut. He started to get out his implements to pick the lock, but then he stopped, and turned the knob. The door opened. It was dark. He flipped the light switch. Suddenly a scene of the splendor of 18th century France came into view, in all its old elegance. The tall Palladian windows, the heavy brocade drapes, the matching chair seats, the Louis XV furniture, the delicate upholstery, the marble fireplace—embers still glowing.

Everything was in perfect order. There was nothing out of place, not a book, not an objet d'art, not a scrap of paper, not even in the wastebaskets. He walked to the door of the bedroom. It was empty—as were the closets, and the drawers.

But to his complete surprise, there on the heavily draped bed, carefully placed there—lay an elegant white satin dress. A long dark wig lay on the floor of the closet, as though it had been dropped there. Biff shook his head and grinned.

"Abby, my dear, you are truly amazing," he said aloud. He walked out of the suite, closed the door, and returned down the front stairs to the front desk.

The manager, visibly shaken and upset, spied him immediately.

"Monsieur, monsieur, je—" suddenly, remembering, he reverted to English. "I have not been able to contact the authorities—but I have left the word—"

"Never mind," Biff said pleasantly, "I've had second thoughts. I think I know where they are. Merci, monsieur, for your trouble."

The manager took a deep breath. A mammoth sigh of relief followed. He continued to look suspiciously at Biff, as if to say, "C'est fou. Il est fou!"

Biff grinned at him. "Au revoir, monsieur, merci beaucoup." He walked swiftly to the front entrance, to the car where François, his contact, was waiting.

Biff opened the car door and sat down in the passenger seat. "They've left with all of their gear," he said. François turned on the ignition and sped off. "Where could they have gone? Where could they leave the country? Is there a harbor nearby where oceangoing ships come and go?"

"Mais, oui! La Porte de Québec. It is nearby—right down the river, maybe twenty-five, thirty kilometers from here."

"Let's go," Biff said.

François came to a sudden fork in the road. "I take detour."

They drove as fast as it was safe on the packed snow. Patches of ice were here and there, but they managed to avoid them. Soon François turned off onto a small road that followed the riverbank.

"The St. Lawrence is the beautiful river, is it not? It is wide and deep. It is said that the Porte de Québec is 51 feet deep.

That is why so many the large cargo boats come and go. It is the deep water, and from here they are the much closer route to the France, to the Europe."

"Then that's where they must be embarking. But how did they know we were on their trail?" Biff said.

"Perhaps they *didn't* know it. But then, they have the spies, we have the spies. We watch them, they watch us."

Biff took his words in—how did Jana know that they were so close? There had to be a leak somewhere. If he didn't know, he had probably guessed that they might have discovered his hoax, but by now he would also know that Suzanne had been declared officially dead. So that should have assuaged his fears. *Did* he know they were so close on his trail? Or was there someone else he was concerned about? He would try to ferret it out when he got back to Abby, to OSS headquarters.

They drove through the cold, cold night. Snowflakes began to fall in a light dusting.

"Can you see the road?" he asked François.

"Not easily, but I go." They continued to speed down the road.

"I see lights around that curve." Biff sat up in full attention.

They drove around a wide curve as the river turned—and suddenly there it was. The lights glowed on a large natural harbor. Several very large ships were moored there. A number of empty docks awaited a new ship arrival.

"Where can we find the port captain?"

"I think in that the building." François drove over to the building. Biff jumped out of the car and entered. The sign on the door read "Porte de Québec."

A uniformed man sat at the desk surrounded by what seemed to be a plethora of official schedules.

"Monsieur, could you help me?" Biff spoke in French.

"Mais oui, I speak the English. What I do for you?"

"I'm from the French Embassy in America." Biff flashed his fake papers. "Can you tell me, are there any ships scheduled to leave for Europe tonight or tomorrow?"

"I look—" The port captain fumbled through a stack of papers on his desk. "There are the two for tomorrow. They sail as soon as they are loaded. Why you ask?"

"I am looking for a man, a French diplomat, accompanied by a young woman. We think they may attempt to leave from here. It is urgent that I contact him before he leaves."

"Non, non! Too, too bad, monsieur. I think you just missed them. The two you described just sailed about 20 minutes ago. They almost missed the ship."

"Can you tell me the name of the ship? And where it was going?"

"The *Marseilles*. It is the big cargo ship. It carries supplies, and at times a few the passengers."

"And can you tell me when and where the ship is due to arrive?"

"Oui, I look." He shuffled the papers again. "It depend on the weather and the convoy it is joining. It is scheduled to arrive in about eleven, twelve days. But, of course, that can change. As I said it could be the longer. It is due to arrive at the harbor in Marseilles, France—non—wait—non, that has just been changed to Liverpool, England—the 29, 30[th,] December, 1942. Eleven, twelve or so days from now, monsieur. If it is that important, I hope you can find them. Get the word to them."

"Merci, monsieur, many thanks for your help." Biff checked his fake French diplomat's papers again to be sure of his alias. "My name is Anton Swift. I may call you about this matter at a later date and I would appreciate it if you could make note of any word you receive about this ship, or the two we're looking for. In the meanwhile, I will appreciate it if you will keep this confidential. Official business, you know. My colleague François will contact you."

"I should be happy to do so, monsieur! Vive la France!"

Biff smiled broadly. "Vive la France!" *A patriot*, he thought. Biff returned to the car. François was rubbing his arms to keep the circulation going in the cold, freezing night. "They were here, but we missed them. Let's go back to the hostel. I have a feeling we should stay there tonight. But on the way, let's see if we can find a place to dine and phone in to headquarters."

"To phone, no way. But to dine, mais oui; I know the old couple who have hostel. They take the care of us—magnifique cuisine!" François turned the key in the ignition and the car started up after a few coughs.

"Bon, but first, I'll pull out my wireless kit and send a coded message. Then we can head out."

They headed back to La Petite Maison, the old bed and breakfast where they had planned to stay if it became necessary. It was getting late and the drive was long—almost to the border.

It was a lovely old house, large and very French. Now, with the snowflakes falling steadily, like down from a pillow, it resembled an ancient provençal country house, something one might see on a treasured postcard.

They would rest a while, at least until dawn. They needed their energy for the drive back tomorrow and the unknown days ahead.

Biff awoke to the aroma of fresh bread baking in the old oven. Dawn was breaking in the distant horizon, spreading an array of warm colors, shades of pinks, reds across the white snow.

Company of Spies

"What a beautiful sight," he said as he looked out the quaint old window. He stretched his weary muscles and yawned. "Oh, for a cup of hot coffee!"

François, always an early riser, knocked on the door. "Allons, allons—nous mangeons!"

"Bon! Je viens."

Madame Picard had always taken great pride in her cooking, having been taught by one of the premier French chefs of the Cordon Bleu in Paris. In spite of the rationing, she had outdone herself this morning: Canadian bacon, Eggs Benedict, hot curried fruit and cheese and that wonderful French bread, hot and fresh out of the oven. They were the only guests there, she had made a special effort, and they relished the wonderful meal she had prepared.

François hugged her as they left. Biff followed suit and the old lady was beaming as they backed out of the courtyard on the packed snow.

They waved their goodbyes and started the short drive to the border. François would drop Biff there and return to his post in Montreal, while Biff would pick up his car and proceed to Washington. It could be a long tedious drive; visibility was poor. Even though the snowfall was light, it was accumulating on the roads, though there was virtually no traffic and ongoing vehicles were sparse.

They reached the border just before six. François pulled into the Border Patrol Station and stopped. They got out of the car and checked with the border guard. Then sat in the car to keep warm and munched on fruit from the great box lunches Madame Picard had prepared for them, while François chatted with the guard there, whom he knew fairly well.

Biff left him, knowing that any upcoming information was in good hands and would be forthcoming immediately to him. François would be his link contact between the Port de Québec and the Border Patrol. He had his instructions. He knew what to do.

Biff thought of Abby. He had missed her terribly. They were indeed a team now; they seemed to think almost as one. He could hardly wait to tell her all that had happened.

The strains of *That Old Black Magic* wafted up from the car radio, Frank Sinatra, in all his glory. *She's got me under her spell, all right! I wonder if she knows it.*

Biff drove on through the snow.

Chapter 25

It was early, not yet five o'clock, but it had begun to snow, and those who could leave were instructed to do so before the roads became impassable.

Abby gathered the materials on which she was working, donned her coat and gloves, and was ready to leave the office for the day. She had waited for a call from Biff all day, but none was forthcoming, and she was beginning to worry about him. Suppose he had had an accident. Having checked on the Canadian weather, she knew the news was bad; a real blizzard was approaching. She recalled that Buffalo had had past storms with an accumulation of up to eight feet. Suppose he were stalled out on some forsaken road somewhere. He could freeze to death.

Goodness, you would think I was his wife, or something.

Then the query. *Are you in love with this man?*

"Good question," she said aloud.

She had had many boyfriends. A girl could be very popular with the opposite sex safely enough in these times, when ladies were ladies and gentlemen were gentlemen and adhered to the codes of behavior. Young ladies were expected to keep themselves pure until marriage. That was the strict rule of social behavior that she had known; and barring a few battles with a very few uncouth "gentlemen" in the past, she had been met with respect and courtesy.

She had had a few crushes before, even two or three proposals of marriage, but it seemed that the instant a young man had shown too much of an accelerated interest in her, she had begun to shy away.

But this time, it was different. She had never felt this way before. She and Biff shared so many of the same interests. They shared the same kind of humor. They seemed to think together. If one came up with a question, the other could come up with the answer. They *were* a team now—not just in name only. There was some kind of—bond between them. She knew he was fond of her, but he had never made any romantic advances toward her.

Abby was closing the office door when the phone began to ring. She dropped everything in her arms and ran to answer it. It was Biff.

"Thank God! I was worried about you."

"Little ole me?"

"Yes, you, you idiot. Little ole you." Abby laughed.

"Well, that's just about the most wonderful thing I've heard today. I'm just getting all those warm goose bumps."

"You stop that! I'm serious."

"So am I, little one." His tone became more sober. "Look, with the weather like this it makes no sense for me to double back over there to the office. Why don't you take a cab here and I'll see that you get home safely. My apartment is only a few blocks from yours. We need to talk. It's urgent."

"Where are you?"

"Watergate Apartments. I'll alert George, the doorman, to bring you up to my flat."

Abby hesitated. All of her teachings against being alone in some man's rooms were kicking in. But this was business, and it was urgent, and it was Biff, whom she trusted.

"I'll be there in about 30 minutes. Get the coffee going."

Biff laughed. "Yes, ma'am."

"You're impossible. What am I going to do with you?"

"I don't know, but I wish you'd do something."

"You just wait till I get there, Russell Bifford!" Abby hung up, laughing. She gathered her things up off the floor and ran down the steps to the front desk. "Cordelia, can you call a cab for me?"

"Sure thing." Cordelia gave her a look. "Going to see the Wizard?"

"Oh? Is he in town?" Abby said.

"The one I'm referring to is. Just blew in on the North Wind."

"Oh, that one. Maybe, if I can find his yellow brick road."

"Well now, let me just call a Yellow cab. They know where all the yellow brick roads are." Cordelia picked up the phone and ordered a cab.

"Cordelia, you're a scamp," Abby said, laughing.

"You mean prophet, don't you? I've seen this coming for weeks now. I think it's wonderful! You're obviously so well suited to each other."

"But, Cordelia, our relationship has never reached that level."

"It already has. Only you don't know it yet."

"Is it that obvious?"

"It is to me."

"Madame Cordelia, the prophetess! And what else does the future hold, madame?"

"Hmmm—You're about to take a long trip. You'll see."

"Now, Cordelia, you know something! Tell me."

"Non, ma petite. I see it in my crystal ball."

They heard a horn blowing.

"Well, now that must be my Yellow cab to take me down that Yellow Brick Road." Abby pulled on a glove. "Farewell, prophetess. Better get your own Yellow cab soon, it's still snowing."

Abby fastened her coat, headed for the door, and picked her way through the snow-packed walkway to the cab.

"Where to, Miss?" the cab driver asked.

"Watergate Apartments," she said.

The cab driver pulled up to the marquee at the Watergate.

"Here we are, Miss." Abby reached for the door handle but suddenly the door opened, as a uniformed doorman offered his gloved hand.

"Be careful, Miss Abby. That curb slippery—step ovah heah on the carpet. The marquee'll keep y'all dry." He handed her out of the cab and onto the covered carpet.

"Thank you," said Abby as she tended to her books to keep them from falling.

"I'll carry them for ya, Miss Abby" said the doorman. He took her books, leaving the files with her.

"Thanks, you must be George?"

"Yes'm, I am. Mista Biff tole me ta look out for ya. Heah, ma'am, follow me." She followed him into the building. He asked one of the desk clerks to watch the door while he ushered Abby to the elevator and up to the top floor. From the elevator they went down a long hall. He knocked. Biff opened the door.

"Heah she is, Mr. Bifford."

Company of Spies

"Thank you, George." George took off down the hall.

They stood there speechless, just looking at each other. Words did not come. No words were needed.

Biff held out his arms and Abby threw her arms around his neck.

At last he said, "I thought I'd never get back to you."

"I was worried, I thought you'd never come." A tear rolled down her cheek.

He kissed her for the very first time—and they stood there, wrapped up in the moment, in each other's arms. He stroked her hair and kissed her cheeks, her lips.

Finally, Abby said, "It was like you'd been away forever…. I missed you so!"

"I missed you too, more than I could ever have imagined. It was as though I had left the other half of me here with you." He loosened his hold enough to look directly down into her eyes. "I love you, Abby. I confess I fought it because of the work we're doing. But I give up. I can't fight it any longer. I'm yours if you'll have me."

"Oh Biff! I've waited so long to hear you say that. I knew you were fond of me but you kept so distant. I couldn't tell how you felt. I love you too, so much."

She snuggled back against his shoulder. "I knew I cared for you but I didn't realize how much until you left." Abby suddenly pulled herself away and addressed him directly. "Don't you dare go off and leave me again!"

"Yes, ma'am!"

"Oh Biff! You rascal!" They laughed together, filled with joy, eyes brimming with love.

"Come," Biff said. "I made a pot of coffee."

"Wonderful." Abby pulled out a chair and sat down at the table. "Tell me what happened. What did you find out?"

As they drank their coffee Biff told all that had happened in great detail. Abby sat back and listened, never taking her eyes from him. When he came to the point of the Fontainebleu hotel, he pulled out an old brochure. The colorful pictures said it all.

"Unbelievable," Abby said. "That's it. That's the building I saw in my dream. And there's the fountain; only, I didn't see it. And just look at the interior; there are the marble stairs, and the decor. It's just as I saw it in my dream."

"Yes, it was just as you had described it. While the manager was calling the authorities, I slipped upstairs and found their rooms. I entered but they had left, apparently only minutes before. When I went in the suite, it was empty; all the closets, all the drawers, everything was empty. Sounds familiar, doesn't it?"

"Absolutely. Typical, I'd say."

"But it was absolutely fabulous. It was decorated in the Louis XV period. The Palladian windows were heavily draped with a beautiful brocade fabric. The furniture was all Louis XV, and was covered with some of the same brocade. The colors were soft and elegant. One could easily have felt like a king and queen if they were staying there. It was truly lovely."

"Yes, that was what I saw in my dream. Incredible, isn't it?" she mused.

"Extraordinarily so. But then, when I went in the bedroom, I couldn't believe it. On the bed lay a beautiful white satin dress carefully arranged, and on the floor of the closet lay a long dark wig, as though someone had dropped it there. It was all in your dream, Abby. You *are* amazing, my love!"

Abby smiled. "*We* are amazing, remember? I would never have known which hotel without you."

"That's true. Looks like neither of us can solve this puzzle without the other."

"Then what happened?" Abby leaned forward in anticipation.

"We thought that they had to have gone to some port to embark. The weather was too bad to fly because of the approaching blizzard. The only port nearby was Porte de Québec, so we sped there as fast as possible, but when we arrived they had just sailed on a large cargo ship, the *Marseilles*. We missed them by about 20 minutes."

"Oh no! That was *so* close." She paused in thought. "But you know, even so, it's absolutely remarkable that we were able to discern where they were. It was really a miracle."

"I agree, completely…. but then, I've come to know that being with you is like living in a miracle. There is something about you that transcends time and space. You know things others don't know. You see things others can't see. There's something magical about you. I knew it the first moment I laid eyes on you."

"You know, I think I knew it too, the first time I spied you with that ridiculous sling on your arm."

"Yes, that was the day. I'll never forget it either. I was told to look for the most beautiful girl in the room, so naturally I expected some old hag. They're always teasing, you know. But when I saw you I knew you were the girl I'd waited for."

As they sat, night was closing in. It was getting quite dark, and shadows of the skyline were reflecting on the white snow.

"Perhaps we should turn on some lights." Biff began to go from lamp to lamp.

Abby rose and looked out the window. "It's still coming down, only this time in enormous flakes. This must be the beginning of that blizzard that was predicted to come here."

Biff went to the window and looked out with her. "I think you're right. We have at least eight to ten inches of snow already. This is going to put a real stranglehold on the city." He looked at his watch. "What happened to the time. Let me check with

George to see if the cabs are still running." Biff called downstairs to the front desk.

"Lawd 'a mercy, Mister Biff, we got a blizzard coming down all over the place. Ain't no cabs or buses gonna make it through this stuff till the snow plows get through. An Lawd only knows when that's gonna be. "

"Oh dear," Abby said. "I have to call home. Miranda will have the dogs after me."

"It's not that bad, is it?"

"No, not really. But she's very protective, like a bloodhound at times."

"She wants to keep you from harm." Biff thought for a moment. "I have a solution—Cordelia has an apartment in this building. Let me call her—I know she would love to have you stay there tonight. It looks like we're snowed in all over the city. So no one is going anywhere. Then you can call your mother." Biff tracked Cordelia down at the office number.

"Well now, if it isn't Mr. Wizard. I heard you just blew in on the North Wind."

"Cordelia, what *are* you talking about?"

"Why don't you ask Mrs. Wizard. I called a Yellow cab to take her down your yellow brick road."

"I'm beginning to get your drift." He laughed.

"I'll be happy to have Mrs. Wizard stay in my apartment. We're snowed in over here too. I may not even get back tonight. Tell George to give her my key."

"Thank you for that, Cordelia. You answered my question before I even asked. Incidentally, it's still Miss Wizard, but I'm working on it."

"Good. Any magic spells floating around?"

"We're completely spellbound over here."

"Wonderful! My crystal ball never fails." Cordelia sighed. "Bye, Mr. Wizard. Give my regards to Miss Wizard."

Biff hung up the phone. He related the gist of the conversation to Abby. She shook her head in amusement.

"Cordelia, the prophetess." Biff said. "Madame Cordelia and her crystal ball."

"I suppose I'd better call Miranda." Abby dialed the number. No answer. She dialed the main switchboard. There was a message from her mother. Abby left a message and hung up. "Believe it or not she's snowed in at the captain's house. I left a message and my number here for her if she gets worried. My mother would have a fit if she knew I was snowed in with a handsome, wonderful, adorable man like you."

"Flattery will get you everywhere." He hugged her, eyes twinkling. "And as a reward I may even feed you. Hungry?"

"Ravenous."

Biff pulled two steaks out of the freezer and some salad greens out of the hydrator. "Can you wait for the potatoes to bake, or shall we do with this?"

Abby handed him a can of cut corn. "This will be faster. I'll do the salad. Gee, I didn't know you could cook, too."

"The fate of a perennial bachelor." Biff handed her an apron. "I dine out for the most part, so don't get any ideas."

Laughing, they hurriedly put their dinner together—chatting and chuckling all the way through—delicious, simply because they were together. Biff put some soft music on the record player and pulled out a bottle of wine while Abby made a pot of coffee. It felt right, comfortable.

After dinner, they took coffee to the living room. Through the tall windows, they could see the lights of the city sparkling on the shimmering snow—a picture of a winter wonderland.

The strains of "White Christmas" came over the player. Abby leaned against him as he put his arm around her.

"We are so lucky to be here together," she said. "I can't help thinking of all those brave men and women overseas who can't get home for Christmas. Some are so cold and wet and hungry and filled with fear. There are bloody battles going on, some of them will be wounded and maimed, and some will never get home at all. I pray for them and their families that somehow God will comfort them in their hours of loneliness and need, and that He will bring them back safely to their loved ones."

"Amen to that!" Biff looked at her lovingly. "You are so dear to me. You will never know how long I have longed for someone like you. It's as if God has sent me a wonderful gift because I waited for Him to make me sure. And I am sure, Abby. Sure that we were meant for each other. Sure that I want you to marry me, so that we can spend a lifetime together."

"Oh Biff, I think I'm going to cry."

"It's not that bad, is it?" Biff looked at her, his eyes smiling with mischief.

"Now you stop that! Of course I'll marry you. I wouldn't dream of letting you get out of my sight, Russell Bifford! Certainly not after that beautiful proposal. Give me your handkerchief."

"Now blow your nose like a good little girl and let me wipe those tears away."

"They're just tears of joy." Abby blew her nose obediently. "I guess this means we're engaged."

"That's what it means. I love you, Abby. We'll have a great life together."

The phone began to ring. Biff reached for it.

"Mr. Biff, Miss Cordelia's trying to reach you. I told her you was in your apartment but she asked me to tell you to call headquarters. And I'm on my way up to give you her key."

"Thanks, George. I'll tend to it right away." He turned to Abby. "I have to call headquarters, they must have gotten my messages. I'll only be a moment." Biff went to his secure phone in the bedroom. George brought Abby the key to Cordelia's apartment and then Biff returned from his call.

"Any news?" Abby sat down on the couch.

"Yes, we're to meet with the Old Man tomorrow. I thought he was in London but apparently he's just returned. He knows that we tracked them down but that we missed them. It means that either he will have someone else try to apprehend them when they reach land, or he will send us."

"So if they left from Porte de Québec, where are they headed?"

"They're scheduled to join a convoy of ships. They'll go the great circle route, which is the shortest distance to Europe."

"Still, sounds like a long trip." Abby frowned, thoughtfully.

"Yes, those ships only travel at about 8 to 10 knots, and joining the convoy will slow them down considerably. Too, the weather this time of year can be treacherous and with this blizzard, who knows. They can never know when they'll run into a German submarine or an air attack. It's a tricky trip "

"Sounds dangerous."

"Yes it could be. It usually *is* dangerous these days on the open seas. But they might luck out."

"So when and where are they due to arrive?" She looked at him quizzically.

"Originally it was Marseilles, France, but that was suddenly changed." Biff thought for a moment. "That would have suited

Jana perfectly, to debark in Vichy. Now he has a *big* problem—landing in England!"

"Lucky for us his destination *is* England instead," said Abby. "Won't that make it easier for us?"

"Indeed it will. They're now due in Liverpool in about eleven to thirteen days, if they're lucky." Biff wrote down some figures on his note pad.

"Eleven to thirteen days! But that would only give us—maybe nine or ten days to get there before they debark. And we have to set up for this mission. But with so many ships waiting to unload, mightn't it take longer?"

"That's true. The only way we could make it is if we fly. And that's going to depend on the weather and whether we can hitch a ride out or not. However covert ops pay very little attention to the weather. If we need to go, we'll go."

Abby thought for a few moments. "So what do we do now?"

"That's the problem at hand. Do we try to apprehend them at landing, or do we wait and try to track them down afterward."

"What does the Old Man think?"

"We'll see him in the morning. Then we'll know what we can plan on."

"So there's really no time for us at all, is there?" Abby looked wistfully aside.

"We'll stretch the time. As long as we're together, that's the important thing."

Biff went to the record player. The strains of Frank Sinatra singing "That Old Black Magic" began to sound through the room.

"I feel like I'm in a whirlwind," Abby said, laughing.

"So do I. I want to shout it from the rooftops: 'I love Abby and Abby loves me.'"

"Me too! 'I love Biff and he loves me!'" She whirled around in a gleeful gesture.

"Shall we dance?" Biff reached for her hand.

Abby began to sing, "That old black magic has me in its spell—that old black magic that I know so well." Biff took her in his arms and they danced around the large room. They melted into the music, lost in the wonder of the moment.

The world, the war, and time vanished and they were alone together.

They were in love. And for a moment, the world stood still.

It was 7 AM. Abby called Biff's apartment. No answer. She drank a small glass of orange juice and was finishing dressing when the phone rang. It was Cordelia.

"Good morning, Miss Wizard, hope you slept well."

"Cordelia, I can't thank you enough for letting me stay here last night."

"You're more than welcome."

"Are the roads clear yet?" asked Abby. "You must have gotten stuck."

"True, but we've managed, and now the snowplows are working overtime. I'm leaving to come home and dress in a few minutes. In the meanwhile, I have a message for you."

"From your crystal ball, madame?"

"No not exactly. It's from Mr. Wizard himself. He says you two are to meet with the Old Man at 9 o'clock. He wants you to wait there, he's coming to pick you up shortly."

"So, he's at the office. I should have known. He didn't answer his phone this morning."

Dr. Margaret S. Emanuelson

"Oh yes, he was here early. And he's walking about 10 feet off the floor. I'll bet you're engaged."

"Could be. But it's probably better not to tell anyone right now."

Cordelia laughed, a big guffaw. "You won't have to, if your behavior is anything like Mr. Wizard's. When two people begin to walk ten feet off the floor everyone knows."

Suddenly Abby felt a rude awakening. "Cordelia, I've just realized. Here we are engaged to be married and I still don't know anything about Biff."

Cordelia laughed. "You mean he's never told you? Typical Biff. Well, my dear, you're in for the surprise of your life. Russell Bifford is the catch of the century. I'll try to remember to bring you his vita. See you!" She hung up.

Abby found coffee in Cordelia's kitchen cabinet and made a pot. As it brewed, the aroma filled the air, delectably. She arranged cups and saucers, cream and sugar on the table and waited.

Soon Cordelia swept in, dripping with melting snow and her usual panache. "Coffee? Smells wonderful! How thoughtful of you, Miss Wizard." She looked at Abby. "Oh yes, it's there! That ten feet off the floor look."

Abby hugged her. "Oh Cordelia, I'm so happy. Biff is so wonderful!"

"You don't know the half of it. I grabbed a copy of his vita on the way out. Wait till you read it." Cordelia picked up her coffee and headed toward the bedroom. "I'm off to the shower. Have to get back to the office."

Abby picked up the cup to finish her coffee as the phone began to ring.

"Good morning, darling. Bring your things down the hall to my place, there's something here waiting for you."

"Oh, Biff! You're always full of surprises. I'll be right there." Her excitement mounted as she gathered her belongings; she could hardly wait to see him. Walking to the shower door, she called out, "Cordelia, thank you for everything. I'm off to see the Wizard."

Cordelia stuck her head around the shower curtain. "O.K., ma petite, don't forget that vita. It's on my bed." Her voice trailed off as the shower curtain fell back into place.

Abby hurried down the long hall to Biff's apartment. Biff met her at the door, kissed her, and took her by the hand. "Come, I have something to show you." He led her to the sofa and sat her down. Out of his pocket he pulled out a small black velvet box.

"This was my mother's, given to her by my grandmother, and given to her by her mother. My mother gave it to me several years ago. I remember her every word. She said: 'this is a special ring. It has been in our family for at least two centuries. My wish would be that the girl you marry would wear it proudly as a token of your love and the full support and affection of your family—past and present.'"

Biff opened the small box. Abby gasped. Perched on black velvet was the largest diamond she had ever seen. It was at least 12 karats, emerald cut, flanked by two large emeralds and smaller diamonds on either side.

She looked at Biff in disbelief. "For me?"

"Yes, for you. Just for you."

"I don't know what to say." Her heart jumped. "It's exquisite! It's absolutely the most beautiful thing I've ever seen."

"Yes, isn't it? I had always admired it. My mother took it out of her collection early to be sure that I would know her wishes. But she also said that if for some reason the girl I chose wanted something else, she could choose from the others."

"Something else? I would have to be out of my mind. Oh Biff, I feel like a princess. Let's see if it fits." She held out her right hand.

Biff looked at her and laughed. "It's the left-hand, sweetheart."

Abby obediently presented her left-hand.

"Will you marry me, Abby?"

"Oh Biff, you know I will. I love you."

"Then this makes it official." Biff slipped the ring on her finger. It was a perfect fit. "See there—it belonged to you all along."

Abby flung her arms around his neck. He held her close and kissed her.

"The future Mrs. Bifford. Doesn't that sound absolutely wonderful? But I'm almost afraid to wear it. It must be worth a fortune."

"Don't worry, it's insured by Lloyds of London."

"But I would die if I lost it."

"I'd just buy you another or you could choose one from my mother's collection."

"I know! I'll just never take it off." Her hand at arm's length, she admired her ring. "I would never have believed I could be this happy!"

Biff went in the study and came back with another briefcase. "Here, little one, you need this for all your books and papers."

"Thank you, darling." Abby looked at the case. It was obviously handmade of fine leather. Under the handle it was inscribed with a number of initials and a coat of arms. "Goodness, Biff, don't you think it's time you told me something about yourself? I said something to Cordelia and she brought me your vita, but I haven't had a chance to read it yet."

Biff laughed. "Read it later, we have to go. I'll tell you whatever you want to know later."

"Yes, your Majesty!" Abby curtsied in playful deference.

Biff gave her a curious look, and smiled. "Come, darling. We have very little time to get to Headquarters. 109 is expecting us."

"109? Who's that?"

"Actually 109 is the office number of the Old Man. We refer to him either way. Come. We don't want to keep the Old Man waiting."

Chapter 26

The ship had sailed down the St. Lawrence River at a good clip. The river was busier than usual, even at this time of year, because of the escalation of the war effort. The need for supplies was imminent if the war was to be successful on both sides of the continent.

The Atlantic was bitter, cold, and damp with winter in full sway. Once they had cleared the mouth of the river the winds were brisker and more noticeable on the open sea. It would take a day or so to reach the convoy forming in its designated spot. Perhaps they would meet with some clearing and sunshine. It would certainly be welcome. Spirits could get gloomy at sea in cold and dismal weather.

Suzanne had found the accommodations on board surprisingly pleasant, even more than adequate. Apparently, in peacetime, it was not at all unusual for a few travelers to book passage on these cargo ships. It was pleasant, afforded more privacy, the food was excellent, and the small staff was friendly and accommodating.

There were few passengers these days. Only those who were on official business were allowed to travel back and forth across the Atlantic. It was impossible for other types of travelers to obtain a passport or visas in or out of either country.

Now, during wartime, the captain was delighted to assist one of his distinguished countrymen and his wife in their return to France. He knew better than to ask many questions of them, knowing a diplomat's work was secret. Too, he felt this was an additional way he could assist in bringing the war to a more rapid close. They made a handsome couple. He with his dark mustache and well-trimmed beard, and she with her fair, fine beauty. But they had kept mostly to their cabin except at the end of the day during late twilight when sometimes they would walk the deck together.

The weather had been cold and cloudy for the past two or three days. Unfortunately, the forecasts warned of a storm on its way. That could mean problems when they joined the convoy. It would mean spreading out to prevent colliding, and they would be in constant danger not only from the storm but from attack. German U-boats were plentiful in the Atlantic and always on the prowl. There was nothing a wolfpack liked better than a whack at nice fat convoy.

But perhaps the storm would pass them by. The North Atlantic was hectic enough in winter, without the onslaught of a horrific storm.

Jacques had been stunned at his reaction to the incident at the hotel. More than that, he was horrified. He had always been in control of his emotions. His mind was keen and quick and he had never before had an experience that disabled his ability to take hold of the situation immediately. But this one had completely overwhelmed him.

Dr. Margaret S. Emanuelson

When he had walked into the room that evening, it was not Suzanne he saw in her beautiful white satin dress—it was his mother in all her glory, standing there. And then, from the past, he heard those suffocating words—"Das ist verboten." And the entire incident came back to him. He had never realized how profound or deep his feelings had been buried, pushed back, hidden—even from himself.

It was 1916. He was 10 years old again. His mother in all her ethereal beauty, was dressed in a long white satin gown. A diamond tiara held back her long pale golden hair, done up for a festive evening. She stood there beside his bed, eyes aglow with tenderness. She leaned down and her lips brushed his cheek.

"Guten abendt, liebchen, gut nacht." She patted his head with a white gloved hand, and rose to give that same gloved hand to his father. His father stood in all his grandeur, his dress uniform perfectly tailored. He recalled having played with the ribbon across his chest, and the colorful medals as he cuddled in his father's lap, listening to the stories he told in that rich baritone voice—of bravery and chivalry in past battles fought, exciting a little boy's fantasy.

He felt safe as they stood looking down at him. And then they left his room. He could envision them as they wafted down the marble stairs.

But then the moment vanished, shattering the serene aristocratic grandeur that was rightfully his inheritance. Shattering a little boy's security, his trust, and turning it to sheer panic.

He heard the excruciating noise of the front door crashing in, the yelling of the soldiers as they burst into the house. He rushed to his door and peered out. He saw astonishment on his mother's stricken face as the soldier grabbed her around the waist and dragged her away. He watched as his father tried to protect her while the soldiers struck him from behind and dragged him off, limp.

His nurse enfolded him in her arms, and pulled him away from his open door. From his window, they could see down below, hear the screams, hear the explosion of the bullets, the crumpled bodies, the blood flowing over the beautiful white dress. He had cried out at the sight. But he heard again the frightened admonition of his nurse, "Shuh! Ruhig!" But he kept screaming.

Suddenly, a large hand covered his mouth. He heard a deep voice from the courtyard below demand: "Nein! Nein! Das ist verboten."

Flames began to engulf the house, everything that he held dear—and the smoke began to seep up, up, blinding their hurried escape, down the back hidden staircase, across the gardens, past the fountains, the clipped shrubbery, and into the woods, as they fled. He, Nurse Gisela and Carl, the old butler, as they ran to safety.

Now, on the ship, he was still shaken. He had not counted on this. He was used to being in constant danger, and that had never bothered him before. But this was different. Suppose he had another panic attack in the middle of a critical moment—would he be able to handle it?

It had taken him a while to put the pieces together, but now he knew why he had been immediately so deeply attracted to Suzanne. She was the epitome of his mother all over again; he knew from that moment what a terrible dilemma he was in. He had fallen hard for her and it was completely mutual. But he had had to deceive her in order to keep her.

He had had to arrange her "murder" so that she could be declared dead. He had done it to protect her not only from the U.S. Military Intelligence, to keep them from following her, but most of all, he had had to protect her from Senator Downs's determination to assassinate her. She knew too much about him.

But what Senator Downs did not know was that he, himself, had now become expendable. He could expose their whole operation. He had made a fatal mistake when he went after Suzanne's lovely head. He didn't know with whom he was dealing.

Jana knew he was walking a tightrope. Suppose she found out that she was officially declared dead? He was sure he could explain that to her. But if Senator Downs found out that she was still alive, he would want to know why and become suspicious. He might even try to take matters into his own hands. He would surely begin to rattle more bones with his contact, Louis. Not only was he a despicable traitor to his own country, but he had become a pest and a liability. Besides, he had already served his purpose, as far as the Third Reich was concerned.

Jana sighed. *I suppose it's unavoidable. Something "appropriate" may have to be arranged for Senator Downs unless he settles down.* He hated strong measures but this was war, and the enemy would do the same thing if it were deemed necessary.

Yes, he had done it all to protect her. She was the answer to his emptiness, his years of discipline and denial. For the very first time in his life he had allowed himself to fall in love. He knew the day of reckoning would dawn. He knew the day would come when she would realize he was a German, not a French spy. But he hoped the war would be over by then and all would be forgiven.

So far the war was going well. Germany would be victorious. At some point, he and his fellow aristocrats would dispose of that maniac Hitler, who would have served his purpose by then. And with the war's end, he would reclaim his rightful titled place in society; he would marry her and take her home to his beautiful Schloss. They would restore it completely and live there happily, as his parents had done.

He had been able to teach her many of the ropes of espionage—how to be an effective counterspy. Like himself, she was an accomplished linguist. She was intelligent, quick to learn. She would not only support him and comfort him in his endeavors, but she would be an invaluable asset.

He had been lonely most of his life until he met her. All he had done to keep her with him had been worth it. And he would continue to protect her from harm. If it ever became obvious that he could no longer do so—

Suzanne had resolved most of her fears over the past few days. She had listened as Jacques had explained that early, repressed incident in his childhood. He had related it to her exactly as it had occurred. Carl and Gisela had told him that his parents were killed in the Great War. But the details of that night of horror had disappeared from his conscious memory. Through the years he had asked many questions of them. But the old butler and his childhood nurse had tried to spare him details of the bloody, terrifying, fiery holocaust that surrounded the incident.

At first, whenever they got too close to the truth, he would begin to panic. And later his nightmares were too frequent and horrifying for him and they had backed off. Time to explain it all later. But the time never came. They had loved him, comforted him, protected him, and raised him.

They had crept back to the chateau after the fire had burned itself out. Because of the stone and marble, the destruction was minimal. They had emptied the hidden safe of the deeds, of the money, the valuables. They would keep these things safe for him. They would survive. And when the war was over they would see to it that he was educated properly as befitted his station, and that his heritage was protected with the deeds and credentials they had rescued. They had done it to the extent that they could manage it. They had done so with the guidance and help of his godfather, Prinz Hollenhauffen, an influential aristocrat of the Old Order.

They had survived the Great War in one of the small cottages on the estate. And when the war was over, in 1919, they had returned to the chateau and tried to restore as much of it as they could, within reason. But the old grandeur was gone. And their lives could never be again quite what they once were.

He loved them both. Though they had been his family's servants, they had been faithful and he knew he owed his survival to them and his godfather. When he had reached manhood, he had seen to it that their fortunes were substantial and legally executed. And he had deeded two of the cottages and a small part of the land on the estate legally to them. They were his closest family—all that he had left, aside from his godfather.

Suzanne understood how an early trauma of that magnitude might be completely repressed. She understood how terrifying it could be. It had happened to her when she witnessed the plane crash of her parents. Aunt Kippy had found a good psychologist for her, who had helped her work through her panic episodes.

If anything, his explanation made her love him more. It simply gave them one more thing in common. Ironically, they each had suffered the tragic loss of their parents at the age of 10. The shock of the loss and the feelings of abandonment were devastating for child of that age; but to witness the actual devastating deaths of the two people upon whom one totally depended was overwhelming.

She now understood his adoration of his lost mother, and how much she resembled her. She understood how the sight of her in that magnificent white satin gown had suddenly brought the whole episode back to his memory.

She understood how he had relived the whole episode over again. She understood the dissociation with the present, the blurring of his sight, the iron fist gripping his heart, the galloping heartbeat, the compulsion to flee, the panic. Even the repetition of the words "Das ist verboten," when he heard the captain's brutal command to his mother, and Carl's large hands had covered his mouth, nearly suffocating him to keep him from screaming. She understood the panic perfectly. How a seemingly unrelated stimulus could bring an entire traumatic experience back again in full force. A similar response had happened to her.

He had never meant to hurt her. She had done nothing wrong. It was simply a malevolent old demon raring its ugly head from out of his past.

Once they were aboard ship, Jacques had told her much about his background. His mother and father were aristocrats, royal blood flowed in their veins, being part of the aristocracy of Europe. For centuries before and during World War I, their family had been high up in nobility, government, diplomacy, and society, but the enemy had ruined all that. The enemy had robbed them of their lives, their status, and some—their estates. The enemy had indeed robbed *him* of his parents, his inheritance, his heritage, and his future. The enemy had ruined his life. And he hated them with a passion beyond comprehension.

Suzanne understood. He had good reason to hate them. Jacques had told her everything exactly the way it was, except for the fact that his arch-enemies were not the Germans.

She had suspected that Jacques D'Arcy was an alias, and that they would use several before this mission was over. There was only one thing that she continued to question. Why in the throes of panic would he instinctively speak in German instead of French? Of course, they *had* been speaking and thinking in German at the time. But still, it was curious. Nevertheless, she would let it go for now. They loved each other—and she would trust him.

Suzanne, though her suspicions had been aroused, was not prepared to relinquish this man whom she loved so completely. She would give him the benefit of the doubt. He would explain away her questions, as he always had.

Chapter 27

Abby was pensive in the cab on the way to headquarters. "You know, I was just thinking of what you found in their suite at the Fontainebleu. In my dream the dress was red and the wig was pale blonde. So the symbolism has to mean something."

"Yes, I've thought of that too." He took her hand in his. "What do you associate with the red dress?"

"Well, I suppose it could be a number of things. On the bright side, maybe joy, celebration, festivity. But on the negative side—danger, blood, terror. Maybe it's a combination of all of those things. When I first had the dream, I didn't know that it was about Suzanne, because I didn't know that she was missing. But when I found out upon my return to Washington that she was AWOL, the red of the dress told me she was in danger."

"Yes, that was my thought when you first told me."

Abby looked away, pondering the idea. "But the white dress is real. It would seem to me to be a symbol of formality, elegance, purity, good. So, you have a synthesis of the pure, the good and the elegant being in danger from a threatening source—the enemy of the pure and the good."

"Yes, that makes sense. And who, then, would the enemy be?"

"Why whoever is against the pure and the good. We would say Hitler's regime, wouldn't we? But it *could* be more personal to a 'Jana'. It could be something else, couldn't it?"

"Yes, it might very well be." He nodded in agreement. "And what about the dark wig?"

"The only thing that makes sense to me is that he's teaching her to disguise herself. He has to be skilled in the art of makeup and disguise. I don't see how the wig has any other significance. But I get the feeling that the dress is a key—perhaps to something very personal to him, and that if we knew the significance of the white dress, we might better be able to understand him, track him down, psyche him out."

"I get the same feeling—perhaps something in his history, his past." Biff paused in thought. "My other question is—why did they leave them behind? Everything in the suite had been completely cleared out except the dress and the wig."

"That *is* strange, isn't it Maybe it's because they left in a big hurry and they were upset about something. They might have missed the wig because it had been dropped on the floor of the closet. But if I know Suzanne, she would *never* leave a beautiful dress like that behind—unless there was something wrong with it. If only we had the dress—I think it would tell us many things."

Biff began to chuckle.

"You didn't."

"Oh yes I did!"

"Biff, you rascal, why didn't you tell me yesterday?"

"If you recall, darling, yesterday we were quite occupied with other things. I think I could probably be forgiven for letting the dress slip my mind."

Abby laughed. "To tell you the truth the only thing I remember about yesterday is you. Everything else is a blur. It's as though my life really started yesterday from the moment you told me you loved me. And now that's the only thing in this world that's really important. Everything else will just have to take second place."

"I wish it could," he said wistfully, "but for now I think we're stuck with a war and a master spy we're trying to find."

"Of course, you're right. But in my heart, you'll always come first from now on, no matter what."

"That's true for both of us." Biff smiled and reached over to brush an ink smudge off her cheek.

"Looks like we're here." Biff got out of the cab and reached a hand in for Abby. "Careful. It's icy."

They held on to each other as they climbed the stone stairs to the main building. There were patches of ice here and there. Washington was obviously in a state of flux; the snow had finally stopped but it would take quite a few days, depending on the temperatures, for the city to thaw out and return to normal. Not that anything was ever "normal" in Washington.

They produced their badges for the guard, even though he knew them, reported in to the receptionist, and headed for 109, the Old Man's office.

"Ah, there you are. And on time too. Seems everyone else is running late today because of the weather." The Old Man rose from his chair to greet them. "Some are still snowbound and can't get in at all. Our secure phone lines are even busier these days. So the show goes on anyway."

"The war stops for no one, unfortunately." Biff helped Abby off with her coat and pulled up a chair for her.

The Old Man resumed his chair with an amused look at them. "Very true. But it doesn't seem to have deterred a certain young couple I know from becoming engaged. Congratulations, Biff. You are one *fortunate* man." Biff smiled, leaned over the desk, and shook the Old Man's offered hand. "And you, young lady, I hope you realize what you've captured."

Abby laughed. "You mean the only rare species left in captivity?"

"Something like that. But I knew the moment I first saw you two together that it was just a matter of time, even for a rare species."

"Truth is, I still don't know exactly what *kind* of rare species, but it doesn't matter. He's all I'll ever want."

"So, Biff, you haven't told her? Typical Biff!" The Old Man looked straight at him.

"I will. I intend to. There just hasn't been time. All this has happened so fast. And, you know, we don't have a lot of time if we're going to track down these two operatives. Believe me, if I could take Abby off to some paradise somewhere I'd do it in a second, but we both know that will just have to wait." The Old man eyed them, amusement in his eyes.

"Well, how does a quick trip to England sound? It might not be paradise but where you'd be going it's close to it. I understand Cameron and Robert are at their country estate, and there are …others there you'd like to see, Biff."

"Sounds wonderful to me," Abby said, in delighted surprise.

"Capital idea!" Biff leaned forward. "How would that work out logistically?"

"Well, let's see. Our culprits are due to arrive at some port in England around the 30th or later. They left Quebec the 18th, according to your report, Biff. There's no way in a convoy they could possibly arrive in ten days. Ten days would be a miracle in itself. The convoy is going to slow them down and a bad storm is predicted—in fact the blizzard that just left here is traveling east and it has probably already hit them. That could slow them up another two or three days. So, I would project that we have till the 29th at the absolute least and probably more like the 30th or 31st before they dock—11 to 13 days or more."

"How will we know where they'll dock?" Abby asked.

"We can find that out from the Navy Department," he answered.

Biff was already thinking of the possibilities. "The port captain at Porte de Québec said they were due to arrive in Liverpool."

The Old Man continued. "Yes, but the convoy will have to break up at a certain point so that these ships will be able to go to their separate ports to unload. We're talking about 75 to 100 ships. If there's a storm, or an enemy attack, the Commodore of the convoy not only has to see to it that they move apart for safety during a storm, but if some of the ships are lost in an enemy attack, he may have to reassign some of the ships' dockings."

"Yes, of course. That *could* happen." Biff thought for a moment. "This is the 20th of December. Do you think—?"

"Yes, I certainly do think. If we can fly you two out today, you would be there the 22nd, spend Christmas with your families, have time to coordinate this caper, and still be on time in Liverpool or wherever they're scheduled to dock to apprehend these culprits when they arrive." He stood up and walked to the edge of his desk.

"Oh!" Abby rose, threw her arms around his neck and gave the Old Man a big hug. "You *do* care about us, don't you?"

Biff laughed and shook his head. "What a woman. What a woman." Only Abby could get away with a gesture like that. She had just given the top brass of all the Intelligence for the entire wartime United States a spontaneous unexpected hug.

The Old Man laughed and hugged her back.

"Abby, before I know it, you'll have me doing a jig at your wedding. I'm not so sure you couldn't persuade Adolph Hitler, himself, to surrender. Now, let me contact our flight resources and see how soon we can get you two off. In the meanwhile, throw some clothing together, you'll have to travel light. We'll ship your luggage over as soon as possible but it won't arrive soon. And remember this is TOP SECRET."

They looked at each other. There was no need for words, no containing their joy. They half walked, half ran out of the office down the hall and down the stone steps to a car waiting for them.

The Old Man shook his head and smiled as he picked up the phone to schedule their flight.

"What do we do first?" Abby said, as the driver pulled away from the curb at headquarters. "I don't know what to pack. What will we need in England at this time of year?"

"Something warm. After all it *is* December. Your three-piece suits are great for this time of year. I'll see to it that we have fleece-lined parkas for the flight. It could be freezing up there at 20- to 30,000 ft."

"Thanks, darling. That's very thoughtful of you. We hardly want to arrive frozen."

"Absolutely not. Those parkas are worn by the flyboys when they're on heavy winter flying duty, otherwise they *would* freeze. Incidentally, Abby, you might try to take at least one or two formal gowns. It's Christmas, you know, and your family and mine will want to celebrate."

"Your family is in England?" she asked, surprised.

"Yes, and they're going to love you, and you'll love them. I'll see to it that they know we're coming. I can send a coded message to Robert. He and Cameron have been close friends of my family for eons. They'll alert them."

"So, now I find out that everyone knows everyone else. And I suppose you've known Robert since you were a toddler."

"True. I didn't know at first that he had a hand in our meeting one another. But I thank God he did." He smiled down at her, lifted the hand he'd been holding and kissed it.

"I wondered what magical stroke of fate threw us together. Now I'm beginning to see—it was all a conspiracy. Well, I don't care. I've never been so happy in all my life." Abby snuggled up against his shoulder. "And I'm about to find out who my fiancé actually is, not that it matters. I would love you if you were the garbage man."

"Egad! Surely you're not saying you'll expect me to take out the garbage?" He gave her a mischievous glance.

"Oh Biff, you're always spoofing." She sat up, suddenly alert. "You know, I really can't seem to get my mind around this. Your family lives in England and I'm going to meet them. How absolutely wonderful. Miracles do happen, don't they?"

"They happen wherever you are, my love."

The cab drove on through the morning traffic. "Where are we going?" Abby said absently, settling back in his arm. "Where is the driver taking us?"

"To your office first. You need to collect your things."

"Of course, and I couldn't possibly leave without seeing Cordelia."

"Of course not. But you do realize, we really have very little time to talk or do anything else. You have to finish packing, say goodbye to your mother, call your father and your grandmother. You can tell them you're shipping out soon, but you can't tell them where you're going or how you're going to get there."

"I know. Luckily, I called them last night. It was very easy because, actually, I don't know myself exactly where I'm going or how I'm going to get there. Miranda already knows I'm on alert, so she's really been expecting it. She seems resigned to the fact at this point." She sighed. "I'm so glad she has the Captain now. He's a lovely man and seems extremely interested in her. That will make it easier." Suddenly she sat straight up, with a look of distress. "Oh dear. She hasn't even met you yet. Neither has my father."

Not completely ignorant of Abby's problems with her mother, he sought a line of caution. "Perhaps we should wait for that until we have more time, don't you think?"

"Yes, I think you're right. But I really can't tell her that we're engaged. My leaving will be enough of a shock At least she knows about you. I've told her you were my boss."

Biff began to chuckle. "Amazing. I wonder if you don't have that backwards."

"Now you stop that!" Abby smiled at him. "Actually, I'm already pretty well packed. My trunk is ready to close and I have two bags that are already half packed. How many bags can I take on the plane?"

"I'll let you know as soon as I hear. We should know within the hour. Have you finished your shots?"

"All but the last typhoid."

"Then we'll get that done in England."

Abby's emotions welled up to the surface and she let them go. "Oh Biff! Christmas in England with you and your family. I'm so happy I could cry."

"Sorry, sweetheart, you don't have time right now. Come here." Biff hugged her and kissed her soundly. She settled into the curve of his arm.

"Where did you say the driver's taking us?"

"To your office." Biff said, amused.

"Oh. It's so wonderful to be helpless."

Biff chuckled. "Helpless? Is that what this is? Helpless like Wonder Woman." The cab pulled up to the curb. "Here we are."

Cordelia spied them as they walked in the door. "Well, I declare. If it isn't the Wizards!"

"Cordelia, bless you. Your prediction came true." Abby held out her left hand, showing off her magnificent ring.

"Heavens, Miss Wizard, all the girls in the office will be pea green with envy. Biff, you lucky guy. I knew from the first day what was coming. And I think it's wonderful."

Abby gave Cordelia an affectionate hug. "Thanks, Cordelia, I don't know what I would have done without you here. I hate to leave you, but we're running out of time. Let me run up to get my things. I'll be back in a moment."

Cordelia turned to Biff. "I know what's up. You know I love you both. You'll have a wonderful life together." She hugged him affectionately. "I'm so happy for you."

"I know you are," Biff said, returning her hug. "And we're both going to miss you terribly."

Abby came flying down the steps with a few items in her arms. "Cordelia, could you see that my luggage is shipped without anyone knowing where?"

"Sure. We'll pick it up but we won't disclose its destination to anyone. I'm to tell you that your plane leaves at noon today. A car will pick you up at 11:00 to take you to the airport. The weather reports are a little fuzzy but we'll know later whether it's safe to take off. Safe or not, Special Ops go anyway. Abby, you're allowed to take two bags only. Your other things will be shipped immediately but don't expect them to arrive anytime soon. We'll send everything to your Uncle Robert in England."

Choking back the tears, they embraced one another.

"Now, better hurry. You don't have much time." She looked at them fondly. "Bon Voyage. Viva the Wizards!"

Cordelia wiped a tear from her eye. She hadn't had the heart to tell them of the "missing in action" telegram she had received just that morning.

An official car was at the apartment building promptly at 11:00 AM. Miranda answered the door to find a young ensign, prepared to carry the luggage down to the lobby. She was resigned to Abby's departure. They had already discussed all that would ordinarily pass between a mother and daughter; embraced each other and declared their love. Miranda had asked no questions because she knew that Abby really didn't know any details. She had known for two weeks that her daughter was on final alert and could go at any moment. She also knew that it would be to some unknown port, by some unknown means of transportation, and to some unknown place.

Miranda also knew the dangers. Reports were coming into G2 every day of capture, torture, death, and destruction. But though she knew nothing of Abby's actual assignment, in a way she admired her daughter's courage, her willingness to risk all for her country. All she could do now was pray for her protection and safe return.

Abby had called her father and her grandmother the night before and told them she was shipping out soon, which was all she could say except to wish them a Merry Christmas and that she would miss them both terribly. Her father had ended their conversation with his familiar phrase she remembered so well throughout her childhood.

"I love you, Abby. Be a good little soldier!"

Chapter 28

The car stopped at the Watergate Apartments, collected Biff, and they were on their way. They arrived at a small airport on the Virginia side of Washington, just shy of noon. A small private plane was waiting for them.

Abby looked impishly at Biff, "Surely we're not going to England in *that*!"

"No." Biff smiled. "Apparently we're going to meet a transatlantic flight somewhere. Probably north of here. OSS has all sorts of means of getting almost anywhere."

"And what do the weather reports say?"

"Cloudy in the States and turbulent to the east. I understand that storm is hitting the convoy now but I hope we'll fly over or around it. Might be a little bumpy for a while. With a bit of luck, it should clear once we're beyond it."

"Are you two ready to go? Let's load your luggage and we're off." An aviation pilot, rank of chief petty officer, took their bags and helped Abby onto the plane. It could seat seven relatively comfortably. APs were enlisted personnel who performed all sorts of flight tasks. He was the pilot and would fly the small plane back to base after they had reached the other flight.

Dr. Margaret S. Emanuelson

A young woman in uniform was aboard. A badge on her arm spelled out WASP. Abby had heard about the WASPs. These were women who were taking up the slack in the shortage of male pilots, releasing them to fly combat duty. They were ferrying all sorts of planes to England, Africa, and other destinations as they came off the assembly lines, or other planes as they were needed in a variety of other strategic areas.

Begun by Jacqueline Cochran, and Nancy Love, two of the most famous early women flyers, the WASPs were providing a vital service to the war effort, while other women worked in factories as mechanics, riveters, and so forth to build and assemble all sorts of ships and transports, including planes. In at least one airplane factory alone, one B-24 bomber was being assembled and released every hour, an unimaginable accomplishment.

It took pilots to fly these planes to the European or Pacific Theaters of War, and the WASPs were there to see that they were promptly delivered. There were planes of all kinds, bombers, transports, fighters, and sometimes personnel, as well, being ferried. The WASPs picked up the planes and flew them to their destinations to provide, replace, and refurbish the much-needed supply overseas.

In the 20 years since World War I the airlines industry had been growing slowly, but it was World War II that realized its importance in a developing world. Now, aeronautical engineers and others were concentrating on developing more efficient and faster fighters, cargo planes, bombers, helicopters, passenger planes and other means of transit aimed at providing the means to win the war. The DC-3 became the major boon to ferrying personnel, both civilian and military.

Thousands of ships were being produced at incredible speeds. In one shipyard alone, a 550-foot Liberty ship was being built and completed in *one* day. The number of ships being built was staggering, almost beyond human imagination. Newer and more efficient weaponry was also being developed. Rocketry, napalm bombs, weapons of all kinds and their means of delivery was changing the way wars were fought.

And secretly, one weapon was being developed that would change the future face of the entire world. The atom bomb.

The nation was showing the kind of stuff of which she was made. The entire population was filled with the 'Spirit of America.' The pride of country, the patriotic loyalty of an entire nation was coming forth to support its brave men and the few women who were on the front line.

And America's women stepped up to the forefront to fill in the gap. In the factories, the shipyards, the supply depots, the administrative offices of the Army, Navy, and Marines, the women of America took up the arms of battle in whatever way they could be most effective.

Though women in OSS were few in number, they became a primary example of the strength, ingenuity, and determination of America's women, who risked all to protect and defend their country. Into the middle of the conflict they charged, working as spies, saboteurs, cryptographers, propaganda experts, agent recruiters, and communications technicians.

And it was World War II that demonstrated to a man's world that this war could not be fought to victory without its women as well as its men. Indeed, the traditional role of the American woman would never be quite the same again.

Abby had wanted to talk to the young WASP, but the noise of the plane made it difficult to carry on any kind of conversation. Before she knew it they had landed again. Abby had absolutely no idea where they were. Probably somewhere north, Biff had said. There was snow on the outlying terrain but the runways had been partially cleared. They taxied over to a small building where the control tower was housed. It turned out to be Stuart Air Force Base.

"Come, darling, we can run in and grab a cup of coffee before we take off."

"Wonderful. I'd like to use the rest room too."

"Good idea. I don't think you're going to find one on the plane. And it's going to take many hours from here to England."

"Oh, horrors, I never thought of that. Well, there has to be some kind of accommodations. In case of emergency."

Biff laughed. "I'll check and see."

They sat at a counter and had their coffee. The place was somewhat makeshift, as though it had been constructed in a hurry. Abby looked out the window. There was an enormous four-engine plane taxiing out on the outer runway.

"What is that?" she asked Biff.

"Looks like a B-24."

"Do you think that's our plane?"

"Could be. Here comes our young WASP. Why don't you ask her."

Abby engaged the young woman in conversation while Biff attended to other things. The young woman was from the Midwest. She and her husband had been flying for about ten years before the war broke out. He was now a Navy pilot overseas in the Pacific and she was doing her part to help end the war sooner by ferrying new and old planes to various battle stations.

Yes, it was she who would be flying them to England in the B-24. She would also have a co-pilot, a navigator, and a radio operator, but she hadn't yet been informed who they were. As soon as the plane was ready they would take off—probably very soon, since the plane had already been refueled.

An Army car came speeding up to the building. An Army major jumped out, with four other servicemen of different ranks. Among them were a Navy commander, a Navy lieutenant j.g., an Army lieutenant, and an Army specialist enlisted man, all in full flight regalia. They all bore the insignias of OSS on their sleeves.

Biff had returned with their lamb-lined parkas, and a heavy lap coverlet. "These are all our guys." He looked closer as they piled into the building. Suddenly he saw Jordan Jenkins. "Well, well if it isn't old Jinx! What brings you here?"

They slapped one another on the back, as good comrades sometimes do. "And look at those bars! A promotion, I assume, Major Jenkins." Biff saluted.

"Absolutely." Jinx returned his salute. "Looks like I'm your co-pilot today. This is *our* B-24 assigned *to us*, OSS, and I'm to familiarize myself with it as we fly it to England. Then it's *mine*. I'll be its captain. We're going to use it for some very interesting sorties—I think."

"Good grief, Jinx. How are they going to do without you at headquarters?"

"Oh, they'll manage. The Old Man finally gave in and replaced me." He suddenly spied Abby. "And who is this delectable creature we have here?" His eyes devoured her with one scan.

"Oh, no, old chap. Hands off! This is Abby St. Giles, my fiancée."

"Biff," Jinx said. "You old son of a gun! You finally did it. But then, I can certainly see why."

"Abby, this is Jordan Jenkins, an old school buddy of mine," Biff said.

"Delighted to meet one of Biff's old school buddies." Abby held out her hand.

"The pleasure is indeed mine," said Jinx as he kissed her hand with great aplomb.

"And may I ask where you two became buddies?" She made an effort to be cordial, though she had not liked his look, or his manner.

"Why Yale, of course, Miss Abby. There *is* no other school." Jinx's voice had an unmistakable arrogance.

Yuk! One of those. "Oh, deah," she said, with feigned innocence. "You will just have to pardon my Southern accent. I distinctly thought you said Jail."

"Touché," said Jinx, laughing. They all joined in.

Jinx turned to Abby. His manner abruptly changed to one of respect. "It is indeed a pleasure to meet you, Miss St. Giles. Biff is a most fortunate man."

Abby smiled graciously, but she wasn't too sure she liked Biff's old school buddy. He was too forward, too arrogant.

Jinx suddenly became serious. "I must go and check out the plane. Time is short—we should be leaving immediately." Jinx trotted off to attend to his duties.

Abby turned to Biff. "Where in the world did he get the name 'Jinx'? It has a rather ominous sound."

"I suppose it does. He played football for Yale and every time he was on line the other team was jinxed. The opposition always lost. That's how he got his nickname. He's a fine flyer too; we're in good hands."

"Good. I'd just as soon we arrive in England in one piece."

The plane took off about 2:00 with an extra full load of fuel. A plane this size would need the extra petroleum to make the 12-hour distance. They would land once in Greenland to refuel. To accommodate for the extra fuel, no guns or bombs had been installed. Fresh off the assembly line, the plane was pretty much bare bones except for flight equipment. Once in England, it would be fully outfitted with equipment and weaponry for whatever awaited its destiny.

Abby's two bags had been strapped in the back along with Biff's one and his garment bag, which was mostly taken up by two of Abby's formal gowns. He had insisted that a plentiful wardrobe awaited him in England and she would need the room in her two bags for other things until her trunks arrived. But they all guffawed hilariously at Abby's enormous hatbox.

"I couldn't possibly go anywhere without my hats and gloves," she said.

"Spoken like a true lady," quipped Jinx. "OK, I suppose it's not *that* heavy. We must be sure to dress properly for English society—and particularly the enemy."

Abby gave him a dirty look as she climbed up the ladder. Two temporary jump seats had been rigged behind the radio operator and navigator to accommodate straggler passengers. Abby and Biff crawled in and secured themselves with their safety belts.

Lieutenant Pierce Abbott, the navigator, made his way in after them, and immediately became occupied with multiple charts and celestial maps. A nice looking, amiable young fellow, Abby guessed that he wasn't much older than she. The radio operator, looking every bit like a teenager, was already settled in, testing and checking his equipment. The young WASP and Major Jenkins were up front in the pilot's and co-pilot's seats, running through a checklist. Shortly, they revved up the motors to full power; the noise was incredible. Finally, the power let down and they began to taxi to the one long runway and stopped.

The pilot turned and addressed the four other passengers: "We're just about ready to take off. All engines and equipment check out, so we're in good shape. Remember that England is on Greenwich Meridian Time, five hours ahead of EDST, which means we will gain approximately five hours by the time we land in Britain. We will land at least once on the way, to refuel. Fortunately, we have a tailwind almost all the way, so we should make excellent time. However, we *are* in for considerable turbulence ahead. I will alert you when to expect it—that will be your signal to hold on tight. As you know, this plane is not fully equipped yet so your seats are installed as temporary and they may not prove too sturdy in severe turbulence. O.K. here goes!"

With that the motors revved up again and the plane began to roll down the runway, picking up speed as it moved along. The roar of the motors was deafening, but finally they were airborne and the noise decreased somewhat.

Abby thought, *there will be very little conversation on this flight. Probably better either to read, or doze off.*

They had been airborne about an hour and twenty-five minutes when the pilot suddenly said, "Here it comes! Hold on! We're really in for it for a while."

The plane began to rock from one side to the other. It was up, dropping down, jolting side to side—no way to keep one's equilibrium. There was no calming of the thermals, it was getting worse by the moment. The winds were unpredictable and the cloud cover was heavy. They couldn't see the sea below but it had to be that terrible storm that was upon the convoy. The pilot was having trouble controlling the plane even with the help of the co-pilot. Suddenly, the plane dropped about 2500 feet.

An iron fist squeezed all stomachs; heartbeats became rapid; blood pressures rose dramatically—all the symptoms of terror. It was a normal response, but an unsettling, frightening one, even for veteran flyers.

Biff let go of Abby's hand and grabbed her with both arms.

Suddenly Abby said aloud, "Lord, please take the bumps out of your air road and give us a smooth, safe flight."

Within a minute or two the airways became smooth and steady.

After a few minutes, the pilot turned around and looked straight at Abby. "I don't know what it was you did back there, but keep at it. For a moment there, I thought if this gets much worse we could be done for."

The navigator exchanged looks with Abby. He smiled knowingly; he knew what was abreast. He, too, had been silently praying.

Biff squeezed her hand. During the drop he had held onto her with both arms. His first instinct was to protect her. But he knew there was a limit to his ability to do so. Ultimately, there was only One who could. He had always believed completely. But somehow he knew that Abby had been touched by the hand of God in a special way. He had given her certain gifts. He had seen them in operation; and this instance confirmed it.

It was fascinating to watch Abby. She went along as though these were completely normal events in a believer's life. If one needed healing, or something else, or even a miracle, one simply had to ask. It was there for the taking—if one truly believed. She was totally unassuming. She never talked about it. Her belief system included the indisputable, undeniable Word of God.

Abby had not always known these things. But she had an inquiring mind. From time to time during her life she had had a not so gentle nudge from an Unseen Hand, which set her mind exploring. Student that she was, as she began to ask and study, the answers came, one by one, and sometimes in a torrent. But she had always known whence the knowledge came, as well as the miracles.

Yes, his Abby was unique. God had given him a miraculous gift, and he would always treasure her.

The landing in Greenland was uneventful and very welcome. While the plane was being refueled they made a quick run for coffee, food, and the restroom. Just to stretch one's legs was a blessing after a 12-hour flight.

Since this was a covert operation, the pilot ignored the 12-hour layover rule and opted for four. All hands stretched, ate ravenously, and fell asleep immediately on makeshift cots, gearing up for the next leg of the tedious journey.

Before takeoff, the pilot turned and addressed them. "For some reason we've been instructed to land in Edinburgh instead of London, our original destination. Could be the Germans are attacking our other airports, as well as the cities again. They get itchy every now and then and spring more massive offenses. Anyway we're making excellent time. Flying time eight hours more. This will have been a long flight from Washington. with the layover and time change … about 32 hours in all. But we should be landing on time, even with the weather and change in landing instructions. That means about 7:00 London time."

Biff turned to Abby. He shook his head. "That will delay us. Robert was sending a car to the London airport to meet us. But he'll be informed of the change sooner or later. When we arrive in Edinburgh, I can phone him from there. We may have to stay overnight and be picked up in the morning."

"Sounds wonderful to me." Abby clapped her hands. "Do you realize we've had practically no time alone together since we became engaged?"

"True, we have been pretty busy, haven't we. Let's see, this is now the 21st of December. I returned from Québec the evening of the 19th. And you accepted my ring, the 20th. Then we left immediately."

"Incredible! Was it only day before yesterday? Why is it I feel like at least a month has gone by, and I've hardly seen you."

"I suppose because at this point we don't want to be separated for even a moment. I'll be happy when we're married, but I suppose as long as this war is rearing its ugly head, we have no assurance that marriage will solve that problem either. Most young couples are being separated every day—sometimes for long months while their spouses are sent away to fight."

"Then promise me that I will be part of whatever your assignment may be. We've been joined together as a team, you know, and whom the Old Man hath joined together, let no man put asunder!" Abby gave Biff an impish smile.

Biff laughed. "Of course, darling. I shall be sure to remind the Old Man of those orders. I'm sure he'll be impressed that his word is omnipotent. The important thing is that we're a team for life. That has to take precedence over everything else."

"But since that is true, they should never try to separate us under *any* circumstances." Abby had made up her mind. She would be with Biff wherever they were sent, and the top Brass had better not try to interfere.

But Biff was well aware that once they were married, military regulations would prevent their serving in the same theater of war. His natural instinct to protect her was becoming more persistent. He thought they might finish this assignment without too much risk to Abby, but what would their next assignment be? No matter what they would be required to do, the risks of survival were high.

Espionage was a dangerous business. They both had known that. There was no way to avoid it. Her welfare now was paramount in his mind. But he would have to wait and deal with it later.

For now, their agenda was full enough. He put his arm around her and hugged her tightly. They boarded the plane and were airborne again.

Chapter 29

Their landing approach in Edinburgh was in total darkness. Before the lights of the runway came on at the last moment, Abby was beginning to wonder how in the world anyone could see the ground, much less anything above it. However, the landing was uneventful and all those aboard felt a new respect for the young WASP who was piloting the plane. After landing, the runway lights were immediately turned off. And Abby was about to learn that the blackout was essential to the safety of all.

They stood around for a while stretching their legs, while the radio operator and navigator unloaded all the luggage and handed it to Biff. The young WASP, finally finishing her tasks in the cockpit, approached Abby. She said, "I want to thank you for whatever it was you did back there. Did you know the turbulence was predicted to become a lot worse, and no matter what we did trying to fly over or under it, nothing was working. Both Jinx and I were becoming more and more fearful that if it got much worse this could be our last gasp."

Abby gave her a big hug. "I think you know very well what I did. I simply asked the Lord to take the bumps out of the air road. And so He did." Abby smiled.

"Does He always answer your prayers?" she asked.

"Oh yes. But frequently I don't know *how* He's going to answer, or *when*. Of course sometimes He simply says nothing so I just have to trust Him."

The young WASP looked at her intently. "I've always thought I was a believer, but I'm beginning to realize there's an awful lot I haven't been taught—I want to know what you know. Tell me, how do I find what I'm looking for?"

"It's really very simple. Ask Him to send you a teacher, and He will."

The young WASP laughed. "Oh, but I think He already has. At least I've received an object lesson. I hope we meet again."

"I hope so too," Abby said. "I admire your spunk, your magnificent courage. This ferrying service you're providing is vital to winning this war, and I, for one, want you to know that it's truly appreciated. I'm sure we'll meet again someday." She saw Biff returning. "In the meanwhile, I wish you God speed!"

"You too." The young WASP reluctantly turned and walked toward the airport building.

Biff returned from attending to their luggage. "It seems a car has been sent for us. Apparently Robert received my message and has arranged lodging nearby for us tonight."

"I hope it's *in* Edinburgh. I would love to see something of the town before we travel on."

"I think that can be arranged. We have very little time, but we'll see what we can do. Ah. Here we are now."

A Rolls-Royce drove up with a uniformed chauffeur. They said their goodbyes to Jinx and the rest of the crew. The chauffeur, Carsbrooke, attended to their luggage and opened the door for them. Biff greeted him as though he were familiar, spoke a few words to him, and came back to assist her into the car. They settled in for the drive ahead.

Abby feigned an exaggerated sigh. "I'm beginning to realize what a privilege it is to be part of the diplomatic service, as well as OSS. I feel like a princess, being catered to at every turn."

Biff laughed. "Enjoy it while you can. Come here!" Biff pulled her close to him.

Abby put her arms around him. "At last I have you all to myself, at least for little while." They snuggled close to each other. Biff kissed her.

About 30 minutes later, the chauffeur, a bright young Scotsman, drove up to the entrance of a charming and very old structure, an ancient inn. In full Scottish brogue, he announced that they had arrived at their destination. He opened the car door for them and began to unloaded their luggage. Biff thanked him.

"Aye, Your Grace, my instructions are to pick you up in the morning, take Miss Abby to Allistair, and then drive you to Mountford."

"That will do very well. I suppose the other car did not have time to make it by the time we landed."

"Aye, sir! That was not the only reason. Some of the roads have been blocked by the Germans' bombing. There has been a rather steady air attack for the past three days. The destruction is severe in some areas."

"Has there been any damage to Allistair or my family's estate?"

"I have heard of none. May the Lord be praised. And none has come this far, at least from this attack."

"That's something to be thankful for. Perhaps the bombing will stop now, at least for a few days. That would be a great Christmas blessing!"

"T'would be that, sir" He picked up two of their bags. "I'll just carry these in." He returned with a service boy, who took the rest of the luggage.

"Your grace, your lodging here has already been arranged. They are ready for you."

"And yours as well?"

"Aye, sir. Is there anything else?"

"No, I don't think so. Very well, then. We shall see you in the morning. Goodnight, Carsbrooke, sleep well."

"And you also, Your Grace." Carsbrooke bowed, tipped his hat to Abby, boarded the driver's seat, and disappeared into the night.

The innkeeper greeted Biff as they entered. "Everything is arranged, Your Grace." He motioned to a young man in uniform to take their bags to their respective rooms. "If you have need of anything else please ring for service. Dinner will be served in the dining room until 10."

They followed the young porter up to their rooms on the second floor, where he deposited their bags.

"How absolutely charming," Abby said as she entered her room, which was furnished in antiques. She could almost visualize its ancient occupants. The bed looked to be from the Tudor period, canopied and draped with the same beautiful old English print as the hangings, now drawn because of the blackouts, which covered the tall windows. But the most delightful thing about the room was the foot-high down covering on the bed.

"I feel like jumping right in the middle of it and never getting up."

"Then why don't you, darling. I think we both need a lie-down after that long trip. Take a few minutes and rest. Then perhaps you can freshen up and we'll go down for dinner. I'll be across the hall if you need me."

"That sounds very inviting. How about 30 minutes?"

"Perfect. See you then." Biff kissed her and left the room.

Abby looked resolutely at the puffy down covering on the beautiful old bed. Impulsively she took a flying leap up the bed ladder and landed right in its center. It sank beneath her body like hundreds of windblown feathers.

"This has to be what Heaven is like." She closed her eyes and immediately drifted off to sleep.

The persistent knock at the door finally registered. She awoke in a fog, not quite sure of where she was. "Come in," she said sleepily.

Biff looked at her and laughed. "So you took the plunge. I knew you would get into trouble the moment I left you."

"Oh dear. What time is it? I really didn't mean to go to sleep." Abby jumped up off the bed. "I'll only be a moment," she said as Biff headed out the door. She splashed water on her face, freshened her makeup, quickly changed her clothing, and appeared for approval.

"Am I presentable?"

"You look lovely, as usual, my dear. Shall we go? We'll just have time to dine and then perhaps take a stroll around the town."

They went down hand-in-hand to the dining room. There were few diners that evening, and by the time they finished dinner, it was 10:45.

"You know," he said, " I think we're going to have to put off our stroll around the town until tomorrow morning. I never thought of it until now, but there's a curfew and a blackout which keeps people off the streets at this time of night."

He helped her from the table, pulling out her chair. "You need to be aware that now you're in a country with much tighter security regulations than in the United States. Here, we are definitely at war, and have been since 1939. Spies have been plentiful here. Sabotage has been rampant, and the bombings from the air are totally unpredictable." They walked out to the lobby, arm in arm.

"Of course, I keep forgetting. Here you're right in the middle of it, aren't you?"

"I'm afraid so. I forget too, when I'm in the States, but we're here now, and it's a different story." He pointed to the exit signs. " When you hear the sirens go off you must take cover immediately. I'll show you the signs in town that indicate where the shelters are. I won't always be at your side, you know, so I want you to be very careful and alerted to any kind of danger."

They continued up the stairs and arrived at the door of her room.

Abby said, "Don't even think such things, darling. It's too horrible to contemplate. I promise to be careful, but you must promise as well. You know, it's only prudent for us to take precautions, but Biff, I believe that God put us together for a purpose and that He will protect us, no matter where He leads us." Abby smiled, her eyes shining.

Abby rose early the next morning at the phone message: "Breakfast in 30 minutes." She went to the window and drew open the drapes. The bright colors of the old English chintz suddenly came to life in the warmth and the rays of the clear winter sunlight.

Abby's room overlooked a beautiful formal English garden with myriad boxwood and a large pond surrounded with flowering evergreens. Though not in bloom in December, Abby could visualize the entire garden in the season of its greatest glory. *It must be lovely in spring,* she thought, as she stretched her weary muscles.

The trip had been long and arduous, and with the delays, layovers for refueling, and the time change, it had taken the better part of two days. Now it was the morning of the 22nd and they still had one more leg of their journey. But she was content. She was with Biff and that was all that really mattered.

She bathed, dressed, finished packing all of her things, and was finishing her makeup when the knock came at the door.

"Are you ready, my love?"

Abby opened the door and threw her arms around him. He hugged her tightly, picked her up, and planted a hearty kiss on her forehead.

"I think, after that harrowing flight, we'd better go down for breakfast and get fortified for our next adventure."

"Great idea. And what did you have in mind, Your Grace?"

"Uh oh. I guess the jig is finally up." He sighed. "My questionable past has been revealed. You finally read my vita."

"On the contrary," she said, "I simply overheard someone addressing you as 'Your Grace.' I'm still patiently waiting for you to tell me the terrifying truth." She tilted her head and gave him an impish look. "But don't think for one moment that whatever you've been hiding is going to matter to me."

"I don't think you'll be too disappointed. I'll fill you in at breakfast. I suppose it's inevitable before you meet my parents." Biff took her by the hand and they skipped, like children, down the empty hall, to the stairs leading to breakfast.

Biff suddenly stopped and offered his arm. They proceeded to descend the stairs in the manner of well-bred aristocrats with the most proper decorum, eyes twinkling with mischief.

During breakfast Biff began to tell her his past history and the history of his family. By now, Abby was used to his surprises so that when he told her that he was English but born in the United States, she was not that overcome. Abby had always known that he was English, but she had attributed it perhaps to an English parent or growing up in Boston or some other city in the East where the long A was generally spoken. Biff explained that though he was English, his parents had lived a good deal of the time in America. She realized then that spending so much time in America had softened his accent somewhat.

He had been educated in private schools in America for his first two years of school, then later at Eton. When time came for college he had matriculated from Trinity College to Yale undergraduate. Done a hitch in the RAF, and then returned to Yale law school. In fact that's how he became known to General Donovan, who was a very successful New York attorney prior to his appointment by President Roosevelt.

Abby sat sipping her after breakfast coffee while he continued.

But when he told her that his father was the Duke of Mountford, Count of Argonne, and Baron of Argyle, it was totally unanticipated. Like a bolt from the blue, she suddenly realized the implications. She sat forward.

"Merciful Heavens! I always knew you were well brought up and were from a good family, because you were always such a gentleman in every way. But I never dreamt you were a titled nobleman. You've always been so unassuming." She sat silent for a moment, turning what he had told her over in her mind. "So then, what does that mean for you?"

"I am the only offspring, only son, and the only heir. That means that all of those titles are also mine. When my father dies I will take his place as head of the family and of the estates." He looked directly into her eyes, waiting.

"Then, that means that whomever you marry will take on a joint responsibility with you to continue the family traditions and practices as those of the past." This was something she hadn't anticipated. There was much to consider.

"Yes. I never meant to deceive you, Abby, but knowing how independent you were I didn't want to frighten you away either. Besides, all the titles in the world do not impress me that much, and I think you know that. I am an American citizen as well as English. The titles simply happen to have been imposed upon me by the circumstances of my birth." He paused, then went on, "The world is changing and all of us are going to be forced to change with it…. But I have always been proud of the high principles and purposes of my family. And I believe that you also will be."

Abby looked at him, deep in thought—*is this what I really want?* But she had given him her promise. She had made her choice long ago. Come what may she knew he was part of God's plan for her. Suddenly, she smiled at him reassuringly. "Biff, darling, it is *you* whom I'm marrying. If a few little old titles come along with it, who am I to complain? Actually, my family's history is deeply rooted in England, and there are a number of titles in its history. You and I will build a future together regardless of what the future brings. I *love* you, and I will always stand by your side."

Biff heaved a sigh of relief. "I must confess, I have dreaded this moment, and I know that the full impact of what I've just told you has not yet settled in. But in the next few days I'm sure you'll begin to accept what's ahead. I believe you'll be very happy with it, once you meet my family."

"Your Gracey, at this point, I'll believe anything you say."

"That's my girl." Biff began to laugh. "A few little old titles! Abby, darling, you're priceless." He took her hand and squeezed it. He was relieved, glad his revelation was over. She had reacted the way he had hoped. "Now I have a surprise for you. How would you like to take a walk down the Royal Mile of Edinburgh? We'll simply take an hour out of our schedule before we travel on to Allistair and my family's estate."

"Oh could we? I've always wanted to see more of Edinburgh."

"We could, indeed! And along the way there will be a very special surprise for you."

The Royal Mile was a famous historic site that beckoned to all travelers interested in the history of Scotland. It stretched from Holyrood House at the bottom to Castle Hill, upon which the Castle sat on the historic crag overlooking the town and the harbor.

They started at the west end, and as they walked, hand in hand, Biff began to read from the brochure he had obtained from the front desk.

"'Situated at the bottom of the Royal Mile is Holyrood House, a site of much of the turbulent Scottish history of royalty, opulence, horrific murders, and religious significance. It serves as a reminder of Scotland's volatile history. Famous incidents include the murder of the secretary of Mary Queen of Scots.'"

"Goodness. So much gore in its history," Abby said.

"Oh, yes, all of Britain is drenched in it, I'm afraid." He continued as they walked, observing the sites.

"'The Augustinian Abby was commissioned by Queen Margaret in approximately 1153. In 1768 it was partially destroyed by a hurricane, leaving the ruin that we see today. The Palace of Holyrood House, today the official Scottish residence of Britain's royal family, was billed as a guesthouse for royal visitors. The Palace and the Abby have survived numerous fires, repairs, and restorations.'"

As they walked Biff continued to point out the historical highlights of each of the edifices they passed.

"'Next, on the left, is John Knox's house. Originally a Catholic priest, he was greatly influenced by Calvin during the mid-16th century. Under his strong leadership, the Church of Scotland adopted a declaration of faith, a form of government, and a liturgy. After the time of the Reformation, he became the first Protestant minister of the Cathedral and stands today as one of the most famous and influential Protestant clergymen in history.'"

"What a fascinating place this is." Abby said as they walked along.

"I knew you would love it—but wait, the best is yet to come." Biff continued from the brochure.

"'At the junction of Northbridge and the Royal Mile, stands Tron Kirk, traditionally the gathering place of Edinburgh folk on the New Year for many a Hogmany celebration.'"

They walked along as Biff continued to point out the historical significance for each of the buildings they passed.

Then, suddenly, they came in front of a large cathedral.

"Darling, this is what I particularly wanted you to see. This is St. Giles Cathedral, *your* cathedral. 'It is the High Kirk of Edinburgh. It was officially consecrated by the bishop of St. Andrews in 1243 but its massive central pillars date back to approximately 1120. This church was named after St. Giles, one of the earliest followers of St. Francis of Assisi, from whom he received the habit in 1208, and who was part of the auld alliance of Scotland and France against England, their common and much hated enemy, during the Reformation.'"

Biff and Abby looked at the façade of St. Giles. It was magnificent. Every pillar, every stone, every window whispered of its ancient origins.

"Oh, Biff, it's wonderful. What a surprise. Can we take just a few minutes to go inside?"

Biff looked at his watch, "Why not, we've come this far. A few minutes more could hardly make that much difference." At least that's what he thought.

Abby took his hand and led him into the church. Biff continued with its history, as they moved along, exploring. "John Knox became the first Protestant minister of St. Giles Cathedral," he said. "His was the house we saw on the way here."

"Yes, I remember," she said. They walked along slowly, viewing the vast magnificence of the interior, the ancient architecture, the Gothic arches, the delicate intricacy of the moldings.

"Isn't it splendid? I've been so anxious to show it to you. We will come back one day and saturate ourselves with St. Giles and the entire city."

"It's breathtaking," Abby said quietly.

They wandered through the different parts of the large cathedral until finally they came to the sanctuary. Walking down the long aisle up to the front altar, they stood there, hand in hand, in silence. The light filtering through the stained-glass windows surrounded them with a mystical ambiance.

Then, unexpectedly, a glorious golden light filled the entire place. Strangely, nothing else could be distinguished except that mystical golden light that encompassed them. Everything had disappeared, there was nothing there at all, except for their awareness of their own essence and the presence of God. And then at that moment they felt an awesome power flowing through their beings. Overcome, they sank to their knees before the altar, becoming aware that in an instant they had become one with God, and one with each other in Him.

How long they knelt there they could never tell. It could have been moments, it could have been hours, but what *was* evident was that their lives would never be quite the same again.

At last, they rose from their knees, and began to walk slowly, still hand in hand, toward the back of the sanctuary. As they neared the vestibule an old priest approached them. He was smiling as though he had seen it too. He said nothing until they reached him, and then he reached out, laid his hands upon their heads and said, "In the name of the Father, and the Son and the Holy Ghost, ye who have been blessed exceedingly, walk in the anointing which ye have received."

The old priest looked at them intently for a moment. And then he turned and slowly disappeared from view.

Outside, everything seemed different.

Abby finally turned and looked at Biff. "I could never feel closer to you than I do at this moment."

"I feel it too. It's breathtaking, ecstatic—one with you and one with Him. What an experience! How could anyone doubt the power of God after that?"

"Only one who has never experienced it," she said. "I know I'll never be the same again."

"Nor I." Biff was quiet, thoughtful. "I know I'll never doubt Him again."

They walked along for a long while, slowly contemplating what they had witnessed and felt. Out of the blue, Abby felt a tremendous exhilaration. "I'm walking on cloud 59! Want to come along?" She laughed and smiled and skipped a step or two.

Biff grinned. "Wait a second till I come down off cloud 60."

"Who wants to come down at all?"

Biff laughed with her. "I think when we do we'll need a golden parachute." He looked at his watch. "It's almost 10. This has been incredibly wonderful, but I think we'd better meet with Carsbrooke, or we'll never make it to Allistair or my parents' estate before nightfall. We'll have to save a tour of Edinburgh Castle till later."

"Yes, Your Gracey, your wish is my command."

"All nonsense aside, as much as I'd like to linger, we'd better get going."

Carsbrooke was waiting at the end of the Royal Mile. He had packed the car with their luggage, made sure there was nothing left behind, and had included a picnic basket with lovely sandwiches, delicacies, and drinks prepared by the chef.

"Your Grace, I've checked the roads again and they are now all cleared to our destination."

"Carsbrooke, you're a jewel," Biff said as he and Abby settled themselves in the back compartment. "You've thought of everything."

Chapter 30

On December 20th, two days out, the storm hit. It was not a simple squall or thunderstorm. It was a full-blown winter's tempest. At first, Suzanne began to notice more vigor in the pitching and listing of the ship's normal movement, but within the half hour the winds had increased from gale to on-coming hurricane speeds.

As the storm approached, the commodore instructed the convoy to span out to greater predetermined distances to avoid collision. The lineup of the nearly 100 ships was on a carefully predicated format, but the final say was the responsibility and at the discretion of the commodore, who was stationed on the lead ship.

Generally, the number of ships traveling together in a convoy determined how many rows were assembled. With so many in this group, there were four rows. In the center were the baby flattops, equipped with F-4Us, providing air cover as needed, and the tankers, which needed priority protection from ambitious U-boats seeking to slither in and blow up the entire assembly. The next outer layers were composed of transports, cargo, and whatever supply or other vessels were involved. The outer perimeter consisted of destroyers, and the outer-most, the corvettes, both of which monitored the safety of the convoy and provided protection from attack. Both were vital if disaster was to be avoided.

Supply was the backbone of the fighting units. Without sufficient men, guns, ammunition, vehicles, food, and equipment in place to supply and sustain them, there was little hope of overcoming a highly developed and efficient German War machine, which had been preparing its men and its armaments for ten years. Meanwhile, the rest of the world had either played politics, entertained, and lived in a fool's paradise, or during the depression, worked at whatever job they could find and tried to keep food in the mouths of their children.

In 1939-1941, the early days of the war with Germany, America, not yet in the war, but under lend lease, had stepped up its production and shipping to meet the needs of its European allies. Hundreds of ships were utilized to complete that task. But it became quickly obvious that the North Atlantic was mainly under the control of the Nazis, whose superiority reigned because of the overabundance and ingenuity of their submarine power. In two months alone they had sunk 142 American ships en route to the aid of our allies. It was this type of debacle during WWI that had prompted the idea of the convoy as a means to protect and defend supply efforts.

As an additional result, the English threw everything they had into developing anti-submarine warfare. By 1942, the English emerged with a new radar invention that could detect the exact position of the U-boat before it could attack, and with sonar provide the direction for counterattack.

Supply was, then, the keynote to maintaining and winning a worldwide operation, both in the European and Pacific theaters of war. And America, both before and after her entry into the war, stepped up to the bat. With the estimate that 15 to 20 persons are required to back up and supply one man on the battle front, the race to equip and reinforce America's, England's, and France's fighting men overseas became mainly an American project. As the war continued, gargantuan efforts were required of its people at home and on sea to provide speedy production of the needed items and rapid delivery and deployment to their needed destinations.

Thus, every effort was made to utilize every inch of space on every vehicle en route to any theater where the war was being fought. As a result, many of the freighters and cargo ships had tanks, planes, and other heavy equipment secured to their decks by enormous 2" cables. At the height of a severe storm, many of the cables broke and the vehicles cascaded onto the deck, crushing and destroying essential structures and then, skidding off into the water, became projectiles in danger of causing serious damage to other ships.

Another hazard became obvious in extremely stormy weather when it was discovered that some of these ships were breaking apart with not only the loss of the contents but the crew as well. Because of speeding up the production of Liberty ships by the method of weld-fitting two complete halves of the vessels together, there were degrees of stress that these ships were simply unable to withstand. In extreme weather conditions, rescue was impossible, to say nothing of the added danger of the broken ship's wreckage jetting into other vessels. After a number of incidents proved catastrophic, a solution was found by fitting a wide steel band around the perimeter of the decks to reinforce stability.

But storms sometimes had their own malevolent agendas.

As the waves climbed higher and higher, Suzanne thought that they would surely be swamped completely. Only those things that were secured remained in place. Everything else was flying off shelves and rolling from one side of the cabin to the other, including the passengers and crew, and violent seasickness became another impediment in an already extremely threatening situation.

Suzanne had always considered herself a seasoned sailor, but she had never experienced anything that even approached the enormity of this intensity. She was petrified. She knew that this was a treacherous situation, that at any moment their lives could be at stake.

Always solicitous to her needs and her feelings, Jacques tried to comfort her and soothe her fears, but she knew he too was alarmed. She was convinced by now that he loved her deeply, and she knew that her emotional responses toward him were not just infatuation. There was a profound, indefinable bond between them.

In a state of inner turmoil with her perceptions heightened, she decided, once and for all, that if this experience were to be her last she had to know the whole truth. It had been lurking in her intuition for some time that Jacques was holding something back from her. There was too much that was mysterious in his background and in their relationship. True, he had been able to explain away whatever questions she had had up to now but still—

Ever since that episode at the Fontainebleu, her confidence in Jacques had been shaken. Where she had trusted him implicitly at first, now there was doubt. She had tried to rationalize her fears, but they had been intensifying. There were too many unanswered questions. Now she had to know. She would put the question to him, but how she could approach it and when to do so was a quandary.

She knew this was hardly the time to press her intentions but as the storm's power increased, her anxiety became unleashed to a fever pitch, and Jacques' efforts at light-hearted banter did nothing to calm her. On the contrary, she became more and more agitated, and her imagination knew no bounds.

"Too bad we're not on a submarine," he said. "Then we could weather this storm without the pitch and roll. It's relatively calm the deeper one goes."

How does he know what it's like on a submarine? Suzanne suddenly remembered the accounts of German U-boats patrolling off the eastern coast of America. *Oh, my God! What if he's a German spy? What have I gotten myself into?*

He had been holding her in his arms for the past hour, bracing against the bedposts for stability. But now he was looking for some kind of rope or cord to fasten them to a secured chair or the bed to keep them from being thrown from one end of the cabin to the other. Suzanne recoiled at the idea of being battened down.

Suppose he's going to tie me down and then strangle me? But I know he loves me! That wouldn't make sense. I'm getting hysterical with fear. I've got to calm down.. He'll know what I'm thinking if I don't get a grip on myself. For now, he'll simply think my reactions are because of the storm.... I'll simply have to wait until the storm is over—until I can think straight.

She remembered the instructions given her by her psychologist so long ago about breathing into a paper bag to prevent the hyperventilation associated with panic. She decided this was one of those times. She began to practice concentrating on regulating her breathing. And eventually the worst of the panic anxiety subsided.

Che sera sera, she thought. *My overreacting will not solve anything. I can at least have some measure of control, even if it's only over my breathing.*

The storm continued for the remainder of the day and into the night. The profound darkness hung like a heavy mantle over the assembly of ships as they were tossed back and forth like children's toys on the angry waters. While on the bridge the only perceptible thing those on watch could see in the distance was the little blue light on the back of the preceding ship, which cautioned not to come closer.

On the afternoon of December 23rd, the 5th day out, the storm subsided and the commodore signaled the ships to return to formation. They had been delayed two days in crossing, which meant they would probably not arrive in port until the 31st, New Years Eve. Even so, with so many ships involved, they could be delayed another day or two anchored in harbor, awaiting their turn to be unloaded.

Jacques began to review his plan to leave the ship before it docked to unload. There would have been no problem had the ship not been reassigned at the last minute from Marseilles to Liverpool, but unfortunately that was the fortunes of war. When he had found out, he had immediately devised another plan before leaving Québec, and sent a message alerting his operatives in England to be prepared to pick them up by water taxi on the scheduled day, but now that they were delayed he felt the need to do some rethinking.

He knew that his lead operative would monitor the ship's landing instructions, so he had no qualms about that part of his plan, but now he had to be sure that he would also instigate the alternative plan to ensure that they could get away without being detected.

Enemy operatives were always suspicious of any unusual requests for debarking. He knew it was too risky to use his own radio to alert him. He would simply have to resort either to asking the captain to send a coded message—or rely on his operative to use his own judgment. He had always proved insightful and totally trustworthy in the past. But to avoid a foul up, he decided on the former.

During the storm, he had become more and more concerned about Suzanne. He realized that this cataclysmic experience in itself had been devastating for her, but now his antennae was picking up more than her emotional upheaval from the storm. She had clung to him, but there was now a questioning fear in her eyes he had not seen before, except during that episode at the Fontainebleu, and her response to him seemed more guarded. He would have to make a decision about her soon, and time was running out.

Chapter 31

Senator Downs had felt a brief reprieve from his fears after he ran across the announcement of Suzanne's death in the official accounts of casualties and deaths published in the newspaper. But by three days later, the more he thought about it the more curious he had become. Over the years, he and Suzanne had made contact with one another every month or so, in keeping with his policy of "keeping one's potential enemies close." But from early September, even while he was secretly sending demanding messages to his German contact to eliminate her, he had not heard from her.

In late October he had had his secretary call Suzanne at Logan's office to "chat" and was told she was on leave, but there was something strange about the fact that she had not told him and did not return his call when she supposedly returned. Two weeks later, he had prompted another call, only to be informed that she had been reassigned. He was alarmed. To what had she been reassigned? And why hadn't she told him?

Finally, two days after reading about her demise, and filled with curiosity, he placed a message asking for details of her death in his German contact's drop zone. His only answer was: "Mission accomplished!"

ee. Thank you, Commander, that makes sense. It's
gh. If that is so, why is she dead? But you have not
ed of her death?"

d I doubt anyone else has. She had no next of kin,
 know…. But I will try to check it out and get back
ay take me a little while, as you know with so much
 and disjointed information due to the war. Certainly
 I know anything, I'll contact you immediately. You
n it."

felt somewhat soothed by Logan's attempts at courtesy
 at placating. Over the past few months he had felt
 been demeaned by the situations in which he found
ately the respect due to him, his position as a United
tor, and his importance to them, had been ignored by
 contacts. How dare they keep him in the dark? And
med to be cut off by his own government.
ation was the key to power. He had known that long
had entered the political scene. In fact capitalizing on
edge that he had acquired about the weaknesses and
es of some of his opponents had gotten him where he
 was no room for mercy in politics. If one in power
d by rumor, even truth—that was his tough luck. Yes,
n was the key; even if it were false.
 very kind of you," said Senator Downs in a syrupy
ice. "I shall anticipate your call." He placed the receiver
 cradle and slammed his fist on the desk. There was
 do now but wait.

---

ander Logan shook his head, sighed a deep sigh, and
 phone again. He called his contact at OSS. With

Frustrated, he felt that he was being kept on a leash, not allowed to be in the know. He was an important man, a United States senator, privy to all sorts of secret U.S. governmental information. How dare they treat him like this! Didn't they realize with whom they were dealing? Besides, he did not like this indirect method of communicating with them. He had no idea who his contact was. Their messages passed only through his assigned drop zone. He could pass his contact on the street and not know who he was. It was maddening. He desired more personal contact.

All of his careful indirect attempts to find out about Suzanne through his own governmental information sources had been abruptly curtailed. It was as though an iron curtain had descended on the life and death of Suzanne Davenport. As though she had never existed. He smelled a rat. No one had even mentioned her. He wondered if anyone in his office had read the notices of her death. Someone had to know. But he didn't dare ask. If he showed too much interest, someone might focus their attention on him.

Still, he *was* an old friend, why wouldn't it be considered normal for him to inquire about the circumstances of her death? It was a perfectly rational thing to do. Finally he decided to call Commander Logan, and pretend he had just seen the notices and was totally "shocked and saddened" to hear the terrible news. Yes, why would anyone question his interest?

He had his secretary put in a direct call to the commander. It was two days before Logan returned his call. Downs was infuriated but he managed to feign affable courtesy.

Logan voiced his apologies. He had been "out of town" on an assignment. Actually, alert to what the senator might want, he had been in contact with OSS for instructions as to his reply to any inquiries about Suzanne.

"Yes, Senator, what can I do for you?"

"Commander, I know that Suzanne Davenport has been your personal confidential secretary for a number of years. If you recall, her appointment in your office was primarily upon my recommendation."

"Yes, I do recall that she came highly recommended by you, and I have found her an extremely bright and efficient young lady."

Senator Downs's thought was: *I wonder if he had an affair with her too.* "Yes, indeed. I was saddened to lose her at the time. In fact she has been not only a former employee of mine, but in addition a close personal friend and has kept in contact with me every couple of months since she left my employ."

"Yes, she always speaks of you most highly."

"She does?" He decided to do a little fishing. Try to get him talking.

"Oh yes, from time to time. Some of the girls in the office are aware that you are friends. It's no secret that she's attended some of your parties."

"I see. Yes. Well, Commander, I have just become aware that she was recently reassigned to another post, without my knowledge. It would not be likely that Suzanne would do such a thing without advising me. And, if that were not mysterious enough, now I find her listed as 'deceased' in the official Navy lists of obituaries and casualties. I am totally shocked and saddened to learn of her death."

"Suzanne is dead?" Logan reacted with genuine shock. "I cannot believe it! How terrible! Where did you see this publication? Could it be a mistake?"

"Apparently not," Downs answered. "She's listed under war casualties."

"I'm devastated," Logan decl[ared]
Suzanne is such a lovely girl. Ever[y]
of her. I cannot believe she's gone.

For a moment Logan had believe[d]
then he knew enough of the facts t[hat]
on the shore of Lake Erie was *not* Su[zanne]
him of that. Now, whatever was goin[g]
was strictly on a need-to-know basi[s]
he was willing to accept it. There [was]
Why was this man so curious about [Suzanne?]

"Yes, well I'm having trouble [with that,"]
Downs. "Who do you suppose cou[ld]
probably not a good idea to spread [it until]
confirmed."

"I agree with you completely. Th[ey]
certainly know. Would you like me t[o find out? I'd like to]
know for sure myself."

"Yes, would you? That's a fine ide[a. Let me]
know." He paused, "Incidentally, what [is this]
about?"

Logan hesitated, "Senator, you [know that]
information concerning assignments of [our people is]
confidential, so obviously I would be [wrong if I]
divulged that kind of information, even [to you."]

The senator bristled. "Commander[, I am a United]
States senator. Surely you do not intend [to—"]

"Sir, I do not mean to offend you." Yo[u know that]
there *is* one thing I can tell you. Perhap[s you know that]
Suzanne was up for a promotion to lieute[nant, so]
that you might surmise that her reassignm[ent was to]
head up a personnel department somewhe[re that]
needed filling with higher level personne[l."]

Robert away, another senior officer, Thomas Grafton, had been assigned to him. They met at five in a safe house on Connecticut Avenue. He reiterated the afternoon's conversation to him.

"Looks like he's becoming strangely agitated for some reason," Grafton said. "We've had suspicions about him for some time. Now he's under full secret investigation and surveillance. We're beginning to find out some very interesting things about Senator Downs. His background is beginning to spring leaks and his methods of being elected were questionable. The man is a self-centered opportunist. We can't trust the welfare of this country to the likes of him."

Grafton paused. He liked the Commander. He was "Old Navy," all spit and polish, but his manner was gracious and cooperative. A true officer and gentleman.

"I'll get back to you and give you further instructions. In the meanwhile, we'll find out what he's up to. If he calls again, you've heard nothing yet. But you're expecting some information soon."

"Roger, I'll wait for your call," said Logan. "I'll keep my eyes open and contact you only if necessary."

Logan took his leave. At least he had been assured that Suzanne was alive, but that's all he had been told. Obviously, the Navy Department had issued the report of her death because they thought the body *was* Suzanne's. They didn't however list the cause of death, probably because they were continuing to investigate her murder.

But apparently OSS thought there were those out there somewhere who needed to think she was dead. OSS was completely capable of keeping the whole truth from Navy Intelligence if they had their reasons. And he was beginning to think they had. Obviously, they were still looking for her. That in itself opened up a whole new scenario.

As for that arrogant bastard, Downs…. Logan walked to his car, got in and drove back to the office.

Frustrated, he felt that he was being kept on a leash, not allowed to be in the know. He was an important man, a United States senator, privy to all sorts of secret U.S. governmental information. How dare they treat him like this! Didn't they realize with whom they were dealing? Besides, he did not like this indirect method of communicating with them. He had no idea who his contact was. Their messages passed only through his assigned drop zone. He could pass his contact on the street and not know who he was. It was maddening. He desired more personal contact.

All of his careful indirect attempts to find out about Suzanne through his own governmental information sources had been abruptly curtailed. It was as though an iron curtain had descended on the life and death of Suzanne Davenport. As though she had never existed. He smelled a rat. No one had even mentioned her. He wondered if anyone in his office had read the notices of her death. Someone had to know. But he didn't dare ask. If he showed too much interest, someone might focus their attention on him.

Still, he *was* an old friend, why wouldn't it be considered normal for him to inquire about the circumstances of her death? It was a perfectly rational thing to do. Finally he decided to call Commander Logan, and pretend he had just seen the notices and was totally "shocked and saddened" to hear the terrible news. Yes, why would anyone question his interest?

He had his secretary put in a direct call to the commander. It was two days before Logan returned his call. Downs was infuriated but he managed to feign affable courtesy.

Logan voiced his apologies. He had been "out of town" on an assignment. Actually, alert to what the senator might want, he had been in contact with OSS for instructions as to his reply to any inquiries about Suzanne.

"Yes, Senator, what can I do for you?"

"Commander, I know that Suzanne Davenport has been your personal confidential secretary for a number of years. If you recall, her appointment in your office was primarily upon my recommendation."

"Yes, I do recall that she came highly recommended by you, and I have found her an extremely bright and efficient young lady."

Senator Downs's thought was: *I wonder if he had an affair with her too.* "Yes, indeed. I was saddened to lose her at the time. In fact she has been not only a former employee of mine, but in addition a close personal friend and has kept in contact with me every couple of months since she left my employ."

"Yes, she always speaks of you most highly."

"She does?" He decided to do a little fishing. Try to get him talking.

"Oh yes, from time to time. Some of the girls in the office are aware that you are friends. It's no secret that she's attended some of your parties."

"I see. Yes. Well, Commander, I have just become aware that she was recently reassigned to another post, without my knowledge. It would not be likely that Suzanne would do such a thing without advising me. And, if that were not mysterious enough, now I find her listed as 'deceased' in the official Navy lists of obituaries and casualties. I am totally shocked and saddened to learn of her death."

"Suzanne is dead?" Logan reacted with genuine shock. "I cannot believe it! How terrible! Where did you see this publication? Could it be a mistake?"

"Apparently not," Downs answered. "She's listed under war casualties."

Company of Spies

"I'm devastated," Logan declared. "I'm so sorry, Senator, Suzanne is such a lovely girl. Everyone here is so terribly fond of her. I cannot believe she's gone. What a horrible loss!"

For a moment Logan had believed that Suzanne *was* dead. But then he knew enough of the facts to know that the body found on the shore of Lake Erie was *not* Suzanne's. Robert had assured him of that. Now, whatever was going on with her disappearance was strictly on a need-to-know basis. He understood that—and he was willing to accept it. There was something wrong here. Why was this man so curious about Suzanne?

"Yes, well I'm having trouble believing it myself," said Downs. "Who do you suppose could confirm this report? It's probably not a good idea to spread the word around until it *is* confirmed."

"I agree with you completely. The Navy Department would certainly know. Would you like me to check it out? I'd like to know for sure myself."

"Yes, would you? That's a fine idea. And then you can let me know." He paused, "Incidentally, what was this new reassignment about?"

Logan hesitated, "Senator, you know that any kind of information concerning assignments of naval personnel is highly confidential, so obviously I would be breaching security if I divulged that kind of information, even to you."

The senator bristled. "Commander Logan, I am a United States senator. Surely you do not intend to deny my request."

"Sir, I do not mean to offend you." *You arrogant jackass.* "But there *is* one thing I can tell you. Perhaps you did not know that Suzanne was up for a promotion to lieutenant commander. From that you might surmise that her reassignment might have been to head up a personnel department somewhere, wherever a vacancy needed filling with higher level personnel."

"Yes, I see. Thank you, Commander, that makes sense. It's strange though. If that is so, why is she dead? But you have not been informed of her death?"

"No. And I doubt anyone else has. She had no next of kin, as you must know.... But I will try to check it out and get back to you. It may take me a little while, as you know with so much bureaucracy and disjointed information due to the war. Certainly as soon as I know anything, I'll contact you immediately. You can count on it."

Downs felt somewhat soothed by Logan's attempts at courtesy and efforts at placating. Over the past few months he had felt that he had been demeaned by the situations in which he found himself. Lately the respect due to him, his position as a United States senator, and his importance to them, had been ignored by his German contacts. How dare they keep him in the dark? And now he seemed to be cut off by his own government.

Information was the key to power. He had known that long before he had entered the political scene. In fact capitalizing on the knowledge that he had acquired about the weaknesses and peccadilloes of some of his opponents had gotten him where he was. There was no room for mercy in politics. If one in power was ruined by rumor, even truth—that was his tough luck. Yes, information was the key; even if it were false.

"That's very kind of you," said Senator Downs in a syrupy tone of voice. "I shall anticipate your call." He placed the receiver back in its cradle and slammed his fist on the desk. There was nothing to do now but wait.

Commander Logan shook his head, sighed a deep sigh, and picked up the phone again. He called his contact at OSS. With

Chapter 32

It was December 22nd, 1942, three days before Christmas, the time of year when all people, whether young or old, felt a different spirit in the air. The spirit of joy and anticipation, the spirit of love and hope, even in the midst of sorrow, loss, and the devastation of war.

And England had certainly had her share of devastation, sorrow, and loss. In the summer of 1940 France had fallen and was now occupied by the Germans. It was obvious that England was next on Hitler's long hit list of acquisitions in conquering the entire world in his mythical 1000-year reign. England was the crown jewel. England was to be the absolute pinnacle of his victories. Then all of Europe would be under his domination.

In the summer of 1941, the German high command began its attack on the British Isles. With an air force five times superior in strength, the bombing began. From southern England to beyond London, terror rained from the sky continually. Outnumbered and against incredible odds, Britain had met every assault upon her sacred soil with honor, from the rescue at Dunkirk to the unrelenting Blitzkrieg from the south to London, as the Germans attempted to prepare for invasion of the islands.

The Brits had fought with every fiber of their beings, at unbelievable odds, knowing that if Hitler gained a toehold on England's soil, the war was lost. The Battle of Britain will go down in history as one of the most astonishing feats ever undertaken by a militarily unprepared people against an efficient, overpowering War Machine.

During the summer of 1941, with only 650-odd planes and a paucity of trained pilots against the Germans' 2500 superior Luftwaffe, the Royal Air Force weathered 16 weeks, four months, of constant bombardment, finally causing the Germans to withdraw because of the enormity of their losses. But at the end of the siege, the RAF had lost one out of every four pilots sent into battle. This astonishing feat prompted Prime Minister Winston Churchill to declare: "Never, in the annals of human events, is so much owed by so many to so few."

Four million homes were destroyed, to say nothing of the factories, schools, hospitals, ancient landmarks, and other essential institutions vital for the survival of a nation. Even Buckingham Palace had sustained several hits from the constant bombardment. But King George and Queen Elizabeth won the very hearts of their countrymen by refusing to move their children or themselves to the north country and safety, choosing to remain with their subjects under fire.

The Blitz of '41 had left England severely crippled, but not defeated. The enemy found that it had awakened a sleeping lion, who now would defy the political complacency of its past leaders and rally all its power and resources and that of its ally, the United States, to bring the enemy and its malicious leader to his knees in total defeat.

Now, as Christmas approached, all of the Christian world felt the pull of the Christ child and the warmth and joy of His message. That indomitable spirit prevailed, despite the carnage. The mystery of the Christ child had its own power to uplift and inspire. And Abby felt it drawing her closer as they drove through the villages and hamlets to their destinations. Beautiful old traditional Christmas carols wafted across the air from the car radio, reminders of other seasons when peace on earth prevailed and the winds of war were not blowing near hurricane strength across the world.

The estates of Allistair and Mountford were both situated in that glorious part of England called Derbyshire. With its pastoral countryside, rolling hills, ancient trees and forests, rivers and streams, it was no wonder that the nobility of centuries past had built their palatial homes there. The areas in and surrounding Derbyshire boasted of many such splendid structures; Chatsworth, Hardwick, Wollaton, Packwood, Burghley, Althorp, Wightwick, all within a fifty-mile radius.

Carsbrooke drove happily through the snowy countryside. He had always loved his position as official chauffeur of the family's Scottish estate. He loved the sounds of the great car as it sped along, the purring of the motor gave him a sense of power. There would never be another automobile built to equal a Rolls Royce, and this one he considered *his*. He took care of it as one would a baby. And now *he* was driving the young duke and his forthcoming bride to Allistair, and then to Mountford, the main residence of the family. One day he too would be assigned to the main house with all its potential staff advantages.

Yes, Carsbrooke was a happy man. He entertained his daydreams as they sped along, applying more pedal from time to time as he felt it prudent to do so. The distance from Edinburgh to Derbyshire was about 200 miles, and it would take them until late afternoon at best to reach their destination.

Abby and Biff had settled down in the back seat of the Rolls for the long drive. Carsbrooke's compartment was closed off from them, which gave them privacy to speak candidly with no fear of being overheard. They were both in that peculiar state of existence between rational thought and insanity—called being in love. Nevertheless, because of the impending events, the conversation between them had wafted back and forth between a number of approaching events, both trivial and pleasurable, troublesome and serious.

Abby's first meeting with Biff's parents and Christmas celebrations were not only a source of excitement but anxiety for Abby as well. She did so want them to be pleased with her as their son's choice. But always lurking in the background was the search for Suzanne and her master-spy, Jana.

"You know, I just had a horrible thought," Abby said. "Suppose we do find Suzanne and bring her to safety—what will happen to her?"

"That's a good question. If I recall she was AWOL when she disappeared. The Navy thinks that she has been murdered and they're still investigating. In fact I think they're still looking at every person she ever worked for, and everyone she ever knew. But they really don't want to divulge the nature of her death until they can get their theoretical case lined up, and a definite suspect. I'm sure they wouldn't want to give up too much information either. It could snafu their case."

"True," Abby said. "Obviously OSS has kept the Navy in the dark. They still think that it was Suzanne's body that was found.

So now, if she's found alive and they find out, she will have a lot of explaining to do."

"Yes, indeed she will." Biff nodded.

"Then the Navy will want to know why she went AWOL and where she has been all these weeks. And who *is* that murdered woman they thought was Suzanne?"

"Exactly. Of course, the Navy doesn't know about Jana or her affair with him. Only OSS knows about that. And we have to keep it under wraps in order to track him down. He's very clever and has bright people working for him. They're constantly trying to find out what we're doing and what we know about them."

"Yes," Abby said, "I sometimes wonder who's out there following us."

"I know the feeling. If they knew about us and that we had tracked him down, they would relay our information to him immediately. Then he would be alerted to change plans and appearance. And truth is—he may *be* onto us. So far, he's been like a slippery eel, impossible to hold on to. He seems almost like Proteus, in that he can change shape at will." *He would also have us eliminated*, Biff thought, but he said nothing.

He yawned and stretched his long legs. "We think we know where they've been and where they are now. What we don't know about Suzanne is whether she has become a counter spy or whether she's totally ignorant of who Jana is."

Abby frowned and shook her head. "We know that she believes his name is 'Jacques D'Arcy.' He may have been able to keep her in the dark until now," she said. "I still believe he has somehow deceived her into thinking that she's going undercover for the United States and that the two of them are working together for the good of the Allies. After all, he's been posing as a French diplomat, and she believed that. I will never believe that

Suzanne, as patriotic as I have always known her to be, would spy upon her own country for the benefit of the Germans."

"I know, it's hard to believe that someone you love could possibly be a traitor. But darling, I think it's time you accepted the possibility that you may be faced with that very fact once we find them," he said.

She sat straight up, horrified. "But that would mean—treason! And the punishment for treason is a firing squad."

"Yes—for both of them."

"But there would be a trial first?"

"Yes, a full court-martial for her. But don't you see how difficult it will be for her to convince her fellow officers that she did not *know* he was a spy?"

Abby slumped back in the seat. Her face reflected her feelings about the hopelessness of the situation. "Poor Suzanne, what has she gotten herself into? I suppose we will have to take it step-by-step. Perhaps, if she can convince OSS that she did not know, maybe we can help her. When and if she discovers that he really *is* a spy, then she will have some stark decisions to make. Even though she loves him, she will have to choose between her love for him and her love for her country."

"This whole affair is a terrible dilemma. But we have to do what is right for our country and unfortunately no matter how much we care about those who might betray us, even inadvertently, we have to put the safety and security of our own people first."

"That's true." Abby sighed. She snuggled up close to Biff and laid her head on his shoulder. "Something like this simply makes me know how fortunate we are to have found each other. I thank God for you every day."

"Yes, we've been truly blessed." He laid his cheek on the top of her head. "Come here, sweetheart." He pulled her closer and kissed her, and soon they fell asleep as the car gently rocked them by its perpetual motion.

They arrived at the gates of the original Allistair about four o'clock. One of the estate's caretakers was there to welcome them, since they were expected. As they drove the mile long drive to the main house Abby roused up on the edge of her seat to take in the scenic view. Even in winter, it was magical. Around a bend in the drive the manor house came into full view. There it was, in all its classical, symmetrical elegance.

"At last. I thought we would never get here. You know, darling, we've been constantly traveling for hours and hours." Abby twisted her shoulders from side to side, trying to relax her spine.

"Indeed we have. It will be good to get home again. I still have another half-hour to go." Biff stretched his arms over his head.

"That's right. Mountford is your *real* home. I'm still putting the pieces together."

Carsbrooke pulled up to the front portico and stopped the car.

Robert and Cameron rushed out to embrace them, ushering them out of the cold December afternoon into the warm interior.

"How wonderful! Just in time for tea," said Cameron as she gathered her little flock into the library.

"Hear, hear, Biff," said Robert. "What's this we hear about you and a certain young lady we know?"

Biff laughed. "Now don't play innocent. You know very well. Abby has finally agreed to marry me."

"Now you stop that, Russell Bifford. Finally, my foot. I thought he'd *never* ask me!" Abby gave Biff an impish look.

"Yes, it really was a terribly long courtship, an eternity, wasn't it? After all, the two of you have known each other for all of three months." Cameron smiled, her tongue-in-cheek humor, as always, right to the point.

"Only three months? I can't believe it. I feel like I've known him all my life," she said.

"I knew the first moment I saw her," Biff said.

Cameron said, "Yes, it was that way with Robert and me. Love at first sight is like that. And a day seems like years until both parties declare it to each other.... Well now, we are absolutely delighted. Had we had the opportunity, we could not have chosen better for you ourselves."

Abby and Biff looked at each other and simultaneously burst into laughter.

Biff said, "Yes, well, we decided some time ago that we wanted to thank the two of you for making sure we met one another. Of course we know that you couldn't possibly have had any ulterior motives."

"Horrors, Cameron! We are found out. To the dungeon, for sure." Robert put his hand up to his forehead in a mock gesture of despair.

"Nothing to fear," Biff said. "The punishment is a big bear hug and eternal gratitude."

They embraced one another, then Cameron served tea in her courtly and traditional manner. "Your trip must have been terribly long and tedious," she said. "You two must be exhausted."

"Actually, we both fell asleep in the car on the way here. I think I've recovered, probably because of all the excitement," Abby said. "Of course it was worse for Biff. He had that terrible all-day drive from Canada the day before, didn't you, darling?"

"Surprisingly enough, I feel fine. Must be your magic touch. Very refreshing." Biff took her hand and squeezed it.

"Oh yes! Of course. My love potion No. 9. It's always very effective."

"Russell dear," said Cameron, "I know you must be off to Mountford, so perhaps we should discuss our plans for the next few days."

"Yes, it's getting late and my parents will be waiting. Tomorrow, Abby and I must head for headquarters in London. There are a number of loose ends we should tie up. I think we should take the train, it'll be much easier than driving. Carsbrooke and I will fetch Abby in the morning and he'll deliver us to the train. But we should return by tomorrow afternoon."

"That will be lovely. Tomorrow evening your parents are coming here to dine with us and a few of our close family and friends. Then, of course, our usual New Year's Day celebration will follow a week later. Abby, dear, I know you remember. It's one of our traditions here, and we always look forward to it."

"Of course, I remember," Abby said. "Your fabulous parties have always been part of the delight of the season."

Cameron turned to Biff. "Then, of course, Russell, your parents always give their annual Christmas Eve affair. I'm sure it will be a very special one this year, in spite of the war, with all of the excitement about you and Abby. Are you going to allow us to announce your engagement?"

"Oh dear," Abby said, "everything is happening so fast. I really haven't given that a thought. And you know I still haven't met Biff's parents."

"They'll love you." Biff smiled at her. "There will be no problem there. But as a matter of fact I haven't met your parents either." He looked to Robert and Cameron. "What would be the correct protocol in this situation? Even if it's appropriate I think the final decision should be Abby's."

"Spoken like a true gentleman," said Robert. "I agree with you completely. Of course this *is* wartime and we are all being forced into relaxing some of our usual protocols. What do you think, Abby?"

"I really don't know what I think. I've never been formally engaged to be married before. We've been in such a whirlwind we really haven't had time to think or plan anything."

"Of course, my dear, how could we possibly expect either of you to have thought this out so soon. Perhaps you should sleep on it and discuss it later. Russell, I think we and your parents are so happy for the two of you we're just overly anxious to share it with all of our family and friends." Cameron smiled reassuringly.

"I know. I feel the same way." Biff looked at Abby affectionately. "I want the whole world to know that this is *my* Abby!" Biff grabbed Abby's hand. "Shall we dance?" They all convulsed in laughter as Abby and Biff danced around the library, laughing and giggling like two little children.

Robert and Cameron joined in. Finally, out of breath, Robert stopped, and with his arm still around his own ladylove, he said, "I pray we shall always be as happy as we are this day."

In unison they all shouted, "Hear hear!"

Chapter 33

Abby was waiting early the next morning when Carsbrooke arrived with Biff to pick her up. They would take an early morning train to London to meet with the prearranged contact provided for them by the Old Man. Since this was a top-secret assignment there was as little communication or involvement with others as possible. Particularly some of the key figureheads, including Lord Smythe, who usually wound up infuriating those American and British agents who had been forced to make contact with him.

Biff, in particular, always tried to steer clear of Lord Smythe, because, besides being insufferable, he always made a big to do about bowing and scraping to him, addressing him as Your Grace and introducing him always as His Grace, Duke of Mountford. Biff had asked him many times to call him Mr. Bifford—not only because of the clandestine operations with which he was involved, but also because it could be dangerous to do anything that might inform the enemy of any title, either political, titled, or military. But it never seemed to make any difference to Smythe, who had his own agenda, and his pompous attitudes and political and social climbing agenda knew no limits. As a result, Biff tried to stay away from him entirely.

They boarded the train promptly at 7 a.m. It was quite crowded, partly because of military transit, and partly because of the Christmas season, but Biff had managed to find an empty compartment for the two of them. The clatter of the train on the tracks muffled all conversation. Even so, they kept their voices low.

"So, darling, where are we headed now?" Abby placed her briefcase and her coat on the seat beside her.

"We're off to Baker Street."

"Baker Street?" Abby sat up in surprise. "Shades of Sherlock Holmes! Are you sure we're dressed appropriately for this venture? It seems to me we should have worn deerstalker caps and caped Macintoshes."

"Good thought," Biff said, amused. "But that would simply draw attention to ourselves, something a good operative would never do."

"I can see this is not going to be any fun at all. How can I be a good spy if I'm not dressed appropriately?" She feigned an impish pout.

"Now darling, you know very well that to be a *good* spy you must never let anyone suspect that you *are* one."

Abby sighed. "I suppose that's the safe way to go, but it won't be nearly as much fun. I've always wanted to be an assistant to Sherlock Holmes."

"Well, you'll simply have to settle for Sherlock Bifford."

"Yes, Your Gracey."

"That's it!" Biff said. "A perfect pseudonym. Abby, you're priceless. Mr. and Mrs. Gracey. That's who we'll be." Their laughter rang out and joined the bells of the old church they were passing.

The train rocked along the tracks. As they came closer and closer to London the destruction of the countryside and the buildings became more and more evident.

"I had no idea how horrible that Blitz in '41 must have been," Abby said. "It's one thing to read about it, but another to see it. For miles and miles we've seen nothing but ruins. I cannot even imagine what these people must have gone through."

"Yes, about 4,000,000 families lost their homes; some of them were killed or wounded. It was terrible. Almost total devastation for miles and miles. Wait till you see London. So many of our landmarks and beautiful buildings in ruins. It will take years to clear away the debris and rebuild. And the bombing is still going on in spots—to say nothing of the sabotage. This country is teeming with enemy agents up to all sorts of tricks. We must be on our guard constantly. There are eyes and ears everywhere and we can never know whether or not they are the enemy's."

"I'm beginning to realize how close the danger is. I suppose this is not a venture to be taken lightly."

"No. But if you can see the humor in some of these ridiculous situations it can save your sanity."

"Dr. Warner said that to me not long ago. I assumed that he must have had some hair-raising experiences of his own. I found him a perfectly delightful, unassuming, and brilliant man. I wondered what he was doing in the position of Director of Training. Someone must have known how much he had to offer."

"Your hunch was correct. Dr. Warner is an icon of many of us. He was in the thick of it, even in Germany, from before 1937. His contributions to our espionage efforts there could never be surpassed. When the Germans finally caught him they tortured him unmercifully but he never gave them a shred of information. A few of our agents managed to rescue him and get him out of

Germany with the help of the Resistance, but he was deeply wounded—physically and psychologically. Nevertheless, he refused to give up. His recovery has been a true miracle, although physically he can never be the man he was. Still, he shows no bitterness or resentment and he makes it clear that it is his faith that brought him through."

"I always sensed that he had a deep faith. I can see now why they placed him in that position. Who could be better to see that others are trained properly than someone who has been captured, and lived to tell about it. I noticed how he was always cautioning to be on a constant alert and never give oneself away by some silly inadvertent gesture or word."

"Yes, the slightest mistake can signal disaster. He wanted to protect you."

They fell into silence for a few minutes, thinking of the gravity of some of the activities they would be required to undertake.

Finally, Abby turned her thoughts to the assignment at hand. "Who is our contact in London? Have you been told yet?"

"We're to report in to a Colonel Mathersby. He'll lead us to the team we're to work with. We will discuss the entire venture, both what we might expect immediately, and what alternatives may or may not develop in the future. This is a very iffy business. Sometimes events are completely unknown until the spur of the moment. And the plans must allow for all sorts of variations so that our agents won't get caught without some sort of alternative if the primary plans don't work. We also need to know the possibilities of escape in case it becomes necessary. And we need a cover story that makes sense."

"Yes, I can see how that might be necessary." Abby sat forward. "I cast my vote for Mr. and Mrs. Gracey."

Biff laughed. "They probably already have one cooked up for us. Whatever it is, we'll probably have to stick with it until after Suzanne and Jana have been apprehended. There's too much of a chance of running into the same enemy contacts again in Switzerland, Germany, or France, or even Spain. If you're recognized under another cover, you've blown your identity. And I might add your operation and even your safety."

The clickety-clack of the train began to change its cadence as they slowly began to pull into King's Cross station. It seemed to Abby to take an eternity for the train to come to a full stop.

As usual, Abby was anxious to get on with it. She longed for closure. There were so many things going on in her mind with their recent engagement as well as the job at hand. She felt some very definite decisions needed to be made soon so that she could get her feet firmly on planet Earth again.

But Biff was used to dealing with OSS and the War Office. One never knew from moment to moment what to expect. It was, as Abby had said, like taking a stroll in Wonderland—exciting, intriguing, sometimes dangerous, and at times utterly frustrating. One's own plans could be curtailed at a moment's notice, so that a change of plans in an operation could take place.

The train lurched, slowed, lurched again, and made a final stop. Biff helped Abby on with her coat. She gathered their briefcases and handed Biff's to him.

He looked out the compartment window. The station was noisy and busy, with myriads of people from countless nationalities and walks of life darting here and there. There were men and women in uniform, civilians, and a few children. Some time ago, most of the London children had been sent north for safety, but some of the older students were risking returning home for the holidays, and their parents were there to greet them.

"I think I see our escort now. They've sent a car for us."

"Makes one feel very important, doesn't it?"

"Well now, who could be more important than you, Mrs. Gracey? Certainly you're the most important one in *my* life. And, who knows, you may be the key to the success of this entire operation."

"How you do run on, Mr. Gracey. Of course, flattery will get you everywhere." She peered out the window. "Our driver, what does he look like?"

"You mean what does *she* look like."

"So our escort is a girl. Is she pretty?"

"I don't know. I'm completely blind." Biff began to chuckle.

"You'd better be, Russell Bifford. I'll bet she's absolutely beautiful."

"Beautiful? Well, if you call flaming red hair and an hourglass figure beautiful, I suppose you could say that."

Abby frowned and stuck her head out the window. The red-haired 'girl' turned out to be a chic grandmother in uniform, assigned to drive the military and VIPs to their appointments.

"You rascal! You'd better watch out, Russell Bifford. This assignment may not be the most dangerous situation you can run into."

"You know very well I have eyes only for you, darling."

"That's the correct answer, Your Gracey. You always know the right thing to say."

Abby and Biff alighted from the train and greeted their driver. She whisked them into her waiting vehicle in a military and no-nonsense manner, as though she were commanding a battalion of troops. But through her crisp and formal approach, one could sense that this was a formidable woman who was secure in her mission as well as her identity. She was still quite beautiful, despite her 59 years. But her real identity came forth after they got under way.

Biff addressed her. "You don't remember me, do you, Countess?"

"Of course I do, Russell Bifford. It's simply a matter of precaution that I don't recognize whom I'm chauffeuring. King's Cross station is full of enemy agents in disguise. Even the sidewalks are full of eyes and ears these days. One of our drivers inadvertently identified one of our agents who was later abducted by the Germans and tortured unmercifully. Of course, we could never be sure that she was the reason for the leak, but the circumstances pointed that way. We've learned to be more prudent since then."

"I see what you mean," Biff said, "but, of course, as you know we're simply innocent, run-of-the-mill civilians."

The countess responded with a wry smile. "Of course, Your Grace, I know." She continued to drive in silence past the entrance to Regent's Park and on to headquarters on Baker Street.

"Here we are," said the countess. "No doubt the earl and I will see you two at your parents' affair on Christmas Eve." She opened the door for Abby. "I know who you are, my dear. We'll talk later." With that she returned to the driver's seat and drove off.

Abby looked at Biff and laughed. "Merciful heavens! What was *that*? I feel like I've just been in a whirlwind."

Biff joined in the laughter. "That was Hermione Whitehall. And she *is* a whirlwind. Hermione is one of the movers and shakers of English society. Her father is a duke and a multi-decorated naval admiral. Now he's mainly involved in quieter activities."

"Maybe Naval Intelligence?" Abby asked as they walked into the entrance of Baker Street headquarters.

"Could be. No one says what they do, these days." Biff said. "Her husband, the earl, is the absolute opposite of Hermione. He is the most gentle, relaxed, pleasant man you'll ever meet. And he adores Hermione. Together they make a perfect pair. They are completely devoted to one another, full of fun, and wonderful company. You'll see."

"Is this the place we're looking for?" Abby turned to read the captions on the door fronts, as they walked down the long corridor.

"This is it." Biff opened a door for Abby to enter, and followed her into a small reception room. He handed his and Abby's badges to the receptionist.

"Yes, Mr. Bifford, Colonel Mathersby is expecting you." The receptionist picked up the phone and buzzed the inner office. "You're to go right in," she said.

Colonel Mathersby sat at a long conference table. He rose to greet them. No one else was present. Abby wondered why the long table if no one else was to be there.

"Do sit down and make yourselves comfortable," Colonel Mathersby said. "I can have my secretary bring tea, if you like." They declined politely.

"Well then, let's get down to business. As I understand this assignment, you two are here to apprehend a 'French diplomat' and his escort, supposedly his wife. I've been told that this is a matter of the utmost secrecy. Even I have not yet been fully informed of all the adjacent facts. I will assign several others as needed to assist you in your mission, but they too will not be informed fully unless they need to be.

"We're here today to map out what procedures we're going to need in order for you to accomplish your mission. Can you tell me what your thoughts are on the subject?"

Biff leaned on the table. "First, Colonel Mathersby, tell me how much do you know about this assignment other than what you have already told us."

"I know that this couple is aboard a ship called the *Marseilles*, and that they are due to dock in Liverpool, somewhere between December the 29th and the 31st. Or thereabouts. I know that you and Miss St. Giles are here to make contact with them, and apprehend them. I know that the two of you will need your identities camouflaged and that you will need cover stories. And I suspect that you will require some protection backup as soon as we've mapped out how we need to proceed."

"Yes, Colonel, you're absolutely correct. This is a critical assignment. Unfortunately, we don't know exactly when the ship will dock because of the storm that delayed them for probably at least two days. Also, we don't know how busy the harbor will be at the time that they arrive, nor how long they will be anchored out at sea until there's room at the dock for them to unload. So you see, there are a number of problems facing us."

"Yes of course. Well, suppose we come up with a tentative plan and move from there? We know there are certain aspects of this assignment that will have to be done regardless of the timetable."

"Exactly! There are only two plans that I can see at this point," said Biff. "One is that we apprehend them while they're still anchored at sea. The other is to wait until they dock in the shipyard. At present, I favor the former. If we wait until they dock, there's a much greater possibility that we could lose them, and we can't allow that to happen."

"I'm inclined to agree with you, however of course that sets up a number of problems. How are we going to get you two to the ship without attracting attention? And how are we going to get Miss St. Giles up a rope ladder unless she's been in training and is accustomed to such physical activity? Bear in mind this is not a large naval vessel that provides boarding stairs to board from a small boat or water taxi. This is a merchant vessel, which may not have a boarding stair and will let down a gangplank only after it docks. And wouldn't it look rather strange for a young woman to be climbing a rope ladder to board a ship?"

Abby began to laugh. "I'm just picturing the scene now. It would be rather undignified, to say the least. I'd say that should cause more than *a little* attention, and we certainly don't want that. Although I'm sure I could make it up the ladder if it were necessary."

All three joined in the merriment. Biff looked over and shook his head laughing.

"Well I think that's settles that. Abby will not be climbing up a rope ladder. I, on the other hand, may have to do exactly that, but I'm up to it. I continually stay in training. But even so, that kind of boarding at sea should be done under cover of night with no fanfare to avoid spooking them. Guess we'll have to rethink that one." Biff leaned back in his chair in thought for a few minutes. "First we need to know if this vessel *is* equipped with a boarding stair. However, it could arouse suspicion if we try to board at sea, unless we have an excuse so as not to alert them. I think it is probably best for Abby to wait on the dock. But we will need to provide protection for her, just in case someone gets wind of our plans. Their operatives seem to have eyes everywhere."

Mathersby frowned. "I can assure you that the people I assign to this task will be the best, and will most assuredly have top-secret clearance. We're keeping our eyes open on this one to know whose lurking in the shadows."

"I have every confidence in you, Colonel Mathersby. A great deal hangs in the balance on this one."

"I've gathered that. All right then, let's enumerate the bare essentials of what we need to do:

"No. 1. We need to provide identity disguises for each of you and a cover story to match. We may have to alter your ideas, but if we do, you'll know why.

"No. 2. We need to provide at least two or three undercover agents to keep Miss St. Giles under surveillance and provide protection if necessary. Someone may try to interfere with her or pick her up—the shipyards are hardly a place for an attractive young woman.

"No. 3. We need to provide an 'official' water taxi manned by our undercover agents to get you, Bifford, to the ship and back to shore with your suspects, in case that's the way we decide to go. If there be any physical violence, or attempts to escape, we'll be sure you and they are armed and able to handle any problem that arises. And they should be informed to provide consistency with your cover.

"Can you think of anything else we may have overlooked?"

Biff said, "You know, of course, if he's planning to debark here, he's going to be backed up by his own operatives. They'll be waiting to whisk the two of them away, and protect him. We could get into a rather sticky situation if he suspects that we're onto him. Or if we make the wrong moves."

Mathersby thought for a moment. "You're right. So, we need to have an adequate backup of our own operatives disguised as longshoremen to 'unload the ship.' When they come into the dock, if things get nasty we might pick up not only the suspects but several other culprits. We'll have to think this through. Anything else?"

"Not at the moment, but I'm sure there will be small details that need to be covered as we go along. We can take it step-by-step." Biff appeared confident.

"Good. Well then, first I think I should send for the people I've already contacted in each section to review the plans we have so far. I will speak to each of them individually, or as a group as to what is required. What kind of cover do you think is appropriate for you and Miss Abby?"

"Abby and I thought that we should pose as a French diplomat and his wife seeking passage on this ship for its return to Canada. That cover story should dispel any doubts or suspicions that our suspects might have until we've been able to identify and apprehend them. But that would depend on whether we board together or not. Bear in mind, we believe that the captain of this ship doesn't know who his passengers really *are*. But we don't want to alert him either, in case he or some of his crew could be a German sympathizer. His ship operates out of Vichy France at the present time.

"If for some reason the ship is able to dock immediately, then Abby and I would board immediately, posing as a French diplomat and his wife seeking passage to the ship's next destination, which is our next diplomatic assignment."

"We seem to have a lot of ifs," Mathersby said. "We'll have to provide for immediate shifts in plans if it becomes necessary. But I think for the moment we're in pretty good shape. Of course, we don't have much time left either, but I think we can pull this whole thing together in a few days, less if necessary. The first thing we need to do is get your disguises ready ahead of time, so give me your measurements, sizes you wear, height, weight, so forth. I suggest we try to make Abby look as plain as possible. She is too beautiful and will attract too much attention."

"That's the first time I've ever been accused of being too beautiful," Abby said, playfully. "Perhaps you can provide me with a false nose or something."

"Well, you know, my dear, it can present a problem. We don't want to attract any undue attention." The Colonel continued, "All right then, I've been assigned to coordinate this entire project, so

I'll get your data to the proper persons. Your clothing will have to be authentic, tailored and cut the French way. The enemy is onto any slight difference. Even the way the seams are sewn or the buttons are attached could give you away. And, I suggest you start practicing your French.

"I've called a meeting for after lunch today, to handle each of these components separately. Each will be assigned only their component part and will be given specific instructions. I think we're in pretty good shape. For now, there is really no need for you to be at that meeting. The less exposure you have, the better. In any event, they will have no knowledge of your real identity.

"Let me pull all these parts together and then we will meet on Monday the 26th to consolidate. That should give us at least five to seven days. Be sure to leave your measurements with me before you leave. In the meanwhile, have a very happy Christmas."

"Thank you, Colonel, and the same to you." Abby held out her hand.

Biff followed suit. "Yes indeed, thank you, Colonel Mathersby. I can see you have everything very much under control. It's always a joy to work with such efficient people…. Particularly, when our very lives depend upon it. I wish an exceptionally happy holiday to you and your family. And again, thank you for your help and assistance."

Biff took Abby by the arm. They left the conference room, heads spinning with all they had heard. But they were satisfied that their project was going well and that all the details would be worked out as near to perfection as possible.

Abby and Biff were met this time by another driver who sped them back to King's Cross. Thoughts of each other and the upcoming festivities crowded out their concerns for the dangers of their assignment.

At least for the next three days they could try to forget the world out there and the horror of the war, and sink into the joy and contentment of their old familiar world. They were in love: their young spirits were soaring, and they felt exhilarated, like two little children, eyes all aglow, expecting Santa Claus to come.

Chapter 34

Senator Downs sat tapping his pen on the top of his desk, having signed the last of the Christmas cards his secretary had prepared. He was late at everything this year. Here it was, two days before Christmas and he had still not finished his cards or his shopping. He had been so depressed he had no incentive. He had heard nothing from Commander Logan regarding Suzanne's death.

"Nothing gets done in Washington during the holidays," he said under his breath. The ringing of the telephone interrupted him. It was his private secure line. What was it now? He reached for the receiver.

"Senator Downs here. How can I help you?" He used his most syrupy voice. *How's that for catching flies with sugar?*

"Senator, this is Max Scheller. I'm so glad I was able to reach you."

"Ah yes, Max." He was surprised. "Good to hear from you. It's been quite a while." How did Max know the number of his secure line? No matter. He realized that Max had taken the utmost precautions. Downs had trouble keeping his voice modulated as his excitement escalated.

Max Scheller was the CEO for a large international conglomerate that Downs had been courting with government favors for six or more years since 1935. Max had shown his gratitude off and on by arranging a number of perks as rewards.

"Yes, it *has* been quite a while. Too long, I'm afraid. But maybe we'll have an opportunity to catch up with old times. Senator, I'm arranging a little holiday house party for a number of dignitaries and VIPs next week. And we were hoping you'd be able to join us."

"I see." His heart jumped for joy. "How nice of you to remember me. My schedule is rather full of the usual holiday affairs—" *No point in seeming overly anxious.* "—but perhaps I *could* manage to sneak away for a few days. I'm sure my wife can handle any engagements we have on our schedule."

"Wonderful! How does an R & R to the Grand Bahamas sound?"

Senator Downs sat forward in his chair. This was getting interesting. The Duke of Windsor had been the Governor of the Bahamas since he had abdicated the English throne in 1936.

"Ah, the Governor's Islands. It sounds absolutely divine. I can think of nothing I'd like better. It is indeed one of most beautiful spots on earth."

"Indeed it is. Of course it will be known as a fishing trip out of Miami. That will be your cover. No point in giving away the store. I'm delighted that you are interested, Senator. We can have a car pick you up and bring you to one of our planes. There's a little private airport we use right outside of Washington. It avoids publicity and affords us and our friends the privacy they desire. Since the war's been underway we find it more prudent to keep a low profile."

"Yes, Max, I couldn't agree with you more. These so-called investigative reporters have gone berserk. They put two and three together and come up with 17. We are all potential victims of their malicious attacks. Believe me, I appreciate your efforts to protect your guests." He thought for a moment. "Anyone else I know who's attending perhaps?"

"There's only one from your area. A young Frenchman. You may have met him, but I rather doubt it. His name is Louis Cabot."

"Oh yes, I *have* met him several times at the French Embassy. A very interesting young man."

"Yes, indeed he is. There are others I'm sure you have met in the past from meetings overseas."

"Max, I'm delighted. Sounds like a fortuitous opportunity to get away from all the stress here in Washington for a few days. I shall most certainly look forward to it."

"Good! Then we'll send a car for you at 7 a.m. on the 29th of December, and return you on the day following New Year's. And Senator, be sure to bring your clubs. We'll take in a few rounds of golf while you're there."

"Right." The senator chuckled. "I intend to beat you this time!"

Max Scheller responded with a light laugh. "We'll just see about that. Good, Senator, I'll be in touch."

Senator Dudley Downs hung up the phone. Obviously his fears were unfounded. Max Scheller was an important cog, high in the wheel of the future New Europe. Max himself had always kept a very low profile. Though he commanded a huge conglomerate of businesses and banks, he presented himself as a simple businessman, with little, if any, influence over corporate or governmental affairs. But those who knew his connections knew that this was simply his cover, and that when the war was over Max would emerge as an important world leader.

Max was a mover and a shaker. If one wanted something done, Max could accomplish it. Though he had never asked Max for any special favors in the past, perhaps he might venture to ask for one this time. In case he did not hear about Suzanne from Commander Logan to his satisfaction before the trip, he just might risk it.

For the first time in quite a few months, his spirits soared. No one was invited to the Governor's Island without the duke's personal permission. He was very particular. And so was the duchess.

Downs had met them before on several occasions, both in Europe and in the Bahamas. He had gotten to know the duke fairly casually. He was a most personable and gracious host. But the most interesting occasion he remembered was a highly secret meeting in Europe shortly after the duke's abdication in 1936. Although the duke himself was not present, Downs had been sure that he was listening or somehow was privy to the discussion that ensued. There was nothing said directly, but Downs deduced that the duke had ambitions to return to the throne, and that certain promises and assurances had been given him.

Downs was anxious to secure his position with his European friends. This invitation, coming at this particular time, had lifted his spirits. He was obviously still very important to them. Important enough that they would invite him to meet with them again. He had been foolish to be so paranoid. If something untoward happened, they would protect him. Even help get him out of the country.

A few years before, he had, as a precaution, purchased an elegant and secret little sanctuary in Argentina, set up under another name. It was here he had shipped a few precious art treasures he had received as "gifts" from his "friends." He had also set up an account in Switzerland, which he could be sure was secure.

Yes, he had been very careful. But that was ridiculous. No one knew of his plans for the future. He had been discrete. No one had ever known—except Suzanne.

Louis hung up the phone, with a wry smile. So, now Max was getting involved with the senator again. Maybe he knew that Downs was getting fidgety and wanted to reassure him. Max was cunning. He knew when to gather his people close to him, and Louis suspected that Max was onto Downs' pesky insecurity.

He wondered when and if ever his orders would come to take care of that pompous, arrogant, old buzzard. He, for one, was fed up with him. A real "pain in the neck" as the Americans would say. Not only a pain, he was getting dangerous.

Louis had recently seen him strutting around with his wife at the annual Embassy Christmas parties. As usual, he was bowing and scraping for political favors. But everybody knew that his new mistress was there as well, and that he had her stashed in an elegant apartment. Louis wondered if his wife knew. So many political marriages seemed to have an arrangement in which each went his own way but kept up the usual traditional appearances simply for the sake of political career insurance.

Louis might have his own moral failures, but he felt that Downs' behavior toward his wife was completely obnoxious, and sharply indicative of the degenerate character that he knew him to be.

Max had given him the skinny on the holiday trip. Officially, it was to be a fishing trip out of Miami. Max would arrange hotel accommodations there so that it would look authentic. No one would know of their real destination. Any phone calls from the States would be picked up by their agents planted there and relayed to the Grand Bahamas. He knew he could rely on Max to provide complete and safe cover.

But now he had another problem. The fact that Max had told Downs that Louis was accompanying him on the fishing trip could start Downs wondering what Louis' connections were to this group.

Of course, Senator Downs had no idea that Louis was the agent who picked up his messages at the "drop" zone. Up until now, he had known him only casually at the Embassy as a French diplomat. They had simply passed the time of day.

He certainly had no idea of his connection to Jana. Louis wasn't even sure that Max knew that. Jana had a way of keeping his links completely separated. It was imperative for security, and Louis had felt safe until now. But perhaps Max had done it to make the old jackass feel comfortable. Louis was absolutely sure that Max had no idea that he was Downs' contact.

Of course, Max knew about the senator's relationship with Suzanne in the past. Max had been present at the trade meetings in 1935 when they first met and began their negotiations. But he also knew that it had ended and that Suzanne had moved on. He doubted seriously that Max had any idea of the senator's present fears or demands regarding Suzanne. Jana would have kept that close to his vest. But if that were true, why was Max getting involved with him again?

Yes, the plot was certainly thickening. Louis knew he would have to be ready with a story to tell the senator when he telephoned. He was sure there would be a call coming soon. Though he had never been in that kind of touch with the senator before, he knew the senator's curiosity couldn't be quieted for long.

The telephone began to ring. Louis smiled and shook his head. *See there! I told you so.*

Chapter 35

Carsbrooke was waiting at the station when the train pulled in. Even the train station showed signs of the Christmas spirit with bowers and garlands tied with red ribbons and berries on the building and the quaint old lampposts. The little village was abuzz with people scurrying here and there engaged in last minute shopping. They made a quick departure and sped merrily down the country roads to Allistair.

"You know," Abby said, "I just remembered. I have gifts for you, Cameron, and Robert, but I ran out of time to find something for your mother and father. What should I do? I don't like not having anything for them."

"Actually, I already have their gifts for Christmas and we could simply give them jointly. I suspect we'll be doing a lot of that in the future." Biff smiled and took her hand. "After all, soon we will be 'as one' and everything we do will be done 'as one.'"

"What a lovely thought." Abby squeezed his hand. She looked into the distance, deep in reflection. "I never thought I could be this happy. This has to be one of God's little miracles. I'm sure I don't deserve it. It has to be His grace."

Biff chuckled. "That must be the real reason you decided to nickname us Mr. and Mrs. Gracey."

Abby laughed. "You rascal! Now who's spoofing! You know that wasn't the original reason—however it *does* fit, doesn't it?"

"Yes, Your Gracey," he said tenderly. They enjoyed the moment as they sped along toward the Christmas festivities of the next few days.

Allistair was radiant with signs of the holiday. Though they must be turned off after dark because of the blackout, electric candles sat in each window, defiant of the war raging beyond their cheery glow. Each candle seemed to represent the valiant spirit of the English in their determination to defeat the enemy. Carlisle, with assistance of the staff, was hanging a large decorated garland over the ancient carved door.

Abby's eyes lit up with delight. "Oh, what a wonderful sight. We know it's Christmas now, don't we, darling?"

"We do indeed," Biff said.

Cameron and Robert were there to greet them with afternoon tea already prepared. After teatime, Robert took Russell off to his study to discuss diplomatic affairs. Cameron and Abby sat with their after tea cigarettes pondering future events.

"Abby dear, have you thought any more about announcing your engagement tomorrow night? Russell's parents and we are eager to do so, but we cannot proceed until you've made your wishes known."

"I know, and I'm so sorry I haven't come to any conclusions yet. As a matter of fact, Biff and I have been too busy to discuss it. However, this is a good time, why don't we discuss it now? When I think about it, the only thing that prevents my saying yes immediately is because I hate to do this to my mother and father. They should really be the ones to know first and to make the announcement themselves. In addition, neither of them has ever met Biff."

"Actually, my dear, they have both met Russell. Your mother met him here when you were in school in Switzerland. I'm sure she'll remember who he is and who his parents are. Once she thinks about it, I'll wager she'll be absolutely delighted. He *is* quite a catch, you know."

"And what about my father?"

"Your father has known the duke and duchess for many, many years. In fact, he used to bounce Russell on his knee. Your father will be ecstatic and so will your mother. There is hardly anything more that parents would wish for their only daughter than a good marriage to an honorable man."

"I suppose you're right," Abby said. "Still, they don't know yet, and I really don't want to hurt them. It's my mother in particular I'm concerned about."

"I understand completely, my dear. I was sure it was your mother who made you so hesitant. She might also resent the fact that we English are taking what she would feel is her rightful place." Cameron paused. "There's only one solution, my dear, and that is to let her know immediately. Your father has already been informed by Robert. And he is delighted, I must say."

Abby began to chuckle. She felt as though a heavy weight had been lifted off of her. "It seems that all my worries were unfounded. That the choice has already been made. All I have to do is tell my mother—but I won't tell her that it's being informally announced here. That way, she and my father can make the official announcement in the States."

"That's wonderful, darling. We can do it here at the annual Christmas Eve Ball at Mountford tomorrow evening. The duke and duchess will be overjoyed. It can be done on an informal basis here, and your parents can confirm it later, officially, in the States with engraved announcements, if they wish. Of course, you know I don't believe in long engagements."

"Yes, I know, but we've hardly had a chance to enjoy *being* engaged. It's only been a few days. Besides, there are things we have to do before we could consider a wedding." Abby thought of their assignment. *Who could know how long their search for Jana and Suzanne would take?*

"Of course, my dear. Well now, suppose you and I tell the men the happy news. The duke and duchess will be here about an hour before our dinner party. We can tell them then before the guests arrive. They're bringing Russell's formal clothes so that he can dress here without having to return home."

Abby smiled affectionately at Cameron. "As usual, you've thought of everything." Abby reached over and patted her hand, and together, arm in arm they walked to the study to inform their two men.

Promptly at 7, Biff's parents arrived at Allistair. After the initial greetings, Biff excused himself and disappeared upstairs to dress for the evening. His mother, always efficient, had remembered to instruct Carstairs, their butler, to include everything needed for formal dress.

Abby, already dressed in a long dinner gown, waited upstairs for Biff so that they could come down together. Her gown, a deep red, matched the ruby and diamond pin and earrings, both family heirlooms, her mother had given her. The dress was classic and becoming.

She met Biff at the top of the stairs. Biff held her close for a second and then, hand in hand, they descended the staircase. Any apprehensions Abby might have had were quickly dismissed when they entered the drawing room. The duke and duchess sat chatting with Cameron and Robert, but when she became aware of their entrance, Beatrice Bifford approached Abby, her arms open. She embraced her.

"My dear, we couldn't be happier. Cameron has just told us that we may announce your engagement tomorrow evening at the ball. We're delighted. What a handsome couple you make!"

"Thank you, Your Grace, we were hoping you'd be pleased," Abby managed.

"We are indeed." Beatrice stepped back and observed her at arm's length. "You've grown up to be an exceptionally lovely young lady, Abby. And the prospect of joining our two families in marriage is even more than we had hoped for. Soon we must get on with plans for the future."

Biff spoke up. "All in due time, Mother. With the war raging around us, right now we're just happy to be here with you."

"Of course, my dear. Of course. There is plenty of time."

The duke came forward to greet Abby. He was charming and immediately made her feel at ease. She could see the resemblance between father and son, and particularly in the duke's brand of humor.

The guests began to arrive. Carlisle announced them as they entered. Cameron's small annual pre-Christmas dinner party turned out to be 24 of their "most intimate old friends" plus the six of the family. Thirty in all.

After one round of cocktails, dinner was announced promptly at eight. Placement at table was arranged according to protocol and Abby wondered if she would ever master all the details of a formal seven-course dinner. She had attended many but she realized it was something else to host one. Cameron, of course handled the entire proceedings with the ease of a veteran, having grown up with the formality of the aristocracy in her family, and then having married into it.

Even so, after everyone had gone through their usual paces, one could immediately sense a shedding of all the folderol as the guests relaxed into the camaraderie and humor to which old friends were accustomed. Dukes and duchesses, earls and countesses, marquis and marchionesses, lords and ladies shed their feathers and completed the metamorphosis, becoming a delightful group of intelligent people who obviously held one another in high esteem. The conversation ranged from the arts, politics, coming festivities, some not too malicious gossip, and funny spoofs. Talk of the war was avoided altogether, except for an imitation of part of one of Winston Churchill's famous speeches, given by Sir William Hedsbey, the celebrated Shakespearean actor.

All in all it turned out to be a fun and festive evening. The dinner lasted three hours but the group interaction was so stimulating that one felt refreshed when it ended. After Irish Mist coffee in the drawing room, the guests began to leave promptly at eleven, except for one or two stragglers who apparently had had a touch too much of the wines served with every course. Gracefully having seen them off, Cameron and Robert joined Beatrice and the elder Russell for a last minute chat before their departure. Abby and Biff stole away to be alone for a few moments.

"I hate to leave you, even for a few hours. This is getting bad isn't it?" Biff hugged her close to him.

"Not bad, it's horrible, I think our 'disease' is getting worse." Abby looked straight into his eyes. "What's to be done?"

"A wedding might help."

"Yes, that would help. But we'll have to wait until after this mission is over, and then—let's do it! We'll go to the priest to post the bans."

"Hallelujah! I've been waiting to hear you say that. It's getting harder and harder to wait. But maybe I can hold out a little longer. We want it to be right, don't we?"

"Yes, darling, we do. We'll be together for the rest of our lives, and we'll know we did it right."

They heard Cameron calling, "Come, Russell. Your parents are waiting."

"Till tomorrow then, sweetheart." The young lovers kissed goodbye and Biff ran down the staircase to join his parents on their trip back to Mountford.

Chapter 36

On the fifth evening, December 23rd, just before twilight, the sun began to peek through the clouds, promising a reprieve from the deadly storm. It seemed to leave almost as suddenly as it had overtaken them. From their cabin Suzanne and Jacques could hear cheers go up from the crew. It was a joyous sound. A release from the fears of the past two days, when at times all had seemed lost to the occupants of the ship.

Spirits began to lift as the crew realized the storm was over. The cheers were followed by singing, carol after carol. Many of them were the lovely old ancient French folksongs handed down from generation to generation. They wafted across the approaching brisk twilight air as the crew set about to repair the damage and set the ship straight. Tomorrow was the day before Christmas and its spirit invaded every heart. Tomorrow was another day, another chance for peace and tranquility in a world gone mad.

Suzanne's spirits began to soar as well. She had been foolish to be so afraid, and she realized that some of her fears were not from the storm alone. Some had touched on that old fear, the feeling of abandonment that had regenerated the early traumatic panic. It had hit like a bulldozer after she had witnessed the death of her parents.

Now that the storm was over, her thoughts during that period of time had vanished as well, including her fears about Jacques and their future together. She knew that he loved her and that he would protect her. She would simply trust him implicitly. She had burned all of her bridges now and she would handle the future step by step. They were engulfed in a world war and the future was unpredictable, and she would do what she could to end it, even in her small way.

As she heard the cheers go up from the crew, she turned, smiling to Jacques. And speaking in French, as they had since boarding the ship, "Something wonderful is happening. Let's go up and see."

"Bon, ma cherie. Indeed, the storm must be over. Now we can enjoy Christmas with our own celebration. It will be our first together, you know. Something to remember forever." He took her hand and led her up on the deck.

The crew was laughing and joking and singing carols. Even the captain had joined in. "Noel, Noel"—the music rang out amongst the laughter and gestures of the men rejoicing. The captain laughed as he saw their exhilaration. There would be time for discipline later. This was a wonderful moment, let them enjoy it while they may. Who could know what disaster would overtake them tomorrow?

Jacques hugged Suzanne close to him. He was reminded of other Christmases as a child with his parents in their beautiful chateau overlooking the icy river, its banks covered with snow. He could almost hear the strains of "O Tannenbaum" as they gathered around the beautiful tall Christmas tree, decked with candles and colorful ornaments. He could hear the strains of "Stille Nacht," his mother's beautiful voice ringing out its sweetness through the vast halls. Jacques found himself voicing his thoughts.

"Ah yes, the all-healing miracle of the spirit of the Christ Child. How precious it can be! This is a Christmas never to be forgotten. None of us will ever experience another like this one, in the middle of the high seas of the Atlantic, in the throes of a world at war."

The captain nodded in agreement. "Mais oui, monsieur. We shall remember this Christmas all the days of our lives." He moved back to the bridge as the orders came from the Commodore to resume their positions in the convoy.

Suzanne, touched by the beauty of the carols, looked up at Jacques, her eyes brimming with tears. She whispered, "You believe in Him, don't you, the Christ child?"

"Oui, ma petite. I have believed since I was a very young child. Our priest was a godly man. He taught us many things. The rest I learned at the knee of my saintly mother."

Suzanne looked at him tenderly. "Somehow I knew in my heart that you believed. No one could hate the enemy and the evil that has beset us as much as you and not be a believer."

Jacques looked off into the distant sea. "Yes, I hate the enemy who killed my mother and father before my very eyes, and I hate that madman Hitler who has Germany and Europe by the throat. He is massacring and slaughtering thousands of innocent people, burning books of wisdom, and bringing our beautiful European cities and culture to ruins. One day we will rid the world of him and restore our land and all of Europe, and the world will be at peace again."

Suzanne settled in the crook of his arm as they stood there. There was a brisk wind sending December's kisses across her cheek from the spray of the water. She laughed as she brushed them away. She felt safe in Jacques' arms. She felt safe in her Lord, and she knew that the future was in His hands.

Jana looked down upon the pale, golden head nestled on his shoulder. She was so beautiful, so like his mother.

He remembered the last time he saw her, standing in her regal beauty next to his handsome father, as she leaned over to kiss his cheek good night. Then her protests as the soldiers broke into the front entrance. And then her screams as the soldiers dragged them both down the marble stairs and into the courtyard. He could see them from his window, lying there as they reached for each other. He heard his father's voice call out to her, "Jana, Jana."

Then Carl and Gisela had carried him down the back stairway as the flames began to rise toward them. He remembered running—and then nothing more.

It was all those years later that the memories had finally come together. When suddenly he saw Suzanne in that lovely white satin gown. She had brought it all back— and he was glad. He had known that his hatred was focused on the enemy, but now he could pinpoint it to a fine T. He would find the one man who slaughtered his mother and father and he would bring him to justice. He would make him pay dearly for his crimes.

Jana was at peace. He knew what he had to do. He had two specific enemies—the French captain, now probably a general, who had brutally defiled his mother—and that madman, Hitler, who was defiling and dishonoring his beloved country in the eyes of the whole world. He was caught between two enemies, one at home and one abroad, but he knew what he had to do. There were plans already underway to remove the madman, but the other venture was personal. His and his alone.

Jana placed his cheek on her golden hair. How sweet was the scent. But then everything about Suzanne was precious to him.

It was almost Christmas Eve. He would surprise her. On his last trip abroad he had prepared for the day when he would act. He had waited… until now. But today was the right day. He took her by the hand and led her to their quarters. It was the right time.

He looked deep into her eyes and smiled. Silently, he slipped the ring on her finger. It was a rare and ancient treasure, the most beautiful of his mother's jewels rescued long ago from his parents' secret safe.

There was no need for words. They both knew its significance. They were now one, bonded to one another. The future was uncertain, but their love would remain, no matter what happened.

Chapter 37

Christmas Eve turned out to be a bright sunny day, reflecting off the snow that covered the countryside. At Allistair, Abby and Cameron had decided on the dresses and gowns and all the other items they must take to Mountford. Then also, there were the gifts to be packed for the two-night stay.

They would arrive that afternoon in time for the annual children's Christmas party at 4:00, an affair instituted by Beatrice Bifford for the children of the school she had established prior to the Blitz, which she had accurately predicted was imminent. Beatrice, always one step ahead of the times, intended to save as many children as possible from the onslaught of the German Blitzkrieg. And many owed their very lives to her efforts. Some, after arriving, had lost their parents in the prolonged attack and were now orphaned, but Beatrice would keep them until after the war when they could safely be placed with good families.

She had not only prepared one wing of the enormous house for a large number of live-in children, but had staffed it fully as well with governesses, teachers, and caretakers to provide for the children's needs. In addition to the children sent for safety by their frantic parents, there would be other children today from neighboring estates with their parents, for the celebration. They were frequently invited to help make the other children feel loved and accepted in the community.

Abby was touched when she learned of Beatrice's school. She wondered if she would be that self-sacrificing or that brave, to take on the responsibility of so many children not her own.

She now had a fleeting remembrance of meeting Beatrice at Allistair, many years before. It was only an impression, but when they had met last night, the old initial thoughts had returned. Here was an striking woman whose very presence commanded attention. Beatrice Bifford, Her Grace, Duchess of Mountford, was an extraordinary woman. She was educated, cultured, and brought up in the most elite circles. Although she held to the old notion of noblesse oblige, she was nevertheless generous by nature and thought of the welfare of everyone other than herself.

She was admired, respected, loved, and feared by some. She was a loyal friend, but she could be a fearful enemy. She and Cameron had been close from childhood. From similar backgrounds, they had shared the same experiences, the same schools, the same friends, and the same philosophies. They were more like sisters than friends. They had always shared the same hopes and dreams and fears for the future, and now they shared a special joy—the joining of their families in marriage.

Abby wondered if she would measure up to the task when she became Biff's wife. She knew she was young and that there would be much to learn. Although all of her life she had been in and out of aristocratic and diplomatic circles, Abby was an American, through and through. She was not accustomed to rolling over and playing dead when she heard the titles "admiral," "duke," or even "king." The Europeans demanded a stricter protocol, and she was beginning to realize that she might find this kind of life much too confining.

She was grateful that Biff had the same attitudes, although that might be because he had grown up under different circumstances and it was simply a way of life for him. Yet, she knew that those titles could be very important and could be a source of offense to some if they were not used correctly.

It was easy to make a mistake. For instance, in France a count was a count and his wife was a countess. But here, a count was an earl and his wife was a countess. Then, there was the matter of how to address them. One would need to know all the families' histories, their titles, which sometimes were multiple, and how to address them formally and informally, and when to do so. It was all very confusing.

She knew she could count on Cameron to help her make a smooth transition, and she had a feeling that Beatrice would take her under her wing, once they were married, but here again, that could prove to be a problem. In the meanwhile, she would simply have to observe and keep her wits about her. She would simply have to ask Beatrice how she would like Abby to address her when they were alone.

Abby spoke out into the empty room. "Oh dear, I hope I know what I'm doing."

"What ho! It seems like our Little One is feeling some pressure," Robert said as he entered the room. "I can certainly see why. After all, you've had quite a bit thrown at you lately. An engagement, the exhausting trip across the Atlantic, all these introductions and festivities, and of course your upcoming mission. Any one of those things would be enough to rattle you. But you know, my dear, all of us understand, and we're here to lean on, whenever you need us."

"Uncle Robert, thank you. That's exactly what I needed to hear at this moment. I'll simply take one step at the time— and worry about it later."

Robert laughed. "If you can do that you're a genius! But knowing you—I'll wager you'll come through it all with flying colors."

"You're just prejudiced in my favor." She smiled at him affectionately.

"You're exactly right. And I always shall be." He strode over and gave Abby a hug. "You'll always be our precious 'Little Abby,' and we'll always be proud of you and your accomplishments."

Abby suddenly felt at peace. She knew it was silly to anticipate the unknown. She felt comforted and supported by those she loved. And she knew that she could cope with the future. But she realized, all of a sudden, that it was different now—that the only one she really wanted to lean on was Biff. He was now her protector, her comforter. He was the one human being she called out to in times of stress.

The phone began to ring. "Shall I answer it?" she asked.

"Go ahead." Robert walked out of the room to attend to the luggage.

"I got your message," Biff said. "You did send one, didn't you, darling?"

"Yes, that's amazing. I was wishing you were here."

"Not so amazing anymore, is it? We've begun to think the same thoughts. A wonderful way to communicate!"

"I feel better already. I can hardly wait to see you."

"My sentiments exactly! Hurry the troops and be on your way. I'll be waiting."

They drove through the gates of Mountford and continued down the long drive to the main house. The countryside was enchanting with its snow-covered landscape and white dusted greenery. When the main house suddenly appeared, Abby caught her breath at its size. Even at this distance, it seemed overwhelming in its dignity and majesty. Behind the main structure were other buildings and she could also make out a large stable off to the side, a considerable distance from the house. Signs of Christmas were everywhere, even on the stable doors.

An avid student of architecture, Abby had studied the classics—Greek, Roman, Romanesque, Gothic—and had visited many of those cherished edifices Throughout Europe, the castles and churches had always been a delight, with their mystery and romance. She had lived in a treasured old home, but now she suddenly realized that she might live here one day. She might one day be its mistress and might be responsible for running a large part of this entire estate herself, as the wife of a duke. She wondered how large a staff was required to cover all the myriad tasks demanded to maintain such an establishment.

Yes, she had a lot to learn. It would be a fascinating adventure, though she had never quite pictured herself in this kind of role before. It was beginning to dawn on her that marriage to Biff carried some completely unexpected side effects. She wondered if all young women felt the same trepidation when they thought of the complete change in their lives a marriage could make.

The St. Gileses settled into their respective suites as the staff delivered their luggage and assisted in the unpacking. Elsma, a French maid, had been assigned to Abby. She had escaped from France as the Germans had invaded. It seemed that Her Grace was always rescuing the oppressed and persecuted, and Elsma was obviously both grateful and devoted to her. Abby was serendipitously acquiring a portrait of her mother-in-law to be that added to her already growing admiration. Beatrice Bifford was quite a woman.

Settled in for the two-day stay, Abby ventured down the long staircase and entered the great room, where the children were already assembled for the festivities. They were gathered round the enormous Christmas tree, standing off to the center of the hall, in front of two of the tall French doors. They were singing Christmas carols, giggling and bustling about as children do.

Abby noticed how beautifully they were dressed and how brightly their eyes sparkled as they anticipated the coming treats, games, and gifts. But there was one little girl in particular who caught her eye. She was sitting on the side with Elsma and seemed to be separated from the others. She was a beautiful child, about five years old, with long golden hair and blue eyes. Even so, her face was pale and she seemed frail and delicate. Strangely, Abby immediately warmed to her. She smiled at Elsma and stooped down to speak to her, "Are you having fun? May I get you more cake?"

"Are you an angel?" she asked, abruptly. Abby was surprised.

"Why do you ask?"

"Because you look like *my* angel," she said in her little girl's accent.

"You have a special angel?"

"Oh yes! She visits me often."

"How exciting. I'd like to hear more about her." She saw Beatrice coming toward her. "I have to go now. But we'll talk about her later. I'll come to see you very soon. Bye bye for now." The child looked up at her and smiled.

"There you are, my dear," said Beatrice, approaching her. "Come, join in the entertainment." She took Abby by the arm, introducing her to her friends from the community who had accompanied their children to the party.

"Tell me, Your Grace, who is that little girl over there? She seems so fragile." Abby nodded toward the child she had noticed so specifically.

"That is Amy, a true little darling. She was orphaned after her parents sent her here for safekeeping. Had she stayed with her parents, she too would have been killed in the Blitz. So she belongs to us now. But you're right, she is very frail. She has a heart condition that may take her life at any moment. Unfortunately, we can do nothing until a particular heart surgeon in London can operate. He is so inundated with life threatening cases where he is, but he has promised us a date soon. We can do nothing but wait, and watch her carefully. I can see you're taken with her."

"Yes, for some strange reason, I noticed her right away. I'll keep an eye on her until the party's over, if you like."

"Wonderful, my dear, but Elsma is watching her. Still, she seems to have eyes only for you." Beatrice continued engineering Abby around the group of guests and parents.

"Incidentally, Russell will be here shortly. I sent him on an errand to the village. He says he has a surprise for us—a little bit of America for Christmas." Beatrice turned as the entrance came into view. "Cameron, Robert, you two, come join the singing."

Abby looked for Amy but she had vanished. She walked into the hall to look. Biff suddenly appeared in the front entrance, his arms loaded with packages, and carrying an enormous sack stuffed with more. He was dressed in an overstuffed St. Nicholas costume, white beard and all.

Abby convulsed in laughter when she spied him. She leaned over and whispered, "May I be the first to kiss Santa?"

"Absolutely! But you do so at your own peril. I think I can do a better job of it once I get this beard off. Come, darling, give St. Nicholas a hug!"

"I see what you mean, it tickles."

"You're not the only one it tickles" He scratched his nose. "Is it time to make my entrance?"

"Let me check with your mother." Abby signaled to Beatrice. She nodded. When the carol had ended, the musicians sounded a fanfare as she pointed to the hall behind the children.

Biff scratched his nose again and stepped into the center of the great room entrance. "HO HO HO!" announced Biff. "Where are all my good little boys and girls. Aha! I think I see one or two."

Sounds of "Oooo" came from their excited voices. Every child's eye turned toward him as he strode into the center by the tree. The sack remained intact but the packages kept falling out of his arms as he swaggered forth. Abby trailed behind him at a distance, retrieving the fallen packages. It was impossible for her to contain her laughter. Biff looked so adorably ridiculous in that stuffed Santa suit.

The children began to clap their hands in anticipation. The animated chatter of children filled the air.

"And who is going to be St. Nicholas's helper?" Biff said.

Several hands of the older children were raised. "Very good! HO HO HO! Step right up. We need you to pass out the gifts. St. Nicholas has several *very large* bags this year." Another "Oooo" went up from the children as their eyes widened. Carsbrooke and Carstairs entered with two more large sacks.

Abby stood in the background, laughing, and watching with delight. She felt like a child again waiting for her turn to sit on Santa's knee. *How wonderful for all these children alone with no parents in a strange place on a war-torn Christmas Eve.* She felt the tears begin to well up but at that moment Biff leaned over to pull a gift out of his sack—when suddenly his beard got the better of him. He began to sneeze. He kept on sneezing, but the last sneeze was so hard half his beard came loose and dangled. As he stepped back his boot landed right in the middle of a plate of Christmas cake left on the floor. Suddenly, he began to laugh uncontrollably. All the children and adults joined in and became consumed with hilarity. The sounds of laughter rang out, filling the great hall to the rafters with overwhelming joyousness.

Finally, one of the older children piped up and said: "Aw, we knew it was you all along, Mr. Biff!"

But it didn't matter. Nothing could ever spoil the delight of that glorious day. And none who were there would ever forget that Christmas Eve of 1942, when His Grace, the young Duke of Mountford, alias St. Nicholas, stepped in the Christmas cake, almost lost his beard, and everyone there convulsed in laughter.

Last minute preparations for the ball were underway. The staff was busy arranging the last of the decorations and had cleared the great room of the last vestiges of the children's party.

Abby put the last touches on her attire for the evening. She lifted the top of the old antique perfume bottle and dragged the cold crystal across her throat and behind the nape of her neck. As she rose from the dressing table, the full-length mirror reflected her image in the black taffeta ball gown. Cut low off the shoulders, it was fitted snugly through the small tapered waist. From there the dress ballooned in yards and yards of rustling fullness to the floor.

Elsma smiled at her, clapping her hands, "Oh mademoiselle, c'est parfait."

There was a knock at the door. "Come in," Abby said.

Beatrice Bifford stood in the doorway looking at her with admiration. "My dear, you *are* lovely." She walked over to Abby. "I want you to have this." She held out a wide diamond tiara with an emerald set in the center surrounded with diamonds. "Would you wear this tonight—for me?"

Abby caught her breath. "It's absolutely exquisite. I would be honored to wear it."

"Then allow me." Beatrice placed the tiara carefully on Abby's head. Its sparkling presence completed the elegance of the portrait. "Oh my dear, you look magnificent. We are so proud of you. You and Russell do make a most handsome couple. I know that you two will be extremely happy together."

"Thank you, Your Grace, you are too kind and generous. I shall never forget how graciously you have received me, even though I am almost a perfect stranger to you."

"Not really, my dear. I knew you years ago when you were just a tiny little girl visiting your Uncle Robert. And again very briefly when you were in your early teens, in school in Switzerland. Even then you were a beautiful and gifted child. We have heard of your growing up adventures ever since. No, my dear, you are no stranger. You are to be my daughter, the wife of my son. Now you are an integral part of this family. You and Russell are its future. It can give me only pleasure to see that you take your rightful place in the family… I want you to have the jewels that should rightfully be yours."

She held out her arms. Abby embraced her, deeply moved, speechless.

"I should go now, the last of our guests are arriving. We shall expect to see you in a few moments." She left the room, softly closing the door behind her.

Abby was silent, overcome by her emotional reaction to Beatrice's gift.

"I'm absolutely overwhelmed. I should be nervous," Abby said to Elsma, "but instead I feel like I'm living in a fairytale."

"And you look like the princess." She paused. "But downstairs you should start shortly."

"Of course. Thank you, Elsma."

Abby took one last look, pulled on her long white gloves, and went through the door that Elsma held for her.

"Bon chance, mademoiselle."

The last of the guests arrived, announced by the old butler, Carstairs. As they began to circulate, chatting with one another, they tasted the delectable hors d'ouevres and sipped from the tall Louis XIV flutes of champagne offered by footmen who moved amongst the assembly. This was a gathering of old friends and dignitaries—the aristocracy and royalty of old England.

The receiving line had not yet formed in its usual place and all were aware that this was not the usual sequence of events for such a gathering. Curiosities were aroused, and people were wondering what surprise was in store. One or two thought they had an inkling of what was to come. The grapevine was quite active within such an elite group, and everyone wanted to be in the know.

Abby walked slowly down the hall to the grand staircase. She stood briefly at the top, watching the last of the guests arriving. The duke spied her as she hesitated at the top of the stairway. She saw Biff, his mother, his father, Cameron and Robert at the foot of the stairs.

One by one the guests began to look up at her. Abby began to descend the tall, wide staircase. Biff moved up the stairs to meet her halfway. She took his arm and they continued to descend. All at once, all eyes were on the two of them. She could hear gasps of surprise and admiration.

The duke met them at the third step. A hush came over the grand hall. The duke began to speak: "This is a grand day in the annals of this family. Due to a slight interference caused by the war, we could not do this in our traditional way. Nevertheless, on behalf of her family, it gives me the greatest of pleasures to announce the engagement of my son Russell to Miss Abigail Adelaide West St. Giles."

A roar of "Hear, hear!" went through the hall.

The duke took Abby's hand and kissed it. Then he lifted his glass. "Let us drink to the health and happiness of these two as they take their place in the future of this house and the victory over the evil that has come upon this world. May God bless them and keep them all the days of their lives, to His honor and glory."

All lifted their glasses. There were numerous toasts from different old friends and heads of families. One of the most powerful was that of the Prime Minister, Winston Churchill, who could never be surpassed when it came to eloquence.

The six of the family formed a reception group at the foot of the stairs. Couple by couple filed by to greet their hosts and to meet Abby. The gentlemen kissed her hand, bowing. The ladies curtsied and made complimentary remarks.

This is like a movie about Old England, Abby thought.

The last to come through the line was Colonel Tilbrooke. He bowed, kissed her hand, and in his typical brusque manner, looked her full in the face and said, "My God, Bifford, where did you find this magnificent creature! My dear, you are a delight to behold."

Biff laughed. "Now Tilly, no poaching! You will be allowed a tete a tete later."

"Oh, very well, foiled again," said Tilly, in jest. "I intend to hold you to it, old chap."

Biff took Abby by the hand. "Come, darling, we're to begin the dance. After that we'll have a late supper."

The orchestra started with a waltz. All eyes were on Biff and Abby as they whirled gracefully around the floor.

Chapter 38

Christmas morning arrived on time to the faint sound of church bells ringing. War or no war, it was the birthday of the Christ child and no red-blooded Englishman was going to let a little thing like a catastrophe interfere with celebrating it properly.

The old church had bravely withstood the bombings and the vicar had courageously refused to stop services thereafter, regardless of the sections of missing roof, some of the ancient leaded glass windows and the ruins of almost one complete wing. The parishioners, outraged at the idea that their archenemy would dare to encroach upon God's territory, immediately began repairs, and despite the shortages of building materials, what was required had appeared miraculously.

Out of the blue, skilled craftsmen appeared from within the community, and the old church building slowly began to recover. True, the south wing would have to wait, but at least the congregation was now protected from the snow and the rain. Two of the stained glass windows had been entrusted to old Michael, who, everyone knew, could repair anything. Temporarily they had been boarded up to protect from the cold and the other repairs.

At the first service after the Blitz, the vicar had pointed out that the *people* were the true church and not the building itself, and that the rock upon which the church was established was their belief in Christ and their confession of Christ as savior. It was an object lesson that many needed to hear. It drew the congregation closer together, and they had reached out to each other in a way never seen before.

On this Christmas day, the parishioners began to arrive with an unconscious sense of expectancy. Families filed into their accustomed pews. Neighbors gathered together in one accord to worship. An atmosphere of camaraderie and love pervaded, and an unspoken acceptance overcame the envy and prejudice so often seen in any diverse community. The war had brought devastation and personal loss into every home, and made evident how interdependent the villagers were upon one another and on those of the outlying estates, who came to worship together as one spiritual family.

The congregation, having greeted one another, settled down to their preliminary prayers, kneeling on the old needlepoint cushioned prayer benches provided a century ago by some of the church women. Soon the old organ sounded the opening hymn, "Hail, Thou Almighty King," and the congregation stood to receive the processional entourage as it headed slowly toward the altar. The service progressed in an orderly fashion. The music was mainly the timeworn carols that everyone loved so much. The children from the parish, including Beatrice's school for the orphaned and other students, provided a special part of the musical program.

Abby spied little Amy sitting on the altar cushion, singing "The Little Lord Jesus, Asleep on the Hay." The sight of her brought smiles and tears and prayers to those who knew her tenuous condition.

At the first service after the Blitz, the vicar had pointed out that the *people* were the true church and not the building itself, and that the rock upon which the church was established was their belief in Christ and their confession of Christ as savior. It was an object lesson that many needed to hear. It drew the congregation closer together, and they had reached out to each other in a way never seen before.

On this Christmas day, the parishioners began to arrive with an unconscious sense of expectancy. Families filed into their accustomed pews. Neighbors gathered together in one accord to worship. An atmosphere of camaraderie and love pervaded, and an unspoken acceptance overcame the envy and prejudice so often seen in any diverse community. The war had brought devastation and personal loss into every home, and made evident how interdependent the villagers were upon one another and on those of the outlying estates, who came to worship together as one spiritual family.

The congregation, having greeted one another, settled down to their preliminary prayers, kneeling on the old needlepoint cushioned prayer benches provided a century ago by some of the church women. Soon the old organ sounded the opening hymn, "Hail, Thou Almighty King," and the congregation stood to receive the processional entourage as it headed slowly toward the altar. The service progressed in an orderly fashion. The music was mainly the timeworn carols that everyone loved so much. The children from the parish, including Beatrice's school for the orphaned and other students, provided a special part of the musical program.

Abby spied little Amy sitting on the altar cushion, singing "The Little Lord Jesus, Asleep on the Hay." The sight of her brought smiles and tears and prayers to those who knew her tenuous condition.

Chapter 38

Christmas morning arrived on time to the faint sound of church bells ringing. War or no war, it was the birthday of the Christ child and no red-blooded Englishman was going to let a little thing like a catastrophe interfere with celebrating it properly.

The old church had bravely withstood the bombings and the vicar had courageously refused to stop services thereafter, regardless of the sections of missing roof, some of the ancient leaded glass windows and the ruins of almost one complete wing. The parishioners, outraged at the idea that their archenemy would dare to encroach upon God's territory, immediately began repairs, and despite the shortages of building materials, what was required had appeared miraculously.

Out of the blue, skilled craftsmen appeared from within the community, and the old church building slowly began to recover. True, the south wing would have to wait, but at least the congregation was now protected from the snow and the rain. Two of the stained glass windows had been entrusted to old Michael, who, everyone knew, could repair anything. Temporarily they had been boarded up to protect from the cold and the other repairs.

In all, it was a glorious service, and when the procession had exited the church they began slowly to leave with the feeling that they had been filled by the love and presence of the living God. Each stopped to greet the vicar as they departed. Abby and Biff, engaged in conversation with neighbors and friends, were almost the last, waiting to leave.

Abruptly, they became aware of some kind of commotion going on outside. Abby wondered what it could be, but no one seemed to know and there was no sense of alarm. The church was crowded that day and it was ten or fifteen minutes before they reached the entrance. But immediately it was clear that the vicar was no longer there to greet them.

"What do you think has happened?" Abby said. "Why are those people gathered over there?"

"I don't know, but there is the vicar and—isn't that the village doctor, Tisdale? Yes, it is. Someone must be ill."

"Let's ask," Abby said. "There must be some one who knows."

Almost immediately, Beatrice Bifford, obviously struggling with tears, approached them.

"Mother, what has happened?" Biff took her in his arms to comfort her.

"It's little Amy. She collapsed about fifteen minutes ago and there was nothing the doctor could do to save her. I'm afraid she's gone. And I had so hoped that we could persuade that London surgeon to operate on her."

Abby didn't hesitate. She practically flew over to where Amy's lifeless little body lay in the arms of the vicar as he performed the last rites.

"No, no!" she cried out. "She must live and not die." She reached the vicar holding Amy's body. Dr. Tisdale was kneeling to one side.

"It's too late, my dear," the vicar said gently, "The doctor has pronounced her dead."

Abby ignored his words. She quickly knelt beside him and laid her hands on little Amy's heart. "Pray with me," she commanded the priest. He responded immediately. It was as though some higher authority had stepped in to intervene.

Together they prayed. Abby felt an overwhelming current going through her arms into her hands—and into Amy's heart. The priest looked at her. He felt it too, as did the congregation, as the power of the Holy Spirit swept over them.

Old Doctor Tisdale stood by observing, and soon all who were gathered near joined in silent prayer. Within a few seconds Abby felt little Amy's heart begin to beat. Stronger and stronger, it beat, as the life's blood circulated through her little body.

Kneeling again, the old doctor checked her heart; he smiled and shook his head. He had witnessed a few miracles, in his lifetime and this was one of them. A gasp went up from the parishioners when they realized what had happened. In an instant their sorrow had turned to exultation.

Abby's eyes met the vicar's. They began to laugh. In obedience they had asked for a miracle and the Lord had answered their prayers.

Little Amy opened her eyes. She looked straight into Abby's. "I knew you wuz my angel," she said. "I saw you there wiff me, standing 'fore the Lord."

"Did you?" Abby said, happy tears streaming down her cheeks. "And what did the Lord say?"

"He said I mus' go back—tell the people."

"Of course He did! He had a special purpose for you all along." Abby squeezed her hand. "It will be all right. He's going to heal you completely!" The ambulance pulled up to take her to the hospital. Amy looked at her with her big blue eyes, expectantly.

"I'm coming with you," Abby said.

Biff took her by the hand and helped her up. "Come, we'll follow the ambulance, darling"

"Could we take her to London? That doctor is going to operate on her *today*." Abby was resolute.

Biff laughed. "All right, Mrs. Gracey, if you say so. After this, I'll believe any thing you say."

Abby took Amy's little hand. "We'll be following you to the hospital. Don't be afraid!"

"Oh, I never be 'fraid again." They lifted the stretcher into the ambulance. Amy smiled at her.

"See you in a little while," Abby said.

Doctor Tisdale climbed in the ambulance with Amy, still shaking his head, and they were off.

London was fairly quiet on that Christmas afternoon. Families had gathered in their homes to enjoy the day after their traditional church services and family dinners. Despite the widespread rationing of food and delicacies, the ingenuity of the English mums had engineered a repast for each home as nearly like "old times" as possible.

The hospital received little Amy with tender concern, reassuring her and providing a very large stuffed bunny for comfort. Beatrice had phoned ahead and had alerted the staff to contact the heart surgeon. He had promised to stop in and check on Amy.

Abby and Biff awaited his appearance in the outer room. Magically, he arrived within minutes of their arrival, and, after giving Amy the once over, came out to talk to them.

"From what I hear, this child is a living miracle. I've decided to operate immediately. She's holding her own right now but I don't want to delay her surgery any further. We'll run a series of tests first and then go for it."

Abby gave Biff a knowing look and smiled at the doctor. "Wonderful! Somehow, I knew you would do it."

"Well, you were right, young lady. Seems this is a very special child and a very special Christmas Day.

"You don't know how right you are, doctor!" Biff said. "But I can't tell you how grateful we are that you've taken her on. It's a great comfort, knowing she's in your competent hands. She's an orphan, but we have arranged to take care of her expenses at the hospital and your fee, of course."

"That won't be necessary, Your Grace. My fee will be a Christmas gift to a little orphaned girl. It will be my pleasure."

"Then we'll set up an account for the next of your patients who can't afford your services," Biff said.

"Excellent. I have another child on the waiting list now. That may very well save his life. There are so, so many, and so few of us who've been left to treat them. I simply cannot get to them all."

He turned to Abby. "She calls you her angel, you know. You may go in to see her now. I've called in all my staff, we'll run all the tests and then we'll be operating within the hour."

Abby and Biff spent the next few minutes with Amy, laughing and giggling about all of the wonderful things that were happening. Amy was not in the least afraid of the operation. She was convinced that she was already healed completely. Once the nurses and attendants took her into the operating room, Abby and Biff wandered down to the ground floor to have tea.

"How long did he say it would be?"

"He said it could be hours. He didn't know."

"Well, there's no need to get impatient, is there?"

They had their tea and talked about what had happened. It was almost too good to be true.

Finally, Abby turned to Biff. "Let's go back up and see if there's any word." They walked hand in hand to the elevator and on to the surgical unit on the fourth floor.

Biff looked at his watch. "It's been only three hours. I think we may have quite a long stay ahead." They sat down on a sofa and settled in to wait.

In a few seconds the head nurse came rushing toward them. Biff's heart sank. *She can't have died, Abby will be crushed.*

"The doctor wants to see you," she said, breathlessly.

Abby and Biff followed her down the long hall. They waited apprehensively outside the door to the operating room. Soon the doctor came out, removing his mask.

"I am truly amazed! I have never seen anything to equal this. Not only did this child have a grossly malfunctioning heart when I examined her a few months ago, but very little chance of survival even with an operation. But I have to tell you, not only did you pray life back into her, young lady, to get her here, now she has a completely new and perfect heart. We ran all the tests twice, examined her thoroughly, compared her last X-rays, fluoroscopes, all other tests, and checked all her heart functions over and over. We couldn't believe it. There's nothing to operate on. She'll be a little sore for a few days but she's a perfectly healthy little girl, with no restrictions on her activity. She is a *true miracle.*"

Abby took the surgeon's hand. "I don't know what to say. Thank you, thank you!"

The doctor laughed. "No need to thank me, young lady. With you around, my dear, there won't be any need for my profession.

I'll have to tend to other kinds of plumbing.... Why don't you go in and see her. She should be back in her room by now."

Biff shook the hand of the doctor. "Then you'll send her home soon?"

"Yes, she can go home tomorrow evening or the next day. We'll keep her at least overnight." He began to remove his gown. "Now I'll leave you to return to my family's Christmas dinner. This will be a wonderful Christmas story to tell *my* children. Goodbye, and a jolly good Christmas to you."

"And to you as well," said Abby and Biff almost in unison. They slipped into Amy's room. She was sound asleep from the sedatives.

A nurse was tending her. "I'll tell her you were here," she said. Abby bent over and kissed her cheek. She saw a faint smile as Amy responded.

"Tell her someone will be here tomorrow evening to take her home," Abby said.

"Yes, and that is not all I'll tell her. The entire hospital is calling her our 'Christmas miracle.' She doesn't even know it yet." She smiled at them her eyes shining as they left the room.

They met Doctor Tisdale in the hall taking off his gown. He had observed the tests and procedures. He beamed with wonder and exuberance, as though he had discovered a long lost treasure after years of search.

He reached for their hands. "This is a Christmas we'll never forget. God is good!"

Chapter 39

Dudley Downs was getting more and more excited about his trip to the Bahamas. He had been careful to cover all the bases. His associates had been informed that he was going to Miami on a weekend fishing trip. He needed a short R & R from the demands of the wartime Congressional upheavals and this was right up his ally. They had all expressed similar desires.

He had been in excellent spirits over the past few days. Ever since his "invitation" from Max two days before Christmas, he had been like a changed man. Betsy, his wife, was amazed at the change in him. He had been so morose over the past few months, she had begun to wonder if he were near a nervous breakdown. He had not only been curt, even insulting, to her but hateful to the children.

Now suddenly his spirits had lifted. He had lavished them all with lovely Christmas gifts and had been loving, affectionate, and considerate for the first time in months. He had even presented Betsy with an exquisite diamond pin on Christmas morning. The family had had a wonderful time together this holiday for the first time in years. Even when the two of them had attended the Washington parties, Dudley had been courtly and affectionate to her. She hadn't noticed his mistress anywhere either, which was a great comfort, but she had to wonder what had overtaken him. Was it a new fling? A new mistress? Or something else?

Betsy wasn't really sure what it was but she knew something had happened to lift his spirits. She knew him too well. After all these years, she knew all the signs. Then, finally on the morning of the 26th he told her about the "fishing trip." Could she handle their engagements through New Year's? Could she do this, could she do that? He even promised her a week at a posh resort as a peace offering.

Oh yes. It was the same old Dudley. Even the diamond pin had been quid pro quo. It was always that way with Dudley—you do this for me, I do that for you.

She was used to it by now. She had loved him deeply once but he had betrayed her too many times. She had agreed to stay with him after one particularly horrible episode, for the sake of his career and the sake of the children. But now she felt only sorrow and pity for a man who could have been so much more. It was a sad example of how unchecked ambition and the thirst for power had corrupted a potentially true statesman.

Betsy had seen it in him in the early years—that fire of aspiration to serve his country. She had shared it with him. But slowly she had witnessed the evil pull of Washington politics begin to induce him to make deals, cut corners, betray friends. She had even wondered if he had had a part in the disappearance of one of the young women, or even the accidents or scandals of some of his opponents who didn't agree with him. But she had never really known for sure, although she had thought she could connect some of the dots.

She had tried to live up to her part of the bargain and maintain some measure of self-respect, difficult though it had been with a philandering husband. But Betsy knew what divorce could do to a woman and her children. In the 1930s, it was considered something of a disgrace in the eyes of many. It cut the woman off from social functions and from her identity altogether, which her husband had provided for her and the children.

No, Betsy was wise enough to know that remaining the wife of a senator, even a stained one, was far better than the alternative. It was she and the children who would suffer the most while he would lose nothing at all and be totally free to flaunt his affairs with no inhibitions whatsoever.

Dudley could imagine what was going on in the mind of his wife. She was usually waiting for the other shoe to drop. But Betsy was a very wise woman. Dudley admired her. He knew deep down he loved her and respected her. She was his anchor in a stormy sea. Nor could he imagine what he would do if it weren't for Betsy. She had pulled him through many a crisis, emotionally, politically, and otherwise. He would make it up to her someday. Those other women really meant nothing to him. They were just playthings to boost his ego. It was just a mark of the sophisticated politician. A male thing. Everybody did it, joked about it. Another notch on the belt, so to speak.

But recently Dudley had begun to reflect on his past. This last emotional episode had demonstrated how low depression could reach. He had made up his mind. He would secure his arrangements on this trip, and then he would not run again, or resign, and move out of the country. But he knew he couldn't do anything to arouse suspicion. Not now. He had been becoming more and more frightened of the unspoken threats and what they could do to him. Now this trip was his chance to secure his future. He felt like he had a new lease on life.

It was the 27th. He decided to check with Louis Cabot at the French Embassy. He understood they were to travel together. Good excuse for him to call.

Dudley picked up his secure phone and dialed the number Louis had given him. It rang three times before Louis answered. His melodious French accent had always intrigued Dudley.

"Ah, Louis, I caught you there. Have you heard any more about our plans for departure?"

"Oui, Senator, I am so glad you called. Apparently, there's been a problem with the clearance of a private plane. Security, you know. So they have switched us to a commercial DC-3 carrying a number of VIPs with top priority to Florida for the holiday. Unfortunately, I'm going to be delayed at least one day, so I will join you there later."

Dudley was puzzled. "Why haven't I been informed?"

"Oh, Senator, I'm sure the driver who will pick you up in the morning has all the information you'll need as well as your tickets. You know Max, he always arranges everything and doesn't see the need of bothering us with details of changes."

Dudley laughed. "Right you are. He's like that. Cuts to the chase and all that. No wonder he's achieved so much."

"Very true, no wonder."

"Very good, then, I'll be ready. Incidentally, do you know who any of the other people are?"

"Only two or three I can think of. One is Chairman of one of the Senate committees, name escapes me—and, ah, one is a well-known European art dealer, and let's see—an English lord something or other."

"Then some are from our own government?"

"Yes, but they're all destined to go their separate ways once they reach Florida. None are included in our fishing group."

"I see." Dudley chuckled. "All right then, I'll expect to see you in a day or two. Good show!"

"Au revoir, Senator. This should be an exciting trip. Till then."

Louis hung up. He looked pensively out of his window at the majestic buildings below. "Yes, this should prove to be a very interesting and exciting trip, indeed."

He picked up his secure phone to call Max.

Chapter 40

On Monday the 26th Abby awoke early, somewhat disoriented. Then she remembered that they had decided to stay in London rather than return to Mountford and make the trip back the next morning. Her anxiety was mounting—their deadline was fast approaching. OSS had assigned them to a safehouse in London usually used for agents preparing for a secret mission or those requiring cover for some reason.

They would be quite busy the forthcoming week, meeting with Colonel Mathersby and planning with those involved in their assignment. The trip back and forth to Derbyshire would involve precious time they could not afford to waste.

Carsbrooke had returned to Mountford the night before with Doctor Tisdale, whereupon Beatrice had thoughtfully had their things packed and sent down to them by Carsbrooke on Monday morning. He and Elsma would fetch Amy when she was discharged and bring her back to the school.

Abby was glad not to return so soon. From her phone conversation with Beatrice she knew that Amy's miracle was the talk of the town and she really didn't want to answer any questions about it. Abby was just as amazed as anyone else at what had happened. It defied analysis, she had simply been compelled to intervene. She would think about it later. Perhaps it would all become clearer in time. She had never thought about healing before, but now she knew it truly was a gift from God.

Biff knocked on the door, "Are you dressed?"

"Almost. Come on in—just a touch or two more."

"We're due in Mathersby's office in 30 minutes. I ordered croissants and coffee, no time for a full breakfast."

A young waiter brought in a tray and placed it on the table by the window.

"You think of everything, sweetheart. That coffee smells good."

"Yes, doesn't it. Drink up—a car will pick us up in 15 minutes. From then on we'll be in concentrated planning and training."

"You'd think it would be fairly simple, wouldn't you?"

"One would think so, but we have to be prepared for any contingencies should they occur. For instance—suppose you were captured?"

She looked at him, startled at the thought. "How could that be—we're in England?"

"Believe me, it's happened here. England is a hotbed of espionage, sabotage, and dirty tricks. Abduction is not unusual in the least."

"Are you trying to frighten me, Mr. Gracey?"

"Just putting you on guard. I don't want anything bad to happen to my Abby."

"I'll be on alert, darling. I'll be careful, don't worry. Besides, I think somebody up there is looking after us."

Biff looked at her lovingly. "I believe you. He certainly has so far."

A car was waiting for them, and after a short drive to Baker Street, they entered Colonel Mathersby's office. For the next three days they worked on the details of their mission. From time to time representatives of different components of their operation joined them to supply what was needed, but never were they all there together.

SI (Secret Intelligence) tried to look after their agents in Special Ops as meticulously as they could in the form of preparation, planning, and backup. After that, they were on their own and would have to handle any snags or unexpected foul ups with their own ingenuity.

Colonel Mathersby gave them his input as well. "We've decided it will arouse too much suspicion for both of you to try to board the ship at sea so we have arranged for the *Marseilles* to be among the first to dock when the ships arrive in the harbor."

"Good. So that will help to eliminate that problem," Biff said.

The Colonel continued, "Yes, I hope. We'll alert our people to keep watch to see that no one slips over the side unnoticed, but that probably could not happen except during nightfall. Of course it depends on how busy the harbor is as well."

"True. Of course, either one or both of them might attempt to return with the pilot boat. But we'll be ready for that option."

"Incidentally, Bifford, Sir Robert checked again with his contacts at the Vichy French Embassy. Your diplomat is registered there but under 'at large' status. Even so, no one seems to know who or where he is."

Abby was surprised but she said nothing. Why hadn't Robert told them that D'Arcy was registered? Perhaps he had just been informed.

"Are you sure this is the man you're looking for?" Mathersby leaned forward, his eyes questioning.

"He's not the only one we're looking for. But yes, from some of the other leads we have, we're reasonably sure. Even if he isn't, we think we can resolve part of our problem."

"Very well. You would never have gotten this far if top brass didn't think it was ultra important. We know all kinds of strange things are coming out of Vichy. Under Petain it was somewhat loose, but it's heavily German controlled now.

"At first, we didn't like the idea that you pose as a French diplomat and his wife. It's risky. Should one of you be discovered it places the other one in jeopardy.

"Then we discovered that the St. Gileses were anxious to get her mother out now that the Nazis have stopped playing games and replaced Petain with Laval. He is a monstrously strict Nazi puppet and has tightened up controls on Vichy to a strangulation point. We think that day is coming very soon when the time to rescue her will disappear. The countess is into all kinds of undercover activities. She is harboring two of our agents now who've escaped from the Nazis. She may not be able to deceive them much longer. The window of opportunity may close at any moment.

"We discussed Abby going to Vichy as the American grandniece of the countess to check on the state of her health. Perhaps to bring her out under the pretense of a medical operation in Switzerland. Actually she *is* her grandniece. It would simplify matters. Besides the countess has had a great deal of rapport and influence with both the pre-war Germans and the French, having lived there so long. It would afford Abby more protection, at least for the time being. But now, we think perhaps your joint cover is secure enough to accomplish that mission as well."

Biff was alarmed. "Colonel Mathersby, if we cannot apprehend them on board the ship, we plan to do it at the dock in Liverpool. My orders are limited to catching these two. I have no orders to extend this mission at this point. If you are planning another leg to this assignment, please tell me now."

Mathersby persisted. "If for some reason you cannot detain them here, then you might think about changing passage to another ship sailing to its home port, Marseilles. Particularly, if you're unsuccessful in capturing them now. That would put you fairly close to the countess' home in Vichy France. Also, you know they're probably headed somewhere near there."

"That may be true but we don't plan on that." Biff was firm. "It is much more to our advantage to capture them here in England. Trying to follow them to France could be disastrous. They would certainly have discovered us by then. In fact they may already know. In any case, we can be assured that no matter how D'Arcy plans to get them off this ship, he has planned their escape very carefully."

"True. Then I think I've already told you what your next assignment may be."

"Yes, I get the message, but this one takes priority and we need to accomplish it before we even consider anything further. We have to keep this as simple as possible. If we get too complicated it could blow the whole affair. You know very well the three ingredients of a successful attack are simplicity, security, and surprise."

"Besides," Abby said, "if later on I should go under my own identity, that would prevent me from ever risking another assignment in occupied France. Someone would be bound to recognize me."

"Possibly. Well, you realize we have to think of all the alternatives. We'll keep it confined to England then, for now," he said, acquiescing.

Biff said, "That's our plan. If we're careful and don't spook them, I think we can get this done without any hitches. Abby's main role is to identify the woman, alert our operatives to take her in custody. After that, she'll be needed to inform Suzanne about the man she's with and the truth of her own status, interrogate her, and obtain as much information as possible about her traveling companion. Abby can identify her either from the dock or by boarding the ship. There is no need, at present, to place her in any further unnecessary danger."

"I see." The Colonel could see that Bifford was concerned about Abby's safety. "Well, I think I'd have to agree to that. We'll proceed according to your original plan, at least for now."

They were taken for fittings of their clothing, which had been meticulously prepared in the French manner. Given code names and cover stories, which had to be practiced until they seemed authentic and on the tip of the tongue; instructed as to the use of one of the buttons that converted into a compass, the use of a camera the size of a matchbox, and a small easily concealed gun. They were provided French money, cigarettes, toilet articles, passports and visas, and official diplomatic identification, French driver's licenses and other paraphernalia. All personal effects, jewelry and otherwise, had to be replaced with authentic French substitutes. But Abby had already entrusted her engagement ring and other jewelry to Cameron for safekeeping.

They were cautioned regarding French customs, table manners, and multiple instructions for survival should they be captured or abducted, including a little blue pill and a "pencil" that fired a single 22-caliber bullet. Abby recoiled at the thought of either.

By the 28th[th], they were beginning to feel that they had covered most all the bases. Now, there was simply a matter of practice, review of the entire plan with the other elements, and the interminable waiting—a frequent occurrence between operations.

Chapter 41

The morning of the 29th found Dudley Downs packed and raring to go. At 7 o'clock sharp, a uniformed chauffeur pulled up in front of his home. The chauffeur picked up his luggage and departed for the car, while Dudley turned to tell his wife goodbye. He took her hands and looked at her for a long moment.

"You're still a very beautiful woman, Betsy. I wonder if you know how much I love you. I know it's been difficult for you all these years, but after this trip I mean to make it up to you."

Betsy felt tears of joy surging up from her inner being. For a moment she felt all the past humiliating events disappear and they were once again a young, idealistic couple who had come to Washington to serve their country. She knew he was sincere. She knew, this time, he really meant it.

He took her in his arms and kissed her as though they were still the young lovers they once had been. He thought he saw tears in her eyes before he turned and headed for the car.

Betsy watched him as he walked to the driveway.

Maybe there was hope for them after all.

The chauffeur opened the door of the Rolls for him and saw to it that he was comfortable. He noticed the fully stocked bar. He decided to have a scotch and soda on the way to the airport. One for the road. Yes, Max certainly knew how to make one feel elegant.

Dudley was given instructions on the way to the airport. He was handed a package with his tickets, reservations for the hotel in Miami, and details of who would pick him up when he landed. His trip on to the Bahamas was top secret, so he knew he'd have to wait for his contact in Miami.

As he boarded the plane, his euphoria knew no bounds. He nodded to Senator Montrose, who had been his archenemy for years. They eyed each other as each of them found their assigned seats quite far from one another. Dudley was assigned a seat in the back beside Lord Farling, whom he had met before, both in Europe and the United States. A rather handsome, even haughty man, who exhibited many feminine mannerisms, and at times seemed to downright flirt with many of the more attractive male sex.

Dudley was not pleased to have been seated next to him. Before the plane took off he arose and quietly asked the stewardess if she could reassign him. There were two empty seats all the way forward, right behind the cockpit. He accepted one of them and went back for his things.

Lord Farling looked up at him, "My dear chap, are you moving already?"

"So sorry to have to move but I seem to be allergic to something back here." Dudley feigned a sneeze. "Please forgive me."

"It's probably just my perfume. Some of the other fellows are allergic to it too."

"Yes, well. See you later." Dudley hurriedly gathered his belongings and made a beeline for the front where his new seat was waiting. "Damn!" he said quietly to the stewardess, "that guy's a blatant weirdo. I don't even want to be seen near him."

He caught Senator Montrose's raised eyebrow as he passed by. Montrose was softly laughing at him.

"Lover's quarrel?" he asked.

Dudley gave him a dirty look. "Hardly. As a matter of fact, he said he's been waiting for *you* to join him." The old bastard—he'd already done enough to make his life miserable in the Senate. He wouldn't give him the satisfaction of spoiling his high spirits now.

He quickly settled in his seat and fastened his seatbelt. The engines' motors revved up and soon they were off.

It was a clear and sunny day. They flew up, up, into the clean blue air. Dudley wafted off into his favorite daydream—he was a hero and the crowds were waving, shouting, and cheering him—He never once suspected the large briefcase placed in the luggage compartment above his head.

But then, unexpectedly, an explosion abruptly shattered any dreams for the future that Dudley Downs might have had, or those of the crew, or those of the other 25 passengers who unsuspectingly boarded the plane that fateful day.

Truth is—they never knew what hit them.

Chapter 42

On the morning of the 29th, they were meeting with Colonel Mathersby to collate all the final aspects of their venture, when they were interrupted by a messenger.

"We've just been informed by Sir Robert that you are to be alerted to the news reports from America." The colonel handed them a copy of the late morning's *London Times*.

"Sir Robert said you would get the connection."

There on the front page was a startling story. "Thursday morning a TWA DC-3 carrying Senator Dudley Downs, Senator Amos Montrose, Lord Percy Farling, Jean Le Vallieur, and others traveling to Miami, Florida, crashed and burned shortly after take-off. There were no survivors. Observers reported that the plane suddenly exploded in mid-air while in level flight. The mysterious explosion causing the crash is now under investigation."

The article went on to extol the virtues of the two senators, one of whom was chairman of the Senate Intelligence Committee, Lord Farling, a primary influence in English Parliament, and Jean Le Vallieur, a world-renowned art critic and dealer, and a number of other luminaries, also victims of the crash.

"Families have now been notified and identification of the bodies is in progress. As more information is forthcoming the public will be informed."

Biff gave Abby a look. "The plot thickens. There has to be a connection among these four. We can guess old Montrose was close on Downs' tail, but the art dealer—and Lord Farling?"

Colonel Mathersby frowned. "We know Farling's been a terrible embarrassment to Parliament as well as the town gossip. Can't possibly keep his mouth shut—even to a dangerous point. Some suspect he blackmails to make his deals. I have no doubt someone might wish to be rid of him."

"Yes, that figures," Biff said. "The art dealer, Le Vallieur, is a wild card—but he could be part of the plot to sequester the old European art treasures."

"You don't think—" Abby was alarmed.

"Oh yes, I do. It makes perfect sense—kill four birds with one stone."

"But the others—the innocent ones—"

"Ruthless men aren't concerned with innocents if it suits their itinerary, darling."

"Hear hear," said Colonel Mathersby. "I get your drift. And somehow all these incidents are part of this caper?"

"I should think they're dammed well related. Every one of these people knew too much."

"The thought of deliberately bringing a crowded plane down simply to get at four—it's unbelievable!" Abby grimaced. "They're ruthless, all right."

"Yes, they are. There are enemies everywhere. And they'll stop at nothing to achieve their goals and protect themselves. We need always to be sure we know with whom we're really dealing."

The colonel seemed to drop his super calm manner and allow his anger out. "Damned right. We'd bloody hell better ensure that we've planned this escapade very carefully and spare no backup. We're looking at two days from now. The ship is due to dock on the 31st. By the 30th we'll have everyone in place, including you two.

"We're moving about six of our SI men from another port. They've been at Hull investigating a dockside explosion of one of our ships. Blew itself and everyone around it to hell and back. We're convinced it was sabotage, and done deliberately. But we can free them up now and have them here tomorrow to execute backup on the dock for Abby and assist you, Bifford, in apprehending them, or whatever happens afterwards.

"I have four other sailors and a lieutenant in charge of the pilot boat to take you to the ship, Bifford, in case it doesn't dock right away. Incidentally, we checked—it *is* a larger vessel that we thought and it does have a boarding stair."

"That helps lessen the complications," Biff said.

"Yes, still, I think it would arouse suspicion for you both to rush into boarding at sea when they're due in port within a few hours. Maybe you, Bifford, could go first with the pilot boat to deliver a message to the captain from the French Embassy. That wouldn't be unusual. But they'll be in port unloading for at least a day. There would be no need to spend that time on board. Unless you were hiding from something."

"You're right, of course." Biff grew pensive. "We'll wait on that one, and think it over."

"Do you know where this ship is headed when it leaves here?"

"Yes, back to Canada to pick up more supplies from there and the United States. Then they'll head for home port, Marseilles. Vichy is always desperate for more food, medical, and other supplies. No doubt they try to smuggle in anything else they need."

"So our suspects will have to debark here to get out of England. Where do you suppose they plan to go?"

"Most probably to France or Switzerland, then maybe even Germany," Biff said.

"And how do you think they'd plan to get there?"

"You can bet they have two or three alternate plans already in place. Their people will try to pick them up right under our noses. Unless they think we're on to them."

"Could they have gotten wind of us?" Colonel Mathersby said.

"I think our spy is a very clever and cautious man. He would count on it even if he didn't know," Biff said.

"So we have to think like he does. How would he plan to escape us?" Colonel Mathersby leaned back in his chair, elbows on the armrests, placed his fingers together, and frowned.

"Good question," Biff said. "We know they have to leave the ship before it sails unless it's returning to Marseilles, but it isn't. It's returning to Canada. They may not have known that when they sailed."

Abby decided it was time to introduce her theory: "He took a major risk returning to Europe by boat in the first place, and I believe it was because he originally thought this ship was headed to its home port, he couldn't arrange a flight out right away, and he wanted to bring Suzanne with him. Too, he didn't want her to know who he really is, otherwise he could have returned by a German submarine, which I'll wager was the way he arrived in the United States in the first place."

"Good thinking. You're probably right. And if he thought the ship would go to Marseilles, then that would be easy for him.

Instead, it's in England—probably reassigned because of that storm." Mathersby nodded.

"So now, he not only has to continue to deceive her, he has to protect her. Which means he'll probably try to get her to Switzerland and then leave her there or get them both into Vichy France, where he can operate more easily.

"That would make sense. Even so, how is he going to get off this ship and out of England? And with her? That is the question." The Colonel pondered.

Biff finally spoke up. "We can speculate all day long but that won't help us. Obviously, he'll try to leave by either boat or land. We simply have to be prepared for either contingency."

"Very true." Colonel Mathersby leaned forward. "Very well, we'll do this. There will be a pilot boat carrying the harbor pilot to guide a ship this size into the harbor. Bifford, you will accompany the pilot and board the ship as a French diplomat with messages for the captain. We've already arranged a number of official documents for his edification.

"However, he's going to be too busy bringing the ship in to read any of them immediately unless they're marked URGENT. The port has been badly damaged by the air raids, and there will have to be some careful maneuvering.

"You can ask the captain if any passengers or crew desiring to leave the ship before it docks are returning with the pilot boat. I understand there are five on board besides our two. Seven in all. Of course, they'll be required to go through customs, and security checks, so that won't be a piece of cake."

"Maybe for an ordinary person," Biff interrupted, "but this guy has diplomatic immunity. He'll sail right past all of it, and, as his 'wife,' so will she, unless we stop them."

"Yes, for a moment, that slipped my mind. Nevertheless, if he tries an ordinary entrance we've already set up for customs and security to detain him. I believe we've covered everything we could foresee that we'll have to deal with. We have our intelligence officers working as stevedores along with the army to unload the vessel. We have our people in customs, security, military police, fire squads, Red Cross. Our people have been assigned to assist you both. They have been briefed thoroughly and you can depend on them. If you're unsure of them, their code answer to 'Where are you from?' is 'Piccadilly.'"

Bifford nodded. "You're right. We have quite a team. We've tried to think of everything. But not knowing how it will happen, we'll just have to improvise as we go and be ready for the unexpected. All we need now is to review our maps, signals, and plans and we're as ready as we can be. As the Old Man would say, 'Just get the damn job done.'"

"Right you are." Colonel Mathersby rose from his chair. "We're on it. Let's do it! Tomorrow AM, all of you leave for Liverpool. The ship is due to dock the following day."

Chapter 43

Jana stretched his long legs as he looked out through the porthole. The weather was clear despite the fact it was late December. The captain had mentioned that they were due to dock sometime tomorrow, the 31st. New Years Eve, 1942.

He wondered what the New Year would bring, and what would become of them. He had been deep in thought for the past week. He had known it would complicate things to bring Suzanne with him, but the truth was he couldn't arrange a flight on short notice and he simply couldn't bear to leave her. But now, he had to face the consequences of his dangerous choice. Alone, he could have left by submarine and not risk his own discovery. He knew that getting off this ship safely might be difficult. He always had to assume that someone was onto him.

He'd had some very close calls in the past and had managed to bluff them through, but he was alone then and it was simpler. Now he had a double problem: continuing to keep the truth away from Suzanne while protecting her from capture, and eluding the enemy himself.

He had had two alternative plans in the works for weeks. His operatives in the U.S. and Britain were aware and ready for either. Now he would have to let them know which one to initiate. It had to be today.

He turned to Suzanne, who was propped up in bed, reading a copy of *Rebecca*.

"Darling, this is so exciting," she said. "You really must read it. They're on the brink of exposing Max's part in her disappearance."

For a moment he was stunned. It was such a shocking parallel to their own situation. It was almost downright amusing. But then, she had no idea his real name was Max.

"Yes, darling," he said, "it sounds very exciting. But then you would want him to be caught, wouldn't you?"

"Oh no, never. Max is the good one. Rebecca was really an evil woman. I do hope he goes free."

"If that's what you want, I hope so too."

He smiled at her tenderly. With all her sophistication she was really so innocent. She had no idea…. Suddenly, he made up his mind. It had to be Plan Two. He would chance it.

"I must send a cable, cherie. I'll be back in a little while. Good luck with your Max." He smiled, a quirk of fate.

"Don't be too long, darling. I'll tell you all about it when you return."

He knew the plot. He had read *Rebecca* on one of his trips the year before. Ironically, it did have some similar components to their situation. The murder-mystery, the naive unknowing wife, the guilty husband, the attempt to deceive and cover up. The name Max. A mind-teasing paradox.

He went to the bridge. The captain steered him to the chief radio operator, with whom he had established some previous rapport. They greeted one another and made a few comments.

"I need to send a cable to the French Embassy in America. Do you think you could handle that for me?"

"Certainment, Monsieur D'Arcy. I will be happy to."
Jacques wrote out his cable in block letters:

c/o Louis Cabot, French Embassy
Washington, D.C., U.S.A.

Due 2 pm, 31st
Notify Embassy. Meet as scheduled.
J D'A

He handed it to the operator. He read it and looked up at him. "You know, monsieur, we can never be sure of the time we'll dock. Do you want to change the time?"

"Non, that's close enough. The diplomats there can figure it out. They will know where and when we're pulling in. I couldn't put specifics in the cable. Security, you know. Send this in code, urgent, top secret. It must arrive this afternoon."

"I'll get right on it." Jacques waited and listened while he sent the cable. Now he could be certain Plan Two was in place. Louis would see that the others were notified. When he finished he thanked him and took the paper the message was written on.

"I'll take this. You don't need it any more."

Jacques strode along the deck toward their quarters. He greeted a couple of the other passengers taking a turn around the deck. There were only four or five others on board. They hadn't really gotten acquainted at all, partially because of the storm and partially because of the icy cold.

He entered their quarters. "How is Max doing?" He smiled, mischievously.

"Fabulously. He's going to be cleared, I know it."

"Let's hope so. Darling, when we dock tomorrow, there will be a harbor pilot coming aboard to navigate the ship into the dock. It will give an opportunity for some of the passengers to return to the dock on his pilot boat."

"Oh?" she said absently. Suddenly she put her book down and sat up. "Good. We could leave then. I must say I'll be delighted to get on solid ground again."

"I thought you would like that. So I want you to go ahead with some of your luggage and the other passengers. I have some things I need to finish up here. Then I'll join you, and we'll be off. There will be a car from the Embassy waiting to pick us up. You can wait for me with them until I finish up here."

"But Jacques, why can't we go together? I don't want to go without you."

"Just some last minute business, darling. I won't be long. Once the pilot boards it's only a matter of a couple of hours before the ship is in harbor. Besides the pilot boat will only accommodate maybe eight or ten passengers plus crew, so you see it's women and children first." Jacques laughed.

"And I suppose I'm the child," Suzanne said.

"You're *my* little girl, aren't you?"

"Yes I am. But you don't have to be so chivalrous."

"Oh yes, I do." Jacques leaned over the bunk where Suzanne lay propped up and took her in his arms. "You will always be my little girl as long as I live."

He took the book and laid it on the night table. He kissed her and caressed her and soon they were in that suspended place where only true lovers dare to go.

The French Embassy in Washington was abuzz with preparations for their annual New Year's Eve celebration. In this party town, war or no war, no red-blooded Washington politician would allow an opportunity to pass by to celebrate something or other. And this was a special time of the holiday season.

It had been only a year and a few days since America's entrance into the war, and people needed encouragement and a lifting of spirits to continue the effort—no matter which side they were on. So far, German-controlled Vichy France had more to celebrate than the Americans did.

Louis, the party's chairman, was in the ballroom supervising the hanging of the decorations and giving instructions to the chef and kitchen staff as to the timing of the repast to follow.

He had alerted his assistant to relay any messages to him immediately. He knew about the impending arrival of the *Marseilles* in Liverpool. He had his sources and he knew that timing was essential for the success of Jana's escape to safety. He was getting anxious to know if Plan One was still to be executed. If he heard nothing by a designated time it would be automatic.

It was the 30th, the day before they were to dock, and he had heard nothing. Of course he knew that it would be too risky for Jana to use his own radio. It would also be risky enough to send a cable from the ship, certainly not in the German code. It would have to be French to avoid suspicion.

Louis was giving instructions on the placement of the flowers when he saw his assistant rushing toward him. "There. That will be perfect." He turned away from the caterer and headed toward his assistant.

"Monsieur Cabot, this is an urgent cablegram," he said quietly. He handed the cable to Louis.

"What does it say?"

"I do not know, sir," he said in his usual bland manner.

"Merci, Gaston, I'll attend to it immediately. Take over here for me. I will be in my office."

"Yes sir," said Gaston.

Louis knew he could trust his assistant, who didn't know what it was all about anyway, but he didn't want anyone prying into his affairs. Nevertheless, no matter how cautious, Louis had completely missed the inscrutable smile on the face of his assistant.

In his office Louis decoded the message and breathed a sigh of relief. He understood the message. He now knew it would be Plan Two. He looked at his watch. Still time to notify their agents in Britain. He left the Embassy to attend to it immediately.

Jana awoke very early that morning. He rose and checked his gear—everything was ready. Suzanne was still sleeping. He looked long and tenderly at her beautiful face, her pale flaxen hair, growing longer now, just touching her shoulders. How exquisite she was, all pink and white—soft and delicate—like a fragile flower—yet strong in so many ways.

He returned to the bed and took her in his arms. She turned to him sleepily and received him in a lover's embrace. Their passion rose to a height unknown before, as they became one with each other.

They lay there together lost in time. He watched her as she fell asleep again. He knew that would be the last time for a while. But they would be together again. Nothing he had ever experienced in the past could meet the intensity of the past few moments with her. He had dreamed of her all his life, and she had walked into his existence out of the blue. He would never leave her. She was his and his alone. His dream—his reality.

Everything was in place. In a few hours his plan would begin to unfold, and everything would work out.

He carefully placed the package in the secret compartment of Suzanne's overnight bag. He had told her it contained her protection, in case she were apprehended. She was still asleep, but beginning to awaken.

"Jacques?" she said.

He leaned over the bed and kissed her. "Wake up, sleepyhead. It's New Year's Eve."

Chapter 44

By the morning of December 31st, the backup part of the OSS team was ensconced in a variety of posts at the Liverpool docks. A cold brisk wind stung hands and faces as the team assumed their unfamiliar tasks. An extra day had been deemed necessary to secure bearings of the layout and prepare alternatives for any unanticipated events. Somehow, no assignment ever seemed to proceed exactly according to plan. They had to be ready for anything.

Abby and Biff were scheduled to arrive the morning of the next day. They had consulted with Colonel Mathersby and most of the key team leaders in London for the past several days. They had gone over the map layouts to familiarize themselves with the harbor, the placement of the structures, the warehouses, the distances between them, and every detail they could think of. They had tried to accommodate for every contingency. Still, one could only project the possibilities.

The night before they left London, Abby and Biff had dinner in the dining room of the safe house. The excellent service and food escaped their notice as anxiety began to take over. Their usual animated conversation was noticeably absent.

Abby, finally, toying with her dessert, looked across the table at Biff, sighed, and said, "Here's my old friend ambiguity again. Doesn't he know he's an unwelcome guest?"

"Yes, here he is again. But you know that's when he gets his greatest kicks. The more the danger, the more the uncertainty." Biff reached across the table and squeezed her hand reassuringly. He felt it too, but it was different for her. This was her first time out in a dangerous undercover operation. Yet he knew from experience, one never got used to that gnawing feeling of insecurity.

Staring absently, she nodded. "Yes, I suppose so. Still—"

Abby and Biff had their instructions. They would arrive at the docks mid-morning of the 31st, speak only French to each other and as little English as required to communicate to any of the others. Biff would go with the harbor pilot on his boat to the *Marseilles*, a confidential briefcase chained to his wrist, with "official documents" from the Embassy. What he planned to do with them, no one else was told.

There were times when this need to know policy irked Abby no end. How did one know they didn't need to know, particularly with as important an issue as this one?

Nevertheless, Abby, alias Madame Aimée du Pré, would be there with her and her husband's luggage, awaiting passage back to Canada on the *Marseilles*. She would wait right inside, to keep out of the cold, until the ship docked and she could join her husband aboard. It was preferable to occupy accommodations aboard ship rather than the meager ones in this war-torn town. At least that was her cover story.

But in fact, she would wait in the warehouse next to the port master's station. It was the building nearest to where the pilot boat would dock to deliver its returning passengers. She would wait there until she recognized Suzanne—then she would signal the other team leaders. Trying to apprehend her before she reached shore could only alert Jana that they were onto him. Let him think he was safe until they had him cornered.

She had been equipped with a tiny set of binoculars. A window just inside the door had been checked out where she might observe. It seemed there were only two options: either Suzanne would remain on the ship till it docked—or she would return with the pilot boat beforehand.

In either instance, there was no way to know whether she would debark alone or if Jacques D'Arcy would accompany her. Abby had had one of her feelings about this one, and opted for the former. But she had had her instructions. She knew what to do. If the unexpected happened. She knew what the Old Man would say—"if there's a snafu, just get the job done."

And that's what she intended to do.

The Du Prés arrived at the harbor in Liverpool in an "official" Rolls Royce as expected. Abby was astonished at the devastation from the many bombings. The Germans had targeted the town and the harbor during the Blitz, attempting to put an end to the endless ships continuing to supply the armed forces with their rich cargos of ammunition, weapons, medical supplies, and other essentials. Though the total count was not yet confirmed, approximately 730 ships had been destroyed or missing in the area of the Irish Sea.

While not quite as intense, the bombing was still continuing, and at times there were mysterious explosions, only explainable by sabotage or an occasional plane. Signs of the deluge were still visible in the harbor. The bow of a sunken ship peeked above the waterline, and there were others, just below but still visible. Damaged buildings, warehouses, and other structures were abundant. The signs of ongoing repair and restoration were there too, but she could tell it was hard to keep up with the ongoing attacks.

As they drove along, Abby voiced her astonishment, "I never dreamt this was what we were walking into. I never imagined it could be this bad. It's obvious these people have been determined to keep this port open with all this reconstruction and repair. But even so, it's so busy. It could become very confusing for us. For one thing, there is so much constant activity, I'm not sure if I can tell our guys from the bad guys."

"You don't really need to." Biff took her hand. "They'll know who you are, disguise and all. Though I must say, they've done a lousy job of trying to make you look plain. Unfortunately, you're just as beautiful as ever. I suppose they gave up, seeing it was hopeless."

"Oh, Your Gracey, you do always know the right thing to say. Nevertheless, I still feel like English dowdy, or should I say French frumpy."

Biff laughed. He looked at her admiringly. The chic little French designer suit had been tailored to fit her perfectly, partially hidden by a matching mink lined cape. The soft felt fedora, covering as much of her face as possible, merely put an accent on the designer's understatement of her attire. Her hair was pulled back in a chignon, and the dark glasses gave her an additional air of smart sophisticated simplicity. After all, she *was* supposed to be the wife of a French diplomat, some of whom were really quite wealthy. It was a perfect rendition of understated French gentility and position.

Only X-2 would know about the button with the hidden compass, or the matchbox that held a secret camera, or the little blue pill in her handbag. Abby knew that these were tools and on this assignment might not be needed, but it was good to know they were there. Other interesting things had been added to her equipment as well, including a very small easily concealed pistol.

If a life-threatening occasion arises, I wonder if I'll have the courage or the foresight to use it.

The Rolls stopped in front of the port captain's station. The chauffeur, James, one of their agents, opened the door for Monsieur du Pré. Biff got out and went in to speak to the harbormaster. He returned almost immediately.

"The Embassy has booked passage for us back to Québec when the *Marseilles* has finished unloading. The harbor captain estimates that will take two days, but if we wish to stay aboard until then, our quarters will be ready by this afternoon. The harbor pilot will go out to meet the ship within the hour and he's been informed that I will accompany him. So, everything is set. He suggests we come in for a hot cup of tea and English crumpets."

"Oh, that would be lovely, but do you think we should?" Abby asked.

"I think we're O.K., as long as we don't forget our roles. Remember, we speak only French to each other, and English with a French accent. We can wait there for the pilot. Then, when I've left with him, you can suggest that you'd like to take a walk around. He won't suspect you. We've been excruciatingly cleared by security. James will accompany you and take you to the right warehouse. In fact, he has a lunch basket prepared should I be late returning. We want this to look as leisurely as possible."

"Yes, but I'm beginning to get apprehensive. I don't like the idea of your going on board alone."

"I feel the same about you, darling, but we'll be all right. Just pray that this goes off well, and that we get them both."

"Already done. We're covered," she said.

"With His feathers?" Biff smiled at her tenderly.

She smiled back at him. "With His feathers!"

Chapter 45

The early morning fog was lifting and now the ships were vaguely visible in the misty distance, ready to come in. Other unloaded ships, were being escorted out to sea by their pilots and tugboats. Longshoremen were either unloading or taking a break, waiting for the next ships. It was a hectic scene, full of activity.

The harbormaster was busy talking to the pilot and the customs officer when the Du Prés arrived with James.

"Ah, Monsieur and Madame du Pré, here you are. Please help yourself to the tea and crumpets while we finish up here."

Biff recognized one of his team's SI intelligence officers, Wiley, standing on the side, but he pretended to be introduced.

"Monsieur, this is the assistant customs officer, Mr. Wiley. He will accompany us to the ship when the pilot is ready. Our usual assistant has suddenly been taken with the flu." He frowned. "It seems to have taken over the city lately and many of our people."

Biff thought, *that was convenient. Wiley's placement has been arranged.* He could hardly conceal a knowing smile, but, he managed to cover it with a hearty cough.

"Monsieur du Pré, I hope you too are not coming down with this dreadful flu."

"Non, Monsieur Captain. I find my allergies quite unpredictable. They come and go, I'm sure that is what it is."

"Very well, then, we should be off. He nodded to Madame du Pré who was seated at a table with James. "We should return in a couple of hours, madame, make yourselves comfortable," he said as he went outside. Monsieur du Pré adjusted his briefcase, chained to his left wrist, made a few comments to his wife, kissed her hand, and the four of them left the building.

Abby looked at her watch. It was 10:15. She watched from the port master's station as they walked the 300 yards to the water's edge. They boarded the pilot boat and the coxswain began his maneuvers to take them out to the anchored *Marseilles*.

Abby's eyes followed them through the window. She watched until the pilot boat had cleared the dock. She turned to James, "Une autre tasse du thé, James?"

"Merci, mais non, madame, et vous?"

"Non, non. Not now."

Abby calculated that the pilot boat should return between 11:00 and 12:00. That would give her and James time to familiarize themselves with the areas where the activities of this operation were most likely to take place.

"It was a long trip, James. Why don't we stretch our legs a bit? A nice walk around the area would be good," she said casually.

"Oui, madame." James rose and helped her with her coat. Abby turned to the port master.

"Sir? Can you tell me where the *Marseilles* it will be docking?"

"Let's see, madame," he said, obviously happy to accommodate the lovely Madame du Pré. He looked at his schedule. "She should be pulling into Area One." He stepped to the door and pointed. "If you will look to your left at that warehouse next to us, it should dock almost directly in front of it."

"Oh, I see. Merci, monsieur. So, James, in about an hour you may bring the car around and unload our luggage in front of the warehouse. That will be more convenient."

"Oui, madame."

The port master said, "We can help you with that when you're ready to board."

"That's very kind of you, monsieur," she said crisply, ignoring the greedy look in his eye.

"My pleasure," he said.

James opened the door and they found themselves in the cold clear air. They began to walk toward the warehouse on their left.

The pilot boat, weaving in and out of the busy harbor traffic, reached the *Marseilles* in about 15 minutes.

The four officials boarded without fanfare. The pilot immediately set out conferring with the captain and the first mate to work out relinquishment of the controls and command of the ship to him until they were safely docked; a tugboat was already in close proximity, awaiting its orders.

Customs Officer O'Donnell and his assistant, Wiley, conferred with the captain about inspection of the cargo and clearance of those who might desire to debark.

"So, you have passengers and crew who wish to return with the pilot boat, captain?" O'Donnell asked.

"Oui, monsieur, I have six passengers who wish to leave early and four of the crew, who have been given furloughs."

"That makes ten. Very well, Captain, if you will ask them to report within the next 10 minutes or so, my assistant Mr. Wiley and I can clear them to debark. They may take only one small bag each, however. Their other belongings will be unloaded when the ship docks."

"I have already alerted them. I believe they are outside there on the deck now."

"Good. Then we can proceed." O'Donnell and Wiley left the bridge to inspect the passports, credentials, and luggage of those debarking early.

Biff, in the meanwhile, waited for the preliminary procedures to end before addressing the captain. He looked outside at the small group of passengers awaiting clearance. The captain had said six passengers but he knew there were seven aboard.

Abby was right, he thought. *Suzanne is leaving early but Jana is planning something else.*

He looked out on the deck to see if he could tell which one was Suzanne. Out of the ten who were there to leave, it was easy to eliminate the four crew members in uniform, lined up with their duffle bags.

He scanned the passengers. There were two men. Of the four women, there was only one who could possibly be Suzanne. No amount of camouflage could hide that perfect Dresden skin, the long, well shaped, slender legs, or the finely chiseled nose peeking out from under the wide brimmed hat guarding her face.

Though her hair was tucked under, it was clear that this was a natural blonde. She wore a heavy coat with a mink collar, but Biff could tell the inner lining was also mink, a hidden symbol of wealth, but also meant to protect against the severe cold of an Atlantic crossing in mid-winter. Yes, that had to be Suzanne.

His first instinct was to take her into custody at that instant, but he knew that it would be impossible without alerting Jana. He had to be somewhere on this ship. But where? He caught the eye of the SI agent, Wiley. He too had recognized that this had to be the young woman they were looking for. It was soon confirmed when she presented her passport and credentials as Solange D'Arcy, wife of the French diplomat aboard, which, of course, gave her diplomatic immunity.

Officer O'Donnell continued to clear the passengers and crew. Soon they began to descend the boarding stair to board the pilot boat. Some of the crew lowered their duffle bags over the side into the other boat, and offered to help the passengers with any luggage too heavy to handle. Suzanne was immediately surrounded with "help" but she had brought only her small overnight bag.

Biff waited until the captain had turned the ship over to the pilot before approaching him. The pilot boat was still loading the passengers.

"Monsieur Captain, I am Maurice du Pré, from the French Embassy. I believe you have arranged passage for me and my wife to Canada."

"Oui, Monsieur du Pré. Welcome aboard. Your passage is all arranged."

"Merci. That is most kind. Incidentally, I believe you have one of my fellow diplomats on board?"

"That would be Monsieur D'Arcy, a very interesting chap. You know him personally, then?"

"Non, but I have some important papers here sent to him from the Embassy." Biff lifted his left hand with the briefcase chained to his wrist. "Do you think you could acquaint me with him?"

"Of course. Let me see." The captain looked out at the departing passengers.

"His wife seems to be making her departure on the pilot boat. He must be finishing up some details in their quarters, and planning to go in with the ship. I can send for him."

The captain motioned to one of the crew. "Go down to Monsieur D'Arcy's quarters and ask him to come to the bridge, s'il vous plaît."

Biff spoke up. "Merci beaucoup, Captain, but I can accompany your man. It might be simpler."

"If you wish, monsieur."

As they left the bridge, Biff saw the pilot boat pulling away from the ship. He estimated it would probably take an additional few minutes with a loaded boat full of uneasy passengers to reach the dock. Maybe 20 minutes. He looked at his watch. It was 11:10. He caught Wiley's eye as he passed him on the way to D'arcy's quarters. It was comforting to know he had at least one known backup on board.

He followed the crewman to Jana's quarters. He knocked on the door, but there was no answer. He tried the knob—the door opened.

He called out, "Monsieur D'Arcy." There was no answer, no one there. Biff looked around. The place had been totally cleaned out. Not a sign of either of them remained. Nothing left in the closets, the drawers, the wastepaper basket. It had a familiar ring to it. He had run into this before, in Suzanne's Washington apartment, in the Fontainebleu. Typical Jana, he thought.

"He's obviously not here," Biff said. "Where could he have gone? He's not on deck either."

"I have no idea, monsieur, unless he went below."

"But why would he do that?"

"I do not know, monsieur. Would you like to take a look?"

Biff hesitated. "Non, I think not. Let's return to the bridge." Biff thought for a moment. *He's planned another means of escape.*

He looked out the porthole. The pilot boat had almost reached the dock. A very strange feeling came over him. It was as though something was giving him an urgent order: "Get off this ship! Now!"

He was compelled by some strange force to obey—it was time to get with Wiley. He left Jana's quarters and headed hurriedly toward the bridge. He spotted Wiley near the bridge, on the port side. He began to run toward him.

He glanced over the stern only to see a speedboat skimming away in the distance toward the open sea. He thought he saw a fair-haired British sailor, waving and laughing at them. Wiley had seen it too.

"That son-of a-bitch!" Wiley yelled. "Come on!"

They looked around for the prearranged official customs boat. It was there, a few yards off of the port side, with a small motorboat hovering aside.

Wiley signaled. Immediately, the motorboat began the few yards over to reach them. Biff clicked the hidden button releasing the chain on his wrist. The briefcase fell to the deck. He picked it up and shoved it in his coat.

Biff looked at Wiley. Their eyes met. Without a word, quickly they threw a line over the side nearest the customs boat, and shimmied down to the small motorboat which had now reached them. They jumped in and sped to the larger boat, revving its motors in anticipation of their arrival. The crew quickly pulled them aboard, and the larger boat took off, increasing speed to maximum.

"He's on his way to the Irish Sea—and probably Ireland." Biff slumped down on the deck, catching his breath. Wiley slumped down beside him.

"Well, we're right behind him by only a few minutes. We'll catch him. We can signal our patrols all around. They can keep a look-out."

They sped away from the *Marseilles* as rapidly as possible toward the escaping enemy.

No one had noticed the small fuse near the ammunition stacked in the forward hold. Suddenly there was a loud blast. Then a series of explosions. At that very moment the *Marseilles* exploded—scattering men, equipment, parts of the ship, and debris everywhere.

They looked back in horror to see the stately *Marseilles* in flames, already sinking in the harbor.

Abby and James had found the warehouse. Though the large loading doors were closed there was an ordinary door adjacent, which gave them entry. Next to the door was a window looking out across the water. Abby pulled out the small binoculars in her purse. She could see the pilot boat coming nearer, approaching the docks. Out in the far distance was the *Marseilles*. In between and around both of these critical vessels there were many other ships, both large and small. She said a silent prayer that Biff would be safe, and handed the binoculars to James.

"Do you see them?" she asked.

"Yes, the *Marseilles* is almost ready to come in—the tug is lining up to pull out."

"How soon do you estimate we have before the pilot boat docks?"

"They're pulling in now. Only two or three minutes before they debark. Yes, the coxswain is stopping. The other sailors are tying on. They're ready to come on deck."

James returned the binoculars. She could see the passengers. The men had come on the deck first, to assist the women out of the boat.

And then—she saw Suzanne. Her heart jumped for a moment in joy. She stepped just outside the warehouse door for a better look. Unexpectedly, Suzanne looked her way. She frowned and looked around. In unbelief and shock, she recognized Abby. Flustered and confused, she put her finger aside her nose.

Abby smiled—that old signal of distress they had used in the past. She returned her signal. But Suzanne had no idea that this was also the signal of positive identification to the OSS team to pick her up.

Suddenly, Abby had an uncontrollable urge. A voice within her said, "Get out—Run—Run!" She repeated it as loud as she could to James as she began to run toward the water—and Suzanne. James was startled but he didn't hesitate, he burst through the door and followed a few feet behind her.

It was then, almost instantly, they heard the explosion behind them. They felt the ground shake underneath them as they ran. Abby saw two men dressed as longshoremen take hold of Suzanne. Two others in British uniform were trying to get her away from them. There were gunshots. She saw one go down. Men were running everywhere. People were screaming, shouting orders. Sirens were ear piercing. Sounds of distant voices calling "Battle stations!"

Amidst the chaos, Abby saw a large explosion on a ship in the distance. Instantly it was engulfed in flames. Somehow she knew it was the *Marseilles*. Her heart sank. "Biff," she cried.

The explosions continued behind them as they ran. Red and yellow lights, heavy black and foggy smoke began to surround them. All hell had broken loose. A large fireball billowed throughout the whole warehouse. Parts of the building began to fly off into the air helter-skelter, threatening the other structures and the people running.

They continued to run toward the water. Abby saw Suzanne look her way as she was propelled toward a dark vehicle waiting a few yards away. Abruptly, Abby felt a sharp blow to her back. She slumped to the ground. Blackness began to engulf her.

Now, she was drifting in a dark foggy mist. Immediately, the sky lit up with red and yellow lights as a loud roar exploded in the smoky darkness. She struggled to come awake but the effort eluded her. There was an overwhelming feeling of terror, fear, helplessness, confusion in her half-consciousness. Then she surrendered—down—down—into the peaceful blackness.

Eventually, out of the darkness, she felt strong arms pick her up. She caught a glimpse of startling blue eyes looking down at her, as the light broke through the foggy smoke. "Feathers", she mumbled. Then the darkness overtook her again.

Chapter 46

Brett Whitney, in uniform as a Navy lieutenant, and his OSS team some dressed as longshoremen, were on the Liverpool docks and ready to act on the morning of December 31st. He had briefed his team and felt they were ready for anything. But one never knew with these Special Ops.

Part of his mission had been to keep an eye on their agents, James and "Madame du Pré," and rescue them if they got into trouble. She would give the signal positively identifying Suzanne for arrest,

But his other major responsibility was to direct the capture of the other French diplomat, Jacques D'Arcy, and his wife, Suzanne. They both were suspected of espionage.

Suzanne would most probably be debarking from the pilot boat and must be taken into custody and detained for questioning. There were others who had the major responsibility of capturing the husband, but it was imperative that each member of the team work together to protect their targets and not allow any interference in the capture of either.

Did the enemy suspect that OSS knew they would be there, or that they had planned to capture both of them? No one could know. But intelligence was fully aware that the enemy would be prepared for any interference with their agents' safe passage and escape.

Monsieur D'Arcy, Jana, was too valuable for them to risk, and so was his cohort Suzanne—but for different reasons—she knew too much by now. If nothing more, she could identify him.

The warehouse was a good distance away from the docks, hard to see only though the light mist. He could see the coxswain maneuvering through the water and the sailors securing the pilot boat to the dock. Once the passengers began to debark, Brett observed Madame du Pré raise her arm and place her finger on the side of her nose, the signal identifying Suzanne.

Immediately he gave the command: "Take her!" Straight away, two of his team took her in hand, taking hold of each arm.

"We are here to escort you, madame. Come with us."

Suzanne was stunned. Something was wrong. Why was Abby here, in England? And where were the officials Jacques had said would come for her? These men were longshoremen—not what she had expected. The expression on her face was one of complete bewilderment. She dropped her overnight bag and let out a little cry, but otherwise she didn't resist, as she began to be ushered toward a waiting security vehicle.

At that very moment a tremendous explosion occurred in the harbor.

Brett's attention went back for an instant to the warehouse. To his surprise Madame du Pré began to run toward them and Suzanne, with James following. Why? This was not in the plan.

They cleared the building and at that very moment the warehouse exploded behind them.

How could she have known? Obviously she couldn't have, except by instinct. It was a stroke of genius. It had saved their lives.

Immediately, he had turned his attention back to Suzanne's arrest and transport. He saw two officers and several men in full British uniform approaching.

It was a near certainty the British officers and men were German spies, sent to rescue Madame D'Arcy and whisk her off to safety. They obviously *had* to be enemy agents. He knew the British Embassy was not involved.

Brett decided to ask for the password. "Sir, where are you from?"

"We come from the Embassy." he said.

Not Picadilly? Not the right answer, thought Brett. "I see," he said.

In a commanding tone of voice the officer in charge spoke, "We have orders to escort Madame D'Arcy to the Embassy." With that, he drew an official paper out of his pouch and presented it.

"Oh? I think not," Brett said. "Her transport has already been arranged. Sir, you are not needed."

"We are going to follow our orders, lieutenant," said the British lieutenant. "If you will not comply, then we will take her by force. I have my orders." He drew his gun.

Brett did not hesitate, "Arrest them!" His OSS agents, weapons ready, closed in on the Brits.

Brett knocked the Brit's gun upward as it fired. He struggled with the Brit. He was strong and determined. Finally, he wrested away his weapon and secured him with the help of another agent.

Three of the British officers went down, one fatally wounded. The others were arrested on the spot and taken into custody as well as the rest of their men. The enemy agents had been well prepared. They had fought bitterly to accomplish their mission, but his team had been ready for them.

He gave the order for their transport to a holding pen in London for questioning until they could be transferred to a military prison. Suzanne was finally secured and sent on her way to headquarters in London. The wounded and dead, including two of his own men, were taken to the Red Cross trauma center hastily set up far behind the warehouses.

Brett heaved a sigh of relief. He was glad it was over. His role had been critical in Suzanne's capture, providing the plan and back up for the OSS agents who had taken her in custody. *But where was Jana? Was the other team successful?*

Several of his team had been wounded and taken for emergency treatment. He hated to see his colleagues hurt—it was such a waste. Fortunately, none were critical.

As for the British officers and their men—better to sort this out later in the cold light of day. There would be a debriefing when they returned to London. They could sort it out then.

It had turned out to be quite a battle. The confusion had been overwhelming. All this, as they were sandwiched in between two mammoth explosions, the warehouse on one side, and that of the *Marseilles* in the harbor on the other.

His emotions were jumbled—exhilarated for their success, but sorrow and concern for his wounded men—and the dead. The war was relentless, ruthless. It cared not for the bodies or souls of its victim. He hated it and the role he had to play. But it was necessary, imperative, to stop that madman Hitler before he conquered the entire civilized world. He hated it; but he would do his part. Someone had to.

Thank God it was over, at least for the moment. Half of their operation was completed. They had captured Madame D'Arcy. She and those enemy agents were on their way to await transfer to more secure holdings. Now, he hoped, their interrogation could yield the identity and whereabouts of her husband, Jana. He would have to wait to see if the other team had captured him.

Mission Flytrap—accomplished! At least my part of it.

He completed his orders to his remaining team. Thumbs up! They had behaved admirably. Now they could assist in searching the debris for the wounded and seeing that they received treatment. He could turn his attention to loose ends.

He looked back to see what had happened to their fellow agents, Madame du Pré and James. He thought they had escaped the explosion in the warehouse. He had seen them running. But where were they? Visibility was almost nil by now because of the smoke and continuing detonations of stored ammunition and flammable material.

He began to walk slowly back in the direction of the warehouse, where he had last seen them running. The debris from the blasts was everywhere. Some of the larger sections were obstructing the trucks and vehicles attempting to remove the dead and rescue the wounded. He wove his way on through the clutter and smoke, searching. Where were they? Were they safe?

He poked at the wreckage, overturning pieces of debris to see what might be underneath. He knew James personally—a delightful fellow—an engineer in civilian life, and a gifted writer and humorist. He was also an accomplished artist—so many of his OSS colleagues were multitalented.

He knew Madame du Pré only by the pictures provided of her in disguise and general description, but he had never met her. The true identity of so many OSSers was unknown to their closest colleagues. Better for security—if they were ever caught.

Suddenly, almost hidden by a large section of roof, he saw a hand. It was attached to a crumpled figure over to his right. He made his way through the litter there as fast as he could. It was a woman, lying face down in the scorched debris. He knelt and gently turned her over, she was still breathing. Her long dark hair fell across her face, out of the fasteners that had held it back. He brushed it aside from her face, still covered with streaks of soot. Even so, abruptly he recognized her. He could hardly believe his eyes. It was the girl on the train. The girl for whom he had searched for over six months. He cried out in astonishment.

"Abby, Abby, I thought I had lost you." Carefully, he picked her up in his arms and carried her to a place of safety—out of harm's way.

He carried her to the makeshift trauma station the Red Cross had set up some distance ashore, affording greater protection from the explosions and the fire. The place was already filling up with the wounded, and there were a large number of the dead laid out off to one side. He placed her on an empty stretcher and grabbed a medic attending to some of the other wounded.

"This girl needs immediate help!" he said.

The medic looked at him. "Just a moment." He grabbed a blanket and handed it to Brett. "Here, cover her. Keep her warm till I can get there."

"Hurry, I don't know how bad—" Brett bent down, brushing the debris off her face. "Abby, Abby, you're safe now. Can you hear me?"

Her eyelids flickered open for a brief instant. She seemed to be muttering something. Brett bent closer to hear what she was saying. "Sounds like feathers," he laughed. "Imagine that." But then she sank back into oblivion. He turned to find the medic but he had come back.

"I'll give her a quick once over," he said in his brisk British accent. He checked her heart, lungs, head, spine, the rest of her body. "No broken bones or open wounds. Probably just a mild concussion and shock. She should come around shortly, but for now best to let her rest. I'll make sure to keep her warm."

"Are you absolutely sure she's safe? I don't want to lose her again."

"No need to worry. See—her color is already returning. Later, we'll get her to the hospital and X-ray her CNS to rule out any concussion or disc damage."

"All right, then. When she comes to, tell her I'll be back for her. Whatever you do, don't let her out of your sight until I return. I have to go and check on my people. I'll be back as soon as I can."

"Don't worry, she won't be going anywhere for a while." The medic was firm. "I'll look after her. Go ahead."

Brett was reluctant to leave her but the medic had assured him that she would be all right. Now that she was safe, he had to find out what had happened to James and the others and if he was needed elsewhere. He was still in charge of this end of the operation.

He hurriedly traced his steps back to the landing dock. If there were any loose ends or lost people, they should be near there. It was slow going. The smoke hung heavy like a black shroud. Visibility was even worse than before and fires were still raging despite heroic efforts of the Liverpool and other firemen to put them out.

Brett was still incredulous as he pondered the events of the past hour. Almost in shock, he wondered what strange juxtaposition of events had brought Abby and him together again, here, on the other side of the world—and in the middle of a clandestine operation, at that. It was almost too mind-boggling to believe. Nevertheless, after all of his searching for her all these months, suddenly there she was. In England, in Liverpool, in the middle of an OSS special op. It was a miracle—no less! There could be no other explanation. It was meant to be.

When he had met her on the train to Washington so many months ago, he had had no idea that he was being assigned to OSS. Apparently, at the time, she didn't know that she would be either.

Unbelievable, he thought. *Fate has a strange way of unfolding.* He shook his head. *Now that I've found her I'll make sure she doesn't slip away again.*

Chapter 47

Chaos continued to reign unrelentingly on the Liverpool harbor. Smaller explosions continued from the mammoth ones begun an hour ago. Ships in the harbor followed the fate of the *Marseilles*, as the flames of the burning ship spread the fire by falling sparks setting off blazing debris shooting off the victim vessel.

Abby awoke to a blur of smoke stinging her eyes and choking off her breathing. She rubbed her eyes. Where was she? What had happened? Why was she lying on this—what was it—a stretcher? Slowly, recognition of the events of the past hour became clearer.

She looked around. The carnage was unbelievable. The noises of attack were deafening still. She sat up, abruptly. Dizziness and confusion had its way with her and she floundered, catching on to the rails of the stretcher. She fell back.

The medic attending a patient on the adjacent stretcher spied her out of the corner of his eye. "Not quite so soon, miss. You've had a hard blow—let your body adjust for a moment. You may even have a concussion."

Abby looked up confusedly at the medic. She could see the Red Cross emblem on his white coat. Out of the blue she remembered her French, her cover.

"Quelle—what happened? How did I get here?"

"Some fellow, an officer, brought you here for first aid. He seemed to recognize you. Kept calling you Abby, or something."

"Aimée, he must have said Aimée." She remembered enough to stick to her alias. No need to blow her cover at this point.

"Yes, might have been. We were pretty busy then." He looked around them, gesturing toward the other stretchers. Attendants were swarming around the broken and bleeding victims of the blasts. Others, not so fortunate, had been laid far off to one side, in rows, covered by sheets, or whatever clothing could hide their fatal wounds, only their faces left visible for future identification.

Abby looked around at the many bodies. She recognized none of the faces of the dead. The wounded were still staggering in, one by one, being attended by the medics and volunteers. The sounds of their agony gripped the heart.

"Mon Dieu! How horrible! So many." She shook her head in dismay. It was one thing to imagine the slaughter of war, quite another to be in the middle of it. She felt sick. This was horrendous. She couldn't bear to look at the torn bodies for long. It was too awful to stomach. *I must have been insane to get involved in this.* She looked up at the medic.

"I think I recall an explosion behind us in the warehouse—and—and the ship in the harbor—the *Marseilles*—it exploded. Mon Dieu! Where are our people—are they hurt?"

She had to get a grip on herself, she couldn't let this take over. She was still in a fog but it was all coming back to her. Where was James? And Suzanne? Did they apprehend her? And Biff…. She had to find out.

"How long have I been here?"

"A while, about 40 minutes. Maybe longer."

"Almost an hour? Oh, my lord. I've been here all that time?" She struggled to rise. She had to know what had happened.

"Now lie back down, miss," the medic insisted. "Give yourself some time to recover, get your bearings. We'll take you to hospital shortly and get an X-ray."

"The hospital? Oh no, I can't wait for that. I have to go."

Abby tried to stand, everything whirling in confusion . She fell back on the stretcher in a sitting position.

The medic gave her a sharp look. His accent told her he was English, and his manner told her he intended to do a thorough job of protecting his patients.

"Now, look here, miss, take it easy. Give us a little time to get you straight—and then you can track down your friends." Then he smiled reassuringly. "Besides, the young man who brought you here—he said he'd be back for you."

"He did?" she said absently. "The young man? What young man?" She was still confused, disoriented, but her head was clearing. Pieces of the puzzle were falling into place. "I'll be fine. It's just the shock. I think I remember something hitting me in the back."

"Oh, yes indeed, something did. You sustained a heavy blow. For the most part, it simply knocked the breath out of you, and you went under. But you're lucky—no broken bones or open wounds that we can find. Still, it's quite possible you have a concussion, you were out of it a rather long time—and you may have an injured disc. Time alone will tell. We can't X-ray until we reach the hospital."

"But there's no time to waste." Abby caught hold of the medic's arm and pulled herself up to a standing position. She felt wobbly.

"Now look here. Sit down!"

"Oh no! I can't wait for that." With that, Abby found her footing. Unsteadily, she charged off into the dense cloud of smoke.

She trudged on slowly through the smoky mist. Surely soon she would recognize some landmark. The last thing she remembered was running, running toward the dock—the water—toward Suzanne—all the while signaling confirmation to her fellow agents that this was indeed their target. But then she had been hit. She vaguely remembered falling, and the blackness overcoming her.

She recalled a brief moment of semi-consciousness, feeling strong arms pick her up and carry her away. And then—she had gone back again into the darkness.

Suddenly, she remembered her dream of long ago. The dream on the train. The blue eyes—Brett. It had to be Brett. Had it come to pass in reality? But if that were true, where was he?

But why was he here? It couldn't be. He was Annapolis, a naval officer. And she had seen him only once—on the train to Washington. What could he possibly be doing in Liverpool, England, in the middle of an OSS special operation? No, she must have dreamt it, that old dream again. The dream from the train.

She continued to weave her way through the debris and the wandering people. Somewhat aimlessly at first, not sure of how to reach her goal or even what it was she was trying to do. But as she went on her thoughts began to clear.

Abruptly, it hit her fully … the *Marseilles* … she had seen it as she ran, exploding into a thousand pieces. Nothing, no one, could have survived that horrific blast. Or could they? Oh God! Biff, darling Biff. A vise closed in on her middle. Had he been on the *Marseilles* when it blew up? Had he managed to escape or….

Vaguely she remembered feathers, thousands of feathers floating down from the sky, over the landscape—over the harbor—over all that was there. She smiled—he was safe somewhere. He had to be. God had promised "under His feathers."

She stumbled on, avoiding the burning and fallen debris, the stunned people sitting or wandering around on the cluttered ground. Others were rushing here and there helping the wounded or moving chunks of wreckage out of the way.

Out of the smoke in the distance the outline of the dock began to emerge. She began to get her bearings.

Her people, she had to find them. Where was James? Perhaps the landing dock was the best place to start. Yes, she would backtrack. The dock was where she should begin her search.

Chapter 48

The old man bent over and struggled up the steep slope of the rocky crag. The cart was overloaded and his horse, though powerful enough, seemed unsure of his footing on the uneven incline. He hesitated, snorted, and shook his mane in protest, but the old man persisted until, at last, they reached the top, with the cart intact.

From the summit, the shoreline spread out below him in a vast expanse. The sea looked endless, unusually calm today, its whitecaps billowing only a few yards from shore. But the mist was rolling in and he knew the time was short before it would encompass the higher ground as well. He patted and stroked the horse's head, whispering to him lovingly in his thick Gaelic brogue for a few moments, then, taking the reins firmly in his hand, he began to lead him and his cargo forward onto the rugged overgrown path nearby.

He could see the snow-covered rooftop of the old cottage way off in the distance, hidden by a clump of trees gnarled and twisted by the vicious winds from ancient storms. This part of the land was utterly isolated. It was rare that any living being would choose to frequent it; or indeed would ever have any desire to do so.

It was not only remote, secluded, but because of the natural barriers around its peninsula, it was also almost inaccessible. All three sides were surrounded by the sea, but the height of the elevation and the steepness of the access made the land a natural fortress. Its only entrance was protected by a very narrow isthmus, a sand bridge from the mainland, barely yards wide and threatening to disappear next time a Nor'easter or a full-bodied hurricane attacked its eroding underpinnings. Besides, even the sand bridge disappeared at high tide, creating an island of the sinister terrain. It was not an inviting place. It wore an eerie, foreboding mantle. The mists hung over it, obscuring it from view, as though they were hiding some strange dark secret, forbidden to be known.

Folklore had followed the spit down the centuries. Tales of fierce Vikings who had taken it by force, burned the castle and murdered its feudal inhabitants. A strange people with flaming red hair, who practiced weird cult rituals. Who had crossed the sand bridge, killed the men and raped the women, spawning a whole new race of descendants, and then moved on. And long ago the few women who had survived had fled onto the mainland to seek refuge and protection from the householders there, who took pity on them; until, finally, they were absorbed into the population.

But to that day, those with red hair were eyed with a superstitious fear and disdain by the mainland oldsters, who wove their tales into an even more mysterious web, and handed them down to the frightened young with strange and eerie premonitions.

He smiled. Yes, this was a perfect place, abandoned, forbidden, yet particularly right for his purposes. He stopped, rubbed his freezing hands together, and stretched for a moment. He could let down his guard soon, but not until he reached the cottage. He had always adhered to an unbreakable policy—keep consistent with one's disguise until completely undercover. There were eyes everywhere, possibly even in this God-forsaken place.

He gave Gerhardt another pat and a word of encouragement: "Kommen Sie, old friend, we're almost there." He took up the reins and led the horse on down the tangled path to the cottage. The old ruins of the castle loomed up off in the distance, whispering of untold tales of unspeakable tragedy and heartbreak.

The mist was rolling in and a storm was on its way. He would be glad for a roaring fire and a little warm food after the excitement and danger of the chase of the past two days.

Shivering from the cold, he struggled onward down the tangled path to the cottage. Gerhardt seemed content enough, now that the terrain was more level, though from time to time he would whinny in protest at the occasional obstacles which seemed to appear out of nowhere.

Jana patted his mane and spoke to him caressingly.

"There, there, old friend, we'll soon be there. Just a little farther."

Finally, they arrived at the cottage door. He tied the horse to the hitching post and entered, shedding his backpack. He found a bucket near the sink, trudged out to the well and filled it with water. Gerhardt drank his fill and settled down, contentedly still, while Jana removed the heavy load of equipment from him he had carried up the steep crag. Once free, the horse shook his head as in gratitude as his long chestnut mane flowed with his movement.

Jana laughed and hugged his neck. They were old friends. They understood one another. He untied him and led him to the small closed barn attached to the cottage. He led him into the stall, checked the hay, the water, and removed his harness.

Patting his neck, he spoke to him softly, and entered the cottage through the inside door to tend to his own needs.

Securing the doors, he quickly lit the fire already prepared for him. Soon flames filled the enormous fireplace built into the stone wall on one side of the room.

Shedding his heavier clothing, he removed his wig and fake hunchback, poured a stiff Scotch from the waiting bottle on the sideboard, and flopped down in the large chair in front of the fire. He looked at his watch. Too early to signal his radio contact. Well he should soon know how it went down.

He stretched his weary muscles. He was bone-tired. It had been a long and tedious operation, and it had not turned out to his liking. At least he had escaped—but Suzanne—He missed her terribly. He should have known better than to risk it. Even so, he had a plan for her rescue. If that fell through, he had still protected her with the documents placed in the secret compartment of her overnight bag.

He stretched out his long legs and placed them on the soft footstool. The Scotch gave him a feeling of well-being as the warm liquid flowed through his veins. He stared at the fire. The flames were dazzling, hypnotic. As their warmth filled the room, soon overcome with his first comfort in many days, he fell asleep—and dreamt of a beautiful girl in a white dress—with pale golden hair.

Epilogue

This is a story of the brave young lions who ventured into harm's way at a time when their respective countries and belief systems were in critical jeopardy. They risked their futures and their very lives to rescue the world they knew from the onslaughts of an evil regime, the extent of whose power and malevolent intent had never before been seen in the annals of history.

Had it not been for them and for those who led them and provided their support, that evil would have remained unchecked, and, like a hungry fiend, would have spread throughout known civilization and swallowed up the world as they knew it.

To those brave and courageous men and women of OSS we owe a debt of gratitude for what they did in the face of insurmountable odds.

And some of them were we.

About the Author

Dr. Margaret Sells Emanuelson, a clinical, forensic psychologist, attended the University of North Carolina at Chapel Hill, (B.A.), Vurginia Commonwealth University, (M.S.), and received her doctorate from the University of Virginia.

She has served as Chief Psychologist for a large school system, Director of Psychological Services for an accredited Psychiatric Hospital and founder of a school for learning disabled and emotionally disturbed children. For the past 30 years she has been in private practice for children and adults in North Carolina and Virginia. She holds two diplomates: one from the American Board of Medical Psychotherapy and Psychodiagnostics, and one from the American Board of Forensic Examiners. She has been an active participant in the judicial system as an expert witness, examiner, and consultant .

Well known in her field as an educator, scientist and lecturer, Dr. Emanuelson has authored many publications, and has spoken to professional and Christian groups. co-hosted a radio series entitled "God's psychology", has appeared as a guest on the CBN network as well as the American Medical Association Symposium on Medicine and Religion.

An Episcopalian, she is a member of the Order of St. Luke, the Physician, a healing order, and advocates a treatment approach which includes mind, body, soul, and spirit.

Dr. Emanuelson is a veteran of O.S.S., the wife of C. William Emanuelson, retired industrialist and resides in Scottsville, Va.

> 434-2864867
> P.O. Box 759
> Scottsville, Virginia 24590.
> drmarobella@aol.com

About the Author

Dr. Margaret Sells Emanuelson, a clinical, forensic psychologist, attended the University of North Carolina at Chapel Hill, (B.A.), Vurginia Commonwealth University, (M.S.), and received her doctorate from the University of Virginia.

She has served as Chief Psychologist for a large school system, Director of Psychological Services for an accredited Psychiatric Hospital and founder of a school for learning disabled and emotionally disturbed children. For the past 30 years she has been in private practice for children and adults in North Carolina and Virginia. She holds two diplomates: one from the American Board of Medical Psychotherapy and Psychodiagnostics, and one from the American Board of Forensic Examiners. She has been an active participant in the judicial system as an expert witness, examiner, and consultant .

Well known in her field as an educator, scientist and lecturer, Dr. Emanuelson has authored many publications, and has spoken to professional and Christian groups. co-hosted a radio series entitled "God's psychology", has appeared as a guest on the CBN network as well as the American Medical Association Symposium on Medicine and Religion.

An Episcopalian, she is a member of the Order of St. Luke, the Physician, a healing order, and advocates a treatment approach which includes mind, body, soul, and spirit.

Dr. Emanuelson is a veteran of O.S.S., the wife of C. William Emanuelson, retired industrialist and resides in Scottsville, Va.

> 434-2864867
> P.O. Box 759
> Scottsville, Virginia 24590.
> drmarobella@aol.com